SECURING ZOEY

SEAL of Protection: Legacy, Book 4

SUSAN STOKER

CHAPTER ONE

"Mark Wright?" the lady behind the airline counter asked.

"That's me," Bubba said. It still sounded weird to hear someone call him by his given name. He'd gotten his nickname after completing BUD/S training and eating an entire bucket of shrimp by himself at Bubba Gump Shrimp Company....and ever since, no one had called him Mark.

"Great," the woman said. "Your chartered float plane should be ready to board in about twenty minutes. If you'll just wait over there with the other passenger, we'll call you when we're ready."

Looking over at where she was pointing, Bubba saw a woman sitting on a nearby chair. She had a book in her lap and wasn't paying attention to anything other than the words on the page in front of her. She seemed like an island of calm after the very busy main terminal in Anchorage.

Bubba picked up his duffle bag and headed over to where the airline employee had indicated. They were in the part of the terminal that housed the private planes and charters. His father's lawyer, Kenneth Eklund, had sent him the details of the flight. It had been arranged by his assistant, on the direction of the lawyer.

He was on his way home to Juneau, Alaska, because his pop had unexpectedly passed away.

Feeling another wave of sadness threaten to overwhelm him, Bubba concentrated on the woman instead. She looked familiar, but he couldn't put his finger on how he knew her.

Standing in front of her, he waited for her to look up, to acknowledge him. When she continued to read instead, Bubba mentally snorted. How conceited was he? Standing in front of her like she was a serf who should be acknowledging her master.

"Hi," he said.

She startled so badly, Bubba immediately felt bad for scaring her.

"Oh!" she said, looking up at him. "I didn't see you walk up."

That much was obvious. "I'm sorry. I didn't mean to startle you. I guess we're on the same flight to Juneau."

She blinked. "Oh, Mark, hi. I didn't know it would be you sharing the flight with me. I'm so sorry about your dad."

It was Bubba's turn to be surprised now. "Um...do I know you?"

She smiled a little self-deprecatingly. "Yeah. I'm Zoey Knight. We knew each other in high school."

And so it began. One of the things Bubba disliked the most about his hometown was how everyone knew everyone. Juneau wasn't exactly small, but it felt like it most of the time, probably because there were no roads in or out of the city. It was only accessible by plane or ship.

There were also no secrets in Juneau. It had driven him crazy when he'd hang out with his buddies in high school and by the time he got home, his dad already knew where he'd been, who he'd been with, and what they'd been doing. He wasn't a bad kid back then, but just once he'd wished he could get away with drinking a beer and not getting the third degree when he got home.

For a second, Bubba couldn't place Zoey's name. It sounded familiar, but he was having trouble remembering her from high school

She put him out of his misery. "I went out with Malcom a couple times our senior year."

It finally clicked—and Bubba studied the young woman in front of him with renewed interest. He remembered her *now*.

She'd certainly filled out in all the right places since high school. Back then, she'd been super skinny and shy. He estimated she was about half a foot shorter than he was, and he couldn't help but let his eyes wander over the curves she definitely didn't have in high school.

Yeah, Zoey Knight had changed a lot...and for the better, as far as he was concerned.

Aware he'd been ogling her a bit too long, he held out his hand. "It's good to see you again, Zoey."

She shook his hand. "You too. I'm just sorry it's under these circumstances."

And just like that, he remembered why he was headed home. He took a seat next to her. "Yeah, me too. I always thought my dad would live forever."

Zoey nodded. "It really was a shock to all of us since he used to be so healthy."

Bubba narrowed his eyes slightly. "You knew my dad well?"

3

She blinked. "Oh, I guess you didn't know."

"Know what?"

"I helped your dad out around the house. You know, some housecleaning, did some yard work when he needed it, ran errands, that sort of thing."

Then Bubba remembered his dad had mentioned a while ago that someone named Zoey had been helping out with some of the chores he hated. He hadn't made the connection between that conversation and the Zoey he'd known growing up.

"Ah."

She studied him. "What does that mean?"

Bubba held up his hands. "Nothing. I knew he had someone helping him, but I didn't really know who."

"Maybe if you'd come home now and then to visit him, you would've."

That hit a little too close to home for Bubba's comfort, and his response was curt. "Yeah, well, I've been off saving the world, sweetheart. I didn't have much time for visiting my hometown to get berated for not being around more."

Zoey's eyes narrowed and she glared at him. "The big bad Navy SEAL. Yeah, we know all about you and how amazing you are. Too good to talk to the likes of me, I'm sure. So if you'll excuse me, I think I'll continue to read until our plane is ready."

Bubba sighed and ran a hand through his short hair. He hadn't meant to insult her, even if she kinda deserved it for being a bit harsh and piling on more guilt. But once he'd left home, coming back to Juneau had never taken precedence in his life. His dad had begged him to come home to work for his company. His brother practically ignored him; talking once or twice about the business didn't really count. And everyone he came into contact with asked him when he was moving back to Juneau. He'd left to begin with because he'd felt stifled in the small town.

Other than the cruise ship traffic in the summers, nothing much changed and gossip was one of the locals' favorite pastimes. It drove him crazy, and when he graduated, he was more than ready to move on, to see the world.

His twin, Malcom, had been content to stay in Juneau and go to work with their father. Bubba hated that he wasn't as close to his brother as they'd been as children, but after thirteen years apart, it wasn't too surprising.

What hurt the most about his pop's death was that it had been so unexpected. Bubba had thought he'd live well into his nineties. He'd always been healthy as a horse, and his passing away had been a punch to the gut. Especially since Bubba had made plans to visit soon. He'd missed seeing his dad one last time, and that hurt like hell.

"I'm sorry," Bubba said quietly to Zoey's bent head. "I just...I feel terrible that I didn't get to say goodbye to my dad. Hell, I didn't even know he was having issues with his heart. This seems so unreal."

Zoey put her finger between the pages to mark her place and closed the book as she looked up at him. "If it's any consolation, he'd been sick for a while, but seemed to be on the mend. And when I left to go to Anchorage to visit my mom, he was getting better, and I felt okay leaving him. I hate that I didn't get to say goodbye too. And I'm sorry about my earlier comment. It was out of line and a low blow. I'm just a little jealous of you. Not all of us had the option to leave after high school," she said softly. "Although, while Juneau isn't the most exciting place in the world, it's not as bad as you seem to think it is either."

"I know. High school was kind of fun," Bubba said,

trying to lighten the mood. Unfortunately, his attempt seemed to fall flat.

"Yeah, fun," Zoey said unenthusiastically.

Sensing he was missing something, Bubba did what he always did...tried to solve the mystery. "So, why did you break up with Malcom again?"

She rolled her eyes, and Bubba couldn't help but think it was cute. Her brunette hair was pulled back into a messy bun at the back of her head, her hazel eyes full of intelligence and spunk. He liked that. "We weren't really dating," she told him. "We only went out a couple of times."

"Really?"

"Really. I'm sure it's no surprise, but Malcom was a horn dog. All he wanted was to get me into bed."

Bubba asked the question before he could think better of it. "And did he succeed?"

Zoey's eyes narrowed. "Not that it's any of your business, but no. I wasn't that kind of girl."

"Wasn't?"

Shit, he really needed to control himself better. But Bubba was surprised at his level of interest in her answer.

"Wasn't," she confirmed, then went on. "Aren't. Isn't. Whatever you want to say. I don't date men so I can have sex. If I want to get off, I can take care of that on my own. I date men because I want to get to know them. Because I like them. Because I enjoy being with them. He's *your* brother, so I'm sure I'm not telling you anything you don't know, but it turns out after I got to know Malcom, I didn't like him all that much. He was too selfish and annoying back then, and not much has changed. And I'm starting to think his twin isn't too far removed, even if your dad did sing your praises.

"Now, I really *am* going to read my book this time and

try to pretend that we didn't have this conversation." Then Zoey opened her book again, turned a little in her seat so her back was to Bubba, and bent her head to read once more.

Bubba mentally smacked himself in the head. God, he was an ass. Asking if she'd slept with his brother was rude and, frankly, none of his business. Rubbing a hand over his face, he sat back in the chair and sighed again.

He knew Malcom was kind of a jerk. He always had been. They'd been close when they were kids, but as they got older, Bubba realized that his brother used people for whatever he could get out of them. He'd date girls until they'd put out, then dump them. He'd begged Bubba to do the ol' twin switcheroo game so he could get out of taking tests. Bubba agreed a few times, but got sick of the game and refused to do it again after they'd gotten caught one time in the eighth grade. It was juvenile and stupid and, by that time, Bubba already knew he wanted to go into the military, so he'd done everything he could to stay out of trouble.

Malcom, not so much. He'd been caught shoplifting and driving drunk. He'd also broken curfew too many times to count and regularly skipped school. Their dad was constantly punishing him and threatening to kick him out of the house.

But they both knew their pop wouldn't do that. Malcom didn't have anywhere else to go. So he'd apologize, clean up his act for a while, then eventually fall right back into his old habits.

Turning his head, Bubba studied Zoey while she read and did her best to ignore him. Now that he remembered who she was, he very clearly recalled when Malcom had gone out with her. Zoey had moved to Juneau in the tenth grade, and had always been quiet and kept to herself. Malcom had been so smug that he'd gotten her to say yes to a date. He'd claimed she was one of the few girls he hadn't had sex with and was thrilled that he'd finally get the chance.

Bubba told him that he'd probably have a girlfriend longer than a couple of months if he actually treated them nicely and less like a piece of meat. Malcom had blown him off and told him he didn't know what he was missing.

It was only after a couple dates that his brother had come home one night, pissed off. Apparently Zoey had dumped him after he'd felt her up. He'd proceeded to trash her for the next hour, telling Bubba she was frigid and uptight and would end up an old maid.

The next evening, he went out with some friends and they'd crashed a college party, where he'd supposedly had sex with three girls.

Bubba remembered feeling sorry for Zoey for the way his brother had treated her. He'd always liked her back in high school...more than just a little, truth be told.

"Once again, I'm sorry," he told Zoey. "I'd like to think I'm nothing like Malcom. I don't know him as well as I used to. But what I said was out of line and rude as hell. My father had to really like and respect you, because I know he never liked people 'all up in his business,' as he always used to say."

Zoey sighed and closed her book once more. She turned to look at him. "No, *I'm* sorry. We've definitely gotten off to a rocky start here, since we're both doing a lot of apologizing. I shouldn't have said what I did. And I loved your dad. He was always nice to me and really helped me out when I needed it."

Concerned now, and not sure why, Bubba said, "That

sounds like Pop." He wanted to know why she'd needed help, and what his dad had done to help her, but he figured he'd already put his foot in his mouth once and he'd better not push his luck. "So, you're headed to Juneau? Are you visiting your family?"

"You really have ignored *everything* going on back home, haven't you?" she said with a small smile, letting him know she was teasing him. "I still live in Juneau. I rent a small house from your dad. He gave me a break in rent in exchange for helping him out. I only went to Anchorage to visit my mom. Your dad's lawyer called while I was here and told me Colin had passed away, and he said I needed to come back for the reading of his will."

Bubba was surprised at that. "You're in my dad's will?"

She narrowed her eyes at him. "Apparently. But if you say anything rude about my relationship with him, I'm going to hurt you. I loved your dad, but not like *that*. We were friends. That's all."

Bubba shook his head. "No, I wasn't going to insinuate anything, I swear. I'm just surprised. That's all. I obviously don't know much about his life...even less than I thought."

Zoey pursed her lips. "When I left, he seemed happy, and he'd seemed to have gotten over whatever weird illness he'd been dealing with recently. He told me not to worry about paying rent this month, to use it on the plane ticket to get to Anchorage instead. He was the most generous man I've ever known, and he was like a father to me. I'm going to miss him."

Bubba felt like shit. He knew his pop was a good man, but it hurt to hear things about him that he didn't know from a stranger. The regret in his gut that he hadn't visited years ago sat there like a hard lump.

Taking a risk, he reached out and put his hand on

9

Zoey's forearm. "Thank you for being there for him. I haven't been the greatest son, but I've always wanted the best for Pop." When she didn't pull away, Bubba felt a little better. "I'm glad he included you in his will, and it doesn't surprise me. Pop always took care of people he cared about."

Zoey looked up at him with her big hazel eyes—and Bubba was surprised when a jolt of...something...went through him. He couldn't have looked away from her if his life depended on it.

She opened her mouth to respond, but the airline employee interrupted before she could.

"It looks like your pilot is almost done with her pre-check. You should be able to board in about five minutes."

Zoey swallowed hard and shifted just enough that Bubba's hand fell from her arm. "Thanks."

Realizing he needed to call Rocco as he'd promised, Bubba stood. "I need to make a phone call before we take off," he told the airline employee.

"You've got five minutes," she replied, seemingly disinterested.

After she'd walked away, Bubba turned to Zoey. "I'm sorry, but I promised my friend I'd call him before we took off. He's a little paranoid and I'm humoring him."

Zoey shrugged. "Whatever."

Feeling oddly off-kilter at her casual dismissal, Bubba took out his phone and stepped toward the window for a bit of privacy as he dialed Rocco's number.

He answered after only two rings. "Hey, Bubba. You getting ready to leave?"

"Yeah."

"The flight to Anchorage was good?"

"Uneventful," Bubba told him. "The pilot is about done

doing her preflight checks and we should land in Juneau in about three hours." He stared out the window at the woman walking around one of the float planes that were so common in this part of the state. There were at least ten other small planes lined up on the tarmac, as well. They were extremely popular in Alaska, as a lot of communities, Juneau included, had no access via road. A lot of people got their pilot's license around the same time they got their permit to drive.

"We?" Rocco asked.

"Yeah. A woman named Zoey Knight is on the same flight as me. Apparently she was helping my dad out, and was visiting her mom in Anchorage when he passed. She's in my dad's will, and has been asked to come back for the reading too. So the lawyer got us on the same flight."

"That's funny."

"What's funny?" Bubba asked.

"Her last name is Knight and yours is Wright. Hell, if you got married, she'd only have to change two letters in her last name."

"Fuck off," Bubba told his friend with a snort. "We aren't getting married. Jeez. Just because you're about to tie the knot doesn't mean the rest of us are."

"Right. Anyway, things here are good. The commander doesn't see any missions in the near future, although we both know how quickly that can change. Try to enjoy your time back home. I know you haven't been back in years. You'll see your brother, right?"

Bubba winced. He felt bad that he wasn't really looking forward to that. Malcom was his twin. He should be ecstatic to see him and catch up. But if Zoey's words were any indication, his brother hadn't changed much. "Yeah. Mal will be there. As will Sean, my dad's business partner. I haven't seen or talked to him in years either. Oh, and probably everyone else I grew up with who I haven't seen in thirteen years."

Rocco chuckled. "Gotta love small towns."

"Yeah, right."

"When's the memorial for your dad?" Rocco asked.

"I think in two days. He'll be cremated according to his wishes tomorrow. So I think the next day is when the memorial is planned." Bubba saw the airline employee coming toward them and knew he had about thirty more seconds to talk. "I gotta go, looks like it's time to board."

"Okay. Be careful up there. You don't have your team at your six this time."

Bubba rolled his eyes, and that made him think about Zoey. "You worry too much," he told his friend and SEAL team leader.

"It's my job. And just wait until you find your woman. You'll feel the same way. I swear to God, I'm more nervous now about the smallest things than I was before I met Caite."

"Pass," Bubba told him. "I don't want to turn into a Nervous Nelly like you, so I'll just stay single."

"Famous last words," Rocco said with a laugh. "Call me the second you land. And if you need us, we're here. I know this isn't easy for you, and if things get too overwhelming, all you gotta do is call and one of us, or all of us, will be there in a heartbeat. Got it?"

"Thanks, Roc. I appreciate it. And I'll call when we hit Juneau."

"Anytime. Talk to you soon."

"Bye."

"Bye."

Bubba hung up and turned his phone off in preparation

for the flight. He heard the airline employee telling Zoey she could board the plane, and he stuffed his phone into his duffle bag then joined them.

He wanted to offer to carry Zoey's bag for her, but he had a feeling he'd pushed his luck enough for one day.

As they walked across the tarmac, Bubba was glad it was sunny. The temperature was moderate for this time of year, in the lower sixties. The forecast called for rain later, but that wasn't anything out of the ordinary. The saying, "If you don't like the weather, wait twenty minutes and it'll change," was very appropriate for this part of the country.

As they walked, Bubba's eyes went to Zoey's ass. He wasn't proud of himself for ogling her, but she definitely had an ass that was meant for ogling. He managed to raise his eyes just in time when she turned around to ask if he had a preference for which side of the plane he wanted to sit on.

"Nope. You can pick. My plan is to take a nap, so it doesn't matter."

Zoey nodded and turned back around, and Bubba found his gaze dropping to her ass once more.

God, what was wrong with him? He was tired, that wasn't a lie. He'd slept like shit the night before, wondering what was waiting for him in Juneau, but it wasn't like him to be so rudely obvious about staring at a woman's body.

Bubba turned his attention to the pilot as they approached the small plane. She looked young, in her early twenties, but that didn't concern Bubba. He knew people frequently learned to fly at a very young age in Alaska.

"Hi," the woman said as they approached. "My name is Eve Dane. I'll be your pilot today. If you leave your bags at the bottom of the stairs, I'll get them loaded and we'll be on our way soon."

Zoey thanked her and, after dropping off her bag, climbed into the plane. Bubba held out his hand and shook Eve's. "I'm Bubba. That was Zoey. We appreciate you taking us to Juneau today. How long have you been flying?"

She smiled distractedly, shaking his hand even while looking at something in the plane. "I know I look young, but I've had my license for eight years. I started flying with my dad when I was fourteen and passed the test when I turned sixteen."

Bubba nodded. That didn't surprise him at all. "It's good to meet you."

"Same."

He dropped her hand and put his bag down beside Zoey's before climbing inside the small plane. There were two seats in the front and two in the back, the latter of which were bench style, separated only by an armrest. It would put him and Zoey very close together. It was a tight fit, especially for him, but Bubba strapped himself into the seat next to her with little difficulty.

Eve climbed in after a few minutes and turned to smile at them briefly. "Ready?"

"Ready," Zoey told her.

Bubba nodded.

He wasn't a nervous flier, and he'd been in more than his fair share of helicopters, jumbo jets, and even small, private planes like this one. So he closed his eyes and took a deep breath. If he could sleep for the few hours it would take to get them to Juneau, he'd arrive in a much better frame of mind. Which was important, since he had a feeling it would take all his patience to deal with the lawyer, his brother, his dad's business partner, and the countless other people who would want to know everything he'd been doing for the last thirteen years.

He wasn't even there yet, and Bubba was already feeling claustrophobic and wanting to leave. As much as he regretted not making the effort to see his pop before he'd died, he didn't regret not spending more time than necessary in the stifling town where he grew up.

Seconds after he felt the plane's wheels leave tarmac, Bubba was out. Sleeping the sleep of the exhausted.

CHAPTER TWO

Zoey couldn't rest. She glanced over at Mark and saw that he was fast asleep, and quickly turned her attention back to the window next to her. She didn't even see the beautiful landscape. She'd seen it her whole life. Instead, she was lost in the memories in her head.

God, Mark Wright hadn't changed at all since she'd last seen him thirteen years ago.

Okay, that was a lie. He'd changed all right. For the better. He was still tall, around six feet, just like his twin. But even though they were identical, she could easily tell them apart. For one, Malcom was a bully, and there was something in his eyes that screamed "asshole."

Mark's eyes were full of secrets and pain, but there wasn't an ounce of jerk there that she could see. Yeah, he'd said some rather insensitive things back at the airport, but he'd apologized for them almost immediately. She couldn't remember a time when Malcom had ever said he was sorry for anything he'd done.

Then again, she hadn't exactly been Miss Congeniality in the airport either. She felt bad about that.

Being a bully wasn't who she was. She'd apologized, but she still felt bad about it. Maybe she'd immediately acted bitchy because she was used to having to harden herself to deal with Malcom. But Mark wasn't like his brother, she knew that from the first apology that had left his lips. And that wasn't the only difference between the brothers.

Mark was a lot more muscular, and his shoulders were broader than Malcom's.

Sighing, Zoey rested her forehead on the cool window. The only reason she'd agreed to go out with Malcom all those years ago, when she'd been young and dumb, was because she'd had a crush on *Mark*. She'd thought that maybe since they looked alike, going out with Malcom would be just as good. She'd been very wrong.

Shuddering when she thought about the night she'd dumped him, Zoey wanted to kick herself all over again. Malcom wasn't *anything* like Mark. He'd taken her out to eat at a fast food place then driven her up to Lena Beach to hang out and talk. But of course, once there, all he'd wanted to do was get his hands up her shirt. When she'd pushed him away, telling him she wasn't ready and didn't want to have sex with him, he got angry. Called her a prude and a tease. He'd actually kicked her out of the car and left her there. She'd had to call her mom to come get her, which was embarrassing and humiliating.

Of course, at school the next week, she'd heard the rumors Malcom had spread about how he'd fucked her and what a terrible lay she'd been. She didn't care about the rumors, except for the fact that Mark would have heard and possibly believed them.

At the time, she'd wondered how in the world she could still have a crush on someone who looked exactly like the asshole who'd humiliated her and left her stranded.

Luckily for her, Mark had always hated gossip. Everyone knew that. And while it didn't stop the whispering about her, sixteen-year-old Zoey had been relieved at least her crush probably didn't assume she was a shitty lay.

At that point, she hadn't known if she was good or bad at sex, as she'd never had it before. She'd been saving herself. But once Mark left town to join the navy, she realized her chance with him was gone. He wasn't coming back. She knew that as well as everyone. The only thing that made her feel better was that she hadn't given her virginity to Malcom as some sort of consolation prize.

When she'd seen Mark in the airport, she'd been shocked, although she shouldn't have been. Of course he was coming home for his dad's funeral. Colin Wright was as good a man as Mark was. He'd constantly talked about how proud he was of his Navy SEAL son to anyone who'd listen, and most of the time, that had been Zoey. She'd kept Colin company, as well as keeping his house clean and tidy. She was his confidant and friend.

Thinking about Colin and the heart attack that seemed to come out of nowhere—after they'd both thought he was finally on the way back to being healthy after an extended illness—depressed Zoey all over again.

She didn't have the most exciting or prosperous life, but she'd been satisfied. She'd gotten her associates degree in business from the local community college. She worked part-time in one of the tourist shops near the cruise ship docks, but that was only in the summers. Her work for Colin made her happy, and had given her plenty to do through the winter months.

But now that Colin had passed away, she'd have to make some tough decisions. Honestly, the main reasons she still lived in Juneau was because of him. She'd liked him enough to not pack up and head to Anchorage when he'd asked her to stay. He'd seemed lonely and sometimes depressed, and Zoey couldn't bring herself to leave.

She had no idea what he'd bequeathed her in his will, but she assumed he'd left just about everything to his sons. Which meant Malcom would probably kick her ass out of the house before the week was out.

After they'd dated, Malcom had never liked her. Even though he'd been way out of line, trying to force himself on her, he'd somehow twisted everything to make it seem as if she was the one who'd done *him* wrong. He only tolerated her being around because his father liked her.

She could move to Anchorage to be closer to her mom, but that didn't really appeal either. Zoey really wanted to see more of the world.

There had been a time when she'd wanted nothing more than to get married, have babies, and stay in Juneau forever. Her mom had itchy feet—always had, always will—and she hadn't stayed anywhere for long during the first fifteen years of her daughter's life. So Zoey had made a conscious choice to stay in the place where she'd graduated from high school, craving the stability.

But after years of hearing about Mark's adventures in the navy from Colin, she'd slowly but surely started feeling as if she were missing out.

She'd never been to the beach—a warm beach, that was. Had never been to Disney World. Never seen the Grand Canyon. So many things people took for granted, she'd never even thought about doing.

Until now.

In many ways, Colin's death had freed her. Yeah, her money situation wasn't ideal, but maybe she could find a job in Anchorage and save up enough money by living with her mom briefly, then moving to the lower forty-eight.

She turned to look over at Mark and sighed once again. His eyes were closed and his head was tilted, resting on the seat back. His brown hair was cut shorter than Malcom's, and it looked like he hadn't shaved in a few days, which was sexy as hell. She was used to seeing full beards on men, as they were very popular in Alaska. Many guys said it helped keep their faces warm in the winter months, but since Mark lived in southern California, he certainly didn't need to bother.

He was wearing a pair of black boots, and navy-blue cargo pants with pockets that seemed to be packed to the gills with stuff she couldn't begin to make out. He had on a dark green Henley with a few buttons undone near his throat and a thicker long-sleeved shirt over it. The material was stretched tight over his biceps, and Zoey could almost picture him sweating and straining as he worked out, doing pull-ups to make those muscles as big as they were.

His fingers were twined together, resting on his belly, and she couldn't help but stare at them. They were long and rough-looking...and she bet they'd feel amazing on her bare skin. His nose was crooked and looked like it had been broken at some point, and there was a small scar at his temple. He had a few more scars on the backs of his fingers, and she desperately wanted to hear the stories about how he'd gotten them.

She wanted to know everything about him.

He looked tough, and if she hadn't already known him, Zoey might've been nervous to be sitting so close to him in the cramped interior of the small plane. But she *did* know him. Probably knew more about him than he'd be comfortable with because of his dad's bragging.

And even after all these years, the second she'd locked eyes with him, her high school crush reared its ugly head once more.

God, she was pathetic. She was no longer the untried virgin she'd once been, but it seemed she was even more attracted to the man Mark Wright was now than the boy she'd once known.

Sighing, Zoey closed her eyes and looked away from him once more. He'd never glance twice at someone like her. And he was only in town for his dad's funeral and the reading of the will. Once that was done, he'd leave and never look back again. She knew that, but it didn't stop her from wanting what she knew she'd never have.

Just then, the plane lurched, pulling her out of her fantasies faster than anything else might have. Zoey reached up and grabbed the handle above her head.

The plane lurched again, then the engine stuttered.

She held her breath and stared with wide eyes at the pilot.

"Shit!" Eve exclaimed, and Zoey saw her fumbling with the instruments on the dashboard. She'd never really minded being so close to the pilot before. It was just a part of flying in small planes in Alaska. But at the moment, she would've preferred to not be seeing the pilot frantically flicking switches and jerking on the yoke.

The erratic movements of the plane obviously woke Mark, because he leaned forward and asked, "What's wrong?"

"I don't know," Eve responded. "It feels as if we're out

of gas, but that's impossible. I filled up before we left. We should have plenty of fuel to get to Juneau."

Zoey watched as Mark's gaze went from the instrument panel on the plane, then to his left, glancing out the window. "What can I do to help?" he asked.

Zoey almost laughed hysterically. Of course the Navy SEAL would want to help. Hell, he'd probably bust out a trio of parachutes he'd packed away in his bag so they could all escape the plane.

"Are you a pilot?" Eve asked.

"No."

Zoey swore in her head. Why wasn't he a pilot? He should be! If he was, he could probably fix whatever was wrong in a heartbeat.

She knew her thoughts were careening wildly, hysterical and irrational, but she couldn't help it. In all her time living in Alaska, in the hundreds of flights she'd taken in a craft just like this one, she'd never been in this situation. It was scary as hell, and she didn't like it one bit.

"Can you take us down safely?" Mark asked the pilot.

She shook her head slightly, which didn't make Zoey feel any better. "Maybe. If I can find a place to land."

"Water or land?" Mark asked.

"Water preferably," was Eve's response. "Ah, there!" she exclaimed. "There's a small lake in front of us. If we can make it there, I can put her down."

As soon as she finished her sentence, the plane coughed once—and the eerie sound of silence filled the interior of the plane.

"Shit. We lost the engines," Eve announced, her tone now scarily calm. "Take brace positions," she ordered. "Put your head down and cover it with your arms. Make yourself as small as possible back there."

Zoey looked over at Mark with eyes she knew were as wide as saucers. He stared back for a beat before reaching for her.

"Breathe, Zoey," he said softly. "Eve will get us down."

"Of course she will, we're going down whether we want to or not!" Zoey retorted.

Mark didn't smile, but his lips did twitch. His fingers curled around the back of her neck, and he urged her to lean over. In any other situation, Zoey would've had a spontaneous orgasm feeling those calloused digits on her bare skin, but being seconds away from death effectively dimmed her libido.

"Bend over, Zoey. Brace position."

Instead of doing as he told her to do, Zoey's body acted without her even thinking about it. She leaned sideways, burying her head in Mark's stomach instead. The seat belt pulled taut and dug into her shoulders, but she ignored the slight discomfort.

They'd been sitting close enough that she could've reached out and touched him at any time, but she'd refrained for her own sanity. Now, knowing they were about to die, she didn't hold back. More thankful than she could put into words that the plane was so small and that no aisle separated her from another living, breathing human being, Zoey wrapped her arms around Mark's waist as best she could and held her breath.

Instead of pushing her away, Mark curled himself over her back as much as possible. The position was awkward on the small bench seat, but feeling Mark's weight and heat on top of her made her feel way safer than curling up into a ball on her side of the bench would have.

She heard the pilot swearing but Zoey didn't lift her

head to see what was happening out the windshield. She didn't want to know.

Minutes passed, or maybe they were seconds. Time seemed to stand still.

At the first rough bump, Zoey let out a startled and frightened squeak. Mark tightened his hold on her, and she did the same to him. No one said a word.

The sound of the plane creaking and water slapping against the pontoons was as loud as a bomb.

"Fuck yeah, I did it!" Eve exclaimed thirty seconds later.

It had been the longest thirty seconds of Zoey's life. She felt Mark rise up, but she stayed where she was, clinging to his lap as if she were three instead of thirty-one.

"I got us down, but we're not out of danger yet," Eve told her passengers. "I'm going to steer us to the edge of the lake. You're going to have to get out while I see if I can figure out what's wrong and get it fixed."

Get out. Yeah, Zoey could do that. She'd gladly get out of this death trap.

"I didn't hear you call a mayday," Mark said.

"Yeah, didn't have time," Eve said calmly. "I'll do that in a second and radio for help. Our flight plan was recorded, and the route from Anchorage to Juneau is well traveled. I'm sure even if I can't get this thing started again, someone will find us soon. Here we are. I got as close as I could to the shore."

Zoey took a deep breath and slowly sat up. Looking out the window, all she could see was water and trees. She swiveled her head to look out the front of the plane, and she saw they were within feet of dry land.

"It looks like it gets shallow close to the bank. If you

climb out onto the small pontoon on the passenger side, you can get to the shore without getting too wet. I'll then throw you the tow line, and you can tie off the plane to one of the trees so I don't float away while I'm figuring out what's wrong with this damn plane."

Zoey looked over at Mark...and saw that he was frowning. Not that it was a surprise; she had a frown on her own face.

But something was different about his expression. He looked on edge. Alert.

Suspicious.

"Mark?" Zoey asked softly. She wasn't sure what she was asking. All she knew was that she wanted out of this plane. Now.

With one last long look at Eve, he took a deep breath and half stood to lean over her and push open the small door on the front passenger side. Zoey pushed the seat in front of her forward and scooted back as far as she could, letting Mark get around her and climb out first. He stepped onto the float and held out a hand to Zoey.

She gratefully took hold. She wanted to memorize how his fingers felt around hers, but this was no time to give in to a silly crush. They'd almost died, for God's sake. She had to get herself together.

He helped her stand on the tiny float, and Zoey inhaled sharply in fear when the plane bobbed in the water, since their combined weight was now all on one side.

Mark stepped down into the water and reached for her. He plucked her from the float as if she weighed nothing more than a child. Zoey wrapped her arms around his neck and held on for dear life as he took the few steps required to get to dry land.

She was wearing her normal attire—jeans, wool socks because her feet were always cold, Timberland boots, a tank top under a long-sleeve T-shirt, and her fleece-lined plaid shirt tied around her waist, in case she got chilled.

The second her feet were on the ground, Mark turned around to head back to the plane and grab the tow line— and Zoey stared in disbelief at the plane they'd just exited.

Instead of being only a couple feet from the shore, it was now more than five yards away, and getting farther and farther with every second that passed.

When the engine turned on, Mark shouted, "What the fuck?"

Without looking at them, Eve turned the plane around and headed away toward the middle of the lake.

Zoey looked on in confusion for a second before the situation sank in.

"I thought the engine died," she whispered.

"So did I," Mark agreed.

They stood on the bank of the lake watching helplessly as the plane they'd thought was disabled puttered farther away, then turned around. Eve gunned the engine and the float plane skimmed the surface of the water for a couple hundred yards before it slowly lifted up into the air. The engine sounded strong, with no evidence of the stuttering that had been there before.

"Son of a *bitch*!" Mark exclaimed in disgust.

They both watched helplessly as the plane got smaller and smaller in the sky until it was gone, the only sounds that of the water lapping lazily against the edge of the shore and the occasional bird.

Zoey took a step closer to Mark, as if her brain knew they were in deep shit and the only safe place was next to the large, pissed-off man at her side.

"She'll be back, right?" Zoey asked after another minute had passed.

Mark gazed down at her with a look so intense and frightening, Zoey instinctively took a step backward.

"I highly doubt it, since she fabricated that engine failure and got us stranded in the middle of fucking nowhere."

Zoey inhaled sharply. "But...she said it herself. The flight path from Anchorage to Juneau is highly traveled. Someone will find us soon, won't they?"

Mark sighed and ran a hand over the short stubble on his face. The scraping sound it made would've turned Zoey on in any other circumstance, but at the moment, all she could do was stare at Mark and pray he'd agree with her.

"I was tired," he said.

Zoey frowned, not knowing what in the world he was talking about.

"I fell asleep almost as soon as we took off. I wasn't paying attention to where we were going. How long were we in the air before the engine supposedly went out?"

"Um...I'm not sure. Maybe an hour or so?" Zoey told him.

"Fuck," Mark swore. "This isn't good."

"But we should be almost halfway to Juneau," Zoey said, thinking she wasn't going to like what Mark said next.

"Zoey, Juneau is southeast of Anchorage. I didn't realize it until after we'd already landed...but we were flying west."

She stared at him with wide eyes, realizing he was right. Shit. The sun should've been in the pilot's eyes as they were flying, but it wasn't, it had been behind them. "We weren't headed toward Juneau," she said unnecessarily. "Why not?"

"That's a good question. I'm guessing it's tied into why our pilot would fake an emergency so she'd have to land the plane and the reason she stranded us here."

The severity of their situation hit Zoey then. They were in the middle of Alaska somewhere, with no food. No shelter. They weren't on the flight path they were supposed to be on, so if anyone looked for them, they'd certainly look in the wrong place. They hadn't even been going in the right direction. They had no phones, not that they'd work out here in the middle of nowhere. No one knew where they were.

They were going to die.

"This has to be a mistake. She'll come back!" Zoey said desperately.

Mark stepped toward her and took her by the shoulders. She looked up at him, hoping he'd say something positive. Anything that would make their situation seem less bleak.

But he didn't.

"She's not coming back. We're on our own."

Zoey wasn't a crier. Had learned a long time ago that crying didn't solve anything. All it did was make her sinuses hurt and her eyes puffy. But she couldn't have held back her tears at that moment if someone had a gun to her head.

She was going to die out in the Alaskan wilderness. No one would ever find her body. Her mom would always wonder what happened to her. Maybe she'd end up on one of those shows on the ID Channel that she loved so much. How Ironic. And sad.

And even Mark taking her into his arms and holding her as she cried couldn't make this situation better.

CHAPTER THREE

Bubba was pissed and disgusted with himself. He should've known something was up, but he'd been groggy from sleeping when the plane had first acted up. Even when his brain had noted that they weren't headed in the right direction, he'd told himself it was just because Eve was trying to gain control of the plane and had gotten turned around looking for a place to land.

He'd been stupid to leave the plane, but he'd been concerned about the look of panic on Zoey's face and wanted to get her to safety.

Fuck, he'd been an idiot.

He had no idea who was behind this, but he was going to find out. Whoever had planned this had seriously underestimated his abilities.

He was a fucking Navy SEAL, for God's sake. He'd been through cold-weather training and he'd spent more than his fair share of time in the wilderness. And while he had no idea where they were, he'd figure it out as soon as he could get Zoey calmed down.

While his duffle was still on the plane with the deceptively helpful and kind Eve, he never went anywhere without some basics in his pockets. Once a SEAL, always a SEAL.

He felt Zoey take a huge breath as she attempted to get herself under control. He appreciated it. He didn't mind crying women, but he was a man of action. They had a lot to do and everything within him said he needed to get started. Though, holding Zoey wasn't exactly a hardship.

Back in high school, he'd definitely noticed Zoey when she'd transferred to his school. She'd been the new kid, and of course all the guys had their eyes on her. She'd been shy and soft-spoken, and something about her had called to him. But then Malcom had asked her out, and after the way things had ended between them, it seemed weird to pursue her, to see if she might be interested in the *other* brother.

He'd already been burned by girls who didn't care which brother they dated. Even in high school, he'd wanted a woman who wanted him and only him.

And he'd also been more concerned with keeping his grades up and getting into the navy than dating.

But holding Zoey right now, and having her turn to him for comfort when she'd thought they were crashing, felt good. Really good. He was used to being in charge, being someone people turned to in precarious situations, but having Zoey rely on him felt different. Felt right.

Taking a deep breath of his own and mentally telling himself to chill out, that they were about to have an extremely difficult few days—hopefully it would be *only* a few days—Bubba put his hands on Zoey's shoulders and gently pushed her back so he could see her face.

Her eyes were puffy and her face was blotchy from

crying, but he didn't see panic, which was good. He could deal with her being scared and unsure, but panic was a harder emotion to combat.

"Feel better?" he asked.

She nodded, but said, "No."

Bubba couldn't help it. He chuckled. That was one more thing he remembered about Zoey. She could make him laugh at the most surprising times. "Right. First of all, I need to apologize."

She frowned. "For what?"

"I should've been paying attention. I know better. But I was tired, and I let my guard down. It won't happen again."

"Mark, this isn't your fault. How could we know this would happen?"

Much like it had in the airport, hearing his given name on her lips made him feel...odd. He couldn't put his finger on why, though, so he simply ignored it. "Well, we both know my pop had plenty of money. So I'm guessing someone didn't want us to make it back to Juneau for the reading of the will."

"That's stupid," Zoey said. "I mean, making us disappear isn't going to automatically make the money go to someone else...is it?"

Bubba shrugged. "I have no idea. I don't know what was in Pop's will or how he worded it. If he set up a trust, it's possible if I was indisposed—or dead—it would go to someone else."

Zoey's eyes got big. "Who do you think is behind this?"

"That's the million-dollar question, isn't it?" he asked. "And something I should be asking *you*. You spent a lot more time with Pop than I did. Who do you think would want to get rid of us?"

"Us? I'm nobody. I wasn't even related to Colin. Why would anyone include me in their scheme?"

"Another good question," Bubba told her, glad she'd stopped crying. "And maybe you just had the bad luck of sharing a plane with me. But as far as you being a nobody, that's definitely not true. I hadn't seen Pop in forever, but I know that you've been by his side for over a decade. You were very important to him, and since he included you in his will, you definitely weren't a nobody to him, either."

Zoey stared at him in silence, and Bubba couldn't read what she was thinking.

Eventually, she closed her eyes and sighed. "So someone wanted us both dead, or at least out of the picture so we couldn't claim your dad's inheritance? It's a stupid plan."

Again, Bubba chuckled. That definitely wasn't what he thought she'd say. "I agree. Because if we *are* declared dead, whatever Pop left us will go to *our* heirs."

"But it still leaves us with the question of who wants us dead," Zoey said.

Bubba nodded. "Yes. But we have bigger things to deal with at the moment."

Zoey looked around them. She hadn't pulled out of his grasp. Bubba saw that she had a fleece-lined shirt tied around her waist, and he moved his hands down to tug at the knot.

"What are you—"

Before she could finish her question, he moved behind her and helped her shrug on the shirt. The temperature was in the lower sixties right now, but he was glad she had the extra layer because it would get quite chilly at night.

"Thank you," she said when he walked back around her.

"We aren't going to die out here," he said in a sure, serious tone.

Zoey tilted her head up to look him in the eyes. "You don't know that."

"I do. Whoever was behind this messed up."

She raised an eyebrow at him.

Bubba felt his lips curling upward again. God, she was adorable. "Their first mistake was thinking dropping us off in the middle of nowhere was going to get rid of us."

"I hate to break it to you, Superman, but we have no food. No transportation. No way of contacting anyone. No shelter." Zoey looked around comically. "And I don't see any Ubers lining up to take us home."

"Oh, ye of little faith," he chided. "On a scale of one to ten, how comfortable are you with the outdoors?"

She frowned and wrinkled her nose. "Maybe a four. Four and a half," she said.

Bubba beamed. "Perfect."

"Perfect? Has anyone ever told you that you're insane?"

"My teammates, actually," he told her, straight-faced. "If you had said zero or one, then things might've been a little more difficult, but I can work with a four."

Zoey shook her head and rolled her eyes, making Bubba suddenly want to grab ahold of her head and kiss the look of exasperation off her face. He didn't have time to examine that reaction before she was talking again.

"Seriously, you're crazy. I mean, I live in Juneau, so of course I'm somewhat familiar with the outdoors. You know as well as I do that we all like to be outside as much as possible in the summer because it's so miserable, cold, and dark in the winters."

"I do know that. What about exercise?"

"What about it?" she asked.

33

"Do you do it?"

Zoey sighed again, and her gaze slipped away from his. "If you're asking if I'm secretly a triathlete or something, you're going to be disappointed."

Bubba didn't like that he'd embarrassed her. He put a finger on her chin and gently turned her face back to his. "I have a feeling *nothing* you do could disappoint me."

When she rolled her eyes again, Bubba internally sighed in relief. He liked her subtle snarkiness.

"To answer your question, I don't work out regularly. I don't like the gym, I feel too self-conscious there, working out next to the super-buff men and women who frequent the one in Juneau. But I also don't have a car, so I walk a lot. The house I was renting from your dad was a few blocks from his own, so when I went over to help him, I walked. When I had to go into town, I rode my bike."

Bubba nodded in satisfaction. "That's great." At her look of disbelief, he went on. "Seriously. Walking in Juneau isn't exactly easy. Maybe you forgot that I lived there too. Dad's house is at the top of that huge hill, and I know from firsthand experience that it's not easy walking up there. And if you biked into town, you had to go up and down several hills. That will help a lot out here."

Zoey bit her lip and looked around. "Mark, we're in the middle of nowhere. We don't even know what direction Anchorage is in. How in the world do you think we're going to get there? We can't walk. We were in the air for an hour!"

Bubba could hear her working herself into a frenzy, so he reached into one of the pockets of his cargo pants and pulled something out. He held it in his palm so she could see, and said, "We won't have to walk all the way. Eventually we'll run into someone. And I've got this."

Zoey looked down at his hand, then back up at his face. "You have a compass?"

"Yeah."

"Why?"

"Why not?" he asked flippantly. When she didn't smile, he got serious. "It's been beaten into my head to be prepared for just about anything. I might not have my duffle, but I promise that we aren't going to starve or freeze."

She swallowed hard. "Do you think we're really alone out here? What if whoever planned this hid someone out here to make *sure* we didn't make it out alive?"

Bubba had already thought about that. "Honestly? I hope like hell they did."

Her eyes rounded, and she stared at him as if he'd suddenly grown three heads. "What? Why?"

"Because I could capture them and make them tell me who the hell's behind this. They'd probably have supplies I could pilfer, as well. Maybe even a satellite phone."

"You sound so sure of yourself," Zoey said after a beat.

"That's because I am. Zoey, I'm a Navy SEAL."

"I know."

He shook his head. "But I don't think you really understand what that means. Most of the time our missions include sneaking into foreign countries and either rescuing innocent civilians from the bad guys or killing HVTs."

"What's an HVT?"

"High-value target. I've been taught how to survive in the hottest deserts and the coldest arctic terrains. I know how to kill with my bare hands, just as I know how to make fire with two sticks, shelter from just about anything, and how to evade capture. I can't promise this will be all that much fun, but I *can* promise that I will get you home. Do you believe me?"

Instead of immediately agreeing, Zoey studied him for a long moment. Bubba had no idea what she was looking for or what she saw when she looked at him, but he stayed silent and willed her to trust him.

"So what you're really saying is that this is nothing more than a normal camping trip or something for you?"

Bubba couldn't hold back the chuckle. "Well, not quite. When I camped with Dad, we always had a tent and a cooler of beer. But if no one else is out here trying to kill us, then yeah, it'll be a walk in the park to get us to civilization—no matter *how* far that walk might be. We might be dirty and smelly by the time we get to where we're going, but we won't be starving to death, we won't be freezing to death—thank goodness it's not the middle of winter—and we *definitely* won't be cowed by whoever thought they could get rid of us."

"I'm always cold," Zoey told him matter-of-factly.

"Pardon?"

"I'm always cold," she repeated. "That's why, even in September, I'm wearing boots, a long-sleeve shirt, and had my fleece wrapped around my waist. I don't know why, I just am."

"I'll do my best to make sure you're comfortable."

Zoey sighed. "I've been camping exactly two times, and didn't really enjoy it."

"You haven't been camping with me," Bubba told her.

As he expected, Zoey rolled her eyes. "I see the navy taught you humility."

Bubba chuckled again then held his hand out to her in invitation. "Come on, let's get our bearings and make a preliminary plan."

She immediately put her fingers in his, and Bubba realized that her hand did feel quite cold. He covered it with his other hand, trying to warm her up.

"Only a preliminary plan?"

"Yup. I've been trained to not only create a Plan A, but B, C, D, and E as well."

"Right. Of course you have," Zoey said. Then she straightened her shoulders and gestured to their left with her head. "By all means, lead on, oh great Navy SEAL warrior."

"Has anyone ever told you that you're a smartass?" he asked as he gripped her hand tighter and led them away from the lake.

"I'm not. At least, I wasn't until you came along."

Bubba couldn't help but smile at that.

This entire situation sucked. More than sucked. But it could've been a hundred times worse if he'd been stranded with anyone other than Zoey Knight. The longer he was around her, the more he remembered how much he liked her in high school. And while he was being honest with himself, he was looking forward to getting to know her better as they figured out where the hell they were and how to get back to Anchorage or Juneau. At least there was one perk to this situation.

He honestly wasn't too worried about roughing it for a while. They'd be uncomfortable, but he had enough confidence in his abilities to be sure they'd eventually make it home.

Whoever had thought to get rid of them had seriously underestimated him. And he hadn't been kidding when he'd told Zoey that he almost wished someone was out here trying to kill him. He could turn the tables and get more supplies, maybe even a vehicle and a phone. But he had a feeling the pilot had randomly chosen the lake she'd landed in. That it hadn't been planned out in advance.

He'd thought she was acting a little weird, but it had taken him too long to figure out what was going on.

Suddenly remembering that he'd promised to call Rocco the moment he landed, Bubba smiled. For once, his paranoid teammate's insistence on checking up on everyone was going to work in his favor. When Rocco didn't hear from him, he'd definitely try to figure out why. Between him and the rest of his team—and their computer-expert friend, Tex—he and Zoey would be home in no time.

He hoped.

As he tightened his hand around Zoey's when she stumbled, Bubba had a feeling his life wouldn't be the same after this little adventure. Whoever had wanted him out of the picture had also targeted Zoey, and that was something he couldn't forgive.

As if she could read his thoughts, Zoey squeezed his hand and said softly, "This sucks, but if I had to be stuck in the middle of nowhere, I'm glad it's with you."

CHAPTER FOUR

Zoey had no idea how much time had passed, but she was already over this impromptu hiking and camping trip. She was trying her best to stay positive, but as each hour passed, she became more and more discouraged and scared.

The only thing she was thankful for was the fact it was early fall instead of the middle of winter. Instead of tromping through the wet undergrowth of the forest, they could be trying to make their way through a foot or more of snow.

Thinking about snow made her shiver. Even with all the walking, she was still cold. Zoey thought it was probably because she couldn't stop thinking about where the hell they were going to stop for the night. She'd have to sleep on the ground and would probably freeze to death. She wasn't even going to think about the bugs and snakes that might decide to take up residence in her clothes.

"Stop thinking so hard," Mark said.

She rolled her eyes. She was walking behind him, and

Zoey knew he was purposely walking much slower than he might've if he was alone, just so she could keep up.

Zoey stopped where she was and put her hands on her thighs as she bent over and tried to get control of her emotions. She was hungry, tired, cold, and scared to death. For a while after they'd started, her adrenaline had allowed her to forget about the severity of their situation, or at least put it in the back of her mind, but as time went on, and as they'd walked for miles through a freaking forest in the middle of nowhere, she couldn't help but let her doubts and fears creep in.

"Zoey?"

Mark's tone was gentle—and almost her undoing. He put one hand on her upper back and the other gently grasped the base of her neck, massaging.

Zoey closed her eyes. Why couldn't he be a jerk like his brother? "You need to stop being nice to me," she told him without standing up straight.

"Not gonna happen," he said.

Zoey sighed. "Then maybe you should just go on ahead and find help and come back for me."

He moved in front of her, then forced her to stand up. He kept the hand on the back of her neck, putting his other fingers under her chin and making her look at him. Zoey didn't know what to do with her hands, so she hesitantly put them on his chest.

He opened his mouth to say something, but she blurted, "God, you're so warm!" before he could get anything out. The heat radiating from his chest almost scorched her poor frozen fingers, but it felt so damn good.

In response, he wrapped his arms around her, pulling her into him so they were plastered together from hips to chest.

Zoey moaned and turned her face so her nose was smooshed against his pecs. Of course, that meant she couldn't breathe, but who needed air when there was this much warmth to be had?

She felt him chuckle, and she moaned a complaint when he shifted her so her cheek was against his chest instead of her face. He had one hand on the back of her head, holding her to him, and the other was pressing her lower back closer. She couldn't have easily gotten out of his hold, not that she wanted to go anywhere. He was like a living, breathing electric blanket.

"I'm not leaving you, Zoey," he said after a minute. "Why would you think for a second that I would? Do you think so little of me?"

He sounded hurt, and Zoey hated that. She shook her head against him. "No. But I'm slowing you down. I bet you could be miles farther by now if you didn't have to constantly wait for me or keep checking to make sure I haven't fallen flat on my face. You could go on ahead and find whoever you can and come back."

"I'm not leaving you," Mark said firmly. "That's not how this works. A SEAL doesn't leave a teammate behind."

"I'm not a SEAL," she said immediately.

"Maybe not, but I'm still not leaving you. Look at me, Zoey."

Reluctantly, she tilted her head back and stared into his whiskey-brown eyes. She had the weird thought that he had the longest lashes she'd ever seen on a man.

"I need you to listen to me. To really *hear* me. Are you listening?"

She nodded.

"We're in this together. No matter what, we stay

41

together. We have no idea what will happen, and I need you as much as you need me. This isn't a one-sided thing. You've been doing amazingly well so far. I'm impressed, and believe me, I'm not easily impressed."

"I've fallen several times, and the only things in my pockets are a pack of Life Savers and a receipt from the crappy hamburger I ate before getting on the plane," she said with a raise of her eyebrow.

"You might've fallen, but you got back up. Each and every time," Mark said. "I'm not blowing smoke up your ass when I tell you that I've been in situations very similar to this...walking through a jungle trying to get to an extraction point with someone we've rescued, and the person we're rescuing has no interest in helping themselves. I know this is hard. It sucks. Majorly. But you're doing *great*. And I'm fairly sure you have no desire to see whoever was behind this succeed. Right?"

Zoey sighed. He *was* right, dammit. "Right."

"We're in this as a team, Zoey. I need you to have my back, and I'll have yours. Okay?"

"Sure," she said. "If a bear finds us, I'll throw a piece of candy at him and hope that'll distract him long enough for us to get away."

"Sounds like a plan," he said with a smile, then let go of her chin.

Zoey immediately buried her nose back into his shirt and sighed as the warmth from his body seeped into her face.

Mark didn't move for several minutes. Letting her soak up his warmth and rest. Taking a big breath, she forced herself to step away from him but couldn't stop the involuntary shiver that went through her body after losing his warmth.

He frowned. "You really are cold, aren't you?"

Zoey shrugged. "I think my core body temperature has been permanently affected from living in Alaska. I told you that I'm always cold."

"I'll do my best to keep you warm," Mark said.

And of course, Zoey's mind immediately went into the gutter. She knew she was blushing, but tried to blow it off. "I'll be okay. We should probably keep going. Are we still headed south?"

For a second, she thought Mark was going to ask what she was thinking as he studied her face, but he eventually nodded. "Yeah. The last thing I want to do is head west. We'd run straight into that mountain range, and I'm not sure either one of us is up to any mountaineering anytime soon."

Looking to her left, Zoey saw the large mountain peaks above her head through the trees. "No, I think I'd prefer to stay down here," she agreed.

They began to walk once more, and, as if Mark knew she needed something to keep her mind off of where they were and what they were doing, he asked, "So...what have you been doing for the last decade, besides helping my dad out?"

Zoey chuckled. "Wow, that was an open-ended question," she complained.

Mark turned his head and smiled. "Got anything better to do at the moment?" he asked.

"Actually, I had a hair appointment, but I guess I'm gonna miss that," she quipped.

Mark chuckled back, and Zoey realized how much she loved hearing him laugh.

"Right, well, after graduation, I went to the community college there in Juneau and got my associates degree in

43

business. I didn't particularly enjoy the classes though and wasn't sure what else I wanted to do. I got a job in one of the tourist shops down near the cruise ship docks, and that keeps me busy in the summer."

"How did you start working for my dad?" Mark asked.

Ducking under a branch and jumping over a puddle, Zoey went on. "It was after the shops had all closed for the winter one year. I ran into your dad in the grocery store. Literally, I ran into him with my cart and knocked him down. I felt terrible, but he was really nice about it. I insisted on helping him get his groceries to his car, then offered to cook something for him in apology. I knew who he was; I'd seen him at graduation with you and Malcom, and occasionally around town. He only agreed to let me cook for him, I think, because I admitted I'd walked to the store, and he was trying to be nice and figure out a way to give me a ride without forcing me. Anyway, I made him stuffed peppers that night, and he offered me a job on the spot. I started that week, cleaning his house and doing general chores. And over the next few months, we became good friends."

She stopped talking, wondering how much Mark wanted to hear. She didn't want to say anything that would make him sad.

"Go on," Mark urged.

"I...I know you guys didn't really get along. I don't want to say anything out of line."

"Is that what you think? That we didn't get along?"

"Well...yeah. You never really came home to visit, and Malcom said you two had a falling out and that was why you were never around."

"I loved my pop more than I can say," Mark said without turning around. "I admit that I should've come back at least once after I left, but I didn't stay away because of him. Not really."

"Then why?"

Mark sighed, and Zoey felt bad for asking, but eventually he answered. "Because I was afraid that I'd just continue disappointing him. I knew he wanted me to work with him. All through high school, he talked about me taking a job at Heritage Plastics and working my way up the chain to eventually be his vice president. I didn't even get a college degree. I couldn't bear to see the disappointment in his eyes when he realized that I'd never be interested in doing what he does. He'd talk about all the stuff his company was working on and my eyes would glass over. I couldn't think of anything worse than sitting in a cubicle, or worse, working in a factory."

Zoey frowned and ran a few steps to catch up with Mark. She put her hand on his arm and tugged, forcing him to stop. He turned around and looked at her questioningly.

"Mark, Colin was so proud of you." When Mark looked at her skeptically, she squeezed his arm tighter. "Seriously. I know you didn't email all that often, but when you did, he'd tell anyone and everyone about how great you were doing. He bragged all the time about you being a SEAL, and how you were out doing the hard work so people like him could sit on his butt and sell plastic."

She saw Mark swallow hard before asking, "Yeah?"

"Yeah. He didn't care less that you didn't have a degree. He was as proud of you as he could be."

Running a hand over his face, Mark said, "I should've come to visit."

Zoey shrugged. "Maybe. But he didn't love you any less

45

because of it. He always said you were too busy saving the world to worry about little ol' him."

Mark chuckled, but it sounded kind of sad. "I regret it," he said quietly.

Zoey squeezed his arm.

"I also regret not staying in better touch with Mal. Maybe it's not too late to fix that relationship."

Zoey did her best to keep her expression even, but she must not have done a very good job of it, because Mark asked, "What?"

"Nothing," she said quickly, not wanting to say anything that would turn Mark off his brother. Their relationship was no business of hers. "As I said earlier, I don't know what I should and shouldn't say in regard to your dad. I won't talk about him if it hurts too much."

Mark shook his head. "No. I mean, yeah, it hurts, but I'd like to hear about him, if you're okay talking about him."

Zoey smiled. "How about we walk and talk?"

Mark chuckled. "You sayin' I'm taking too many breaks, woman?"

"You said it, not me," she sassed.

"Ma'am, yes, ma'am," he said and gave her a smart salute, then turned back around and began walking once more.

For just a second, Zoey could totally imagine him standing there in his white dress uniform and saluting. She'd seen pictures of him wearing it. He'd recently emailed his dad a photo of him and his teammates wearing their dress whites. They were standing on a beach surrounding a man and woman who were obviously just married. She couldn't help but drool over him just a bit.

She'd always had a thing for a man in uniform, even though she'd die before admitting it.

"So, there was this one time a girl came by your dad's house. She was selling cookies, and she was crying a little because she'd been turned down so many times. Colin invited her and her mother in and kneeled down in front of her and talked to her for about ten minutes. They talked about what subjects she liked best in school, what her favorite food was, and a million other random things. Then he asked how many boxes of cookies she had to sell —and proceeded to buy *double* that amount from her. When the girl left, she was smiling from ear to ear and telling her mom she couldn't wait to tell her friends that she'd doubled the minimum requirement. He was always doing things like that. Unselfish things. Colin had a lot of money, but he never acted like it. He was just as happy eating boxed mac and cheese as he was a fifty-dollar steak."

"What'd he do with all the cookies?" Mark asked.

Zoey looked at him in surprise. "What do you mean?"

"Pop hated those cookies. Said they tasted like crap. I know he didn't eat them, so what'd he do with all those boxes?"

Zoey smiled. Mark might regret his relationship with his dad, but he still knew the man. Even though he hadn't seen him in over a decade, he *knew* his dad. "He donated them to the homeless shelter and women's shelter in town."

Mark nodded. Zoey couldn't see his face, but she had a feeling he was smiling. "Yeah, that sounds like something Pop would do. What else?"

Over the next hour or so, Zoey told Mark as many stories as she could remember about his dad. Some were sad, but most were silly and happy memories. It felt good to talk about him. When she finally ran out of stories, Mark said, "Thank you. I can tell you loved him very much."

She did. Colin Wright could be grumpy and annoying, but couldn't anyone? And he'd done more for her than just about anyone else in her life. He believed in her and always encouraged her to do whatever she wanted. Of course she loved him.

"Can I ask you something?" Mark asked.

"I think you just did." She heard him chuckle, but then he turned his head and looked her in the eyes and asked, "Why did you stay in Juneau after your mom left? Did you love it there that much?"

They were still walking, and it wasn't until Mark had turned around and wasn't staring at her anymore that she could answer. "I guess because there wasn't anywhere else for me to go," she said. "That sounds kinda pathetic, now that I think about it—"

"No. No, it doesn't," Mark interrupted.

"It does. And don't interrupt me," Zoey scolded, forgetting Mark wasn't his father for just a second. But when he merely smirked at her over his shoulder, she relaxed. "I was going to move to Anchorage, but Colin asked me to stay. That's when he said I could rent the house near his. Honestly, he made it so easy for me to say yes. Probably why I'm thirty-one years old and have no idea what I want to be when I grow up."

"My pop always had a way of making things seem easy," Mark said. "That was one of the reasons I left so soon after graduating. I knew if I stayed and worked with him, even for a couple months, it would be that much harder to leave."

Zoey thought about that for a while as they trudged along. Mark was right. His dad *had* made it very easy for her to stay in Juneau. She didn't hate her life, but it wasn't exactly all that exciting. She met a ton of happy people in the tourist shop in the summers. People who were thrilled to be on a cruise and seeing the world, and there she was, a homebody who'd never even left her home state.

She'd been so lost in her own head that she hadn't realized Mark had stopped, and she literally ran right into him. She would've fallen on her ass if he didn't have super-fast reflexes, reaching back and catching her.

"Oh, thanks. I should've been watching where I was going," she said. Having Mark's arm around her felt amazing. Comforting. It seemed to her that he was slow in letting go, but the second he did, she took a step to the side, not wanting to crowd him...or let him know how much she wanted to stay in his arms. She had to get her shit together.

"It's fine. I should've warned you I'd stopped. I think this is a good place to stop for the night."

Zoey looked around and didn't see any difference in where they were standing now than where they'd been walking for the last half a day. "Here?"

"Yeah."

"Why?"

"Because you're tired. You're breathing harder than you were an hour ago, and you've been stumbling over your feet a little more. There's a clearing over there where I can build a small lean-to, and there's plenty of dry wood we can use for a fire."

Zoey was embarrassed that they were stopping because of her, but remembering his earlier words about him not leaving her, she forced back the thought that he would be able to go a lot faster without her. Looking around, she still didn't see anything that resembled a good place to put up a shelter or make a fire, but she didn't argue. Mark was the SEAL; he would know.

"What do you need me to do?" she asked.

She didn't understand the tender look he shot her way, but it felt good nonetheless.

"Can you see if you can gather up some wood? We'll need smaller sticks and some larger logs."

"Um...Mark?"

"Yeah?"

"I know you said you could do it earlier, but are you really going to start a fire by rubbing two sticks together?"

In response, he reached into one of his many pockets and pulled out a small silver block. He smiled as he showed it to her, but he didn't explain what it was.

Zoey looked at it, then at him. "I'm sure I'm supposed to know what that is, but I don't. A four on the outdoor comfortability scale, remember?"

He laughed, and Zoey couldn't take her eyes off his face. So far, this being deserted in the middle of nowhere wasn't *too* bad. Especially when she had someone like Mark to stare at.

"It's a flint. It'll throw sparks and start the fire for us."

Of course. Zoey felt really stupid now. "Right. I knew that. Okay, I'll find some logs for our fire then." She started to turn around so she didn't have to face Mr. Mountain Man, but Mark caught her arm and spun her so fast, she lost her balance and would've fallen to the ground if he hadn't caught her—again.

He pulled her into his arms, and she couldn't help but burrow close. Once again, he was warm and she was freezing. Just being near him made her body temperature go up several degrees.

"Don't be embarrassed," he told her.

"You can't just say something like that and expect it to be true," she grumbled.

She felt more than heard his chuckle under her cheek. "Yes, I can. I'd never make fun of you, Zoey. Ever. I don't care what you know and what you don't. I said it before and I'll say it again, I'm going to make sure you get back home no matter what it takes. I feel as if I got you into this mess, so I'm going to get you out."

"You didn't hire that woman to fly us into the Alaskan wilderness and leave us here," she said. Then looked up at him and asked, "Did you?"

He closed his eyes and shook his head, but because he was smiling, she didn't think he was upset with the question and had taken it as the joke she'd meant it to be.

"No, Zo, I didn't."

Goose bumps formed on her arms at hearing him call her Zo. No one had ever given her a nickname before. She liked it.

"You gave me something precious today, and I'll never forget it."

She wracked her brain trying to figure out what she'd given him and couldn't think of one damn thing. Was he delirious? Had he hit his head when she wasn't looking?

"Stories about my pop," he clarified. "It's been my experience that when people pass away, no one wants to talk about them for fear of upsetting their loved ones. But hearing about his everyday life, knowing he was happy and that you were there for him, means more to me than I can say."

"Well, don't get too excited, not everyone in your

family liked me all that much." Zoey knew she should've kept her mouth shut when he tensed against her.

"Mal?" he asked.

She nodded. "And Sean."

"My dad's partner?"

"Yeah. I heard him talking to Colin one night, asking why he kept me around. He said if he needed a house-keeper, he could hire a service for your dad."

"Asshole," Mark muttered.

"And I'm not sure his lawyer is all that fond of me either," Zoey went on, not able to stop her runaway mouth. "When he called to tell me about the reading of the will, he didn't sound too thrilled that I was included."

"I don't give a flying fuck about them," Mark said firmly. "I like you, and that's all that matters."

And at that moment, standing in his arms in the middle of wherever the hell they were, that was all that mattered to Zoey too.

Eventually, Mark pulled back and said, "Come on, we need to get crackin'. I know it's still light out, but you're cold. I want to get a fire going so you can get warm."

It was obvious she was more tired than she'd thought when even that little gesture made Zoey want to cry. She took a deep breath and nodded. "The good news is, we don't have to worry about hiding a fire from any bad guy who might be following us."

When Mark didn't immediately respond, she asked nervously, "Right?"

"Sorry, right. You're exactly right. And, who knows, maybe a fire in the middle of wherever we are will alert someone to the fact that people are out here, and they'll want to investigate," Mark said.

Zoey nodded. "I'll gather as much wood as I can find so we can have a big fire then."

"Perfect," Mark told her.

Zoey turned away to start pulling her weight, but when she looked back at Mark a minute later, he was still standing where she'd left him. He was staring at her, but obviously lost in thought.

"Mark?" she asked. "Is everything okay?"

That seemed to shake him out of whatever trance he'd been in. "Yeah, sorry. Everything's great." Then he reached into another pocket and pulled out the knife he'd shown her earlier. He said he'd received special permission to carry it since they were on a chartered flight outside of regular security channels. Though it had been in his suitcase on his earlier flight to Anchorage.

Wondering what else he had in his pockets, Zoey got to work collecting firewood. She daydreamed about him pulling out a meatball sub sandwich. Or a satellite phone, which he'd laugh about, and then say he'd just wanted to spend time with her before calling for help.

Zoey knew she was in trouble. The more time she spent with Mark Wright, SEAL extraordinaire, the more she liked him. And this was no schoolgirl crush. This was a full-on infatuation. She'd just have to make sure she never let him know. The last thing she wanted to see was that tender look cross his face again—right before he shot her down hard.

Her life was here in Alaska, and his was in California. He'd never want a homebody like her. She'd have to enjoy spending time with him now and hold these memories close to her heart if...no, *when*...they finally got out of here.

CHAPTER FIVE

Bubba stared at the dancing flames in front of him without really seeing them. All his attention was on the woman in his arms. They hadn't eaten anything for dinner, except for one Life Saver each, and were now huddled together in the small lean-to he'd made in front of the fire. Zoey was shivering, and he hated that he couldn't do more to warm her up.

She'd been a tremendous help in setting up their small camp for the night, wanting to know what else she could do after collecting wood for their fire. He'd patiently shown her how he was making their lean-to, and she'd watched carefully as he'd used the flint in his pocket to start the fire.

After he'd set up the small snare trap with some of the twine from his pocket and sticks he'd found around the camp, and after he'd set up a system to catch water from the trees, he'd scooted up behind her, wrapped his arms around her, and did his best to warm her from behind as the fire did the same from their front.

She held herself stiff in his arms, but didn't pull away.

"Do you want me to move away?" he asked.

Zoey immediately shook her head. "No. I mean, hugging you earlier was one thing, but lying against you like this is a little...awkward."

"No, it's not," he countered. "Just relax."

"But we're strangers."

"No, we aren't. I've known you for more than fifteen years, Zoey."

She shook her head. "Yeah, but I haven't seen you for thirteen of those years, Mark."

"Then we're just picking up where we left off," he told her.

She snorted, and Bubba imagined she was probably rolling her eyes. "I think I would've remembered us doing this in the past. I had a crush on you, you know."

"You did?"

Zoey sighed. "Shit. There goes my mouth, overriding my good sense again."

"If it makes you feel any better, the second I saw you, I thought you were cute."

She turned her head and stared at him. The sun hadn't quite set yet, and he could see the way she eyed him skeptically. "Are you just saying that to try to make me feel better?"

"Nope," Bubba told her easily. "You had just walked into the school with your mom. You looked scared as hell, and I couldn't blame you. Being the new kid in a high school in a place like Juneau definitely would scare the hardiest soul. But when you saw people looking at you, you raised your chin and met everyone's eyes. I thought it was brave as hell, and I was intrigued. Not to mention the way

55

you filled out the black jeans you had on, and the shape of your...erhm...assets under the pink T-shirt you were wearing."

"You remember what I had on when you first saw me?" she asked, still staring at him.

Bubba tightened the arm around her waist and wrapped the other around her chest, diagonally. She settled back against him once more. Bubba felt more comfortable, now that she wasn't staring right at him. He looked into the flickering flames of the fire as he spoke. "Yeah, I do. You were wearing Chucks, and I knew right then and there you were cool."

"I wasn't cool," she muttered.

He chuckled. "Seriously, from everything that I saw, you were nice to everyone you met. You didn't think you were better than anyone else, and you didn't care if someone was the class nerd or the jock, you treated everyone the same."

"I can't believe you remember what I was wearing," she said with a shake of her head.

Bubba chuckled again. He couldn't remember laughing this much in a very long time. He wasn't a grouch, not like Phantom, but he wasn't exactly jovial either. Even in this shitty situation, being around Zoey had him laughing more than was usual for him.

"Well, shit, if I'd known you even knew I existed, I might not've agreed to go out with Malcom when he asked."

Bubba did his best not to tense. "Why *did* you go out with him?"

Zoey shrugged. "I figured he was as close to you as I was going to get."

Her words seemed to echo around them in the waning light. She quickly continued. "But from the second we met at the mall, on our first date, I knew things weren't going to work out."

"Why?"

"Because he practically ignored me," Zoey said. "He was too busy looking around to see who else was there, and who might be looking at him. It wasn't until he saw one of his friends that he reached out and wrapped his arm around my shoulders. He pulled me against him and practically strangled me as he walked me to the theater. He did buy my ticket, but once inside, where no one he knew could see us, he dropped his arm and told me if I wanted a snack, I'd have to buy it myself. Then, throughout the entire movie, he kept trying to cop a feel. It was annoying, and I didn't want to have to deal with him anymore. He insisted on walking around the mall afterward, doing the arm-around-my-neck thing once more."

Bubba could see the picture she was painting in his head, and he didn't like it one bit. "Mal told me that you and him made out during the entire movie and you were all over him."

Instead of getting pissed off, Zoey laughed. "As if. Anyway, I did try a couple more dates, but they were much the same as the first, and I told him that I didn't think we were compatible. He was pissed I was dumping him before he'd gotten into my pants, so he left me stranded at Lena Beach. I admit that I was disappointed things didn't work out between us...but more because I'd had high hopes he would be more like *you*. Every time I saw you at school, you were considerate of the people around you."

"Me and my brother are nothing alike," Bubba told her,

hating how terrible Malcom had treated her in high school.

"I know."

Bubba had no idea if she realized she was running her palm down his thigh, as if to soothe him, but he couldn't deny it felt good and kept him calmer than he might be otherwise. Listening to her basically tell him that she'd gone out with Malcom because she'd had a crush on *him* was tough.

Hearing that Malcom had treated her like shit was downright infuriating.

"I thought twins were supposed to be really close and a lot alike," Zoey said after a moment.

Bubba shrugged. She couldn't see him, but she could probably feel him against her back. "Mal and I have never liked the same things. When my dad put us in the same outfits when we were little, one of us would always change. Mal was the more impetuous of the two of us, rushing headlong into situations before thinking about them. I was always more cautious. And let's just say there's a reason girls didn't hate my guts when we broke up."

"It was a letdown," Zoey admitted. "I don't think I went on another date for the rest of the year."

"How come you aren't married by now?" Bubba asked. "I mean...you aren't, are you?"

She shook her head against his chest, and he could smell the light scent of her shampoo. Even after their day trudging through the forest, she still smelled good.

"I'm not married. Hell, I haven't even really dated much in the last few years."

"I don't understand that," Bubba admitted. "You're beautiful. Considerate. Smart. What the hell's wrong with the male citizens of Juneau?"

She huffed out a breath. "Thanks. I guess I just want... more. And this might sound stupid, but I didn't want to marry the first man who asked just because he might be the *only* man to ask. I want to be with someone who can't imagine *not* being with me. A man who can't wait to get home at the end of the day because he knows I'll be waiting for him. Someone who will treat me with respect and encourage me to go after my dreams, instead of insisting that I find some crappy job so he can buy all the weed and alcohol he wants."

Bubba tensed under her. "Did someone actually do that?" he asked.

"Yeah. But don't worry, I broke things off with him two-point-three seconds after he suggested it. I know I'm a romantic, I can't help it. I want a partner in life. Not someone who I have to take care of, and not someone who thinks *I* need to be taken care of. I'm a grown-ass woman who has managed to keep a roof over my head and food in my belly for all of my adult life. I might not be a millionaire, and I might not have a dream job, but I think I'm doing okay."

"You are," Bubba told her. "And you shouldn't settle. I think that's a huge issue in our hometown. People think if they don't accept the first person who comes along, there won't ever be anyone else. Excuse the cheesy cliché, but there are lots of fish in the sea, and you shouldn't settle for the first one that jumps into your net."

"Yeah," Zoey agreed.

They were silent for a while, until Bubba asked, "So if I had asked you out, would you have said yes?"

"In a heartbeat," Zoey said immediately.

"I wanted to," Bubba admitted. "But after you went out with Malcom, I thought it might be weird. I didn't want people to think you were going out with me because of *him*. Childish, I know."

Zoey nodded, but didn't comment.

"I think I also didn't ask you out because I knew I was leaving right after graduation. Deep down, I knew if we started dating, it was going to be that much harder to leave." Bubba felt Zoey flinch slightly against him, but she didn't say anything and didn't turn around. "And even though it's years later, I know I was right. It would've hurt both of us when I left, and I didn't want to do that to you."

"I'm glad you didn't ask me out," Zoey said after a minute or two.

Bubba blinked in surprise. That wasn't what he'd thought she would say after hearing his confession. "You are?"

She nodded. "Yeah. It would've killed me to say goodbye to you if we'd gotten close, knowing you weren't ever coming back. And look at you. What you've done is amazing. You've saved countless lives, you're serving your country, and you're doing what you love. Staying in Juneau would've suffocated you. You're a good man, Mark, and I'm proud of you. I know I told you already, but it bears repeating. Your dad talked about you all the time."

Her words felt good. He hadn't talked to his pop much, and hearing that his old man had been proud of him went a long way toward lessening the guilt in his heart for not being there when he passed.

"Thank you," he whispered.

Zoey squeezed his thigh where her hand was resting. "You're welcome."

Bubba could feel how tense Zoey still was against him. He wanted her to relax. To lean on him. "Relax, Zo. I'm not going to bite, and I'm not going to think you leaning against me means you want to strip off all my clothes and have your wicked way with me."

She chuckled. "But what if that's what it *does* mean?"

Her words struck him hard, but he forced himself to stay calm.

"Then I'd say when we get to civilization, I'm more than happy to let you do whatever you want to me."

She chuckled uneasily. "I was kidding," she said quickly.

"I wasn't," he said softly.

To her credit, she didn't leap out of his embrace and berate him for coming on to her. "I don't understand how, in romance books, when the couple is fleeing bad guys in a jungle, they always stop to have sex. I mean, it's only been one day, less than that really, and I feel disgusting and dirty. Not to mention, I'm freezing. The last thing I want to do is take off my clothes to get freaky."

Bubba practically choked. Then he laughed. "Well, that's not my genre, but I'm guessing it's the romanticism of it all."

"No offense, but this isn't romantic," Zoey countered.

"What? We've got a nice fire, beautiful scenery, and great conversation. What's not romantic about this?"

"Um...it's cold, we have no idea where we are or if anyone knows we're missing, someone obviously wants us dead, and we might be out here for weeks."

"All of that is true, but you have to look on the bright side, Zo."

"There's a bright side?" she asked.

"There's always a bright side," Bubba told her. "It doesn't look like anyone is out here with us, trying to kill us; it's not winter, and while it's chilly, there's no snow on the ground and it's above freezing; I've got a compass so we can't get lost; and we aren't going to starve because I can hunt and cook any small animals dumb enough to walk into my snare. And we're not alone. We've got each other."

"True," Zoey said in a small voice. "If I were by myself, I have no idea what I would've done. Probably have a nervous breakdown."

"Nah, you would've done what you've always done."

"And what's that?" she asked when he didn't immediately finish his thought.

"Pulled yourself up by your bootstraps and gotten shit done."

"I think that's the nicest thing anyone has said to me," Zoey told him.

"Then I'll have to work harder to top it," Bubba said. And he wasn't just placating her. Everything he'd learned today had been enlightening. Zoey Knight wasn't someone who let life get her down. "I'm glad I'm not alone either," he told her after a while.

She made a scoffing noise.

"What?" he asked. "I'm being serious."

"As if you need anyone else. All I'm doing is slowing you down."

"Not true," Bubba told her. "Having a team is the most important thing in a situation like this. You've got my back and I've got yours. That's how a team works."

"You got stuck with a pretty shitty teammate then, Mark."

His name on her lips never failed to make his belly do flip-flops. "Don't say that," he scolded. "When I was going through BUD/S, we were taught that every single person is vital to the mission. Yeah, today has been tough for you, but I've watched you get more and more confident in your abilities as time has passed. You know how to start a fire and make a shelter, now. But probably more important, you've kept me company. Losing my dad was like a sucker punch to my gut. I have a lot of guilt and regret about our relationship, and having you talk about him, telling stories about him, made me feel a lot better. So don't think you aren't a vital part of this mission, Zo. Because you are."

"So this is a mission now?" she asked.

The sun had finally set, and the fire in front of them was the only light around for miles and miles. It felt intimate and cozy.

"It's absolutely a mission," Bubba told her. "Someone wanted us gone, out of the way. We need to figure out who and what they have to gain from it. We need to survive long enough to get back to civilization. We're bound to run into someone eventually. Even though this is Alaska, there are thousands of people living off the grid. We don't want to get eaten by a bear or moose, we have to find our own food and water, and most importantly, we have to stay positive. So yeah, Zo, it's definitely a mission."

"I'm glad you're here with me," Zoey said.

"And I'm glad you're here with me too," Bubba returned.

Several minutes of silence passed. Zoey shivered in his arms, and Bubba tightened his hold on her. He should be exhausted, but just like when he was on a mission for the navy, his mind wouldn't shut down. As was his way, he couldn't stop trying to figure out why someone had gone through the trouble of stranding them. He kept going over everything Zoey had said about his dad, and about the people who were closest to him.

"Do you know exactly how my dad died?" he asked

63

after at least twenty minutes of silence. "I mean, I know it was his heart, but that's about all I know."

"I don't know all the details. He'd been feeling under the weather for quite a while. I'd made him chicken noodle soup and stuff when I visited. Some days were better than others. But he'd been feeling better. I was relieved about that. I thought it was safe for me to go to Anchorage. Your dad hated doctors, never wanted to admit that he needed one. If he had any kind of chest pains or anything, I know he wouldn't have gone to the hospital like he should've. Anyway, Malcom went to the house to check on him, since he hadn't shown up at work, and found him in his bed. He'd apparently passed away sometime in the night."

"I didn't even know he was sick," Bubba said softly. "I hate that."

Zoey then did something that blew Bubba away. She picked up his hand, kissed the palm, then put it back around her chest. "He didn't want anyone to know. I only knew because I was at his house every other day getting his mail, straightening up the place, things like that. Sean knew, and Malcom. Oh, and I guess Kenneth knew too, but that was about it. None of his employees were aware of how ill he'd gotten, and that's how he preferred it. I begged him to go to the doctor, but he always said he'd feel better in the morning and kept putting it off. But I swear neither of us thought he'd have a heart attack."

"That's totally my dad." Bubba sighed. "I'm gonna miss him."

"Me too," Zoey agreed. "What's the plan for tomorrow?"

"Same as today. We keep moving south. Hopefully I'll have caught something in the trap and we can get some protein in us. We'll keep our eye out for edible mushrooms and berries, and we can nibble on certain leaves too. There's no danger of us dehydrating because it seems as if every hundred yards we have to cross one stream or another. We'll just keep moving until we either run into some sort of town, or we cross paths with someone."

"You make it sound so easy," Zoey complained good-naturedly.

"One foot in front of the other," Bubba told her. "That's all we can do."

"Do you really think your friends will realize something's wrong?"

Earlier when they were setting up the camp for the night, Bubba had mentioned his team, and how he was sure they'd figure out something was up and come looking for him when he didn't get in touch.

"Yes. I'd bet everything I own that Rocco has already called in the troops."

Bubba felt Zoey finally relax against him. She gave him her weight, and that small step toward trusting him felt amazing. As if he'd crossed some huge hurdle that he'd been working at for days.

He shifted until they were both on their sides. He kept his arm around her waist and pulled Zoey back against him. She had the fire in front of her and hopefully his body heat would keep her warm as well. It was chilly, though nothing that he hadn't been through before. But Zoey wasn't used to this at all, and, like she said, her body temperature seemed naturally low. He'd have to watch her carefully to make sure she was holding up all right.

"For the record?" Zoey said.

"Yeah?"

"The next time we go camping, I want the glamping experience."

"Glamping?"

"Yeah, camping with all the comforts of home. A real bed, real pillows, shower, maybe even a Jacuzzi. Fireplace and room service."

"Is this really a thing, or did you make it up?"

"It's a thing," she told him. "Look it up. Well...you'll have to look it up when we get home. I don't like sleeping on the ground."

"I'm not a huge fan myself," Bubba told her. "But I promise to take you glamping when we get back."

"Good. Mark?"

"Yeah?"

"I don't know how you've managed it, but I'm not freaking out. I'm scared...but with you by my side, I think we might actually make it home."

"We will. I swear to God, I'm going to get you home safe and sound."

"Of course, getting home doesn't mean that whoever orchestrated this little camping trip won't try to get rid of us again," she murmured.

Bubba tensed.

Fuck. He hadn't even thought about that. Of *course* they would. Because someone didn't go to the lengths they had to make both him and Zoey disappear if they weren't serious about it. He had no idea if both of them were the primary targets, but at the moment, it didn't matter.

"I'm going to find out who did this and make sure you're safe to live your life the way you want to," Bubba vowed.

But Zoey hadn't heard him. She was breathing deeply, indicating that she'd dropped off to sleep.

Tightening his hold, pulling her into him until he didn't

know where she ended and he began, Bubba thought about his friends.

Rocco, you better have called in the troops when I didn't call you like I said I would.

"Something's wrong," Rocco muttered under his breath. He'd been half-joking when he'd told Bubba to call after he'd landed. But when the time came and went, and then several hours passed, Rocco got more and more uneasy.

His uneasiness increased when he'd called Bubba's phone and it had immediately gone to voice mail. He'd checked the news reports and found no mention of a plane crash in the Anchorage area. He'd even pulled some strings and tried to find out the details of the chartered flight he'd been on, with no luck.

No one in the Anchorage airport could, or would, tell him anything about a flight that was supposed to have left around the time he'd last heard from Bubba.

His "oh shit" meter had been pinged, and enough was enough.

Rocco picked up the phone and dialed the number of the one person he knew would be able to help him immediately. Tex.

He hoped like hell he was overreacting. That Bubba had landed safe and sound in Juneau and was simply too busy dealing with his dad's estate to remember to call.

Even as he had the thought, Rocco dismissed it. Bubba was a professional. He'd no sooner "forget" to call Rocco than he'd head out on a mission without ammunition for his weapons.

No, something had happened. Something bad. And

Rocco wouldn't rest until he'd found out what that something was and brought his friend home.

Hoping like hell he wouldn't bring Bubba home in a pine box, he held his breath as he waited for Tex to pick up the phone.

CHAPTER SIX

"Tell me more about your team," Zoey asked the next day as they trudged south.

The morning had gone as well as it could. Mark had caught a small rabbit and Zoey had felt terrible for the little thing. She wasn't thrilled about watching Mark skin and gut it, but had refused to turn away. If she was going to be his partner out here, she had to learn how to do more. To pull her weight.

She hadn't thought she was going to like rabbit. Especially when she thought about how cute and furry the little thing had been. But the smell of the meat cooking had made her mouth water, and by the time it was done, she no longer felt any reluctance to try it.

Her stomach had been growling nonstop the entire time Mark had cooked. She wasn't used to not eating anything but berries and a piece of candy for dinner, and while she'd been a little reticent to take the first bite, after that, she was hooked.

Manners that she'd learned from a young age went out the window after one bite of food. It tasted *so* good. A little bland and tough, but so damn delicious. They'd both eaten all the meat they could get off the bones then set off feeling stronger and more determined to find some sign of people and civilization.

Three hours later, her enthusiasm for the adventure had dimmed. Even though her boots and socks kept the moisture from getting in, her feet were still cold. Mark marched on as if he could go another hundred miles, and that annoyed her a little...because she knew he actually could. She'd fall over in an exhausted heap way before that.

To keep her mind off her aches and pains, and from remembering how she'd woken up in Mark's arms that morning—a dream come true—she practically begged Mark to talk. She was curious about the men he referred to as if they were his brothers. She'd never had that kind of bond with anyone, friends or family, and was curious as hell about them.

"What do you want to know?" he asked.

"Everything," she told him.

He chuckled, and the sound wrapped its way around her heart and made her feel a little better about the entire situation she'd found herself in. She didn't remember Mark being especially jovial, but since they'd been stranded, she'd heard him laugh often.

"Well, we're a team of six. We've been together since we graduated from SEAL training. Rocco's the oldest at thirty-five, and our unofficial leader. I'm actually the youngest of our crew at thirty-one."

"Wow, really?"

"Really. And we've been on the team a long time, so we practically know what each other is thinking. Most of the time we act before anyone gives us a command."

"That's kind of cool," Zoey told him.

"Yeah. I love those guys. Would do anything for them, just as they'd do for me."

"Is that how you know they'll be looking for you?"

"It is. And I know down to the marrow of my bones that even if we somehow manage to die out here, they still won't stop until they not only find our bodies, but figure out who got us into this situation and how we died."

"Um...that's a little morbid."

Mark chuckled again. "Yeah, I guess it is. But my point is that they're the best friends ever, and I don't know where I'd be without them."

"Must be nice," Zoey said without thinking.

"You don't have friends like that?" Mark asked.

Kicking herself for bringing it up, Zoey tried to blow off his question. "No, I mean...it's nice you have people you can count on like that."

"And you don't?" he pressed.

Shit. He wasn't going to let it drop. "Honestly? No. You know how it is, if you aren't born and raised in Juneau then you're an outsider. I have some people I get together with now and then, but nothing like what you're talking about."

"You'd love Caite, Sidney, and Piper," Mark said.

She was glad he didn't further question her lack of close friends. It was something she hated, and no matter how hard she tried to cultivate friendships, they never seemed to get any deeper than the occasional drink or meal out. "Who?"

"Rocco, Gumby, and Ace's women."

Zoey shook her head. "I swear you guys have the weirdest nicknames. There's no way I could ever call you Bubba. You are so far from a Bubba it's not even funny.

And I'm sure your friends are probably the same way. Gumby? Seriously? Is he big and green?"

Mark laughed. "No. Phantom's the tall one at six-five."

"He's the one you said is intense, right?" Zoey asked.

"Yeah. He had a horrible childhood, although he doesn't ever talk about it with us. Just enough to know the topic is off limits and if he never sees his aunt or mother again, it'll be too soon for him."

Zoey shivered, and only partly because the air was chilly. She wasn't so sure about meeting his team. She knew Mark loved them like brothers, but she couldn't imagine being around so much testosterone all in one place. She had enough trouble dealing with Mark by himself. "Tell me about the women?"

Zoey listened intently as Mark shared the stories about how each of his friends had met their women. They all sounded awesome, and a pang of jealousy went through Zoey.

"Caite actually saved your friends' lives when they were in Bahrain?" she asked. "Or are you exaggerating for the sake of the story?"

"I'm serious," Mark told her. "Rocco said they'd made their peace with it, and were trying to figure out how to take out the most smugglers before they were shot, when Caite moved the table off the hatch that was keeping it shut tight. If she hadn't shown up when she did, the smugglers could've just stood above the cellar they were trapped in and shot Rocco, Gumby, and Ace one by one."

Zoey shivered. She didn't like to think about how that could've been Mark. Hell, he hadn't told her any other stories from his missions, but she had a feeling that it probably *had* been Mark at one point. Thank God he was still around today.

"I'm so glad Sidney rescued Hannah," she said.

"Yeah, me too. That pit bull had been so abused, but you'd never know it as she's the most loving creature I've ever met...except if someone threatens her humans."

"And I can't believe Piper and Ace were allowed to adopt those girls so fast! That's totally not normal, right?"

"Right. But that's Tex. He's amazing. I swear to God he can find a needle in a haystack without breaking a sweat."

Zoey knew she sounded a bit more unsure than she wanted when she said, "I never thought I'd compare myself to a needle, but I hope to God you're right and he can find us in this haystack of a forest."

Mark stopped then and faced her. Zoey almost wished he'd just keep walking. Then she wouldn't have to try to look braver than she felt. Their situation was sinking in more with every hour spent in these woods. This wasn't some tough camping trip. Someone had actually tried to make sure they'd disappear *forever*. Probably hoping they'd get eaten by a bear or something.

"He's going to find us," Mark said without one shred of doubt.

"You can't know that."

"I do. And you want to know why?"

"Why?"

"Because he's the best at what he does. Because he's a former SEAL. Because he knows how pissed off I'd be that someone dared try to kill me off for something as stupid as money."

"You really think that's why?" Zoey asked.

Mark nodded. "There's really no other explanation. The question is, who? Kenneth? He was the one who'd arranged the charter for us. Sean? Pop's business partner?

He could be pissed if Pop left me part of the business, especially when I haven't been involved in it at all."

"Maybe it was Ashley," Zoey said, getting into the spirit of the discussion.

"Who?"

"Ashley Gilstrap. She was a nurse your brother hired to keep an eye on your dad. She came to see him on the days I didn't."

"I didn't know about her. Is she older? Younger? Married?"

"I'd say probably around our age. Single. I think your brother and her had a thing for a while, but I'm not positive."

"Speaking of which...we can't take Malcom off the list either."

"Do you really think your own brother would try to get rid of you?" Zoey asked.

Mark shrugged. "No. At least, I'd like to think not, but at this point, we have to suspect everyone."

"Sean's wife is a bitch," Zoey volunteered. "Your dad told me that Vivian Kassamali hated the business and was always telling Sean to sell out his half."

Mark looked down at her for a long moment.

"What?" Zoey asked with a tilt of her head.

"You're amazing," Mark told her quietly.

Zoey had no idea what he was talking about. She frowned up at him.

"I know you don't think so, but just being able to talk things through with you helps. This is what my team does. We brainstorm and throw out every possible outcome of every action. It helps us put a plan in place and make sure we come home in one piece."

"Inside, I'm freaking out. I hate this, Mark. No one has

tried to kill me before and it doesn't make any sense," Zoey said honestly.

"And that makes the way you're handling things even more remarkable. To get back to our original subject, Tex and my team will find us...if we don't rescue ourselves first. I half expect them to show up, laughing and joking about how long it took me to find *them*."

"I wouldn't be opposed to them showing up, but let's say they swoop in with a helicopter so we don't have to walk another hundred miles, yeah?"

Mark threw his head back and laughed, and Zoey was fascinated by the way his throat moved. Then he recovered and stepped toward her. He engulfed her in a huge bear hug, and it felt wonderful.

She'd loved waking up in his arms. The ground was cold, the fire almost out, and she couldn't really feel her feet, but sometime in the night she'd turned so she was facing him, and he'd turned on his back. Her nose had been buried in his neck and his arm was around her waist, holding her tight. She could feel his body heat even through both their layers. For just a moment, she'd closed her eyes and tried to pretend they were sleeping together back in her bed in Juneau. That he'd come to visit his dad and promptly fell head over heels for her. He'd made love to her all night, and they'd both fallen asleep from exhaustion.

It was stupid, but she couldn't stop her wayward imagination.

"A helicopter it is, Zo," Mark said, then he kissed her temple and stood back. "You good to keep going for a while longer?"

Zoey nodded. She was tired, but she'd be damned if she let Iron Man in front of her know.

But it seemed he knew anyway. "Just a while. We'll stop soon and I'll find us a snack. Okay?"

"Okay," she agreed.

He looked at her for a long moment, and Zoey would give anything at that second to be able to read minds and know what he was thinking. But eventually he simply nodded his head once, then turned and they were on their way again.

Finding their way through the forest wasn't a walk in the park. There weren't any trails to follow so they had to bushwhack their way as they went. Mark was constantly on alert for the sounds of bears or other animals, and more than once, he'd held up his hand for her to stop then stood listening for a long few minutes. Every time it happened, Zoey couldn't hear anything but her own heart, which sounded way too loud and beat way too fast. But each time, after a moment, they'd continued their trek. So far they hadn't come across any massive bears or moose, but Zoey knew that was just luck.

True to his word, after about an hour, Mark found a large rock for her to sit on and rest while he wandered off to find them something to eat.

"Don't go far," Zoey called out when he was about to disappear into the forest around them.

He stopped and came back to her. He put his hands on the rock next to her hips and leaned in. Zoey could only stare at him in surprise.

"I'll be back as soon as I can."

"O-Okay," she stammered.

"I'm not leaving you out here by yourself," he said.

"I know. But...shit happens."

"I swear on my life, I'll be back."

Zoey's throat closed up with unshed tears, and she

nodded. She couldn't talk without Mark realizing how close to the edge she was.

As if he knew anyway, he brushed her hair out of her face and leaned forward to kiss her forehead. Then he rested his sweaty forehead against her own and put a hand behind her neck.

The position was intimate and personal. Neither of them smelled all that great anymore, and Zoey knew her hair was probably a rat's nest on her head, but at the moment, none of that seemed to matter. It was as if they were the only two people in the world.

"I haven't survived being captured by the Taliban, two helicopter crashes, and countless assholes trying to shoot me and blow me up to be taken out by a bear in the middle of Alaska, leaving my girl to fend for herself. I. Will. Be. Back. If you believe nothing else I say, believe that. All right?"

Zoey wanted to hear all about the Taliban and the helicopter crashes, but figured she was probably better off not knowing. Besides, he probably couldn't talk about them anyway. So she simply nodded once more.

"I know it's not exactly comfortable, but if you can take a nap, feel free. At least close your eyes and try to relax. I'll be back soon with something to eat and we'll be on our way again."

"Be careful," she whispered when he finally stood.

"I will."

And with that, he turned and headed out into the dense forest around them. One second he was there, and the next she was alone. She couldn't even hear Mark walking around. It was scary, and she forced herself not to call out for him. He said he'd be back, so he'd be back.

Taking a deep breath, Zoey did as Mark suggested. She closed her eyes and did her best to relax.

Bubba hated the wild look in Zoey's eyes. He hated that she was scared. She'd done an amazing job so far. She was more than pulling her weight, and he hated like hell they were in this situation in the first place. He didn't like thinking about who in his father's circle might've arranged for their demise, but it wasn't something he could ignore. Someone had hired Eve Dane to fly them into the wilderness and leave them stranded.

He supposed it could be worse. Whoever was behind this could've sabotaged the plane so they'd crashed for real.

The whole situation was so bizarre. Why just leave them stranded if murder was the objective? Whoever had hired Eve had no way of knowing if he and Zoey would die after being left in the wilderness. The possibility that they'd come waltzing out of the wilderness weeks from now might be slim, but it was still possible.

Zoey wasn't a SEAL, of course, and she was right when she'd said she was slowing him down. But the fact of the matter was, he didn't care. He'd rather have her with him than not. Bubba didn't know if they had ten miles to walk or a thousand. He was hoping that Rocco and Tex would work their magic and actually fly to their rescue sooner rather than later. In the meantime, they just had to keep moving, find enough to eat, and stay as dry and warm as possible. He could probably last for weeks out here on his own, but he wasn't sure Zoey could, although she'd held up well so far.

Spying what he'd been looking for, Bubba kneeled by a tree and carefully pulled up the mushrooms growing at the base. His dad had taught him long ago which fungi were safe to eat and which weren't. His pop had taught him a hell of a lot, and for just a moment, Bubba let his head drop as the reality of his father's death washed over him.

He'd never again hear Pop's laugh.

Never hear him talk excitedly about some new plastic.

Would never read another email from him, asking if he'd found a girlfriend yet.

Never hear him tease Bubba about wanting to be a grandfather.

It wasn't fair.

Taking a deep breath, Bubba stood with the mushrooms in his hand. He couldn't dwell on the past or his grief would consume him. Like he'd told Zoey, he had to keep going forward. But he made a vow right then and there to make sure the most important people in his life knew how much he appreciated and loved them.

As he retraced his steps back to Zoey, he thought about all the signs of trouble he'd ignored. How Kenneth had insisted on the charter flight when taking a commercial one to Juneau would've been just as fast. The way Eve, the pilot, wouldn't look him in the eyes as she shook his hand when they were introduced. How she hadn't immediately put out a mayday call. How calm she'd been when they were presumably going down.

Even the sound of the engine sputtering, now that he'd thought about it, hadn't sounded right. He wasn't a pilot, but he'd heard enough plane and helicopter engines failing to know what it sounded like.

Yeah, there had been plenty of things to make him take

extra precautions, but he'd been worried about Zoey and focused on making sure she was all right.

He regretted ignoring the signs, but he didn't regret being with Zoey here and now. If he'd stayed on the plane and Zoey had gotten out, would Eve have left her there by herself? If he'd protested in any way, would Eve have pulled out a gun and simply shot them both?

Shaking his head, Bubba forced himself to quit thinking about the what-ifs. He couldn't change anything that he'd done now, and he had to focus on the present. On surviving and getting both him and Zoey back home.

When he remembered the fear on Zoey's face when he'd left, anger filled him. He knew what humans were capable of doing to each other. He'd seen it up close and personal. But he hated that Zoey had to experience it. She was good down to her core. He knew she'd stayed in Juneau mostly because of his dad. Because he'd needed her.

Her being scared was unacceptable. He'd find out who was behind this half-baked plan to get them out of the picture and make sure they paid. They'd fucked up by not outright killing him. Whoever it was must've assumed both he and Zoey would perish in the backwaters of Alaska, but the joke was on them.

"I'm going to find out who you are and make you wish you were never born," Bubba said between clenched teeth. As if by saying it out loud, it would make it more true.

Taking a deep breath to try to control his anger, Bubba walked faster. Zoey would be worried about him, and he needed to get back. He had to feed her, make sure she had enough water, and maybe even warm her up a bit before they started walking. He'd never met a woman who was always cold like she was.

She probably had blankets all over the house that she could snuggle under. Maybe even an electric blanket on the bed. She'd love Riverton. It wasn't too hot or cold. She could go to the many beaches and lay out on the sand and soak in the rays of the sun. He knew without a doubt that she'd get along perfectly with Caite, Piper, and Sidney. In fact, Zoey reminded him a lot of Piper. When they'd been fleeing the rebels in Timor-Leste, Piper had been amazingly resilient.

When he realized where his thoughts were heading, Bubba grinned ruefully. Despite telling Rocco that he was happy being single, the thought of bringing Zoey back to Riverton with him wasn't distasteful in the least.

Stopping in his tracks, he tilted his head up to the sky. *Did you send her to me, Pop? Was I taking too long to give you those grandkids you always wanted?*

There was no answer, of course, but the thought that his dad had somehow kept Zoey safe for him until he could find his way to her was one that wouldn't leave.

Bubba was a big believer in fate, and now that he'd gotten to know Zoey, and was impressed by what he'd learned, he couldn't shake the feeling that his pop had a hand in this somehow. He probably hadn't meant to die, but Bubba hoped like hell he was somewhere watching over them now.

When the burner phone rang, the Boss swore long and low before answering.

Only one woman had that number.

"Hello?"

"Hey, Boss, it's me. The job is done. Now I need the money you promised me."

Shocked as hell that Eva Dawkins, also known as Eve Dane, was still alive, the Boss knew the shit was about to hit the fan. Eva had been hired to fly Mark and Zoey to Juneau, then pretend to have "engine trouble" along the way and ditch them.

Except the engine trouble should have been real...and Eva was supposed to have died along with her passengers.

It wouldn't do any good for Mark and Zoey to disappear! Their bodies needed to be *found*. But clearly something had gone wrong, since Eva was actually on the phone when she should've been dead. But before the Boss could figure out how to fix whatever had been fucked up, Eva needed to explain what she'd done with her passengers.

"Not so fast. I need details. Where'd you leave them?" the Boss asked.

Eva sighed on the other end of the line. "Mark fell asleep right after I took off, thank goodness. If he'd been as hyperaware as you said he was, he would've known we weren't flying southwest toward Juneau. I flew straight west and circled a bit before heading down into the Lake Clark Preserve and Wilderness. I went down between two mountain ranges and landed on a tributary of Two Lakes."

"And he didn't suspect anything?"

"No. I don't think so. Not until it was too late to do anything. I cut the fuel to the engine and made it seem as if we were crash landing. They went into brace position. I landed on the lake and told them I had to check things out. I had them get out, then when they were on shore, I backed up and flew away." Eva paused. "The looks on their faces will haunt me forever, if I'm being honest. Mark knew what was happening immediately, and wasn't happy at all. Zoey simply looked confused. But after I turned the plane around, I looked back. She had a look of utter disbelief and terror on her face."

"And you didn't leave them with anything that might help them survive, right?"

"No. All they had were the clothes they were wearing. But, I have to tell you, Mark had approval to carry a knife on the plane, and I'm pretty sure the pockets of his cargo pants were full, but I don't know with what. Otherwise, all they had were the clothes on their backs."

"Good."

But it wasn't good. *Everything* was fucked now. For most people, having a knife wouldn't be much help, but this was Mark. Everyone knew he was a SEAL. Even just having a knife in the Alaskan wilderness could give him enough of an advantage to save his life, along with the life of that bitch he was with.

"You're sure no one knows where you went and where you are now?"

"As positive as I *can* be," Eva said. "When I filed the flight plan, I used a fake name and fudged the N and serial numbers. So if anyone goes looking for me or my plane, they won't find us. I left the plane in some backwater town with a dirt runway and convinced a local to take me back to Anchorage, where I boarded the flight here to Seattle. Also, since we were flying in the complete opposite direction than I'd declared in the flight plan, anyone who tries to find them will be looking in the wrong place."

"Serves them right. They have no right to Colin's damn money. *None*. They're getting what they deserve."

But the plan was well and truly fucked. Their bodies were supposed to be found quickly. The plane was supposed to crash not too long after takeoff, so all the bodies would be recovered within hours. Now that Eva had actually carried out what she'd thought was the real plan...there was no telling when, or if, Mark and Zoey's bodies would be found.

And that wasn't good. Not at all. A *motion* to have them declared dead—just to start the process—couldn't be filed for several years. The fucking money left to them by Colin would be tied up in the courts until their deaths were official!

"So...when am I getting my money?" Eva asked.

"You'll get it when I know they're not going to show up and claim their part of that inheritance."

"That wasn't the deal! You said when I finished the job, I'd get paid."

"Well, the job's not finished yet, is it? I'll be in touch."

Not giving Eva time to reply, the Boss clicked off the connection, then turned off the burner phone, and made a mental note to ditch it so the bitch couldn't make contact again.

Eva wouldn't call the cops though. She was stuck. She was desperate for the money she'd been promised. If she dared to go home empty-handed, her ex would disappear with her kids, and she knew she'd never see them again.

Eva had been perfect for the job. Expendable and way too naïve. She'd word-vomited her entire sob story, one that made her the perfect patsy for the plan. When Eva had met Jay, her ex, she'd thought she'd hit the jackpot. He'd swept her off her feet, married her, gotten her pregnant...then his true self came out. He was an abusive asshole who dealt drugs for a living.

It took her a while to get out from under Jay's thumb, and she'd thought she'd succeeded. But then he'd called in some favors and gotten a judge to award him full custody of their kids. He didn't want them. Hated them, as a matter of fact, but he loved having the upper hand. Loved knowing he was hurting her. But he said he'd hand over her kids and disappear forever *if* she repaid him every dime he'd spent on her over the last four years.

It was more money than she could ever come up with on her own. Of course, Jay had helpfully given her the name of a contact—the Boss—who would pay her what she needed if she did one little favor...

Fortunately for Ms. Eva Dawkins, the *real* plan had gone sideways. But unfortunately, she'd never see a dime of the money she'd been promised. She wasn't supposed to have survived. She was supposed to be *dead*, right along with Mark and Zoey.

Sighing, the Boss knew the only hope of getting Colin's money would be for his son and that stupid bitch Zoey to be found. But that would be tricky. Everyone thought they were headed from Anchorage to Juneau, when in reality, they were hundreds of miles in the other direction. This was a disaster...but it might still be salvageable.

It would take careful planning and lots of acting, but with a little luck, poor Mark and Zoey's bodies *would* be found sooner rather than later, and everyone could get on with their lives...a whole lot richer.

CHAPTER SEVEN

The next morning, Bubba didn't immediately wake Zoey. He knew they needed to start moving, but he couldn't make himself get up yet. At thirty-one, he'd been in his share of relationships, but he'd never really understood the allure of cuddling. He was a morning person and was always ready to get up and go.

He'd never felt the urge to lie in bed simply for the hell of it. He always had shit to do. Most of the time he had to get to PT with the rest of the team. But after waking up with Zoey for just two mornings, he realized what he'd been missing out on.

The air was chilly but not frigid. Apparently Zoey didn't know that. She'd once again turned to face him sometime in the night and had buried her face in his chest. Her hands had snuck under his arms, seeking the warmth she knew would be there. Their legs were intertwined, and Bubba couldn't remember ever feeling this...content... simply being with a woman.

Yes, they were in a unique situation, but he had a feeling he would've felt comfortable around Zoey even if they weren't in a life-threatening position. Bubba figured part of the reason he felt so comfortable with her was because they weren't exactly strangers. He'd liked her back in high school, and even though that was a long time ago, he felt drawn to her now.

They knew the same people. Hell, she was closer to his dad than he'd been. The night before, they'd talked about the old hangout spots from when they were in high school, and they'd laughed over the fact the kids today were doing the same things they'd done over a decade ago. Things in Juneau hadn't changed all that much, which was both comforting and a little disconcerting at the same time.

Bubba shifted, trying to dislodge the rock that was jabbing into his ass, and his movements woke Zoey. He smiled as she groaned and slowly came awake. She was so different from him. When he was awake, he was *awake*. He could go from being dead to the world to on his feet, ready to fight, in seconds. It took Zoey several minutes to even crack her eyes open after she woke. He had a feeling she was a three-cups-of-coffee girl before she'd be awake enough to talk.

"You sleep okay?" he asked quietly after a moment.

"No," she mumbled into his chest.

Smiling, Bubba merely shook his head and waited for her to wake up a bit more. It wasn't as if they had to be anywhere at a certain time. He could lie there all day with her in his arms.

It took another five minutes or so for her to wake up enough to think about moving. Five minutes during which Bubba ignored the rock poking his ass and simply enjoyed the curvy body cuddled against him. When she finally lifted her head and looked up, Bubba felt something jerk inside him at the look in her eyes.

She was still sleepy and her hair was in complete disarray. Her cheeks were red, from both sunburn and a touch of windburn, most likely. Any makeup she'd been wearing had long since been rubbed and sweated away. Neither of them smelled all that great, but for some reason, he was more drawn to her than ever.

"Hi," he said inanely.

"Hi," she returned. Then after a moment, she asked, "Do I look as rough as I feel?"

Bubba chuckled, then lied straight to her face. "No."

She rolled her eyes, and Bubba couldn't help but smile at her reaction. He'd never see someone roll their eyes again in his life and not think of her.

"Liar. But I appreciate it." She slowly sat up and groaned once more. "I have no idea how in the world you're always so damn warm, but I have to say that I appreciate it more with every minute that goes by."

"Anytime you want to use me as your own personal heater, I'm at your disposal," Bubba assured in a much more serious tone than he'd intended.

"Thanks," she said with a laugh. "Maybe you can just follow me around and let me stick my icy hands under your shirt whenever I get cold."

As soon as the words were out of her mouth, she closed her eyes briefly, and Bubba saw her cheeks pinken even more than they already were. "Ignore me," she mumbled. "I'm obviously delirious."

Bubba chuckled. Then he stood and held a hand down to her. As she took it, and he helped her stand, he said, "Nah. Tired, hungry, and worried, maybe, but not delirious."

Then he took both her hands in his and slipped them under his shirt at his sides and held them against his skin. They were chilly, but not so much as to really bother him.

The look of ecstasy on her face was more than enough reward for the slight discomfort he might feel.

She closed her eyes and groaned, and Bubba couldn't help but think about her having that same reaction to him doing something *else* with her, but he quickly pushed the thought aside. The last thing either of them needed was adding any kind of sexual tension to their already stressful situation. He needed to be her friend right now.

"Oh my God," she said quietly. "That feels so good."

Bubba stood there with his hands on her waist, hers clutching his bare skin under his shirt, for a couple of long minutes before she sighed and looked up at him. "Thanks. What's on the agenda today? A little fly fishing followed by a nice quiet walk in the woods and a four-course dinner at the lodge when we get tired? Oh, and let's not forget the soak in the hot tub under the stars too, huh?"

He chuckled. "I was thinking we should see if we caught anything in the snare. If so, we'll cook that up, then see if we can't make some more headway to get out from between these two mountains. I also thought we could have a competition today to see who can find the most mushrooms."

Zoey sighed but smiled up at him gamely. "You're going down, SEAL Boy."

"It's good to have confidence," he replied.

Then she blew his mind by getting serious and saying, "Thank you for making this not suck as much as it could. For keeping my mind off the fact someone literally left us out here to die. And thank you for packing more shit in your pockets than I have in my entire suitcase. A knife, compass, twine, flint, and who the hell knows what else you've got in there. Just...thank you. I can't imagine this going very well with anyone other than you."

Bubba couldn't help it. He reached out and palmed her cheek. "You don't have to thank me, Zo. In fact, I'm guessing if you hadn't had the bad luck of being on that plane, you'd be back in Juneau cursing my name because I didn't bother to show up for the reading of my dad's will."

She frowned at him. "What are you saying? That you think *you're* the target of whoever did this?"

"That's exactly what I'm saying."

"Do you know what's in your dad's will?"

"No. You?"

She shook her head.

"Right. Obviously Pop left you something. I can't say what, you'd probably know better than me, but it's most likely not enough for someone to want you dead."

Zoey stared up at him but didn't respond.

"But me being his son...and knowing how much his business is worth, I'm guessing there's quite a bit of money in there for me."

She blinked as if something had just occurred to her. "Oh my God, Mark. Do you think Malcom's okay? What if someone went after him too?"

Bubba had thought about that himself, but he hadn't said anything because he didn't want to worry her. And...if his brother had done this, then he'd obviously *not* be in any danger.

When he didn't answer fast enough, Zoey asked, "Do you think Malcom's behind this?"

"I don't know," Bubba said quickly. "But at this moment, the only thing I'm concerned about is the two of us. We can't control anything else but our own situation.

There's no sense worrying about shit we can't do a damn thing about."

Zoey closed her eyes, and Bubba saw her shoulders slump as she leaned into his hand. He held her gently and waited for her to work through whatever she was thinking about.

Eventually, her eyes opened and she said, "I hate that money can do this to people. *Hate* it. I mean, I'm not stupid. I know money makes the world go 'round, but it's insane how little money it takes to make people do terrible, awful things. I'm not that fond of your brother. He's kind of a jerk. But he works hard and was really helpful to your dad. I don't wish him ill will, so I hope he's okay."

"What about Sean?"

Zoey sighed. "Yeah, I could see him doing this. I know he and Colin had been arguing a lot recently about the business. I think Sean wanted to move the factory overseas, where it would be cheaper to make the products, but your dad was fighting that. He wanted to keep jobs here in America. In Juneau. They'd been fighting a lot about it."

"What side was Malcom on?"

Zoey shrugged. "I don't know. But all the fighting and tension was really eating at Colin. That, along with him being sick all the time, was making him cranky and short with just about everyone."

Bubba hated to think about anyone wanting to kill him, but especially not the people who were closest to his dad. Zoey was right, it sucked that money could make someone want to kill to get it.

Just then, Zoey's stomach let out a loud rumble. She wrinkled her nose, and Bubba finally dropped his hand from the side of her face. She put a hand over her belly and said, "Can you call room service and ask what's taking them so long to get our order to us?"

He smiled down at her, and not for the first time, thanked God that they'd been stranded together. "I'll get right on that."

"And I don't suppose you have any shampoo in those pockets of yours, do you?" she asked with a hopeful arch of a brow.

"Unfortunately, no. But I do have this..." Bubba reached into a pocket low on his pants, near his calf, and produced a small black comb. At the look on her face, Bubba would've thought he'd pulled out a miniature helicopter that could take them out of there.

"A comb! Oh my God, you're my hero!" she exclaimed.

Bubba had never cared much for that word, but hearing it come from her lips and seeing her look up at him like he'd given her the world felt good. Then, looking at her hair, he grimaced and said, "You might need some help."

She grinned, and one of her hands immediately went to her hair to try to smooth it down. "That bad, huh?" she asked.

Bubba shook his head. "Nothing we can't figure out."

"Thank you," she told him again.

"Nope. None of that. We're a team and in this together."

She looked at the comb longingly for a moment, then took a deep breath. "Well, I'm thinking my hair can wait. If you aren't afraid to be seen out in public with me, with my hair looking like it does—if this forest can be considered 'out in public'—then I can wait until later to deal with it. We need to check the snares, get a fire started, and figure out where we're going today."

Putting the comb back in his pocket for later, Bubba had to force himself to not take Zoey in his arms. She was incredible. Practical and down-to-earth. But he could still see the vulnerability and uncertainty in her eyes. It made him want to encourage her to spread her wings and enfold her in his arms to keep her safe at the same time. He settled for asking, "Do you want to check the snare or try to start the fire?"

"Fire. I'm not sure I can do it, but I'll leave the dead animals to you, if that's okay."

"You can sit here and do nothing if you want," Bubba told her. He had no problem taking care of them both. But she immediately shook her head.

"No, I'm not a damsel in distress. I'm helping."

"Okay. Remember what I told you yesterday about the flint?"

"Yeah. But let's not expect miracles this first time on my own, okay?"

He chuckled. "If you need me, I'll be a yell away."

"Right. It's not like we have to worry about being quiet or anything. No one's out here to hear us anyway."

Bubba nodded. Things would've been a lot worse if whoever had arranged for them to disappear had sent in a few snipers to make sure they didn't make it out, but they were either too cheap to follow through, or too sure that stranding them would do the trick. "I'll be back soon." He reached into his pocket and pulled out the flint and placed it in her open palm. "You got this, Zo."

"Yup. Just call me Laura Ingalls."

"Who?" Bubba asked, confused.

She laughed. "Never mind. Go. Shoo. You man, provide meat. Me woman, make fire."

Laughing, Bubba turned to leave their impromptu

camping spot. He loved that she was constantly making him laugh.

Yeah, it was safe to say Zoey had gotten under his skin...and he liked her there. A lot.

Zoey did her best to control her breathing as they trudged through the forest later that morning. As it turned out, she hadn't been able to start the fire. The flint was tricky, and she'd been able to make sparks with it, but they hadn't landed where she'd wanted them and she couldn't get the small sticks she'd collected to catch fire.

Of course, Mark had been able to get a flame almost immediately, which was irritating. He'd been nice enough to tell her he'd just gotten lucky, but Zoey knew that wasn't it at all.

The more time she spent around Mark, the more her high school crush rekindled. But this time it was more than a mere crush. She admired Mark. Liked the man he'd become. He was generous, courteous, brave, knowledgeable about a whole hell of a lot.

He was also very observant. She was losing his "look for mushrooms" game, but that wasn't a surprise. She had a feeling he was well aware of every bird that flew overhead and every small mammal that made noises in the underbrush. He held the compass in his hand and kept them on track, while at the same time pointing out every little thing that might trip her up and finding every freaking berry and mushroom they passed.

If she didn't admire him so much, she'd be mightily annoyed.

But it was the glimpses of the not-quite-so-perfect man

that intrigued her the most. He hadn't been the best son, or even brother, if she was honest. He emailed Colin here and there, but he hadn't called much, and he certainly hadn't visited. Malcom was left to help Colin with the business and his everyday needs.

Ten years ago, it hadn't been a big deal, but when Mark's dad had gotten sick, he'd needed more and more assistance. Zoey did what she could, but Malcom had definitely had to step up more. Mark hadn't even been aware he was sick.

And the man was just a bit too damn positive.

She figured he was doing it for her sake, but just once she'd like to hear him complain about the fact they'd been dropped in the middle of a freaking forest. Or about how he wanted a shower. Or how he wanted something to eat other than squirrel meat, berries, leaves, and fungus. She knew he had to be uncomfortable and irritated, but he'd been almost cartoonishly upbeat all morning...and it was maddening.

Zoey did her best to maintain her own positivity as they continued on their trek. He'd tried to explain what his plan was and where they were going, but Zoey had tuned him out a little. The bottom line was that it didn't matter, because neither of them had any real idea of where the hell they were. North of Anchorage? South? She just didn't know.

The mountain peaks on either side of them stood like prison guards, not letting them go anywhere but south. It was almost as if they were herded in that direction, and Zoey couldn't help but shiver.

She was so lost in thought, she almost ran into Mark's back when he stopped. She caught herself just in time and peeked around him to see why he'd stopped.

Blinking in disbelief, she swore at the huge lake blocking their path. "Shit!" She looked up at Mark to see him studying the area intensely.

Sighing, she saw a rock nearby and trudged over to it. She plunked herself down and pulled her knees up. Hugging them to her chest, she lay her cheek on her knees and closed her eyes. If it wasn't one thing, it was another. Yeah, they could probably walk around the lake, but it would take forever. Not that they had a set time frame. They could take an extra day, or three, and it wouldn't make one damn difference in their situation.

But she didn't *want* to take an extra day or three.

"Things could be worse," Mark said after a moment.

Zoey clenched her teeth in irritation. She knew she was being unreasonably grumpy, but she couldn't take Mark's positive attitude at the moment. She *knew* things could be worse, but hey—things were actually pretty shitty right now as they were.

As her frustration grew, so did her irritation. Just *once*, she wanted to see Mark get upset. It wouldn't change anything, and it wouldn't make anything better, but it would make him a little more human in her eyes.

She knew she wasn't being rational—it would be bad if they were both freaking out—but she couldn't help the way she felt.

When she didn't respond, he continued, unaware of her emotional turmoil. "I think I can see the edge of the lake to the west. It'll take some time, but hopefully on the other side we'll find a fisherman or hunter or something."

When she still didn't answer, Mark asked, "Did you hear me, Zo? This lake is a good thing. We'll have lots of fresh water to drink, and maybe we'll even be able to catch a fish for dinner instead of having to eat another squirrel."

"Great," she mumbled, wanting nothing more than to be back in her little house in Juneau living her boring, yet safe and warm life.

She felt one of Mark's hands touch her calf and assumed he was kneeling in front of her. She didn't open her eyes to see.

"Are you all right?" Mark asked softly.

That did it.

She'd been trying to be so strong, trying to hold in her fear and anger and frustration, but she couldn't handle his compassion right now. "No," she whispered. "I'm not all right."

"What's wrong? Talk to me, Zo."

Lifting her head, Zoey looked into Mark's concerned brown eyes and almost chickened out. She could tell him she was just tired, and then they'd start walking around the huge freaking lake...or she could tell him what was bothering her.

She chose honesty.

"I can't do this anymore."

Mark's brows furrowed. "Do what?"

"*This*. Pretend we're on some fun camping trip or something. You haven't complained *once*. I get that this is probably easy compared to some of the things you've seen and done, but it's not for me. I hate it. Every bit of it! And hearing you be all upbeat and positive without even one complaint is killing me! Are you really that calm inside? Is this really no big deal for you? Because it is to me. Someone wants us to *die* out here, Mark! I need to know you're even a little like a normal human. That you're hurting. That you hate this. That you're hungry, your feet hurt, *something*! And I know this all sounds ridiculous because both of us freaking out wouldn't be good, but I'm so far out of my league here, and I just want you to be honest with me."

He stared at her for a heartbeat, and for a second, Zoey thought he was just going to try to calm her. Then he spoke.

"I'm fucking *pissed*," he said in a tone that more than conveyed his anger. "More so because this has to be related to my dad's death and the reading of his will, which means that whoever is behind this is someone I probably know. Someone who was close to my dad. And that makes me want to literally fucking *kill* whoever it was. I hate that I let down my guard enough to allow it to happen in the first place. I fucked up, and now we're both in this situation. I'm worried about you, but at the same time, I'm so impressed with how you've held up it isn't even funny.

"I'm trying to be upbeat and positive because otherwise you'll see a side of me I'm thinking would scare you. I'm concerned that we might have to walk another hundred miles before we find any evidence of another human. I'm scared we're going to come into close contact with a bear or some other pissed-off animal, and I don't have a weapon to defend us. I *am* hungry, and tired, and I'm missing my coffee—but you're right; none of these things is anything I haven't handled before."

Zoey couldn't take her eyes off the man in front of her. It was as if he were a completely different person...and she was kind of embarrassed that she was as turned on as she'd ever been while listening to him complain.

It was exactly what she'd needed. To see some deep emotion from him. Knowing he wasn't taking their situation lightly, strangely, made her feel better.

"The most important thing during a mission is not to dwell on the negatives, but to look at the positives instead.

That's all I'm trying to do. But I'm human, Zo. Just like you. Don't ever think that I'm not aware of the dangers we face. I'm probably more aware of them than anyone. I'm simply trying to stay upbeat because the alternative is to fall so deeply into our misery that we eventually just sit down and give up. And that's *not* an option.

"I like you, Zoey. I liked you when we were eighteen, and I like you even more now. I hate that I can't ask you out on a date like a normal man. That I can't pick you up at your house and see you all dolled up for me. I want to watch you laugh and smile in the candlelight across a table at a fancy restaurant. To feel the anticipation and excitement when I take you home and try to figure out how to ask for a good-night kiss without looking like an ass. That *sucks*...and I hate it."

Zoey couldn't believe what she was hearing. Mark Wright liked her? *Liked* her? Holy shit. "I don't need that stuff," she said without thinking. "Never have. I want a guy to be happy sitting around reading, while every now and then nudging me with his foot to let me know he's thinking about me. Someone who'll go grocery shopping with me and make me laugh in the cereal aisle. A man who isn't afraid to let me see his emotions, and who will tell me he's not in the mood because he has a headache and his bunions are killing him."

Mark chuckled, and Zoey was glad to see the angry look had disappeared from his face. She could see a hint of his emotions in his eyes, and it made her feel much better.

"I love that you're positive, but I don't want you to hide all your concerns about what we're doing from me. We're a team. Talk to me. I might not be a SEAL, but I've lived in Alaska all my life. I can help. At least, I'd like to think I can. If nothing else, I can be a sounding board for you," she told him. "I don't want to hold you back. I don't want to feel as if I'm a burden and you have to constantly check on my mental well-being."

Mark nodded. He hadn't moved his hand from her leg, and the warmth and weight of it made Zoey feel good.

"You're not holding me back, and you are definitely *not* a burden. But I hear you. I've been trying too hard to be upbeat. Got it. I'll do my best to check that, but you have to understand that I'm trying to protect you."

"I know, and I appreciate it. I just want you to be yourself. Not pretending we're out on some pleasure hike. And I'd like to say I don't need protecting, but I'm obviously out of my element here, regardless of my huge score of a four on the outdoor comfortability scale." She gave him a small smile.

He returned it and moved his hand to the back of her calf. She felt his fingers brush against the underside of her thigh and every muscle tensed...in a good way.

"Understood. And you're doing good, Zo. Really good. I'm not lying about that either. I'd say even after the short time we've been out here, you've moved up to a five, five and a half on that outdoor comfortability scale."

"Thanks."

"You're welcome. Now...about this lake?"

"Yeah?"

"It blows."

She chuckled. "Yeah. That's what I thought."

"But I wasn't just being all Positive Polly when I told you about the fish and walking around it. It sucks that it'll take more time, but large lakes sometimes mean people. So we just need to keep our eyes out for them."

"And if we don't find any?"

"Then we keep walking until we do."

"Do you really think someone will find us? That your friends are looking for you?" she asked for what felt like the hundredth time.

"Looking for *us*. And yes. I know without any doubt that Rocco is losing his mind and has already called in the cavalry to search for us."

"Alaska is a great place to hide dead bodies," Zoey replied in a somber tone.

"I know. But we aren't dead, and my friends won't stop until they find us, no matter if they think we've been murdered and dropped off somewhere or not. They'll track down Eve and figure out where she left us and who's behind this. I guarantee it."

"There you go, being a Positive Polly again," Zoey teased.

"No. That's me being real," he argued.

"If you're so sure your friends will find Eve and will figure out where she dumped us, why didn't we stay near that other lake?"

"Because I don't know how stubborn Eve is. Or how long it'll take for them to track her down. And because even if we walked a hundred miles south, having that starting point means they'll slowly expand their radius for searching. They'll eventually find us...if we haven't rescued ourselves first. I'm not willing to wait for them if I don't have to."

Zoey nodded. That made sense. "So...do you really think you can catch a fish?" she asked. "Not that I don't love your squirrel du jour, but I wouldn't mind a nice fat salmon right about now."

"I'm hoping I can," he said.

Zoey appreciated that honesty, rather than a straight-up yes, more than she could say. She slowly dropped her legs, and Mark stood as she did. "Well, if we have to walk around this fucking lake, we might as well get started," she said.

Reaching out, Mark pulled her into him, and she gladly went, resting her cheek against his chest and listening to his heartbeat. It soothed her at the same time his nearness made her want to latch on to him and never let go. She forced herself to take a step back and gesture to their left. "After you."

"You just want me to go first to break up all the spider webs," Mark complained.

Zoey burst out laughing. "Don't tell me you're afraid of spiders?"

"Can't stand them," Mark replied.

Even though nothing had changed—they were still stuck in the middle of nowhere with nothing but the clothes on their backs—she felt better than she had since before they'd climbed onto the small chartered flight.

"Tell ya what, if I see any crawling on you, I'll be sure to save you from them."

"I appreciate that," Mark told her. "Come on. Let's get this show on the road."

As she set out after him, Zoey couldn't help but feel a spark of hope. He continued to believe his friends would be looking for them, and she had to believe him. She just prayed they'd be able to find Eve and get her to tell them where she'd left Mark and Zoey sooner rather than later.

CHAPTER EIGHT

Rocco paced the small meeting room on the base in agitation. It had been two days since Bubba was supposed to land in Anchorage to deal with his dad's will. But when he didn't get in contact with anyone three hours after he was supposed to have landed, Rocco called Tex and got the guys together, and they'd started making inquiries.

Now, two days later, they still hadn't heard from Bubba, and no one seemed to know where he was. And worse, the plane he'd been on hadn't been seen or heard from either. They all knew that meant it had most likely crashed, but something didn't feel right, and Rocco always went with his gut. It'd saved his life more than once in the past.

"Okay, so we've called all the hospitals in both Anchorage and Juneau, with no luck. The police in both cities haven't had any reports of plane crashes, and the National Transportation and Safety Board hasn't reported any maydays being called in around the time he was supposed to be in the air," Rocco summed up as he paced.

"I contacted Zoey Knight's mother in Anchorage, and she hasn't heard from her daughter either," Rex said.

"And Kenneth Eklund wasn't any help," Ace said on a sigh. "In fact, he was decidedly *unhelpful*. He didn't know the name of the pilot or anything about the plane he chartered. Claimed his assistant arranged the flight. When I asked for a receipt, or *something* to show that he'd chartered the plane, he couldn't produce anything. Then I asked to speak to his assistant, and he said she's on vacation this week. All of that is decidedly suspicious, if you ask me."

Rocco agreed. "Right, but we were able to obtain the name of the pilot and the plane number from the Anchorage airport."

"But we haven't been able to find *anything* on an 'Eve Dane,'" Gumby added.

"This whole thing is suspicious as hell," Phantom growled.

Rocco held up his hand. "I agree. But right now, the main thing is Bubba. The commander has given us permission to head up to Anchorage to start our search from there."

"I hate to be a downer, but we don't even know where to start," Gumby said.

"Well, Juneau is southeast of Anchorage, so we start looking between the two cities. Commander North has hooked us up with the Alaska State Troopers, and we'll start our search from the air."

Phantom stood up so fast, his chair crashed to the floor behind him, but he didn't apologize and didn't pick it up. Like Rocco, he paced agitatedly next to the table. "We're looking for a needle in a haystack," he complained. "There've been no pings from Bubba's cell phone because he most likely turned it off before the plane took flight. So we can't track him that way. If that tiny plane he was in crashed, it would be almost impossible to see through the trees. Or, God forbid, if it went into the ocean, it would've sunk like a stone. And who's to say they even went in the direction of Juneau? We have a flight plan, but if something went wrong, the pilot could've deviated from it. We have no idea if that damn pilot went north, east, south, or west. We need more. *Something*!"

Rocco agreed one hundred percent. He was as pissed as Phantom, but the shit of it was, they had no options other than to simply fly around and search for their friend and teammate. "Look, we all know Bubba. He's a tough son of a bitch. Remember when we were captured by those assholes over in the Middle East on that one op? He was the one who managed to hide his fucking KA-BAR well enough that it wasn't found when they searched us. He had so much shit in his pockets that even our captors were impressed. I don't know what happened to Bubba up in Alaska. But what I *do* know is that if there's even a one percent chance of surviving whatever it was, Bubba would've done it. And he's probably got a fucking tent in one of his pockets that he's using to hole up in. I don't care if we have to search every fucking square inch of the state, I'm not giving up until we find him, dead or alive."

One by one, his fellow SEAL teammates nodded their agreement.

Except for Phantom.

The man looked extremely angry and frustrated and, as usual, Rocco couldn't read what he was thinking.

Finally, he spoke. "Something is very fucked here. It's way too coincidental that Bubba flew up to Alaska to find out about his inheritance and he disappeared without a trace. Someone wanted him dead, probably so he couldn't collect whatever his dad left for him. We all know sex and money are the two things that make seemingly normal, law-abiding citizens lose their minds. Do we know anything about this Zoey chick who was with him?"

Gumby picked up a piece of paper and read from it. "Zoey Knight. Thirty-one years old. She moved to Juneau in the tenth grade and has lived there since. Mother's in Anchorage and her father's not in the picture. Hasn't been for years. She works part-time in one of those kitschy tourist shops downtown in the summers. She's also been helping out Colin Wright for ten years or so. She's been renting a house from Colin, and she makes just enough money to live on. She's got about a thousand dollars in her accounts. No big deposits or withdrawals in the last four months. She was in Anchorage visiting her mother when Colin passed away, and the lawyer asked her to come in for the reading of the will as well. Since she was in Anchorage, he arranged for her to be on the same flight as Bubba."

"So she could be in on whatever happened to him," Phantom concluded. "Maybe she was dating Bubba's dad, and he told her what he was going to leave her. She's pissed that she didn't get more in the will. If Bubba wasn't paying attention, she could've gotten the drop on him and killed him, then worked with the pilot to dump his body some-where before they both disappeared."

"At this point, that's all irrelevant," Rocco said.

"How can you say that?" Phantom asked. "You know as well as I do that no one is innocent until we've found proof they aren't involved."

"I'm saying it's irrelevant because our first concern is finding Bubba. If she's with him, fine. If not, fine. But we've got time to figure this shit out...*after* we find our teammate. Believe me, Phantom. If we find out that his disappearance is anything other than a freakish accident,

I'll be at the front of the lynch mob to take down whoever dared try to hurt him. But until then, all I care about is *finding* him. The longer we sit around here with our thumbs up our asses, the longer it's going to take to bring him home. And if he's injured or trapped in the wreckage of a plane, we need to get eyes in the sky now. *Everything* else can wait."

Rocco stared into Phantom's eyes for a long moment, not willing to back down. Yeah, they could call Tex and get him working in the background to find out the whys and whos—and in fact, he'd already done that—but as for the team, at the moment, their priority was Bubba.

Finally, Phantom nodded. "You're right. We'll have time to figure this shit out after we find him."

Rocco gave his friend a chin lift, then turned to the others. "Wheels up in two hours. Go home, pack, say goodbye to your women and do what you have to do. We're not coming back until we find our teammate. SEALs don't leave SEALs behind. Ever."

Everyone chimed in with their agreement and filed out of the room. Rocco gathered up the papers before taking a deep breath. He pressed his lips together and couldn't help but send a silent plea to his missing friend.

Wherever you are, Bubba. Hang on. We're coming for you.

"That's it. You've almost got it," Bubba praised as he watched Zoey try to start a fire for the fourth time. She was struggling to get the hang of the flint. It took a lot of practice to be able to get the sparks to land right where they needed to, then coax those sparks into a flame.

She sighed in frustration and sat back on her heels,

holding the flint and striker out toward him. "Forget it. I can't do it."

Bubba didn't reach for the fire-starting tool. "You almost had it that time. Try again," he urged.

Zoey shook her head. "No. I suck at this. I'll just go and collect more wood. You're in charge of the fire and shelter. I can gather wood instead."

Bubba reached out and grabbed her biceps to keep her from standing. "Don't give up, Zoey."

She looked at him, and he could see the defeat in her eyes and hated it. "Mark, I appreciate you trying to teach me new things, but I'm tired. And hungry. And the only way we're going to get to eat that fish you caught today is if we get this fire started. Please. Just do it, and I'll go get more wood for later."

Knowing if he continued to push her, it could do more harm than good, Bubba nodded before she gave him a tired smile and got to her feet. As soon as she was a good distance away with her back to him, he leaned over and used the flint to get the fire started within seconds.

She'd helped him with their shelter for the night, and while she hadn't quite gotten the hang of the exact way to bend the twigs and sticks to get them to stay together, she was getting better. He had no doubt by the time Rocco and his team found them, she'd be an expert. She was frustrated now, yes, but most of the time he could see the determination in her eyes not to be a burden and to learn as much as possible so she could carry her own weight.

It had been three days since they'd been abandoned in the wilderness, and if she'd been a four on a scale of one to ten when it came to outdoor stuff when they'd been stranded, she was at least a six and a half now.

Bubba admired her. She didn't let her frustrations get

the better of her and most of the time she stayed upbeat and positive. He wasn't surprised that she was flagging now. They'd had to take cover for much of the day, since it had been raining. The worst thing that could happen to them was to get soaking wet. They had no clothes to change into and even though it wasn't the middle of winter, it wasn't exactly warm. Wet clothes would leech out their body warmth and they could get hypothermia, even though the temperature wasn't below freezing.

The rest of the evening went by fairly quickly. They'd eaten their dinner, which consisted of the salmon he'd caught and more berries and mushrooms. The fish had been delicious and a welcome change from the tough meat of the squirrels he'd caught. But Bubba could tell Zoey was having a hard time shaking off her frustration.

When they'd finished their meal and had built up the fire as far as they'd dared, Bubba held out his hand. "Come here."

She looked at him questioningly, but put her hand in his and let him pull her over to where he was sitting. He situated her in front of him and put his arms around her. His legs were outstretched on either side of hers, and it felt like they were literally the only two people in the world at this moment in time. Resting his chin on her shoulder, they sat cheek to cheek, staring at the fire for a few minutes.

He didn't like to talk about the past events he was preparing to share with her, but he thought at this point, she needed to hear it.

"I told you before that I'd been held captive by the Taliban."

He felt her jerk slightly in surprise in his arms, but she didn't pull away, just nodded once.

"Rex and Ace had been injured, and even with the other four of us healthy and able, we couldn't take on the twenty men who'd surrounded us, so we allowed ourselves to be taken."

"Holy shit, really?" Zoey asked.

"Yeah. We probably could've gotten away, but we weren't going to leave Rex and Ace. No way in hell."

Zoey turned her head to look at him, but he stared straight ahead at the crackling flames. He wasn't sure what she saw, but after a moment, she turned back around, curled her hands around his thighs and held on tightly.

He sighed silently, loving her hands on him, but needed to get his story over and done with.

"They searched us, and much like this time around, I had a ton of shit in my pockets, and they were too busy laughing at me and my huge assortment of supplies to really do a thorough search."

Zoey inhaled sharply. "What'd they miss?"

Smiling because of how quickly she'd caught on, he said, "A knife. It was tucked into a secret inside pocket of my pants."

"So you used it to kill them and get out of there?" she asked.

Shaking his head, Bubba said, "No, unfortunately. They were pretty excited to have us at their mercy and spent the first twenty-four hours beating the shit out of us. They tied us all up in separate rooms—actually, they were more like stalls...there were walls but no doors—next to each other and went from room to room, beating us."

Zoey inhaled sharply and her fingers tightened on his thighs, but she didn't comment.

"We could hear what was happening, but couldn't see each other. We've been trained to withstand torture, so it wasn't the beatings that got to me. I could handle the pain. It was the worry over Rex and Ace that almost broke me.

"I remembered back when we were in Hell Week together. It's the third week of BUD/S training, before the navy makes an expensive investment in SEAL operational training. It's five and a half days of literal pure hell. Four hours of sleep the entire week, running, swimming, paddling, sit-ups, pushups, rolling in the sand, slogging through mud...you name it, they put us through it. The sand was chafing me in places I don't want to remember, and the saltwater from the sea was making the cuts and scrapes on my body burn. We had to perform evaluations that required us to think, lead, make good decisions, and functionally operate while hallucinating, having hypothermia, and while sleep-deprived."

"That sounds horrible," Zoey said. "Why in the world would they do that to you?"

"Because they want to know who *really* wants to be a SEAL. They want to know who has the physical ability and mental fortitude to make it through the training and possibly save their own life, and the lives of their comrades, when shit gets real on a combat mission."

"And you did," Zoey said simply.

"Eventually, yes. But I had gotten to the point where I was done and about ready to ring the bell."

"Ring the bell?" Zoey asked.

"Yeah, quit. The instructors for Hell Week take great pride in doing their best to entice the trainees to quit. They use a bullhorn to basically mimic our inner voices that tell us we can't do it. That we're no good. That it's too hard. They make it seem logical, even honorable, to quit. To come out of the cold, ring a bell that signifies defeat, and to enjoy doughnuts and a cup of hot coffee."

SUSAN STOKER

"But you didn't."

"No. But only because of Rocco, Gumby, Ace, Rex, and Phantom.

"See, Hell Week is more about making it through mentally than physically. The instructors could get anyone to quit if they really wanted to. They truly *want* people to succeed. But the trainees have to have the mental strength to see it through. To ignore the pain and the inner voice that wants them to quit. That says they can't endure anymore. And my teammates helped me find that burning desire deep within me to be a SEAL. To not quit. To not give up and ring that fucking bell.

"I thought about that when I was being beaten by those Taliban assholes. They wanted me to quit, to ring the bell. To give in to the shit going on in my head. I remembered what my teammates had done for me in Hell Week, and I returned the favor. Every time I was hit, instead of groaning or swearing, I yelled out a word that reminded me of Hell Week. Loud enough for my teammates to hear. Sand, cold, log, paddle, boat, food, sleep...it went on and on. My entire concentration was on thinking up new words to use instead of thinking about what was happening to me, or my injured teammates."

Zoey was as still as a statue in his arms. He wasn't sure she was even breathing. Wanting to finish up his story so he could think about something else made him talk faster.

"How long they fucked with us, I have no idea, but eventually they left. We were all still in our own stalls, and I'm sure they'd thought they'd broken us. After a while, I managed to slip my hand out of the rope they'd used to tie me up."

Bubba didn't tell Zoey that he'd had to dislocate his

shoulder and use his own blood to lubricate his wrist in order to do it.

"I got the knife out of my pocket and cut myself free. Then I went from stall to stall and freed the others. We did our best to stabilize Ace and Rex and get the fuck out of there.

"My point with this long, rambling story is that it's *okay* to get frustrated. To feel like you want to quit. But you can't. Even when things seem horrible and you think you can't continue, you can't quit. I know this isn't easy for you, Zoey, but trust me when I tell you that you're doing great. So you can't start a fire, big fucking deal. You're more than pulling your weight. You're making this so easy on me, I almost feel guilty."

"Easy?" she said so softly, he almost couldn't hear her. "You've caught all our food, made the fire and shelter, and you had all the things in your magic pockets that we've needed to survive. I feel like I'm a giant anchor that's holding you back."

"But that's just it, you're not. And I'm not lying, Zoey. No, this isn't a walk in the park for you, and you're out of your element. But you've gamely trudged on and done the absolute best you can. You haven't freaked out much. Most importantly, you haven't given up, forcing me to carry you. And yes, before you ask, I totally *would* carry you if I had to. And most importantly, you've talked to me. I've learned more about my dad in the last three days than I knew about him in the last thirteen years. Thanks to you, I feel as if I know him once more. I regret not finding it all out on my own, but I'll always be grateful for you giving that to me. Your strength lies in distraction, so we aren't constantly thinking about how cold and miserable we are. How hungry. How dirty and in need of a hot shower.

Everyone has their strengths and weaknesses. Please don't quit and ring that bell on me. I need you, Zoey."

Bubba held his breath. He'd taken a while to get to his point, and he wasn't sure he hadn't just rambled on about shit that made no sense, but he hoped like hell she understood what he was saying.

It took a few minutes. A very long few minutes, during which Bubba mentally berated himself for bringing up his capture and Hell Week. She was probably missing his dad just as much as he was, and it had been a mistake to bring him up too.

"I'm not going to quit," she said, making Bubba close his eyes in relief.

"This sucks. And it's harder than anything I've ever done in my life. I don't think my fingers and toes will ever thaw out. I'm scared to death no one is going to find us and we're going to die of scurvy or something, but I'm not giving up. If you're willing to let me keep trying, I'm gonna make that flint and fire my bitch one of these days."

Bubba couldn't help it, he laughed. "First, scurvy is caused by an elimination of vitamin C from your body and it takes at least three months for symptoms to occur. Since we're eating lots of berries and leafy greens, I think we're good. And second, I have absolutely no doubt that you're gonna get the hang of the flint. You almost had it tonight."

Zoey relaxed against him, giving him her weight, and something inside Bubba clicked into place. Having her in his arms was nice. Sleeping next to her made him relax and feel comforted. But when she leaned against him, trusting him to not let her fall, he felt ten feet tall.

He tightened his arms around her chest. She brought her hands up and gripped his forearms hard. It was probably ten minutes later when she said, "I'm sorry that happened to you and your friends. They sound like they're all pretty amazing."

"They are. And you're going to meet them when they find us."

She hesitated, then said, "You're really positive they're going to, aren't you?"

"Find us? Absolutely. I know I didn't do that good of a job explaining what we went through in Hell Week, but it's a bond that's deeper than anything I've ever experienced in my life. I know I could call them anytime, anywhere, and they'd be there for me. No questions asked. Me disappearing without a word won't sit well with them, and they'll move heaven and earth to figure out what happened. They're coming for us, Zoey. We just have to keep doing what we've been doing until that happens."

"That's good because my mom wouldn't have the first clue where to start to try to find me...if she even knows I'm missing."

"I'm sure she does and is probably frantic."

Zoey shook her head slightly and sighed. "My mom is... not like other moms."

"In what way?" Bubba asked.

"She's always been kind of selfish. Don't get me wrong, I love her...but she's always put herself first. We moved around a ton before I got to Juneau, and it was always because she was following a new boyfriend. She never thought about how moving around could be hard on me. She wants to be loved by a man so badly, that she'll give up *anything* to make it happen. But so far, all she's gotten is heartache.

"When I got called back to Juneau for the reading of your dad's will, she'd just met a new guy. I can read the signs. She's completely gone on him already, and if he decided to move to the Alaskan bush tomorrow, she'd go without a second thought. I'm sure she's worried about me—*if* she knows I'm missing—but she'll probably assume the authorities are doing what they can to find me, so it wouldn't be worth it for her to get all worked up about it."

"All worked up about it?" Bubba asked incredulously.

"I know, that sounds bad. I mean, it *is* bad. But I had to beg her to stay in Juneau until I finished high school. She eventually relented, but I knew she was dying inside. She wanted to get back to Anchorage and try to find 'the love of her life.' She hadn't found him in Juneau, and I think she realized she never would. She loves me in her own way, but I'm definitely not the most important person in her life. Once, I stayed at a friend's house for three days before she called me, wondering where I was."

Bubba hated that for Zoey. She deserved to be loved without reservation, especially by her own mother.

"I think that's why I got so close to your dad," Zoey said quietly. "I never missed not having a father, but I did miss that parental love. I got that from Colin. He was my friend as well as my surrogate dad. I'm going to miss him a lot."

Bubba squeezed her, not knowing what to say.

He felt her lean even more heavily against him, and Bubba realized for the first time that she'd completely relaxed. She'd slept in his arms, but when awake, she'd always been somewhat stiff, keeping a part of herself separate from him. As if protecting herself.

He had a feeling she finally understood and believed him when he said that Rocco and the others would eventually find them. "I'm so sorry about your mom, but I'm glad my pop was there for you. And my friends *will* find us. It might take a week," he told her. "Or a month, but they'll do it, I have no doubt."

"I hope I can light that fucking fire before they do," she said after a while.

Bubba shook his head and merely chuckled. "Close your eyes," he told her. "Try to get some sleep. In the morning, we need to take off our boots and let our feet air out for a while."

"Why not now?" she asked.

"I don't want to risk the temperature dropping overnight. It'll make our internal temperatures fall faster without any shoes or socks on."

She sighed. "Yeah, that wouldn't be good. But I have to say, I'm not looking forward to taking my socks off at all. My poor toes are already shivering in my boots."

"Would it help if I promised to give you a foot massage?"

Surprisingly, she shook her head. "No. Ew, gross. Mark, feet are disgusting. I've never had a pedicure, and I never will. I'm too ticklish, for one thing, but for another, I can't stand the thought of someone touching my feet."

He shook his head. Zoey never said what he thought she would. "Fine. No massage, but how about if I promise not to let your toes get too cold in the process?"

She tilted her head back and narrowed her eyes at him. "How?"

"My armpits?" It came out more of a question than an answer.

In response, she grinned. "My God, I'd never thought I'd say this, but I have a feeling sticking my freezing toes in your armpits will be as close to heaven as I can get out here."

Bubba smiled back. "Sleep, Zoey. Tomorrow will be

just another day of our wilderness adventure. We should enjoy it while it lasts."

She shook her head and settled back against him. "You're weird, Mark."

"Yup. Zoey?"

"You know I'll sleep better if you stop talking to me, right?" she quipped.

"Just one more thing."

"Okay. What is it?"

"I'm glad it was you in that plane with me. I can't say that I've missed you since I graduated from high school, but that's only because I didn't *know* what I was missing. Now that I've gotten to know you, I'm even more sorry that I never came home to visit Pop. I thought you were pretty cool years ago, and I regret not trying to get to know you better back then."

He thought she wasn't going to respond when she didn't say anything for several minutes. Finally, she said softly, "Do you think we'll ever see each other again after we get out of here? I mean, is this a situational thing?"

Thinking about her walking out of his life and never seeing her again made Bubba frown. "We're going to see each other," he said firmly. "The situation allowed us to get to know each other again, and I'm not stupid enough to let you disappear from my life now." When she didn't reply right away, he added lamely, "That is...if you want."

"I've known you for years," she said. "Your dad talked about you all the time. So much that I truly felt as if we were friends. I definitely want to see you again."

"Good. Now sleep. We've got a big day of mushroom foraging, armpit wrestling, and fire-making tomorrow."

Zoey pulled her feet up and curled into a ball against his chest. She was still sitting, but curled up like she was, he was supporting all her weight. It wouldn't be comfort-able for him to sleep that way, sitting up, holding her against him, but he'd hold her this way as long as he could before lying them down for the night.

As Zoey's breaths evened out and she slept, Bubba felt more relaxed than he had in days.

They weren't out of danger, not even close, but somehow he felt more at peace with their situation. Zoey wasn't going to mentally tap out, and he'd do whatever it took to keep them both healthy and safe until they were found.

CHAPTER NINE

Rocco and the rest of the SEAL team sat around the table at the Alaska State Troopers' headquarters in Anchorage to discuss how the search had been going so far. There were representatives from the state troopers, the Village Public Safety Officer Program, Alaska State Park Rangers, the Coast Guard, the NTSB, and both Juneau and Anchorage police departments.

It felt as if they'd searched every inch of land between Anchorage and the capital city in the last two days...with no luck.

Bubba had been missing almost a week. A *week*. There was still no sign of a downed plane, and even after spreading the word across the state and all local airports, no one had reported hearing a mayday or having any airplanes make an unscheduled landing.

It was frustrating as hell, but Rocco wasn't ready to give up.

"What do we do now?" Malcom Wright asked.

It was a little eerie having Bubba's twin sitting in the room. But other than looking exactly like Bubba, Rocco would never mistake the men for each other. For one, Bubba carried himself with a confidence Malcom didn't have. And Malcom was conceited at best, irritating as hell at worst. Bubba was physically bigger and stronger than his brother, as well.

Malcom had insisted on being involved in the search and doing whatever he could to find Bubba, which wasn't something Rocco could deny him.

"We expand the search parameters," Rex said firmly.

Rocco nodded to one of the state troopers he'd talked with before the meeting, giving him the go-ahead to discuss the plan.

"Exactly," the trooper said. "We've been in touch with the VPSOs in all the outlying villages, and no one has reported anything unusual. No strangers in town, no one saw or heard a plane go down. It's our belief that since we haven't found anything on the flight path from Anchorage to Juneau, that the plane didn't go that way. Of course, it's possible that we've just missed it, but none of us are willing to ignore the possibility that the pilot deliberately flew in the wrong direction and intentionally crashed the plane in a remote area."

"Oh, come on." Malcom frowned. "Do you really think that's what happened? What would be her motive? That's just crazy."

A detective from the Juneau police department leaned forward and said, "Is it? Colin Wright was half owner of a multimillion dollar company. I haven't seen his will, but I'm assuming that those assets would be split between his two sons. People have been killed for far less money, Mr. Wright."

Bubba's twin paled and sat back in his seat, subdued.

"Right," Rocco said, wanting to move on so they could

get back to finding Bubba. He wasn't sure he trusted Malcom, but now wasn't the time or place to interrogate him about his possible involvement in his brother's disappearance. "So, the troopers and even the Coast Guard have agreed to fly search-and-rescue missions, as they've been doing for the last two days, but this time we'll split up. Some will fly west, some will go north, and others due east. We'll be looking for any sign of Bubba or that plane. Smoke rising, trees bent over or burned, craters in the earth. Anything. It's going to be long, hard work. We can't let our attention lapse for even a second." He paused, then scanned the room, meeting every single person's gaze for a moment.

"Bubba's out there. Somewhere. Our only goal right now is to find him. We'll deal with the will, and Colin's business issues, and everything else once we find him. Right now, we have nothing but our hunches to go on about what happened. And as much as I want to know the whys and have my million-and-one questions answered, the most important thing is Bubba. And of course, Zoey and the pilot, who were on that plane with him."

Everyone nodded in agreement.

"Good. We'll split up and figure out who's going where after we're done here."

"I'd like to go as well," Malcom insisted.

Rocco immediately shook his head. "No. We need you here. You're our go-between with the lawyer and Sean, Colin's business partner."

Malcom frowned again, and Rocco tensed. The last thing he wanted was to get into a pissing contest with Bubba's brother. The man wasn't trained like the SEALs and the law enforcement teams were. They didn't need a civilian getting in the way. He may have lived in Alaska all his life, but it was obvious by looking at him—in the three-piece suit he was wearing at the moment—he wasn't prepared to get on a helicopter or plane and spend hours looking at nothing but trees and water, searching for his brother.

"Fine. But I know people. I'd like to organize my own search party as well. They might not be SEALs, but I've got friends who know a hell of a lot about Alaska's roughest terrains. They might be able to help. And I want to be notified the second anyone learns anything," Malcom said.

Rocco nodded. "Great. We can use all the help we can get. Bubba might be your brother by blood, but he's our brother by circumstance. We aren't giving up until we find him." Rocco couldn't read the look that briefly flashed on Malcom's face, but one second it was there, and the next he was nodding.

"Good. I'll call Sean and Kenneth and update them. The lawyer won't be happy he has to postpone the reading of my dad's will again, but I'll make sure he knows there's no choice."

"And Sean will be all right with running the business?" Gumby asked.

Malcom nodded once. "Of course, why wouldn't he? The factory is covered by the project manager, and anything else that comes up, Sean and I can deal with, just like we've been doing for the last decade. Go find my brother," he said brusquely. "The sooner we find him, the sooner things can get back to normal."

And with that, Malcom scooted back his chair. "If you'll excuse me, I have some phone calls to make." Then he nodded at the room in general and headed for the door.

The second he was gone, Ace shook his head. "If he

didn't look exactly like Bubba, I wouldn't believe they were related."

Rocco agreed, but didn't have the time or patience to discuss Bubba's slightly asshole-ish brother right now. He looked at the senior Alaska State Trooper who was with them, then at the representative for the Coast Guard. "Let's go over the search grid one more time, then we'll figure out who will go where."

Both men nodded and leaned over to look at the maps in front of them.

Rocco wanted to forget the planning and just get into a helicopter and take off, but he knew they needed a plan. He just hoped like hell the extra time it was taking wasn't going to be the difference in Bubba's life or death. If he was hurt and needed medical care, every minute that went by could be precious.

"Hang on, brother," he murmured, before turning his attention back to the others.

Malcom Wright wasn't a happy man. Being away from Juneau for this long wasn't what he'd envisioned when he'd gone to Anchorage because of Mark's disappearance.

He'd already had to arrange their father's memorial by himself and deal with just about everyone who lived in Juneau. He'd planned it for two days after his brother's arrival, and by the time he realized Mark was missing, it was too late to cancel. Everyone in town had been there. All the employees from the factory, all the shop owners, hell, even some of the homeless in the area had shown up, wanting to pay their respects to Colin. Malcom had preferred to go on with the service without his brother, but he couldn't exactly cancel on the entire town.

He knew some had disagreed, namely Sean, but Malcom stuck to his guns. His entire life, everything had been about Mark. Even though the man had left Juneau and never looked back, everyone still knew he was a SEAL, thanks to Colin.

Just this once, the attention deserved to be on their dad.

Malcom didn't like feeling jealous of his twin, but ever since they were little it seemed as if Mark had been the more successful son. Grades, athletics, girls...whatever it was, Mark excelled.

And of course, Pop had no problem comparing Malcom to his overachieving brother.

Why can't you be more like Mark?

Mark got an A, why didn't you?

You're not going to the dance? Maybe Mark can help you find a date.

I got an email from Mark today, he just got back from a mission and saved the lives of two dozen people. That's so amazing!

It went on and on. His pop never stopped talking about Mark, even though he hadn't bothered to come back and visit even once since leaving after graduating from high school.

Malcom did his best to keep his feelings off his face—so no one would discover exactly how much he hated his twin.

No one could ever understand. They'd say he was supposed to love his brother more than anyone else in the world. Insist they must have some sort of twin connection.

Reality couldn't be further from the truth. As far as

SUSAN STOKER

Malcom was concerned, Mark's disappearance wasn't the worst thing in the world.

Heading outside, he pulled out his phone and dialed a number he'd long since memorized.

"Hello?"

"It's me," Malcom said.

"Any word?" the voice on the other end of the line asked.

"Not yet. There hasn't been any sign of the plane or my brother. The assholes today had the nerve to ask if the business would be okay. As if I couldn't keep things running like I've been doing for years. It's fucking annoying."

"What about the reading of the will?"

"Postponed until they find something out about Mark."

"Shit! I can't *believe* those assholes we hired to sabotage the plane screwed up so badly."

"Have you been able to find them?" Malcom asked.

"No. They're in the wind. Believe me, if I could, they'd regret taking my money and not holding up their end of the bargain."

"We should've just had them killed in a drive-by or something," Malcom muttered.

"Oh, *that* wouldn't have been suspicious or anything," came the sarcastic response. "The bottom line is that we have to find them before anyone else. You'll never get the money if they're missing. I'll find someone to search for them, and when they find them, if they're still alive, they'll be taken out before anyone knows they survived. Mark's portion of what Colin left to him will go to you."

"Those teammates of his are pretty damn determined.

126

They aren't going to give up until they find him, alive or dead."

"Well, we'll just have to make sure he's dead then, won't we?" the Boss said.

"We should've done things differently," Malcom said.

"Well, we didn't! What's done is done, and we have to see it through," the Boss snapped acidly.

"Whatever. Just make sure you're ready for the reading of Colin's will after the search ends. I want to get this done and move on with my fucking life already."

"I will. Keep your head down. Don't do or say anything that will tip anyone off."

"Do you think I'm an idiot? I'm not about to risk losing all that money at this point."

"Okay. I gotta go. Keep me updated."

"I will. Bye."

"Bye."

Malcom clicked off the phone and pressed his lips together tightly. Nothing was going according to plan. His brother's charter should've crashed right after it left Anchorage. Malcom would've played up the grieving son and brother, and everyone would've felt sorry for him. He would've gotten half of Heritage Plastics awarded to him and been set for life.

Now he had to worry about the damn pilot opening her mouth and telling someone what she'd done.

They'd meant to kill *her* too, making up the insane plot for her to leave Mark in the Alaskan wilderness. Which made no sense—if his body was never found, it could be decades before he was officially declared dead—but Eva was too stupid to realize that, and she'd taken the bait ridiculously easily.

So now Malcom had to hope the Boss could hire

someone skilled enough to head out to where Mark and that bitch, Zoey, had been stranded, find them, *and* kill them in a way that seemed fitting in the wilderness.

Everything was too damn complicated now, and it was seriously stressing Malcom out.

Taking a deep breath, he told himself to trust the Boss. The entire situation would be cleaned up and, in the end, he'd own half of Heritage Plastics.

"You aren't going to win this time, bro," Malcom said under his breath. "Not this time."

CHAPTER TEN

Zoey had lost count of what day it was. They all kind of blended together now. They'd wake up in the morning, take their shoes off and air out their feet, eat some berries for breakfast, walk for a few hours, stop for a break and a snack, walk some more, Mark would find a place for them to camp for the night, she'd attempt to start a fire—with no luck—then assist with their shelter. Mark would either fish or set a snare for their dinner, they'd sit around the fire talking, then she'd fall asleep in his arms.

She was tired, dirty, and getting more and more worried by the day.

Mark said his friends would find them, and she believed him, but she was beginning to think they'd walk themselves out of whatever area they'd been dropped in before that happened.

"Hey, are you okay? How're your feet doing?"

Zoey looked over at Mark. "They're fine. Your armpits did a great job of keeping them warm this morning."

He grinned, but then sobered. "I know this isn't ideal."

Wasn't ideal? Was he kidding? He was close to getting

back to that too-positive thing that irritated her so much. She grunted in response.

Of course he wouldn't let her get away with that. Mark was the chattiest man she'd ever met. Weren't SEALs supposed to be all closed-mouthed and stuff? God, what she'd give to be able to sulk in peace.

He stopped in front of her and waited for her to look up at him. "What?" she asked, a little more grumpily than she'd intended.

He studied her for a bit before saying, "I know this is hard."

Zoey couldn't help it. She snorted. "Mark, hard is getting up because you know you have to go to work even when you're hungover. Hard is passing a geometry test when you haven't studied for it. Hard is what a guy's dick has to be before any hanky-panky can happen. What this is, isn't hard. It's impossible. We're basically attempting to walk across Alaska with nothing but a knife, a flint, and a few other odds and ends."

She hadn't thought about her words. Had just spit them out. But of course the second she shut her mouth, what she'd said registered and she closed her eyes in embarrassment.

Mark chuckled, and she knew she blushed even harder. She kept her eyes shut, not wanting to look at him right now.

But instead of resurrecting Positive Polly, he surprised her. "You're right."

Her eyes popped open and she stared at him. "I am?"

"Of course, Zoey. This sucks. I'd rather not be here. No one would. I have no idea how much longer we'll have to go before we find any sign of civilization. I've been dreaming of a huge ice cream sundae and, believe it or not, chicken fingers. I'd give anything to be bitching about having to go to the grocery store or about the traffic in Riverton right about now."

She waited for the inevitable upbeat pep talk to start. But when Mark didn't say anything else, she practically gaped at him. "And?"

"And what?"

"Go on. Tell me that your friends will find us soon. That we'll be eating that ice cream this time tomorrow. Be your usual positive self," she told him.

He sighed. "The truth of the matter is, I'm struggling. Just like you are. I'm ashamed to admit it, but I'd almost rather be in the middle of some far-flung country exchanging gunfire with the bad guys. At least then I'd know there would be an end to whatever we were doing."

Zoey reached up and grabbed Mark's biceps and said, "No."

"No, what?"

"No, you can't do this. You're the positive one. The upbeat one. The one who's so sure your friends will find us. As much as it annoys me, and even though I told you a few days ago that I needed you to be more real, I changed my mind. I *need* you to be the annoyingly positive guy right now."

"I'm not perfect," Mark said. "And this does suck."

They stared at each other for a heartbeat before Zoey couldn't help but smile.

"I have no idea what you're smiling at," Mark grumbled.

She took a step toward him and wrapped her arms around him and held on as tightly as she could. She was relieved when he hugged her back. How long they stood like that, she had no idea. Neither of them smelled good and she knew her hair was limp and greasy from going a week without washing it. Her clothes were dirty, as were his, and she could hear his stomach growling.

Looking up at him, she said, "We're going to be okay."

His lips quirked upward. "*Now* who's being the positive one?" he asked.

"Hey, we can't both be negative. And you said that we had to be positive to make it out of here."

"True."

Taking a risk, she reached up and palmed his face. His stubble had grown out until it was almost a full-fledged beard, and she could see how much dirt was under her fingernails, but she forged on. "One thing your dad always said to me when I was sad or depressed was," she lowered her voice, mimicking Colin's deep voice, "Zoey, girl...as bad as things look now, they can always be worse."

She loved the smile that crossed Mark's face. "That sounds like something Pop would say."

"As we both know, things *could* always be worse. It could be December and there could be two feet of snow on the ground. One of us could've been injured in that landing if things had gone differently. We could've been killed outright. There are any number of things that could make our situation much worse than it is. I'm not always the most positive person, but I've still tried to do the best I can. I'm totally out of my element here, but you've made this so much better than it would've been. I like you, Mark. A lot. And I admire you. I did before I even really got to know you, thanks to your dad, but after a week with you out here, I see so much more than I ever would've imagined."

He didn't respond, so she went on. "I see a man who loves his friends enough to know without a doubt that they'll be there for him. A man who has regrets and freely admits them. A man who can also admit when he's wrong, and who has an immense amount of knowledge about keeping himself safe and alive. You haven't complained about me not being able to do my share of the work, and you've been patient with me as I try to fumble through things that you could easily do in seconds. I can be the positive one for a while, but if you fall into your head and I can't pull you out, we're gonna die out here."

That brought a small smile to his face. "We aren't going to die," he said firmly.

"Good. Because there's an amazing ice cream shop in Anchorage I want to take you to when we get back there," she told him.

A genuine smile lit up his face. "Deal."

"Yeah?"

"Yup. And there's a to-die-for place in Riverton, California, that serves the best chicken wings you've ever tasted. I want to take *you* there."

Things were getting serious, but Zoey didn't care. "Okay."

"Okay. And even though we're both tired, we have to go a little farther today. You good?"

"Are *you* good?" she countered.

"Yeah. Your pep talk helped." He grinned. "And you're right, this isn't hard. I'm happy to show you *hard* after we're rescued, and we've showered, eaten, and probably slept."

Closing her eyes, Zoey shook her head. "How did I know you weren't going to let that go?"

He chuckled. "Because you know me."

And Zoey was surprised to realize he was right. She *did* know him. They'd spent a lot of time talking, and she'd gained a lot of insight into his personality and what made him tick. Just as he had her.

"Whatever, Navy Boy." It was a lame comeback, but she couldn't exactly say what she was thinking. That he could show her his kind of "hard" anytime he wanted.

"Come on," he said with a small smile. He took her hand in his and brought it up to his mouth and kissed the back before squeezing her fingers. "Time to get back on the road."

"Road?" she asked sarcastically.

"Road, forest path, bushwhacking through the undergrowth...same thing."

She couldn't help it, she laughed.

Four hours later, Zoey wasn't laughing anymore. She was tired and ready to stop for the day. She wasn't paying attention and ran right into Mark's back for what seemed like the hundredth time, after he'd stopped suddenly.

Looking up, she gasped at what she saw. It was reminiscent of the huge lake that had blocked their path. Directly in front of them was a deep, fast-running, wide stream, a tributary shooting off of the lake they'd been walking around for days. They'd either have to cross the rushing water here, or follow it for who knew how long to find an easier way across. Their other option was to turn around and go back the way they'd came. Which wasn't something she wanted to do.

"Shit," she mumbled.

Mark didn't say anything, instead wrapped his arm around her as they stood shoulder-to-shoulder and stared at the obstacle in front of them.

"What now?" she asked softly.

"We cross it," Mark said matter-of-factly.

Zoey looked up at him in disbelief. "How?"

"Very carefully," was Mark's not-so-helpful response.

"Smartass," she told him. "Got any ideas?"

Mark surveyed their surroundings. Zoey let him think, not interrupting him as he problem-solved. He walked the immediate area, poking at some of the fallen logs nearby.

Zoey just watched, observing as he calculated what they'd need to get across the water. The sun was out today, thank goodness. She was about as sick of rain as she could get. It drizzled just about every night, and they'd almost been caught in a downpour a time or two. Mark had said time and time again that the last thing they needed was to be soaking wet. It was already chilly out, and cold material against their skin would weaken and possibly kill them faster than anything else.

Mark finally came back by her side and sighed. She didn't like the sound of that.

"So?" she asked. "Are we turning around after all?"

"No. I'm pretty sure this'll work. I'll need your help though."

"Of course," Zoey said.

"There's a fallen tree about thirty feet into the tree line that I think will work. It looks like it'll be long enough to get across the water. If we can drag it here and get it up on its end, we can push it over and it should span the stream. Then we can walk or scoot across it to get to the other side."

Zoey looked at him as if he had a horn growing out of his head. "Are you kidding?"

"No."

He looked at her without a trace of the humor and

SUSAN STOKER

silliness she'd come to enjoy over the last week. She turned her head and saw the end of the log he was probably talking about. It was big; there was no way they could drag that thing to the water, never mind pull it upright and drop it over the stream.

"You do know that I'm not a guy, right? That I'm way weaker than you?"

"I'm well aware that you're not a guy...thank God. I've got a plan, and I'll do most of the work. But I know with your help, we can do this. Since the ground is wet, I think the mud will actually help us out in this situation. The log'll just slide right over the ground."

Zoey knew he was sugarcoating the situation, but didn't call him on it. "Fine. What do you want me to do?"

Instead of answering, Mark startled her by reaching out and pulling her into his arms. She went eagerly, not willing to pass up the chance to be close to him. The more time they spent together, the more she liked him. He wasn't perfect, that was obvious after their morning talk, but he seemed to be perfect for *her*.

Which was scary as hell.

Their situation was certainly unusual. And she knew it had cemented her feelings for him. She was pretty sure he liked her back, but the big question was, did he like her as an old friend he was enjoying getting to know again, or as a man likes a woman? She had no idea.

He pulled back, and she did the same, looking into his eyes. She couldn't read what she saw there.

"Have I told you lately how glad I am that it's you who's out here with me?"

Zoey nodded. "Yeah."

"Good. Because I am."

"Me too. I mean, I think it's obvious that I wouldn't have gotten far if you hadn't been with me."

Mark shook his head. "No way. You would've figured out how to survive. I have no doubt about that."

Zoey knew he was wrong, but she didn't say anything. His gaze roamed up to her hair, and she winced, knowing it was a disaster. He smiled and reached up to pluck a pine needle out of her brunette locks. In return, she surreptitiously grabbed a pine needle off his shoulder, then pretended to pull it out of the facial hair that had grown over the last week on his cheeks.

He grinned and took her hand in his. He held their clasped hands together between them. His fingers brushed against the curve of one of her breasts, and she felt her nipple pucker in response. Both cursing and thanking the layers of clothes she was wearing, Zoey simply stared up at him.

Slowly, ever so slowly, Mark dropped his head toward hers. Zoey didn't close her eyes until the last second. His lips brushed against hers lightly, as if testing things out, making sure she wasn't going to pull away.

No way in hell was she going to do anything to rebuff him. She'd wanted to kiss him since she'd first seen him in the halls of Juneau High School over a decade ago. Of course her fantasies were much different than reality, but it didn't matter.

She tightened her fingers around his and clutched at his side with her other hand, going up on tiptoes to try to get closer. She felt him smiling as his lips touched hers again, but she didn't care that she was amusing him. She was kissing Mark Wright.

Holy shit.

And kissing they were. After the first tentative brush

of his lips, any restraint he might've practiced was gone. His head slanted, his free hand came up and speared into her hair, holding her to him, and he devoured her.

The kiss was intense and passionate and almost a little desperate. Zoey moaned in her throat and he pulled her even closer. Their tongues dueled and their teeth clashed in their passion. Neither seemed to notice or care.

All Zoey could think about was getting closer. She pressed herself against him and felt his erection. He was hard, and Zoey wanted to see him up close and personal almost more than she wanted a hot shower and clean clothes.

How long they kissed, Zoey had no idea, but eventually she needed to breathe, more than little inhalations through her nose, and she reluctantly pulled back. Mark immediately let her go, but kept his hand on the back of her head and her hand in his. They were practically plastered together from hips to chest, and Zoey had to crane her head back to look him in the eyes.

She prayed he wouldn't say anything that would ruin this moment for her. Practically holding her breath, she waited for him to speak.

His eyes roamed over her face, then her hair, then back to her lips. Zoey licked them unconsciously, and his fingers on both hands tightened. She felt surrounded by Mark. As if he would literally slay dragons for her. She prayed this wouldn't make things awkward between them. That he didn't regret kissing her. She silently begged him to say something. Anything.

"I've wanted to do that for days," he said after a minute, and Zoey practically sagged in relief at his words.

"Me too," she whispered.

He smiled down at her. "You intrigue me, Zoey Knight.

I want to continue to get to know you. I want to take you out to the fanciest restaurant and to the diviest dive. I want to introduce you to my friends and sit on the deck at Gumby's house and watch you laugh and play with Ace and Piper's kids on the beach. I want to know what foods you like and hate. For the first time in my life, I feel as if a day should go by, and I haven't talked to you, seen you, that I'll be missing out. I've never felt that way about anyone before. Ever."

With every word out of his mouth, Zoey melted further. "It's probably because of the situation," she said softly. She didn't want to believe that, but she had to be honest with herself and him.

He shook his head. "No. That's not it. Zo, I spend my life in situations like this. Life and death. Intense. Not knowing what's around the next corner. We've rescued a lot of women, and not one has touched me like you. Maybe it's the connection we already have because we knew each other before. Maybe it's because I know you loved my pop as much as I did. I don't know. But I can't just walk away when we're rescued. One day, one week, or one month from now. I want to see where this goes when we're back in the real world."

Zoey couldn't say anything else. She was so floored and overcome with feelings for Mark, her throat seemed to close up. She wanted that. More than anything. It seemed like a dream come true.

After a moment, Mark frowned, and she felt his hold on her loosen as he prepared to step away. "If you don't feel the same, that's okay. I just wanted you to know."

Zoey frantically shook her head. She threw herself against him, knowing he'd catch her, which he did. "I want that too," she told him quickly. "I was just in shock. I liked you when I was a teenager, and I admired you simply from the things your dad told me. But now that I've gotten to know you, *really* know you, I realize what I thought I knew about you was only the beginning. You're so much more. You're not just the military hero or the high school hunk I'd built up in my mind. You're *real*. You get upset and worried and your stomach growls just like mine when you're hungry. And as much as I want to be rescued, I also dread it because that means going back to my boring life. I dread not seeing you every day. I want nothing more than to see where this goes too."

The furrows in his brow evened out and he smiled down at her. "Good. Maybe another kiss to seal the deal before we tackle this log and continue our journey?"

Zoey returned his smile and nodded probably a bit too enthusiastically.

His head dropped once more, and then they were kissing again. His beard was scratchy against her face, but Zoey barely noticed. Her focus was on the way he playfully nibbled on her lower lip and, when she opened for him, how he didn't hesitate to sweep his tongue into her mouth.

Their kiss was shorter than before and less intense, but it still made Zoey's toes curl. He pulled back and rested his forehead on hers and said softly, "We haven't talked much about what happens after we get rescued, but hear this— I'm not going to walk away and never look back. We don't know who was behind this, but if there's even a hint that you could be in danger, I'm not leaving you to defend yourself. I'd never abandon you. This is going to sound crazy... but I want you to think about coming back to California with me."

Zoey inhaled sharply, but he didn't give her a chance to speak.

"Don't say anything right now, just think about it. I know you have a life in Juneau. A job. Friends. But anyone who would go to these lengths to get rid of us wouldn't hesitate to try again, and if you're right there, an easy mark in Juneau, I wouldn't be able to live with myself if something happened to you."

"Mark," Zoey protested. "I don't think I'm the person they were targeting here. I'm nobody."

Mark pulled back and brought the palm of his hand up to smooth her hair away from her face. "We've been over this. Don't underestimate your worth, Zo. We have no idea what Pop left you, and I'm beginning to think it's probably more than either of us thought. But even if it's not, it doesn't matter. Pop obviously loved you. You loved him."

Zoey shivered, not wanting to think about someone wanting to kill her. She really *wasn't* anybody important. The thought that someone wanted her dead was crazy, wasn't it?

"Just think about it, okay?"

She nodded.

Mark took a deep breath and said, "Right. Time to get to work. You ready?"

Zoey mimicked his inhalation and nodded. "Carry on, oh fearless leader."

It was his turn to roll his eyes, and the sight made Zoey smile.

"Piece of cake. Let's do this and get on with our day," he quipped. When he turned, he kept hold of her hand, and Zoey knew she'd never forget this moment for the rest of her life. When the guy she'd crushed on for years had kissed her. Then said he wanted to date her. And offered to bring her to California so he could make sure she was safe.

Oh, yeah, this was definitely one of the best days of her life.

Did she say this was the best day of her life? Zoey shook her head. She'd lied. Today sucked. Dragging a simple log a hundred feet shouldn't have been as hard as it was. The thing was heavy. Like, *really* heavy. It had taken the two of them over an hour of swearing, slipping and sliding, and pure brute strength to get it close enough to the stream.

Then it had taken another thirty minutes, and the use of the rope Mark had in his pocket, to roll the log to where they needed it to go. They'd managed to get it up on its end and push it over the creek, which had worked surprisingly well. It wasn't all that stable, but it wasn't in the water and, on paper at least, they could cross it without getting their feet wet, which was the goal all along.

They'd both taken off their outer shirts as they'd worked, as they were warm in the sun and sweating. Zoey was in her tank top and long-sleeve shirt, and Mark was wearing only his green Henley.

She would've admired his bulging biceps if she hadn't been so concerned about crossing the stupid stream. Looking at their makeshift bridge, this suddenly seemed like a bad idea. Especially considering they had no idea what was on the other side. They might cross this thing to find another wider stream a hundred yards farther down and around a bend.

"Maybe we should just turn around after all," Zoey said as she and Mark stood looking at the log and the fast-moving water under it.

"We've got this," Mark said in his familiar positive tone. "I'll go first. Make sure it's safe. I'll anchor it with some rocks on the other side, prevent it from rolling. Then you can come across. Okay?"

Zoey wanted to say no. That she was too scared. But she tried to be positive by swallowing hard and nodding.

Mark put his finger under her chin and forced her to look up at him. "Hey, we got this."

She tried to smile, but knew it fell flat.

"I'll even let you wear my outer shirt. I know you're gonna start shivering in a minute or two, and you'll need the extra warmth."

"And you don't?"

"No. I'm good. I'm way more used to being cold than you are. Which is kinda funny, considering you're the one who lives up here in Alaska. You're the one who's supposed to think this weather is warm enough to sunbathe in."

Zoey shuddered. She couldn't imagine lying around in a bathing suit. Even though the sun was shining, it probably wasn't even sixty degrees. Besides, the clouds would most likely come out any second. That's how it was in the early autumn months in Alaska. It could be beautiful and sunny one second and cloudy and foggy the next.

"A kiss for luck?" Mark asked.

Now that, Zoey could do. She immediately went up on her tiptoes and kissed him. It was short and sweet, but every time his lips touched hers, sparks shot down to her toes. It was a very effective way to get her mind off of where they were and what they were doing, and it went a long way toward warming her up to boot.

Mark pulled back and kissed her temple before turning toward the log. Around his waist, he tied the long rope he'd made by braiding vines, bark and dead plants, and Zoey took the other end in her hands. As far as a safety line went, it wasn't much, but he'd assured her it was merely a precaution. That nothing was going to happen, and he'd be on the other bank before either of them could blink.

Zoey watched as he tested the stability of their makeshift bridge and winced when it wobbled as he lowered himself onto it. Instead of walking upright, which would've been suicide, he straddled it. His feet came up behind him, steadying him. He ever so slowly inched forward, stopping every few inches to balance himself as the log shifted under him.

Zoey couldn't breathe. She tightened her grip on the thin rope, letting out slack as he moved across the fallen tree.

For a minute, she thought he was going to make it. He was moving at a pretty good clip and was halfway across when disaster struck.

He'd just shifted to move forward another inch when Zoey happened to look upstream. Her eyes widened and she yelled, "Watch out!"

But it was too late.

A large tree that had fallen somewhere upstream was rushing headlong toward Mark and their precarious bridge.

He braced himself, and even stuck out a hand to try to push the log away, but it was no use. The branches of the floating log rammed right into Mark, and the tree itself lodged under their bridge. The force of the water and the tree was too much, and one second Mark was perched on top of the log, the next, he'd disappeared into the rushing stream amongst a flurry of leaves and branches.

The rope in her hands immediately went taut, and Zoey fought with all her strength to keep hold of it. She didn't feel the way the make-shift rope left burn marks on her palms; her only focus was Mark. She fell to her ass on the bank and grunted as the water tried to rip him away. For a wild moment, she thought it might be better to let go, to let him ride the rapids down to the lake, where it was calmer, but then she thought about how cold the water was. The water in the stream had to be coming from the mountains, where the snow and ice was constantly melting. There was a good chance he wouldn't make it to the lake, and even if he did, it was possible he wouldn't have the strength to get out because of the cold.

So Zoey frantically held on. She was dragged closer and closer toward the stream. Mark outweighed her by quite a bit, but she refused to let go.

She was pulled ever closer but as luck would have it, a large rock sat between her and the bank. She turned slightly and used her feet to brace herself against the boulder.

It worked. She stopped moving.

Wrapping the vines around her wrists, she vowed to do whatever it took to get Mark to shore. Every now and then, she saw his head pop out of the water in the rapids, and she knew he was fighting on the other end of the rope.

Slowly, ever so slowly, she watched him make progress toward the bank. After he disentangled himself from the rogue tree that had appeared at exactly the wrong time, he was able to move a bit faster. Within thirty seconds, Zoey felt the rope in her hands go slack.

He'd done it.

Unwrapping the vine from her hands, not even noticing the bruises already forming on her wrists, she ran toward where Mark was crawling on his hands and knees out of the stream.

"Mark! Are you all right?"

"Don't touch me," he ground out.

Zoey stopped in her tracks in shock. "What?"

"I'm soaking wet. I don't want you to get near me. Give me a second."

"What can I do?" Zoey asked. Even as she watched, Mark's body began to tremble. Now that the adrenaline from his dunk in the water was wearing off, the cold was already settling in.

"Just step back, sweetheart. I'm okay. I promise."

Hating that she was powerless to do anything to help, Zoey did as he asked. She hovered near him as he crawled even farther out of the stream. He got to a patch of grass and tried to stand but couldn't, falling back on his ass.

"Mark!" Zoey exclaimed.

"I'm okay," Mark said again. "J-Just c-cold."

He looked up at her then, and Zoey could see that his lips were already turning blue.

Shit, shit, shit!

Mark began to fumble with the laces on his boots, but it looked like he was having a hard time.

"Fuck not touching you," Zoey mumbled and went to her knees at his feet. She brushed his hands away and went to work on getting his boots undone. It was hard to get them off his feet, but after tugging for a bit, she was finally successful.

"The s-socks too," Mark said.

Zoey knew he was right, but she hated this. And of course, when they needed it the most, the sunlight had disappeared behind rapidly growing clouds. She stripped off his socks, and when his hands went to the button of his pants, the fact that he was actually going to strip naked sank in.

Quick as a flash, she stood and raced back to where they'd spent the early afternoon working to get the log to the stream. Both their outer shirts they'd taken off were still hanging from a branch. Thankful he had something dry to put on, she sprinted back to where she'd left him.

By the time she got back, he'd managed to get his pants and shirt off. He was sitting on the ground in nothing but his soaking-wet boxer briefs. In any other situation, Zoey would've been thrilled and ogled him, but at the moment, all she could think about was his health and well-being.

He tried to get up on his knees to take off his underwear, but was having trouble staying upright. Zoey dropped their shirts on the ground and reached for him. "Let me help," she ordered.

"I c-can d-do it," Mark insisted.

"Bullshit. Mark, you're shaking so bad you can't even curl your finger around the waistband. Lay down," she said. Zoey wished he could keep his underwear on, but they were soaking, just like everything else. And the last thing he needed was that wet cotton against his most vulnerable parts. He had to get everything off, get dry, and get warm.

Swallowing down the panic that threatened to overwhelm her, Zoey concentrated on doing one thing at a time.

Frowning, Mark lay back. Zoey slid her fingers under the cotton—and jolted when Mark chuckled.

"What the hell are you laughing at?" she groused.

"I w-wanted you to p-put your hands on m-me, but never imagined it w-would happen this f-fast."

"Shut up," she told him, secretly thrilled he hadn't lost his sense of humor.

"P-Please remember w-what c-cold water d-does to a m-man's dick, Zo."

At that, her gaze went up to his—and she was surprised to see a hint of concern in his eyes that he tried to hide with humor.

Shaking her head, she looked back down at what she was doing. "You have nothing to worry about, SEAL Man. I'm more concerned about your blue balls right now than the size of your package."

He burst out laughing, and it made Zoey feel good that she could give that to him. There was certainly nothing funny about their current situation.

She couldn't help but see Mark's dick as she helped him remove his underwear. Even almost frozen, he was still impressive.

She quickly stripped off her long-sleeve shirt, immediately shivering in the cool afternoon air, but she ignored her own discomfort, knowing Mark would feel twenty times worse after his dunk in the glacier-fed water of the stream. She shoved her shirt at him. "Here, use this to dry off as best you can. You can put on your dry flannel and use my fleece-lined shirt to cover your legs. When you're done using that shirt to dry off, it can stand in for underwear for the time being, as well."

It wasn't enough. Zoey knew that. He didn't answer, was awkwardly doing his best to dry himself off with her shirt. His movements were uncoordinated and stiff. She shifted to her ass and started fumbling with her shoes.

"W-What are you d-doing?" Mark asked.

"Taking my socks off. You need them more than I do. The last thing you need is to lose any toes."

"I'm n-not t-taking your s-socks," Mark said gruffly.

"Yes, you are," Zoey told him without looking up.

"Zo, l-look at m-me," he stuttered.

She refused. She stripped off her socks, then quickly shoved her feet back into her boots and tied them once again. She stood and grabbed both long-sleeve shirts and brought them over to where Mark was sitting. Snatching the shirt out of his hands, she quickly finished drying his back and ran it over his hair as well, trying to get as much moisture out of the strands as she could. Thank God it was short; long hair would take forever to dry out here. She helped guide each shaking hand into a sleeve of his warm flannel shirt and sighed in relief.

"Lift up," she ordered, pushing on his shoulder. Mark obliged by shifting until one of his perfect ass cheeks was lifted from the cold ground. She shoved her now-damp long-sleeve shirt under his ass, and went to his other side to do the same. With that done, she did her best to nonchalantly tie the sleeves around his waist, covering his manly bits in the process. Then she draped her own fleece-lined shirt around his waist in the front. Finally, she went to his feet and stretched her wool socks over them. They didn't exactly fit, but they'd do.

"Don't move," she ordered, before standing once more.

"I'm okay, Z-Zo," Mark stuttered.

"I know. You're a SEAL. This is nothing for you," she said, the words more for herself than him. But deep down, she knew this wasn't like Hell Week. He'd told her lots of stories about what they'd been through, but the difference was, there wasn't any bell to ring to quit *this* hell. No medics standing by just in case. There wasn't a hospital just around the corner that someone could be brought to if something went wrong. There was only her. She wasn't going to let him down.

The bottom line was, Zoey knew she couldn't survive out here on her own. Therefore, it was in her best interest to do whatever it took to make sure Mark got warm as soon as possible.

Without another word, she raced away from Mark toward the tree line. She ignored how he called her name and concentrated on the task at hand...namely, gathering as much wood for a fire as she could. The most important thing right now was to get Mark warm. No matter that she was running around in a tank top and no socks. For once in her life, she didn't feel cold. She felt absolutely nothing but determination.

She went back and forth from the tree line to where Mark sat at least a dozen times, ignoring the way he demanded she slow down and take a breath. She'd found some moss hidden inside a tree that seemed relatively dry, which was a minor miracle. She gathered small sticks, medium ones, and some big ones as well. Most of the bigger branches and logs were damp, but that couldn't be helped right now.

After dumping the last load of wood, she nodded in satisfaction at the pile near Mark.

"Zoey, s-stop a second and l-look at me," Mark begged.

Taking a deep breath, she did as he requested. He was still sitting on her shirt, but had managed to bring his knees up and under his oversized shirt. All she could see of him was his feet sticking out—covered in her purple wool socks—and his head. She wished she had a hat for him; it was a well-known fact that people lost most of their body heat from their head. His lips were still blue around the edges, and he was still stuttering, which wasn't good.

"I'm okay," Mark told her.

Zoey shook her head. "No, you're not. You're freezing. I knew that stupid log was a bad idea. Shit!"

"Zo," he said firmly.

Zoey couldn't stop. Couldn't look at him. Couldn't listen. He'd just try to tell her that he was okay, and she knew he wasn't. She went over to his pants lying nearby and rifled through the pocket where she knew he kept the flint. Pulling it out, she sent a prayer upward. *Please let this work. His hands are shaking too badly to be able to light the fire. It's up to me.*

She quickly arranged the fire as close to Mark as she dared. They were in a small clearing near the stream, and while she would prefer to be under the trees, in a shelter, this was going to have to work for the moment.

Mark seemed to finally understand that she couldn't talk right now. That she had to do what she had to do, and him talking would distract her. Goose bumps rose on her arms as she worked, even as sweat dripped down the side of her face. She was both hot and cold at the same time. Zoey ignored everything but setting up the fire.

Once she had the moss in place, and the small sticks ready to catch the fire to set the larger ones ablaze, Zoey sat back on her heels and took a deep breath.

"That's it, Z-Zo. You c-can do this," Mark said softly. He didn't demand she pass the flint to him. Didn't try to take control of making the fire. He had faith that she could do it.

Nodding to herself, Zoey bent over the moss and hit the flint with the metal striker. Sparks flew like they were supposed to, but just like every other time she'd attempted to start the fire, they went every which way, not down at the moss where she needed them.

"Take your t-time," Mark encouraged.

Gritting her teeth, Zoey struck the flint again. And again. With each hit, she got more sparks. She was slowly getting the hang of it and determination set in. She needed this fire. Mark needed this fire. It was going to start, dammit, no matter what.

It took probably two dozen strikes, but finally a spark landed right where she needed it. It was probably luck more than anything specific she'd done, but she didn't care. Smoke rose from the moss and, feeling her adrenaline spike, Zoey leaned over the precious spark and very gently blew on it, just like Mark had taught her.

Within seconds, the spark had turned to a flame.

Not wanting to do anything that would make the precarious fire go out, she moved a few sticks over to the smoldering moss. Slowly but surely, they also caught fire.

Five minutes later, there was a crackling, warm fire burning.

Zoey turned to Mark in disbelief. "I did it."

"Yes, you sure d-did, s-sweetheart."

Hearing his stutter, Zoey brushed off the feeling of accomplishment and shuffled over to Mark. "Come on. You need to get closer to the fire."

Very slowly, and holding her shirt to his midsection, Mark stood. Zoey quickly went to his side and wrapped a steadying arm around him. Within moments, he was sitting once more, this time right next to the fire. She could feel the heat coming from the flames, and for just a second she considered sitting down next to Mark to soak them up, but she had more work to do.

Leaving Mark by the fire, she gathered his clothes and squeezed as much water out of them as possible. Then she draped them over some logs she'd carried to the fire. He couldn't continue on without his clothes, and he couldn't put them on if they were wet. So the only choice was to do everything possible to dry them out. Luckily, the cargo pants weren't one hundred percent cotton like a pair of jeans would've been. She figured they should dry fairly quickly. But his T-shirt and underwear would take much longer to be ready to wear again.

Then she set about seeing what she could find for them to eat. Making a snare and killing a squirrel was outside her abilities, but Zoey did manage to forage some berries, a few mushrooms, and even a bunch of cattail plants. They didn't taste the best, but Colin had taught her that, in a pinch, they could be consumed.

The sun had completely disappeared behind the afternoon clouds, and Zoey shivered. But she did her best to ignore her discomfort. Mark was in much worse shape. She could deal with a little chill.

She brought her bounty back to where she'd left Mark and found him lying on his side. Zoey put more wood on the fire, ignoring the amount of smoke that was curling up into the sky. As long as they had flames, she didn't care how smoky things got.

The sound of her messing with the fire woke Mark, and he pushed himself upright.

"I found some stuff to eat," Zoey told him with a small smile. She saw the look of admiration in his eyes, but ignored it for now. "As well as our usual berry and fungus feast, I found us some cattails."

"Cattails?" Mark asked.

Zoey was pleased that he didn't seem to be shivering as much anymore, and he hadn't stuttered. "Yeah. Your dad taught me. I'm going to roast the shoots, as that's the easiest thing to do out here. The roots can also be eaten, but they're not as good."

"My pop taught you that?" Mark asked.

Zoey nodded as she used his knife to cut the shoots. "Yeah. We were talking one day about all the stuff in the wilderness that was edible. He told me cattails were, but I didn't believe him. So of course, he had to prove me wrong." Zoey chuckled. "Honestly, this isn't going to taste all that good, but since I can't catch any meat for us, this will have to do for now."

"I didn't know about cattails," Mark said.

He sounded so different, Zoey looked up at him in concern.

"You're amazing, Zo."

Blushing, Zoey shrugged. "If I was all that amazing, I would've been able to catch us a moose and make us some moose burgers." She wasn't used to compliments. Not ones that were accompanied by a look like the one on Mark's face. "I need to go wash these. I'll be right back."

"Don't fall in," Mark quipped.

Zoey rolled her eyes. "I think one of us taking an impromptu dunk is enough. Although I *am* kind of jealous that you were able to take a bath and wash off the worst of the dirt from the last week." She couldn't believe she was actually joking about what had happened, but she supposed it was a good way to let off some nervous energy.

Bubba was pissed. At himself. It wasn't as if it was his fault that the tree had come down stream at exactly the wrong time, but he should've at least planned for something like that. He could've taken off more of his clothes, just in case he got dunked. If he had, he wouldn't be sitting on the ground, practically naked, watching Zoey take care of him.

It was a weird role reversal, and he didn't like it. Didn't like the way Zoey was flitting around in only a tank top. He could see how cold she was by the way her nipples were poking through her bra, and the goose bumps that rose on her arms every time she stepped away from the fire. He didn't like that she'd literally given him the shirt off her back, and her socks as well.

If they'd both been soaked, they would've been fucked. Zoey had done everything right.

All his adult life he'd taken for granted that his teammates would have his back. If he'd been with one of them, it would've been a given that they'd have done what Zoey had. But she wasn't a SEAL. Wasn't his teammate. And yet, she'd acted immediately and kept him from suffering needlessly. He wasn't exactly out of the woods yet, but the warmth from the fire was going a long way toward making him recover sooner rather than later.

Bubba was as proud as he could be that Zoey had managed to get the fire started. He couldn't have done it, his hands had been shaking too hard. But she'd managed, and the feeling of accomplishment that he'd seen on her face was beautiful.

She'd started the fire, gotten them food, taught him something he didn't know about edible wild plants, and now it was time she stopped moving for two seconds and relaxed. "Come here," he told her after she'd put another log on the fire. Bubba held out an arm, encouraging her to snuggle up against him.

She came to him without hesitation, which made him feel ten feet tall. His colossal mistake hadn't seemed to diminish her willingness to be near him. When she snuggled against him, he could feel the chill of her body against his own.

He held her tight and moved them a little closer to the flames.

"You know what I'm wishing right now?" she asked when they got comfortable.

"For a large steak and potato dinner?" Bubba asked.

She chuckled. "Besides that."

"No, tell me."

"Back home, when I did laundry, one of my favorite things in the world to do was take the towels and sheets fresh out of the dryer and curl up on the couch under them. The warmth would seep into my bones and warm me from the inside out. They smelled fresh and clean, and it's always been one of those small indulgences that I know other people would think is weird, but I did it anyway. I wish I had a dryer right here, and I could take those warm towels out and wrap them around us."

Bubba could picture Zoey in his mind right now. She'd be smiling and her eyes would be shut as she enjoyed one of the little things in life. He wanted to give her that. Wanted to give her everything.

"When we get to Anchorage, I'm gonna make that happen for you, sweetheart."

He felt her shrug against him. "It's fine. Mark?"

"Yeah?"

"You scared the shit out of me."

Bubba closed his eyes. He'd kinda scared himself. For a second there, when he was trapped under the tree branch in the fast-moving water, he'd thought he was a goner. And once free, the only thing that kept him from being swept away had been the rope around his waist and Zoey holding on to the other end.

He reached out and picked up one of her hands. It was dirty from putting the last log on the fire, and she had debris caked under her nails. He turned it over and saw a dark red burn mark from the very rope she'd used to save his life, and a bruise forming around her wrist, probably from wrapping the rope around it. Bubba kissed both gently.

"Thank you for being there. You did everything right, sweetheart."

She didn't respond, but curled into him tighter.

"I'm sorry I scared you. I can't promise not to do anything in the future that will make you uneasy or frightened, but I do promise to be more careful. To not take chances. We should've just turned around today. Or I should've thought a little more about alternative options to get around the stream. I'm sorry."

Zoey nodded against him. He liked that she didn't say it was okay. Or try to convince him he didn't fuck up when they both knew he had. But he also liked that she didn't berate him or say anything that would make him feel even worse than he already did.

"But you know what?"

"What?" she mumbled.

"I think after today, you're officially a ten out of ten on the outdoor comfortability scale."

She picked her head up at that. "Seriously?"

He chuckled. "Yeah. You pulled my ass out of the stream. You got me warm. You made fire. Started drying my clothes and got us food. I'm sure if you had to, you could also make us a shelter if we needed it. So yeah, I'd say that brings you up to a ten out of ten."

"Well, yippee for me," she said sarcastically. "When do I get my merit badge?"

Bubba felt better right that moment than he had in the last couple hours. He was wearing only his shirt, had on a pair of women's socks, and had her pink and purple fleece wrapped around his waist, but he'd never felt more comfortable.

They sat in silence for quite a while. Enjoying the heat from both the fire and each other's bodies. Zoey had stopped shivering, which relieved Bubba.

He was about to ask her some random question...when he thought he heard something.

For the last week, the only things they'd heard were leaves blowing, birds singing, their own voices, and the wind and rain. What he was hearing now was definitely out of the ordinary.

"Zoey! Quick, put more logs on the fire!"

"What?" she asked, sitting up.

Bubba pushed at her shoulder a little harder than he'd meant to. "*Now*, Zo. Do it! A wet one if you can find it. We need smoke. Lots of it!"

She moved then. Without any more questions, she leapt up and hurried over to the stack of wood she'd dropped earlier and quickly worked on stoking the fire.

Bubba stood, and while he wobbled at first, he quickly regained his equilibrium. He stood in Zoey's purple socks, clutching her fleece shirt to his nether regions, his ass facing the fire as he looked up into the sky.

The clouds were low, which might fuck them, but Bubba hoped not.

Zoey came up to his side and put her arm around his waist. He put his around her shoulders and they both stared upward.

"Is that what I think it is?" she asked, the hope easy to hear in her voice.

"Yeah. It's a helicopter. But there's no guarantee it'll stop. No way to know even how close it is. Sound travels really far out here. It could be miles away," he warned.

"It'll see us," Zoey whispered. "It has to."

Bubba glanced back at the fire and saw Zoey had done an excellent job at making it bigger. There weren't any trees above to block the smoke either. If the chopper got low enough, there was no way it could miss them. But that was a big if. With the clouds being as thick as they were, it was possible the helicopter was flying above them and wouldn't see the smoke from the fire. Or it could be miles away.

Zoey turned into him and wrapped both her arms around his waist. She buried her head against him and held on tight. He knew she was praying as hard as she could, and he joined in.

"Come on," he said softly. "We're right here. *See* us."

CHAPTER ELEVEN

Rex was frustrated. He'd been in an Alaska State Trooper helicopter all day. They'd flown west of Anchorage on their assigned search grid and had been at it most of the day. The weather had started out sunny and clear but had slowly gotten more and more cloudy. The pilot said they'd have to be heading back to the airport soon, as visibility had decreased to the point where it was dangerous to continue the search.

They hadn't found hide nor hair of Bubba or the plane he'd been in. It was as if he really *had* disappeared into thin air. It was frustrating and demoralizing. The pilot had gotten updates from the others, who hadn't found anything either. They'd flown as far east as Whitefish Lake, a fairly large and popular destination for nature lovers and hunters alike, but hadn't seen anything out of the ordinary.

The trooper who was in the back of the chopper, searching with him, hadn't complained about the long and boring work, understanding the driving need to find and rescue a teammate. They'd lost a pair of troopers when the helicopter they'd been on had crashed after rescuing a stranded snowmobiler. There had been no survivors, but they'd all worked around the clock to get to the wreckage and recover the bodies of their brothers-in-arms.

The chopper had descended and was flying much lower than the pilot would've normally flown because of the clouds. They'd crossed the mountain range that housed Denali, the twenty-thousand-foot-high peak north of where they were, on their search earlier that day. It would be much trickier to go back over the mountains, now that the weather was crappy. There weren't any huge twenty thousand foot peaks like Denali, but even an eight to ten thousand foot high mountain was still enough to be concerned about.

They would've already been back in Anchorage, but the troopers got a call from a VPSO about a situation they needed help with, and they'd stopped at the small town for a few hours to deal with that.

Rex had appreciated the break, as it was hard on the eyes to constantly scan the countryside for anything that looked like it might not belong. Now he was getting tired again, and he wanted to lie down for a few hours before heading out again the next day with a new plan. Tomorrow, they'd hug the coastline to see if they could find anything.

Rex was thinking about the huge cup of coffee he was going to pour for himself the second they landed when something caught his eye. Turning his head, he stared hard, wondering if what he was seeing was merely clouds... or something more.

After mere seconds, he was sure it wasn't clouds.

"Four o'clock," he barked into the microphone at his lips. "Smoke. Where are we? Could that be from a house?"

"No way," the pilot said immediately, turning the chopper in the direction Rex had pointed out. "We're directly over the Lake Clark Preserve and Wilderness. There's nothing out here. No hunters are allowed and there are certainly no residences."

Rex's heart began to beat faster.

"Unless that's an out-of-control wildfire, which is unlikely with the amount of rain we've gotten recently, there's someone down there," the other trooper said.

Rex did his best to not get his hopes up too high. It was possible it was a hunter breaking the law, or someone camping. Just because there was smoke, didn't mean it was Bubba. But after seeing absolutely nothing all day, and with the current weather, even seeing the smoke from the fire was a minor miracle.

The smoke continued to roll upward, and the closer they got, Rex could see it was coming from some sort of campfire. The pilot slowed the chopper as much as he could and began to fly in circles above the smoke. They descended slowly, and Rex prayed harder than he ever had in his life.

When the helicopter banked and came back around, Rex saw what he'd been looking for. What they'd *all* been looking for the past week.

Bubba was standing in the middle of a clearing with a woman against him. A fire blazed merrily behind them, belching smoke as if the person making it had no idea that the wetter the wood, the more smoke it would produce.

Rex leaned out as far as he could, knowing the safety line attached to the harness around his chest would keep him safe. Using hand signs, he asked Bubba if he was hurt.

The best sight Rex had ever seen was when Bubba lifted an arm, made a fist, and tapped the top of his head.

He was all right.

Fuckin' A. Bubba was okay, and they'd fuckin' found him.

Rex vaguely heard the pilot radioing in to someone that the targets had been located and seemed to be alive and well. He kept his eyes on his friend as they hovered above them. There was no place to land, so they'd have to haul up Bubba and the woman, Zoey, using a Stokes basket. Rex couldn't wait to get them into the chopper. He didn't know where the plane was, or the pilot, but for the moment, he was relieved that he'd found his friend.

Rex could see that Bubba was practically naked. He wore a long-sleeve flannel shirt but his legs were bare. He had what looked like two shirts wrapped around his waist, one that tied in the front and the other in back, making it look like he was wearing some sort of odd loincloth. He also had purple socks on his feet. Then he noticed what he assumed were Bubba's clothes draped over a log near the fire. The woman wore pants and shoes, but only a tank top otherwise.

Knowing whatever had happened wasn't good, Rex was even more antsy to get his friend in the helicopter and out of the fucking middle of nowhere. His concern was tempered by his excitement and relief. He'd honestly started to believe he'd never talk to Bubba again. He was happier than he could say that he'd been wrong.

The trip up to the helicopter wasn't something Zoey ever wanted to duplicate. Mark had insisted she go first. She hadn't wanted to be away from him, even for a second. The few minutes it took to get her up and into the

163

chopper before the basket returned for him felt like hours.

That irked her. She wasn't the kind of woman who ever needed or wanted to rely on a man for her well-being.

But she decided to go easy on herself, considering what she'd been through over the last week. Besides, she and Mark had been together for literally every minute for seven days. They'd had to rely on each other for just about everything. At this point, it was natural that she'd feel uneasy when he wasn't next to her.

She knew she'd have to get over that feeling...and fast. She could see from the way one particular man in the helicopter kept his eyes focused on Mark, this was probably one of his SEAL teammates. She didn't know which one, but it wasn't hard to see he was very concerned.

When Mark's head finally popped up from below the opening of the chopper, Zoey breathed a sigh of relief. He had tied her shirt backward around his waist, covering his privates, and her fleece shirt he'd tied the opposite way, covering his ass. His legs were still bare, and she hoped like hell someone had an extra pair of pants for him somewhere.

He was carrying his clothes in his lap, and he'd taken care of the fire before coming up to the helicopter.

Expecting him to greet his friend and the other crew members in the helicopter, Zoey was surprised when, the second he was inside the cabin, he came toward her.

Mark's gaze was focused on her, and Zoey couldn't remember when she'd felt more cherished. More cared for. He settled next to her and reached for the metallic emergency blanket his friend was holding. Instead of wrapping it around himself, he shook it out and tucked it around her chest and behind her shoulders.

The noise of the helicopter was loud, and she knew he wouldn't be able to hear her, so she shook her head and tried to make him take it. But Mark simply ignored her and reached for another one of the small, compact blankets his friend was holding out. After he'd wrapped her up in both, Mark finally saw to himself, wrapping himself in the thin but oh-so-warm material. Once he'd settled, the other man in the back of the chopper—who Zoey now saw was an Alaska State Trooper—covered them both with a large, heavy wool blanket.

Mark then took a headset that his friend was offering and gently placed it on her head, settling it over her ears carefully, adjusting the microphone so it was right against her lips. Afterward, he put on a set of headphones himself.

"Good, Zo?" he asked.

She jerked at the sound of his voice in her head. It seemed even more intimate through the headphones. She nodded.

"Bubba, holy shit, man, is it good to see you!" said the man she assumed was his teammate.

"I think that's my line," Mark replied.

Zoey listened to the two men banter back and forth, sighing in contentment when she felt Mark's hand slide over hers under the blankets.

"I can pretty much put two and two together, but want to tell me why you're not wearing any pants?"

Mark went into an explanation about how he'd fallen into the stream and Zoey had helped pull him out. How he'd had to strip off his clothes since they were soaking wet. She saw his friend nod in understanding, and she had a feeling he probably understood better than most would.

"Rex, I'd like you to meet Zoey Knight. Zoey, this is

one of my best friends and teammates, Rex. Otherwise known as Cole Kingston."

"I'd offer to shake your hand, but I'm sure you prefer to keep it under that nice warm blanket. It's very nice to meet you, Zoey."

"Same," she said softly. "I've heard a lot about you from Mark over the last week."

"All lies," the SEAL said with a smile.

Zoey couldn't help but return it.

"Stop flirting with my girl," Mark growled.

Zoey turned to stare at him. His girl? God, that sounded good. But Zoey knew the real world was about to intrude on whatever bond they'd formed in the last seven days. It was one thing to connect with someone when you had no choice and, in her case, were literally relying on them to keep you alive.

"So that's how it is?" Rex asked.

"Yes," Mark confirmed.

She felt him squeeze her hand in reassurance, but he didn't turn to look at her. Zoey suspected she should feel annoyed at his claiming of her in such a chauvinistic way, but she couldn't bring herself to care.

"So, want to give me the CliffsNotes version of what happened?" Rex asked Mark. "Where's the plane? And the pilot?"

"You haven't found her?" Mark asked in surprise.

Zoey was equally shocked. She thought for sure that's how the chopper knew where to look for them.

"No."

"Then how'd you find us? Where were we, anyway?" Mark asked.

It was Rex's turn to look surprised. "You don't know?"

"No clue. I was sleeping when the pilot told us there

was a problem with the engines. She landed on a lake, and we got out so she could see if she could fix the problem. The second we stepped onto land, she backed the plane up and took off."

"Fuck!" Rex swore.

"Yeah," Mark agreed.

"You're in the middle of the Lake Clark Preserve and Wilderness," Rex said.

Mark didn't react, but Zoey inhaled sharply, drawing his attention.

"What? Where's that?" he asked her.

"It's west of Anchorage. There's literally no big towns or cities out here. Eve had to have gone in this direction from the second she took off. I'm so stupid! I didn't even notice we were going the wrong way."

"Not your fault," Rex said, beating Mark to the punch. "And as far as we know, Eve Dane doesn't exist. We've searched every database we can find and there's no one with that name that's listed as having a pilot's license in Alaska, or anywhere else for that matter."

"Fucking hell," Mark swore. "So how'd you find us?"

"After looking at just about every mile of land and sea between Anchorage and Juneau, we all agreed to branch out. Rocco and Phantom went north, me and Ace went west, and Gumby stayed in the eastern part, seeing if we'd somehow missed a downed plane. We actually shouldn't have been out this far, but the troopers got a call for assistance from one of the VPSOs. We were flying lower than normal because of the weather and on our way back to Anchorage when we saw the smoke from your fire."

"Holy crap," Zoey whispered.

"What?" Mark asked immediately. "Are you okay? Still cold? Rex, throw me another blanket."

"No. I mean...yeah, I think I'm going to be cold for another month, but that's not what I meant." Zoey realized that she had the attention of all three men in the chopper. The pilot was even turning to look at her between watching where he was going. "It's just that... today was the first time we made a fire out in the open. Every other night, we were under the trees, in a shelter. If we had turned around today and gone back the way we came, or followed that stream to try to get around it, and if you hadn't tried to cross, or we were faster or slower in getting that log across it...if I hadn't been able to start the fire, or the wood wasn't as wet...they would've flown right over us."

The other men in the helicopter seemed to fade in the background. She was staring at Mark and couldn't look away. His gaze was piercing in its intensity and the hold he had on her hand almost hurt, but she didn't try to pull away. She felt closer to Mark in that moment than she had for the last week, and that was saying something. The realization of how close they'd come to being missed was sinking in.

"I made what I thought was a stupid decision," Mark said.

Zoey knew everyone in the chopper could hear their conversation, but it still felt as if they were the only two people in the world.

"But as it turns out, it was exactly the right thing to do at the right time. I've had some eerie encounters with fate in my line of work, but right now, I'd have to say that there was more than just luck going on."

"Colin," Zoey whispered.

Mark nodded. "Pop," he agreed.

It was hard for Zoey to breathe, thinking about how

lucky they'd been. If they'd done just one thing differently, Rex and the troopers would've flown right over them and never known they were there. It was a sobering thought.

For the rest of the flight, Zoey vaguely listened as Mark talked to Rex about everything that had happened in the last week. How there'd been no trace of Eve Dane or the plane, how the reading of Colin's will had been postponed, and how all five of his SEAL teammates had been sleeping only the bare minimum and looking under every rock and stone to find their friend.

She was practically asleep when they finally landed in Anchorage. Everything happened quickly after that. Mark refused to be separated from her, which was a huge relief, and they were both taken by ambulance to the hospital to be checked over.

After they were declared amazingly healthy, Rex stopped and picked up huge hamburgers, French fries, salads, and two pieces of pecan pie. He drove them to the hotel where he and the other SEALs had been staying. Without asking, Mark had happily agreed they would take over the room Rex and Ace had been sharing.

Sighing in relief that she wouldn't have to say goodbye yet, they entered the hotel room. Mark was wearing a pair of scrubs the staff at the hospital had given him. Zoey was still in her dirty clothes, and was once again wearing her long-sleeve fleece shirt she'd given to Mark after he'd been dunked.

"Shower's all yours," Mark said firmly when they'd gotten inside. "Rex went to get you some clothes and should be back by the time you're done."

Zoey shook her head. "No, you were the one who went swimming. You should go first."

Mark put his hands on her shoulders and turned her to

face him. She looked up into his eyes. "Go shower, sweetheart. You can stay in there as long as you want, the hot water shouldn't run out. Rex said there's extra shampoo and conditioner in the bathroom, feel free to use it all. Rocco also got toothbrushes and toothpaste from the little shop in the lobby. I don't care if you're in there for an hour, as long as you're clean, happy, and warm when you come out. I'll go next door and shower." He gestured to the connecting door with his head. "That's where Rocco, Phantom, and Gumby are staying. If you need anything, just call out. I'll hear you. Okay?"

All Zoey could do was nod. She was numb. Not temperature-wise, but her emotions and thoughts. So much had happened in the last few days. She'd gone from despair, to worry, to extreme fright, back to worry, then excitement.

As if he knew how on edge she was, Mark pulled her into his arms. How long they stood like that, huddled together, Zoey had no clue. But she wasn't nearly ready for him to pull back when he did. "Shower, Zo. You'll feel more like yourself afterward. Promise."

She nodded and headed for the bathroom.

It was at least an hour later when Zoey finally emerged from the steam-filled room. She'd stood under the hot water not moving for at least the first ten minutes. Then she'd cried. When she didn't think she had any tears left in her body, she washed her hair three times before slathering it with conditioner. She scrubbed her body until it was pink and tingling, then scrubbed it once more for good measure. It had never felt so good to be clean.

After she'd finally gotten out of the shower, she had the thought that it was probably a good thing the mirror was steamed over so she couldn't see her hair. She'd tried to finger comb it, with little luck. She'd have to see if Mark could find her a comb or brush. Zoey still didn't have any clothes to put on, so she wrapped one of the huge, fluffy towels around her body and slowly opened the door.

Shivering because of the temperature difference between the bathroom and the bedroom, she walked out. The second Mark saw her, he stood and came toward her. He picked up a stack of clothes sitting on the bed on his way and pressed them into her hands.

"Here's what Rex found. You have a choice. Rex can take your clothes down and get them cleaned so you can wear them tomorrow, or he can go back out and buy more stuff. I wasn't sure how you'd feel about wearing the same thing you've had on for the last week."

Zoey knew she shouldn't be surprised at how considerate Mark was, but she still blushed. "I'm fine to wear the same things. I'd prefer that, actually."

Nodding, Mark said, "Okay, hand them to me, and I'll give them to Rex while you're changing. Then I have a surprise for you."

Her brows shot up. "A surprise?"

Mark smiled, and Zoey felt the butterflies in her stomach take flight. "Yeah, sweetheart. A surprise."

Thinking it had been a very long time since anyone had bothered to try to surprise her, she headed back into the bathroom with her new clothes. She refused to blush when she handed over her dirty clothes, including her underwear. Mark wasn't a seventeen-year-old boy, he was a man who hadn't blinked at stripping naked in front of her when his life was in danger. He and his friends had seen way more intense things than her plain white cotton underwear.

She reemerged from the bathroom a few minutes later

and saw Mark standing by the open door to the hallway. "Go lie on the bed," he ordered with a smile.

"What in the world?" Zoey asked.

"Please? I promise you're going to love this," Mark said.

Shrugging and figuring she might as well humor him, Zoey did as he asked. She walked into the room and lay on one of the two queen-size beds.

"Close your eyes," Mark ordered from the doorway.

Sighing in exasperation, Zoey closed her eyes.

She heard footsteps and whispers, but she was so tired, she tuned them out.

Seconds later, the most delicious heat engulfed her body.

Her eyes flew open in surprise, and she stared up at Mark. He was standing over her, smiling as he piled heaps of warm towels on top of her.

He'd remembered the story she'd told him about how much she loved to do this at home. The towels were obviously from the laundry room at the hotel. How in the world he'd gotten the hotel staff to agree to this, Zoey had no idea, but she couldn't deny the warm and fuzzy feeling that formed inside her heart.

"Mark," she said. The tears she'd thought had been all used up welled in her eyes once more.

"Close your eyes and enjoy," he told her. "I promised I'd fold all these towels if they just let me borrow them for twenty minutes."

God. No one had ever done anything like this for her before. Zoey couldn't talk. Couldn't protest that she could get up and help him fold. Couldn't do anything but lie there and enjoy the warm heat seeping into her very bones.

Rex poked his head into the room and said, "Is it safe for us to come in?"

"Yeah," Mark said.

And before Zoey knew what was going on, the room was full of five more of the most handsome men she'd ever seen. They all had beards and were crazy muscular. They also had an air of competence and bad-assery about them that would've freaked her out and made her find a way to exit the room as soon as possible, if she hadn't been buried under a mound of warm towels.

"Hi!" one of the men said cheerily. "I'm Rocco. We're in your debt for keeping this asshole alive out there."

Zoey opened her mouth to protest, to say that Mark was the one who'd kept *her* alive, when one of the other men spoke.

"I'm Ace. Bubba told us how you pulled his ass out of that stream and literally gave him the clothes off your back. Thank you."

"And I'm Gumby. Using wet wood for that fire was smart, it sent smoke into the air high enough to be seen."

Zoey's eyes went to the last man in the room. He was frowning, and she shivered at the cold look in his eyes. She swallowed hard, almost scared to hear what he had to say.

"By process of elimination, I'm Phantom. Bubba said you weren't a pain in his ass while you were out there. Coming from him, that's high praise indeed. Thank you."

Blinking in surprise, it took a couple of tries before she could speak, but she finally said, "It's nice to meet you all. Mark told me you'd find us. I have to admit that I wasn't completely sold. But I'm glad to know I was wrong. I've heard so much about you all. I'm so happy to meet you."

The guys all gave her chin lifts, then got to work folding the towels lying over her. They were careful not to let their fingers brush against her in an inappropriate way, and Zoey loved hearing the banter between them. She could tell they were close, and she loved that for Mark. She understood a bit more why he hadn't come home after joining the navy. He'd had his family right there with him.

The phone on the small table between the beds rang, scaring the shit out of Zoey. Ace leaned over and answered.

"Hello? ... Yeah, this is her room. Can I ask who's calling? ... Just a moment, please." Then he held the phone against his chest and told Zoey, "She says she's your mom."

Zoey eagerly moved a hand out from under the towels and Ace put the receiver in it.

"Mom?"

"Yes, it's me! Are you all right? When the police called and told me you were missing, I was so worried!"

"I'm okay. It was a little touch and go there for a while, but the state troopers and Mark's teammate found us. Are you going to come by the hotel?"

"Oh, honey, I wish I could...but I'm in the middle of packing."

Zoey's stomach dropped. "Packing?"

"Yes!" her mom said excitedly. "You met Liam when you were here before. He actually lives up in Fairbanks and was only here on a temporary job. He asked me to move in with him, and we're leaving tomorrow! I've only got about half my apartment packed so far, and I know I'll be up all night getting the rest into boxes."

"That's great, Mom," Zoey said with as much enthusiasm as she could muster.

"It is! He's different from anyone I've ever met before. He's so good-looking, and has a great job too."

"Are you sure this is what you want, Mom?" Zoey

asked, knowing what her mom was going to say before she said it.

"Yes! This is it, Zoey. I feel it in my bones!"

"I'm happy for you then."

"Thanks, baby. I'll call when I get settled in and give you my new address."

"Okay."

"I'm glad you're okay!"

"Me too. Drive safe."

"I will. Love you."

"Love you too, Mom. Bye."

"Bye."

Zoey handed the phone back to Ace and scooted up on the bed. Most of the towels had been folded, and she felt six pairs of eyes on her.

Making sure no emotions were on her face, she looked up and said unnecessarily, "That was my mom."

"She's not coming to see you?" Rex asked with a frown.

Zoey shrugged. "Apparently, she's moving to Fairbanks with her latest boyfriend."

None of the guys said anything, and it felt extremely awkward, so Zoey tried to explain. "It's just how she is. We never stayed in one place long when I was growing up. We moved from town to town when Mom met guys. She always thought they were 'the one.' I'm used to it. It's fine."

"She should be *here*," Phantom said harshly.

Zoey flinched, but shrugged. "She does her best. She hasn't had an easy life. We were even homeless for a while when we lived here in Anchorage. I was in middle school and we stayed in our car for about three months, until she found a job and we could move into one of those rent-by-the-week motel rooms. The only thing she wants in life is a guy who will take care of her."

The more Zoey spoke, the more pathetic her mom sounded, and she hated that. "She's not a bad person," she said urgently. "She's...it's just that her goal in life is stability, and she hasn't been able to find that yet. So she moves from town to town, guy to guy, looking for it."

"That's why you moved to Juneau when you were in the tenth grade?" Mark asked.

Zoey nodded. "Yeah. Her latest boyfriend lived there and convinced her to move to be with him. When I was a senior, she broke up with him but stayed so I could graduate. The day after I walked across the stage, she headed to Kodiak with a new boyfriend."

"Jesus," Gumby muttered.

"And you stayed," Mark said. He hadn't taken his eyes from hers.

"Yeah. I liked it there, and I was tired of moving around. Besides, it was way easier for my mom. She didn't have to worry about me then."

"You mean the assholes she was hooking up with had one less person to worry about," Rex said under his breath.

"Yeah, that too," Zoey agreed. She knew she was a third wheel in her mom's relationships. Some of the men had made that more than clear. Breaking up with her mom because she had a kid, or simply ignoring Zoey. "But seriously, she loves me, and I love her. I hope this guy is the one she's been praying for her entire life." She didn't mention that she doubted it, but figured she didn't have to.

"I'll get these towels back to housekeeping," Rocco said.

"I'll help," Ace chimed in.

"We'll all help," Gumby said.

One second, Zoey was surrounded by six hot, bearded men, and the next she was alone with Mark once more. "Thank you," she told him. "I haven't felt that spoiled since I was ten and my mom splurged and bought me breakfast at McDonald's, lunch at Hardees, and dinner at Kentucky Fried Chicken."

Mark smiled, but she could tell it was forced. "I'm sorry about you not getting to see your mom."

Zoey shrugged. "Honestly, Mark, I'm used to it. And I got to see her for a while before I got on that stupid plane. It's fine."

She could tell he was struggling with her mom's inattentiveness, but she relaxed when she realized he was going to let it drop. "I've got another surprise," he told her.

Zoey shook her head. "You've done enough for me. I should be finding ways to spoil *you*. I wasn't the one who took a header into a glacier-fed stream."

Ignoring her as if she hadn't spoken, he said, "Scoot over here and sit on the floor by the bed." He took a pillow and placed it on the floor at the end of the bed.

Frowning, she got off the bed and went to where he'd indicated, sitting slowly on the pillow. He grabbed a bag from on top of the dresser, and then sat on the bed behind her. His legs were on either side of her body, and she could feel his heat radiating into her.

"I had Rex stop at the pharmacy. He got some detangling spray—I think that's what it's called—and different kinds of combs and brushes. I didn't know what would work best on your hair and didn't want to rip it out at the roots."

Zoey stilled for a second, then turned to stare at him. "You did?"

"Yeah. I told you I'd help you brush your hair when we were rescued, and that's what I'm doing...unless you'd prefer I didn't."

She shook her head. "No, I'd love that. But I just..." Her voice trailed off.

"You just what?" Mark asked.

"I thought you'd want to hang out with your friends. They're obviously glad to see you. I'm just kinda confused."

"I'm not leaving you, Zo. Maybe I'm the only one who's feeling a little lost, but I don't want to be away from you."

"Do you think we're still in danger?" Zoey asked.

"Maybe. But that's not why I don't want to be away from you. Something happened out there. I've always liked you, Zoey. Even when we were teenagers, I thought there was something special about you. But spending every day with you for a week made that 'like' morph into something more. Respect. Admiration. I want to see where things between us can go. Maybe being in the real world will make me realize what I was feeling wasn't what I thought it was. But what if it makes me feel even closer to you? If I'm out of line here, now's your time to speak up."

Zoey swallowed hard. She was at a crossroads in her life right this second. She could choose the easy path. Go back to her boring and lonely life in Juneau by herself, now that Colin was gone. Or she could take the winding, bumpy path with Mark. She had no idea where that scary and unknown path would take her, but at least she'd be living.

For a second, she wondered if this was how her mom

SECURING ZOEY

often felt. That the winding road might lead her to heartache, but it also might lead her to the life she'd always dreamed of. She understood her mom a little more at that moment, and felt a little guilty at the way she'd always judged her so harshly.

"You're not out of line," she told Mark. "I admired and respected you before we even crossed paths again because of your dad. He talked about you all the time. To be honest, I've always had a crush on you. But now that I *know* you?" She shook her head. "You're so much more than the stories your dad told. And I'd like to see where things between us can go too, but I'm scared to death of being like my mom. Of moving to another city every time a man asks me to."

Mark smiled, then put a hand on her shoulder, physically turning her so her back was to him once again. He sprayed her mussed hair with the detangler and slowly, and ever so carefully, began to brush her hair.

"How many men have you moved for?" he asked.

"Well, none," Zoey said.

"Right. I've been thinking about this ever since we were picked up. I already told you I wanted you to come down to Riverton with me, both to keep you safe from whoever wanted us to disappear, but also because I could see you all the time. I don't want you to feel as if you're completely dependent on me, I know you want to be independent, and I have no issues with that.

"I have this neighbor... She's eighty-three, and she lives by herself. She never had any children, and her husband passed away about five years ago. She does pretty well on her own, but I've noticed recently that she's been slowing down. I mow her grass and try to touch base with her once a week, but her house hasn't been cleaned the way I know she likes it recently, and I don't think she's been eating as well as she should.

"She's lonely as hell. One night when I went over to visit, I stayed several hours. We played cards and talked. She said she would enjoy having someone stay with her, but she didn't have any family left. Meeting you, hearing how you took care of Pop, got me thinking. What if *you* moved in with her? She's really nice and honestly doesn't need much care. She just needs someone to be there just in case, and to talk to.

"As much as I'd like for you to move in with me, I'm not sure that's the best thing for either of us at this point. So this could be the next best thing. I could still see you almost every day, since you'd be living across the street, but you could be independent and do what I think you enjoy doing...taking care of others."

Zoey closed her eyes. Between his hands on her hair, slowly brushing, and his words, she was practically a puddle at his feet. She wanted to turn around and throw herself into his arms, but a part of her was still scared she might be misinterpreting what he was saying.

"So you want me to come to California because I might still be in danger, and because you want someone to look after your neighbor?"

He stopped brushing and leaned over, putting his hand on her chin and turning her so she had no choice but to look at him. "No. I want you to come to California because the thought of leaving here without you makes me physically sick. And I want you to look after Jess because I honestly think it's something you'd love. I saw how animated you got when you talked about hanging with my dad and helping him out. But more than that, it'll give you some independence, and you'll be near me so I can see you every day."

When Zoey could only stare at him and try to get her thoughts in order to respond, he kept talking.

"I know this is sudden and you have a life here in Alaska. You have a job and all your things are here. But we can figure that stuff out. I heard what you said about your mom, and this is *not* that. You're an amazing woman all by yourself. You don't need me to be successful in life. You don't need any man. But I'm sitting here pretty much begging you to let me be in your life. You hold all the cards here, Zoey. Jess can pay you to help her, so you won't be dependent on me. I just...I can't let you go. Please say yes. At least try it out."

"Yes," Zoey said when he took a breath, probably to continue to say things that would make her fall for him even harder.

"Yes?" he asked.

Zoey nodded.

Mark let out a little whoop of delight that made Zoey chuckle, then he stood, pulling her up with him and folding her into his arms and spinning in circles, laughing delightedly.

"Everything okay in here?" Rocco asked, poking his head into the room from the connecting door.

"Everything's great," Mark told him. "Zoey agreed to go back to Riverton with us."

"Awesome. Oh, and, Bubba, I got in touch with your dad's lawyer. Tomorrow afternoon, he's going forward with the official reading of Colin's will." Then he pulled back and shut the connecting door behind him.

Zoey's enthusiasm dimmed at hearing that. Mark still held her in the circle of his arms. "I'm so sorry about your dad," she said. "I'm not sure, in all the hub bub, that I even told you that."

"I know you are. And honestly, I'm glad we're getting this done. The sooner we know what Dad left us and why someone might've wanted us dead, the closer we are to figuring out who's behind it."

"Do you really think there's going to be any big surprises in his will?" Zoey asked. "I mean, your dad was one of the most straightforward men I've ever met. I can't imagine he's got millions of dollars stashed overseas somewhere. Or that he's a member of some secret organization or something and his 'associates' want to get their hands on his money."

Mark smiled down at her. "No, I don't imagine there will be anything shocking. I'm guessing that his stuff will be pretty much split between me and Malcom. And he obviously left something to you. And since he's a half partner in a business, something will have to be done with that too. I can't think of any reason why someone would want to kill us."

"Oh...speaking of the will, have you seen your brother?"

"Yeah. I saw him for a brief moment while you were showering."

"And?"

"And what? We were glad to see each other. He's been in Anchorage helping with the search for us."

"And did it go okay?"

Mark stared at her for a long moment. "Yeah, it did. He seemed very happy to see me alive and well. It surprised me, actually. He's either a very good actor, or he was genuinely relieved to see me."

"Interesting. Did he say anything about me?"

"What aren't you telling me?" Mark asked, looking concerned now.

"Nothing. It's just...we don't really get along, Mark. And it's not a big deal, but he was mad at me before I left Juneau. He was supposed to come to the house I'm renting and look at the roof, then get someone out to fix a leak, but he never came. I asked him three times when he was coming over before I finally had to go to Colin, which pissed off Malcom. I hated to do it, but the stupid roof wasn't going to fix itself. Anyway...it's ridiculous. Of course he didn't mention it because it's silly to be worrying about that now, when you were missing and miraculously found."

"I won't deny that Malcom and I have grown apart since I left Juneau, but honestly, we weren't all that close while growing up. We were simply too different. He's still my brother, and I love him. But if he gives you any shit tomorrow, or even looks at you wrong, let me know and I'll take care of it."

Zoey sighed. "Thanks. I'm sure it'll be fine."

Mark looked skeptical but didn't say anything more about it. "How about you sit back down and let me finish your hair?" he suggested.

Nodding, Zoey lowered herself back onto the pillow and couldn't help but feel goose bumps when Mark once again began running a brush through her hair. It felt so good, and she felt a true connection with him at that moment.

She was mostly asleep, swaying in position as Mark brushed her hair way longer than necessary. It was practically dry by the time he finally called it quits. "Come on, sweetheart. Let's get you tucked in."

He helped her up and led her to the bed, and when he

started to step back, she reached out and grabbed his arm. "Stay with me?"

"You sure?" he asked. "I was going to sleep in the other bed."

Zoey shook her head. "Please?"

Without comment, Mark shucked off his pants and climbed under the covers. He pulled her toward him until she used his shoulder as a pillow. She twined her leg with his, and his arm around her tightened. "God, this feels so much better than the hard, cold ground," she murmured.

"Agreed. Sleep, Zo. We're safe."

"I've never felt safer than when your arms are around me," Zoey admitted sleepily.

She didn't feel him relax under her, didn't feel him reverently kiss her temple. The second the words left her mouth, she fell into a sleep borne of a week of uneasiness, being cold, and not knowing if they'd be rescued.

CHAPTER TWELVE

Following a nervous flight to Juneau, Bubba sat around a large table the next afternoon and listened to Kenneth Eklund, his dad's lawyer, read the last will and testament of Colin Wright. The room was packed full, with him, his brother, Zoey, Tracy Eklund, the lawyer's wife—who also served as his assistant—Sean Kassamali, his dad's business partner, and his wife Vivian. Also in attendance were Rocco and Phantom. Bubba had asked them to attend to keep watch over everyone there, and so they could relay any particular names to Tex, to see if the computer genius could come up with a reason why someone would want him, and possibly Zoey, dead.

The more he thought about how close they'd come to being missed by the search chopper, the more Bubba was convinced his pop had to have had a hand in their rescue. He was usually never as careless as he'd been at the stream. Nothing had happened the way he'd planned it, and because it had been so FUBAR, it made him think it had all gone down exactly the way it was supposed to.

He was happy to be alive. Happy to have reconnected

with Zoey. He was pleased he was able to see his brother in person. Talking with Sean was also good. The man had always been somewhat of a grouch, but it seemed that Colin's death had mellowed him some. He wasn't the same asshole Bubba remembered him being in the past. He said a lot of great things about his pop, and it was clear the other man loved his friend and was devastated he was gone.

"If it's okay with everyone, I'm going to paraphrase what Colin said in his will instead of reading the legalese word for word," the lawyer said after everyone was seated and ready for him to begin.

Kenneth was in his mid-fifties and wore a gray suit with a red tie that didn't seem to match the solemn occasion. He was around five foot nine inches tall and had a pronounced beer belly. His light hair was combed back and Bubba could see the lines his comb had made in it when he'd last brushed it back.

His wife and assistant, Tracy, stood behind his chair and looked bored out of her mind. She'd said all the right things earlier, telling Bubba and Malcom that she was sorry for their loss, but her tone didn't exactly match her words. She was quite a bit younger than her husband, and stood at his same height in her two inch heels. She had on a black dress, which hugged her slender body, but all-in-all, simply looked as if she was trying too hard to be fashionable and younger than she really was.

When everyone agreed, he continued. "Right, so Colin had about a hundred thousand dollars in cash in his accounts. This money will be evenly split between Mark and Malcom Wright, and Zoey Knight. The house he was living in will go to Malcom; the house Zoey was renting will go to her to do with as she pleases. As for his investments, he's instructed those to go to four different chari-ties in Juneau: The Glory Hall, an emergency shelter and food bank; Best Friends Animal Society, which is a no-kill shelter; Big Brothers, Big Sisters; and this last one he added at the last minute when he was sick...the Hospice and Home Care of Juneau."

Bubba wasn't surprised his pop had decided to give money away to the charities that meant the most to him. He'd always been a sucker for animals and kids. He'd hated how many homeless and struggling people there were in their hometown, as well. Alaska wasn't an easy place to be without a home or food to eat. The last one was a bit more surprising, but he supposed since his dad had been sick, he'd seen the need for care at the end of one's life.

"As for Heritage Plastics," the lawyer continued, "Colin was ever thankful that his friend, Sean, decided all those years ago to go into business with him and to take a gamble. Sean, you're already a fifty-percent owner, but Colin is giving you another five percent of his shares. Malcom, you'll get twenty-three percent; Mark, you get seventeen; and Zoey, you'll receive the last five percent."

Bubba *was* surprised at how his dad had broken up his half of the business. By giving Sean an additional five percent, that gave him the majority share, even if his dad had given all the rest of his shares to Malcom.

"This is bullshit," Malcom snapped. "Seriously. I've been by his side for over a decade. I've hired and fired employees and basically kept things going day to day. What has *she* done? *Nothing*. Not one fucking thing," he spat as he glared at Zoey.

Bubba tensed. He was as surprised as his brother was, but then again, he hadn't worked at the factory a day in his life. He didn't really know anything about running a business the size of his pop's. But he wasn't going to let Malcom belittle and harangue Zoey.

"That was uncalled for, bro," he said in a low, harsh tone.

Malcom shook his head and sat back in his chair with his arms crossed. "Was it?" he asked. "How would *you* know? You don't give a shit about any of it. You haven't bothered to step foot in Juneau since you left. You left us high and dry and didn't care. You were off saving the world, but didn't give two shits about the family you left behind. Did Pop tell you about the time he almost lost the house? No, I can see by the look on your face that he didn't. Things were tough and he fell behind on the mortgage. But it wasn't *you* who came to his rescue, it was *me*. The business took an upswing not too long after that and everything turned out all right, but my point is that you didn't know or care.

"There are countless other times when I was there for him and *you* weren't. But of course, throughout it all, Pop couldn't stop singing your praises! Good ol' Mark, the Navy SEAL hero! God, what a joke."

Bubba was shocked by Malcom's outburst. He had no idea his brother held this much animosity for him. "I didn't know you guys needed help because no one *told* me," he fired back.

"Whatever," Malcom huffed.

Bubba clenched his fist in his lap. He didn't know how to fix this. He'd regretted staying away, but the more time that passed, the harder it was to call up his pop and tell him he was coming to visit. He'd emailed and called every now and then, but of course, that wasn't enough.

If he was being honest with himself...he was afraid his pop would talk him into staying and running Heritage

Plastics with him and Malcom. Which was silly; it wasn't as if he could just go AWOL from the navy.

He'd fucked up, and all the regret he'd felt before this trip crushed down on him even harder.

When he felt Zoey's hand lightly squeeze his thigh under the table, Bubba closed his eyes and drew in a deep breath.

He needed that. Needed her to ground him.

It wasn't as if he'd had an easy life. He didn't tell his pop or brother any of the horrors he'd seen or gone through. Hadn't told them about when he'd been captured by the Taliban. His life hadn't been sunshine and roses, but he'd loved his family too much to burden them with those details. He supposed that was why his pop hadn't told him about his troubles either.

"Er...if we can continue?" Kenneth asked.

Bubba glanced over at Zoey and saw that her gaze was locked on the lawyer. She wasn't looking at him or Malcom. But she kept her hand right where it was.

Moving slowly so as not to draw attention to either of them, he covered her hand with his. As usual, it was chilly, so he wrapped his fingers around hers, trying to give her some of his warmth.

Half an hour later, the lawyer was finished reading the will. They'd signed all the legal papers he'd prepared and everyone was dispersing. Mark had left Zoey standing with Rocco and Phantom in the small lobby. They'd make sure she was all right and no one harassed her or said anything out of line.

He jogged to catch up with Sean and his wife. "Sean?"

His pop's oldest friend turned to face him. "I'm sorry about Colin."

"Me too," Bubba said. "I know we haven't talked much

over the years, but I just wanted to thank you." He stood eye-to-eye with Sean and saw that the man looked tired. He was a few years older than his dad had been, but his brown hair hadn't started to gray yet and his blue eyes were as clear as ever. Living in Alaska obviously agreed with him as he seemed strong and healthy.

"Thank *me*? For what?" Sean asked.

"For being Pop's friend. For letting him do something he loved. I know you guys didn't always see eye-to-eye, but I also know he respected you a hell of a lot."

Sean nodded. Then his lips pressed together and he sighed.

"What?"

Sean's blue gaze met Bubba's, and he asked, "Can I be honest here?"

"I'd prefer it."

"I'm not that thrilled about Colin's decisions regarding the business."

Bubba stiffened as the older man went on.

"Malcom's been a big help, but he's a bit hotheaded. Doesn't think before he acts, and we've lost some good employees as a result. You haven't stepped foot in the factory and don't know the first thing about what it is we do, or the business side of things. I mean, you're his son, and you're certainly entitled to a part of his estate, but I figured he'd leave you money instead of actual shares in Heritage. And him leaving *any* part of the business to Zoey just baffles me."

"But he made sure you had a controlling percentage," Bubba said.

"I know. But that doesn't mean I can sit around and make all the decisions. There's a lot that goes into an organization the size of ours. I can't do it by myself. Colin and

I talked daily about profits and expenses, our employees, and even to brainstorm about new products. We were in talks about expanding overseas when he passed away, and that's something I strongly feel we should still consider. But now, instead of just two people making the decisions, there are four. Are you planning on moving back to Juneau?"

"You know I'm not," Bubba told Sean.

"Yeah. That's what I thought." The older man sighed again. "Even though you've only got a seventeen-percent interest, I'll need your input, and there will be things you'll need to sign. Expect lots of calls and emails while we figure this out."

Bubba looked into Sean's eyes and saw that he was serious. "I could sell you my portion," he said.

For the first time, he saw a bit of friendliness creep into the other man's expression, but he shook his head. "That's decent of you, son, but that's not going to solve the issue of needing help running this thing."

"I could sell to Malcom," Bubba offered. He thought Sean would jump at that opportunity, but instead, he immediately shook his head again.

"No. That would make my problems worse. We'll think of something. Just promise that you'll take my calls?"

"Of course," he agreed immediately.

Then Sean stuck out his hand, and Bubba shook it.

"Again, I'm sorry about your dad. Colin was a good man, and he loved you very much."

Before Bubba let his dad's friend go, he asked, "Can you tell me what happened? I mean, I thought Pop was pretty healthy."

"Yeah. So did I. But you know him. He didn't like to go to the doctor. He came down with a stomach bug and couldn't shake it. Never really recovered. I saw him down at the factory one day, then the next thing I knew, Malcom was calling and telling me he'd passed away in his sleep."

It was pretty much the same thing Zoey had told him. Bubba frowned. "Damn."

"Yeah. Anyway, I'm glad your friends found you. Take care of yourself. Watch your back. Life is short, and any one of us could find ourselves in the same shape as your father."

"I will," Bubba said. He didn't really like Sean's insinuation. Had he been threatening him? Or was it just a general statement? Bubba couldn't tell.

They nodded at each other, then Sean turned with his wife and walked away.

Bubba thought it was a little weird that Vivian hadn't said anything. She'd simply stood next to her husband, watching them as they'd talked. Even though she was five years younger than her husband, Alaska hadn't been as kind to her. She had deep lines on her face and it was more than obvious she dyed her blonde hair. She'd fidgeted in her slight heels as Bubba had talked to her husband as if impatient to leave. Not only that, but Bubba had felt Vivian's intense gaze on him while he'd spoken to her husband. It made him uneasy, but knowing he needed to talk to the lawyer before he left, Bubba put it out of his mind.

He caught up to Kenneth and his wife before they left the conference room. "Can I talk to you for a second?" he asked.

The lawyer nodded.

Bubba looked at Tracy Eklund and raised a brow.

"I'm his assistant," she told him haughtily. "Anything you say to him, you can say to me."

Bubba knew that wasn't how it worked, but since he didn't really have anything private he needed to discuss, he let it go. "I'm headed back to California tomorrow. I won't be around to sign any other paperwork, so I just wanted to make sure everything was good?"

"It should be," Kenneth said. "I'm assuming your address in California will be the same as it was when I contacted you previously?"

"Yeah." Bubba wanted to be sarcastic and tell the man he hadn't actually had the opportunity to move in the last week, since he'd been in the middle of the Alaskan wilderness, but he refrained. "I need a favor, though."

The lawyer arched a brow.

"Zoey's coming to California with me."

"Really?" Tracy asked.

When Bubba glared at her with what he knew was a protective look on his face, she rushed to explain.

"I'm just surprised. I mean, she's spent most of her life in Juneau. It just seems fast. Things must've gone well out there in the bush."

Feeling his ire rise, Bubba did his best to push it down. He knew people would talk about how fast their relationship seemed to be progressing, but he didn't care. Intense experiences had a way of cutting through the bullshit in life and showcasing what was important.

But he had a feeling nothing he said to this blowhard would matter, so Bubba merely said, "We'll be in contact with her new address, but what I was going to ask was if you could recommend a service to look after Zoey's house. We haven't talked about what she wants to do with it, but if she decides to stay in California, she'll need to either rent it out or sell it. And whether she moves to Riverton permanently or decides to come back to Juneau, in the meantime, she'll need someone to look after it for her. Make sure there aren't any leaks or anything."

"I can help," Tracy offered immediately. "I've got a great realtor, and I'm willing to assist in packing up her stuff and helping to stage the house if she wants to sell."

"Thank you. We'll be in touch," Bubba said, wanting nothing more than to get out of the building and out of this state. The hair on the back of his neck was standing straight up, and he didn't know why. He turned and saw his brother was still in the lobby.

Glancing at Rocco and Phantom where they were still standing with Zoey, he gave them a small chin lift, indicating that they should meet him outside.

Nodding, Phantom leaned over and said something to Zoey. He then took her elbow and led her toward the door. She looked back at him, and Bubba did his best to smile. He knew he hadn't really succeeded when she looked extremely worried as his friends led her out of the office.

Taking a deep breath, Bubba wandered over to where his twin was standing. "You okay?" he asked.

Malcom merely shook his head. "Let me guess, you're out of here."

Feeling bad for a split second, Bubba nodded. "I've been gone too long. I had a few days' leave to come up for the reading of the will and Pop's memorial service, but I obviously used more than I'd planned. I need to get back." Bubba had been upset when he'd heard his dad's memorial had gone on without him, but not exactly surprised. He'd told Zoey that would probably happen, but it was still a little sad. He and Zoey would just have to have their own private ceremony when they got back to California.

"Right. I'd expect nothing less," Malcom muttered.

Angry now, Bubba growled, "You want to do this here?

Fine. What are you pissed about, bro? That Pop gave me some of his money? That he gave his investments to charity? That you didn't get all of his business?"

"You really want to know?" Malcom asked.

"Yeah, I really do."

"Fine. I'm pissed that even though Pop worshiped the ground you walked on, you couldn't bring yourself to get up here to visit him even *once*. I'm pissed that he gave you part of the business, since you haven't been involved for even one day in your entire life and made it clear you hated everything about it from day one. And I'm even more pissed that he gave *any* part of it to that bitch who's been milking him from the day she met him!"

Bubba could handle Malcom being upset that he hadn't been to Juneau to visit. He was mad at himself for that. But he couldn't let his dig at Zoey go. "Why do you dislike her so much?" he asked between clenched teeth.

Malcom sighed, and his voice gentled just a bit. "Look, I get that you two had a harrowing experience together. I'm happier than I can say that you're all right. But Zoey's not what you think. You don't know her like you think you do."

Bubba didn't believe one word his brother was saying, but he asked, "And you do?"

"Yeah, Mark. I do. She's been hanging around him since we graduated. She's always got one sob story or another. She talked him into renting her that house for half what he could've gotten from someone else. Then she wheedled her way into his private life too. Coming over and playing board games. Watching TV. She had her eye on his money and business the entire time. I wouldn't be surprised if she knocked him off to get that house. She was probably working with Ashley, that incompetent nurse he hired. Hell, she probably poisoned him!"

Bubba was genuinely stunned by his brother's resentment toward Zoey. It was true he didn't know her like Malcom did, but he honestly couldn't see her doing any of the things he was accusing her of.

"First of all, *you* hired Ashley, not Dad. Secondly, Zoey was in Anchorage visiting her mother when Pop passed," Bubba reminded him.

He snorted. "Right. I thought you were worldly, bro. She could've hired someone to kill him. Like I said, all it would take is one dose of arsenic or cyanide or something. If she was working with the nurse, it would've been easy."

"Seriously? Jesus, Malcom, what's *wrong* with you? I can't believe you're actually accusing Zoey of *killing* Dad! Normal people don't immediately think 'murder' when their loved ones die. I'm sorry you didn't get more of Dad's money than you wanted, but that's no reason to be such an asshole."

Bubba was done with this conversation. "I'm headed back to Riverton in the morning. But I'm going to do a better job of being involved. If you need anything, call. If I'm not on a mission, I'll always be available. I can help with the business and making decisions. I'm sorry I wasn't around for Pop, but I'm here for *you*. I love you, Malcom. You're my brother. My twin. And we might annoy each other, but that doesn't mean we aren't family."

He saw Malcom struggle with some inner demon for a moment before nodding. He held out a hand, and Bubba shook it.

"Thanks, bro. I'm going to take you up on that. And don't be surprised if I ask you to come back up here at some point in the near future. There's a lot of behind-the-scenes shit that has to happen now that Pop's gone. And since the two of us are the second and third biggest owners of the business, we have to be involved in those decisions."

"Understood," Bubba told him. "Be careful out there, Mal. Someone wanted me and Zoey out of the way. You could be targeted next."

"You think Sean is pissed he didn't get Dad's shares?"

Bubba should've been surprised at how quickly Malcom jumped to that conclusion, but after his accusations of murder, he wasn't. "I have no idea. All I'm saying is for you to watch your back. You're my only family now. I don't want to lose you too." Then Bubba surprised both of them when he reached out and pulled Malcom in for a quick hug. It was a little awkward, but it felt good. Right. "I've missed you," he told him when they stepped back.

Malcom nodded and said, "I'll be in touch." Then he turned on his heel and left.

Taking a deep breath, Bubba looked up at the ceiling for a brief moment. "I'm trying, Pop," he whispered, before exiting the room to go find Zoey and his teammates.

Late the next morning, Zoey sat on a commercial flight next to Mark. They'd all spent the night in her little house. She'd felt guilty that Mark's friends had to sleep on the floor, but they'd reassured her they'd slept in much worse places. She'd headed to bed early, unable to keep her eyes open, and didn't even hear Mark when he came in later. She'd woken up with her nose tucked into his neck, feeling warm and cozy.

But she hadn't been able to laze around and appreciate it, as they had to head to the airport to catch a plane to California. After packing two suitcases full of as many clothes as she could fit, she'd soon found herself boarding another plane...this one much bigger than the tiny float plane that had changed her life forever.

Mark's teammates were sitting in the seats all around them, but that didn't make her feel any better. It was her second flight since the crash, but she was no more relaxed than she'd been on the flight to Juneau the morning before. Her hands clenched the armrests as if that alone could keep the plane from crashing.

"Relax, Zo," Mark said softly into her ear. He peeled her hand off the armrest between them and held it in both of his on his thigh.

"I can't," she whispered. "This plane is nothing like that float plane, and we didn't crash, but I can't help remembering how it felt when I was hunched over in the crash position, and how I thought we were going to die."

"But we didn't," Mark said calmly. "We're alive and well and we had a fun little adventure in the process."

Zoey rolled her eyes and Mark chuckled. "There's the Zo I know and love."

Her heart about stopped at his words. He didn't try to take them back, merely stared into her eyes steadily.

Had he meant it? No, he couldn't. It was just a saying. She frantically tried to think of something to say. "Maybe I should just stay here. I mean, now that everyone knows I didn't get all that much from Colin, I'll be fine."

"Breathe, Zoey," Mark ordered. "And now that everyone knows exactly what you *did* get, you could be in even more danger."

She glared at him. "How do you figure? I mean, a house

isn't exactly cash. And as much as I love that place, it needs a lot of work to update it. And five percent of his business isn't that big of a deal."

"Zo, five percent equals about a quarter of a million dollars. And don't forget about the thirty-three thousand dollars in cash you'll be getting. Don't you pay attention to the news? Or watch that true crime channel on TV?"

"Yeah, but that's TV. This is real life," she said.

"Those shows are based on actual cases, you know that. People kill for way less money than you just got from Pop."

She stared up at Mark. "But...you and Malcom got way more than I did."

"And that's why I warned him to be careful too."

Zoey could hardly believe this was her life. That someone might want her dead. She still mostly thought that it had been Mark who'd been targeted though. "I can't believe he left me anything, to be honest," she said, trying to ignore how they were on their way to the runway.

"Why not? From everything I've heard, you were a big part of his life."

"I guess." She looked up at him. "Was Malcom really that pissed that I got anything?"

She could tell he didn't want to admit it.

"Never mind," she mumbled. "I know he was."

"What is it between the two of you?" Mark asked.

Zoey sighed. "I guess it started when I broke up with him back in high school. He pretty much didn't like me from that point forward. He also didn't like that I spent a lot of time with your dad, but I refused to let him scare me away."

"He scared you?" Mark asked sharply.

Zoey shook her head. "Figure of speech. He just let me know by his looks and snide comments here and there that he wished I wasn't around. I know he tried to talk Colin out of renting me the house, but after your dad heard that I was thinking about moving in with my mom in Anchorage, he offered the house to me at an insanely low price. I knew he was giving me a huge break, and I was ashamed to have to accept, but I really didn't want to leave."

She blushed, then turned her head to look out the window as she felt the plane speed up and start to race down the runway.

Mark put his fingers under her chin and turned her face back to him. "Then what?"

"Then what, what?" Zoey asked.

"Did he raise your rent after a while?"

"No. But I told him to. I even started writing my rent check for more than we'd agreed on, but he always snuck cash back into my purse when I visited. So I gave up on that, but got more sneaky." She smiled.

"How?" Mark asked.

"I started leaving money around his house. A twenty here, a ten there. Places where I didn't think he'd notice." She shrugged self-consciously at the tender look on his face. "I think he figured out what I was doing, but by then it was kind of a game between us. He'd pretend not to notice I was doing it, and I'd pretend I was still being sneaky about it."

"That sounds like something Pop would do. So Malcom didn't know about it?"

Zoey scrunched up her nose. "No. I wasn't going to talk about my finances with him. We didn't get along, and he wasn't thrilled with me having such free access to Colin's house, especially when he was still living there. But it's not like he did a lot to help out around the place. Our relationship only got worse when I caught him with some mystery woman a couple years ago. To this day, I don't know who it was, but he was *not* happy with me. I'd been looking for Colin, to get his opinion on an investment I was thinking about making, and I called the factory. Sean told me he'd gone home. So I went to his house and found Malcom there instead. Anyway, I used the key Colin had given me, and I caught the back side of a woman as she ran into the room Malcom was using. He was furious at me for walking in.

"I was embarrassed that I'd almost caught him making out on the couch. I mean, we were both in our late-twenties, it wasn't like it should've been a huge deal, but he made it one. He screamed at me to get out and told me I was trespassing and I had no right to be there. When he knew very well I *did* have a right, as I was helping Colin out a lot, doing things that, frankly, your brother should've been doing. But I just left. Things were even more awkward and tense between us after that."

"I'm sorry, Zo. That sounds stressful."

She shrugged. "You know, I have to admit that despite all the good stuff your dad said about you, I was nervous to see you again."

"Why?"

"Because I was afraid you might've been like Malcom. That you'd take one look at me and think I was a gold digger or something. I loved your dad, Mark. I swear I did. I never wanted anything from him but his friendship."

"I know, I believe you. And...what did you think of me when you saw me again?" Mark asked with a grin.

Zoey knew she was blushing, but she forced herself to meet Mark's eyes. "I recognized you immediately. I could always tell the difference between you and your brother. You carry yourself differently. You're more confident.

More...I don't know...open? Anyway, I didn't think you'd recognize me."

"I remembered you pretty quick," Mark said. "I probably shouldn't admit this, but there were many nights back in high school when I fantasized about you."

Zoey's mouth fell open. "You did?"

"Yeah."

"Well, shit, if I'd known that, I might've actually had the nerve to approach you."

He smiled. "So that's it? You knew I wasn't Malcom and thought I was more confident?"

"Well, I was nervous at first, but when you didn't say anything snarky or look at me like I was the devil incarnate, I relaxed. And I admit to watching you while you slept on the plane, before...you know...we fake crash landed."

Mark winced. "Not my best moment. I shouldn't have been sleeping."

Zoey rolled her eyes. "Whatever. You had no idea Eve, or whatever her name is, would do what she did."

He shrugged, and Zoey knew he'd always blame himself for letting down his guard. "So, what did you see when you studied me while I was sleeping?"

Zoey broke his gaze and realized that they were in the air. He'd distracted her while they'd taken off, to help her relax. Once more, something inside her shifted. Making her want to melt at how considerate he was. It was the million-and-first thing that made him different from his twin. Malcom would go out of his way to make sure she was as uncomfortable as possible if he could.

She ducked her head and saw her hand still securely ensconced in his. It made her feel safe, which was crazy, because it wasn't as if he could actually do anything if *this* plane went down.

Realizing he was still waiting for her to answer his question, she decided to be honest. "I thought you looked twenty times better than you did in high school. More seasoned, if that makes sense."

He gazed into her eyes, and she couldn't look away. When he didn't respond for several seconds, she felt stupid. She opened her mouth to say something else, something more acceptable, but he interrupted her before she could take it back.

"You want to know what I thought when I saw *you?*" he asked.

She didn't. Not really. But she nodded anyway.

"I regretted even more not going back to see Pop. And that's saying something, because I'd already regretted it more than anything else in my life. I told you that I'd liked you when I was a teenager, and that wasn't a lie. But the woman I saw sitting in front of me at the airport was a hundred times prettier than she'd been a decade ago. Like you said...more seasoned. I liked that. A hell of a lot."

Zoey couldn't think of one thing to say in response. Not one. She was flabbergasted and shocked...and more turned on than she could remember being in her life. She was pretty normal on the "pretty scale." She had some killer curves, more than she'd like at times, and she liked her thick hair. But generally she thought the rest of her features were mostly underwhelming. Not to mention, she'd spent most of her life bundled up because she was always cold. But nothing had made her feel more special than Mark's words.

As if he knew how much he'd just rocked her world, he pushed the armrest between them up and out of the way and tugged her toward him. Zoey went willingly, resting her cheek on his chest, glad that she didn't have to say a word.

He smelled good. Really good. She'd gotten used to his musky male scent after their time in the wilderness, but now, fresh, clean soap and mouthwash had never smelled sexier.

"Why don't you take a nap?" he said softly, and Zoey could feel the reverberations of his voice under her cheek. She nodded against him. She'd gotten used to sleeping against Mark, and the thought of going to bed without him wasn't pleasant. But she had to get on with her life, as did he.

She had no idea how things would go with his neighbor, Jessica Martens, but she hoped the older woman would like her. It was scary flying off to a new city to start a new life. Zoey had no idea how her mom did it all the time.

Deciding she'd close her eyes for just a minute or two, she relaxed.

"She asleep?" Rex asked Bubba from the seat next to him.

Bubba nodded. He'd been surprised when Zoey had fallen asleep as fast as she had. She'd been stressed and nervous about the flight, and he'd done the only thing he could think of to help her relax...talk.

"I'm glad you're bringing her back with you," Rex said.

Bubba raised an eyebrow at his friend in question.

"First, it's obvious how much you two like each other. You connected out there, and you'd be crazy to not do whatever you can to see if this is it for the both of you."

Bubba was surprised. Rex didn't talk a lot about women, but then again, he didn't date much either. Everyone knew he had his eye on one of the nurses at the hospital on the base, but he hadn't asked her out for some reason.

"Second, whoever schemed to leave you two in the wilderness to die hasn't been caught."

Bubba nodded. Now *this* was something he could talk about. "Assuming you guys called Tex."

"Of course. Rocco has been in contact with him almost from the beginning."

"And?"

"And he hasn't been able to track down the pilot or the plane yet."

Bubba frowned. "Wow, seriously? She can't have disappeared into thin air."

"*You* almost did," Rex retorted.

"She faked that engine dying," Bubba said. "She had the ability to cut both engines and still bring that plane down smoothly. She's a skilled pilot, not some fly-by-night kid."

"So what's your theory?" Rex asked.

Bubba shrugged one shoulder, the one that wasn't currently being slept on by Zoey. "Someone didn't want me, and/or Zoey, to inherit. They hired Eve to fly us into the middle of nowhere and leave us there. They didn't bother placing anyone on the ground to kill us, figuring the Alaskan wilderness would do their dirty work for them. That tells me whoever it was is either a coward or just plain stupid. And I have to assume the pilot probably needed money for some reason, and was desperate, if she agreed to the crazy scheme."

"We *have* to find the pilot," Rex sighed.

"Yeah. I'll call Tex when we get home to tell him everything I can remember about her. Maybe it'll help."

"Can't hurt," Rex agreed. "And Zoey? What about her?"

"What *about* her?" Bubba asked.

"If this is just a sex thing, it's not a good idea."

Bubba scowled. "Not cool, Rex."

His friend held up a hand. "Hear me out." After Bubba gave him a brusque nod, he continued. "You're both feeling a ton of emotions. You went through some serious shit out there, especially after she basically helped save your life after you got dunked. You're both probably feeling especially vulnerable and needy. You like each other. It seems like a good idea to have her come home with you. But, Bubba, I see it in her eyes every time she looks at you. This isn't casual for her. She's into you. Big time. All I'm saying is to think about this before you take things so far that you can't back out without destroying her."

Bubba wanted to rip into his friend, but he knew he was simply looking out for Zoey. He couldn't get mad about that. Besides, even Bubba knew they were moving fast. "You sound like you're talking from experience."

Rex shrugged. "I've made my share of mistakes in the past, and I'm determined not to repeat them."

"That why you haven't asked out that nurse you've been flirting with?"

"I'm not good relationship material," Rex said. "I can be a dick, and the last thing I want to do is get her hopes up for something to happen between the two of us. I like her. She's funny, cute, and she seems like a hell of a nurse, but I haven't had one relationship in the last five years that's worked out. I don't like making women cry. All I'm saying is, don't make Zoey regret coming back to California with you."

Bubba looked down at the woman against his side. She was still using him as a pillow, her body curved sideways in a position that didn't look all that comfortable, but she still slept like the dead. He looked back at his friend. "I think you're wrong about you not being relationship material. If you were the dick you seem to think you are, you wouldn't care about that nurse's feelings. You'd go out with her, enjoy the physical side of the relationship, and then walk away without a second glance.

"But you're right in that Zoey and I like each other. We went through some serious shit, but not once did I wish she wasn't there with me. I liked this woman in high school, and in the time that's passed, she's only gotten more amazing. And I'm shocked as hell that she's still single. I'm bringing her to Riverton with the hope that she'll stay. She can live with my neighbor for a while, until I can convince her to move in with me."

"Do you love her?" Rex asked.

Bubba didn't hear any humor in his friend's voice, or snark. He was serious.

"Love? I'm not sure I know what that is. I mean, I thought I'd loved women in the past, but nothing I've felt compares to what I feel about Zoey. She confuses me and excites me. I wake up wanting to see her and go to sleep loving how she feels in my arms. I worry about her constantly, wanting to make sure she's warm enough, that she's eating enough. And I sure as hell don't want anyone to kill her for the money Pop left her. Is that love? I don't know. But I'm sure as hell willing to see. And I can't do that if she's back in Alaska and I'm in California."

"Just be careful," Rex said. "Zoey's lived in Alaska all

her life. This will all be new for her. Go easy. If you really care about her, give her what she needs, not what she asks for...which will probably be nothing."

"Got it. Thanks for the advice. And seriously, I really think you should ask that nurse out. I haven't seen you so interested in someone in a very long time."

"I'll think about it," Rex said. "But rumor has it she's going to head over to Afghanistan on a special mission to help educate the local nurses about prenatal health and other issues unique to women."

"How long?"

"How long's the mission?" Rex asked.

"Yeah."

"I'm not sure. I think it's just a short-term thing. Maybe a couple months."

"So let her know you're interested before she leaves, then when she gets back, maybe you can take her out," Bubba said.

"It's not that easy," Rex complained.

"If there's something I've learned over the last week or so, it's that nothing worth having is easy. I have a lot of regrets, Rex, and I wouldn't wish that on anyone. If she heads overseas and something happens, you're going to regret not at least letting her know that you like her and want to go out with her."

"You're an asshole," Rex complained. "If something happens to her over there, I'm blaming you."

Bubba smiled. "Ask her out," he ordered gently.

"I'll think about it," Rex said. Then, changing the subject, he asked, "You gonna bring Zoey to meet the other women?"

"Yes. Absolutely. As soon as we can arrange it, actually."

Rex smiled. "I'm sure that won't be a problem. They already know about her, since they were as worried about you as we were. Rocco called Caite after you were found, told her you were safe—*and* he's told her Zoey's coming home with you to Riverton."

"Think they'll be at the airport when we land?" Bubba asked with a grin.

"It wouldn't surprise me," Rex replied.

"I should probably wake her up and warn her," Bubba said, looking back down at Zoey.

"Let her sleep," Rex disagreed. "From what I've seen, she'll be able to hold her own and adapt."

Bubba nodded. Yeah, his Zoey was adaptable, that was for sure.

His Zoey. He liked the sound of that.

Closing his eyes and resting back on the head rest, he tightened his arm around the woman at his side and breathed a contented sigh when she mumbled something under her breath and snuggled even further into him.

CHAPTER THIRTEEN

It was early evening when the plane landed in Southern California, and despite the nap Zoey had taken, she was still exhausted after the events from the last week and a half. She gathered the backpack Rex had bought for her while in Anchorage, hoping it wouldn't take long for the rest of her things to be packed up and sent. She had two suitcases full of clothes, but there were still a lot of things she'd had to leave behind.

She'd arranged for Tracy Eklund to go to her house and send the rest of her clothes and a few personal items. Everything else, she could get later...if she stayed in California.

It seemed unreal that she'd made such a spur-of-the-moment decision, but honestly, she felt more at home, safer, with Mark than with anyone she'd met in her entire life. The fact that he understood that she needed a purpose, couldn't just go to California without some sort of plan and job, said a lot about how well he knew her already.

SECURING ZOEY

She was looking forward to meeting his neighbor and hoped they'd get along half as well as she and Colin had.

Thinking of Mark's dad made her sad, but she pushed the emotion down as they walked hand in hand toward the baggage claim. None of the SEALs had checked luggage when they'd rushed up to Anchorage, carrying only enough to last them a few days. They'd managed to do laundry at the hotel while they'd been there searching for Mark, and it was obvious they were all anxious to get home.

After they'd collected her bags, the team headed down the escalator toward the exit. Zoey and Mark were bringing up the rear when she saw what seemed like a small welcome party waiting at the bottom. There were three women and three kids—and Zoey knew at a glance that they were waiting for the SEALs.

The second the women and kids saw the group on the escalator, the excitement on their faces more than communicated how happy they were to see the team. The kids started waving energetically, and the women shuffled in place, impatient for the escalator to hurry up and deliver their men.

Zoey felt uncomfortable as she didn't know anyone, but Mark didn't leave her side. His hand on the small of her back soothed and made her feel a little more relaxed. But the second they reached the bottom, Mark was engulfed by all the women and little girls. Zoey took a few steps back to give them room. They surrounded Mark and took turns hugging him.

"I'm so glad you're all right!"

"Was it super cold?"

"I heard you thought you were Aquaman!"

"Bubba safe?"

The last came from the smallest of the little girls, and Zoey watched as Mark leaned over and picked her up, holding her against him. She patted her hands on his cheeks, the top of his head, and even his chest, as if she were checking for herself that he was safe and in one piece.

"I'm good, Rani," Mark told the little girl. "Were you worried about me?"

She bobbed her head up and down enthusiastically. "Mama said you were lost. But you gotted found."

He chuckled. "Yeah, something like that."

She squirmed and Mark put her back on her feet, and Zoey watched her run over to the woman who she figured was her mom.

Zoey was used to fading into the background, so she was reluctant when Mark turned to her and held out his hand. But she took his hand, and he pulled her into his side, wrapping his arm around her waist.

"Everyone, this is Zoey Knight. She helped look after Pop up in Alaska and saved my life while we were out in the wilderness."

Zoey shook her head, knowing he was completely overstating what she'd done after he'd fallen in the stream, but the women didn't give her a chance to explain what had really happened. The next thing she knew, she was being pulled away from Mark and engulfed in a group hug.

"I'm Caite," said a woman with light brown hair, who was about the same height as Zoey. "Blake is my fiancé."

"Blake?" Zoey asked in confusion.

She laughed. "Sorry, Rocco."

Zoey nodded. She looked over and saw the tall black-haired SEAL had his eyes on his fiancée.

"And I'm Piper. The girls are mine. Ace and I have had them only months, but it feels as if they've been ours forever." She put her hand on her belly as she spoke, and Zoey realized that she must be pregnant. "I had to spend a few nights in the jungle in Timor-Leste, but I have a feeling my experience was nothing like yours." She shivered. "I can't stand the cold."

Zoey smiled. "I can't say I'm all that fond of it myself. Even though I live in Alaska, I'm not a fan."

The two women smiled at each other in kinship.

"And I'm Sidney," a petite woman with long black hair said. She smiled widely at Zoey, and unlike the fake smiles of the tourists and many people she came into contact with back home, she could tell Sidney was genuinely happy to meet her. "We're so glad you're all right. You had to be so scared."

Gumby came up behind her and threw an arm around her chest. Sidney immediately brought her arms up and grabbed hold of his forearm. "I'm thinking she's doing her best to forget it," he chided gently.

Sidney tilted her head back and smiled at him, then brought her gaze back to Zoey's. "She's safe to think and talk about it with us," she told Gumby.

Zoey saw something in the other woman's eyes. Something that actually made her believe she *was* safe. That Sidney wouldn't think less of her if she admitted to being scared to death the entire week they were lost in the wilderness.

She remembered Mark telling her that Sidney had been through something traumatic herself, and something in the other woman's facial expression made Zoey feel as if she would understand her. Understand her fear.

When she turned to look at the other two women, she could sense they'd understand as well. Zoey had never felt so welcomed, so at home with a group of women before.

She'd been the "new girl" more times than she could count, and she really hoped she'd finally found a group of friends she could fit in with. That she wouldn't be an outsider.

"I have to say, it wasn't exactly a walk in the park," Zoey said after a moment. This wasn't the time or place to get into all the details about what happened, but she did say, "If I'd been alone, I don't think I would've made it. But having Mark there with me made it a hundred times more manageable."

She felt his arm tighten around her waist, but she kept her eyes on Sidney.

"Yeah, our guys tend to make any situation better. I'm looking forward to getting to know you, Zoey."

"Same here," she replied.

"Hey! I know! What's everyone doing this weekend? How about we all go over to Gumby's beach house for a 'thank God Bubba's stronger than some jerkhole thinks' party?" Piper asked.

"So you're just inviting yourself over now?" Gumby asked with a laugh.

Zoey glanced at him, hoping the other man wasn't offended, but she relaxed when Rocco said, "Like you care, man. I think you're happiest when you have a houseful of people enjoying your paradise by the sea."

"True," Gumby agreed. "So...barbeque at our place? Saturday? Around two?"

Everyone agreed, and Zoey was content to lean against Mark and observe the dynamics of the group. Even though Phantom and Rex didn't have women there to meet them, they weren't excluded. The oldest of the three girls was standing next to Phantom, clutching his hand, and Rex was holding the middle girl on his hip.

Everyone seemed genuinely pleased to be with each other, which made Zoey's heart happy.

"I don't know about you guys, but I'm more than ready to take my wife home and get her settled," Ace said. He now had his hand on her stomach, his thumb gently stroking back and forth over her slight baby belly. "I've also got three little girls who I need to catch up with, and lots of snuggles to give."

Zoey would've laughed at the big bad SEAL being all mushy, but it was one of the most tender things she'd ever seen. Ace wasn't afraid to admit that he wanted to take care of Piper, and he freely admitted to wanting to spend quality time with his kids.

That's what she wanted. A man who could kick some serious ass, but who wasn't afraid to show his tender side when he was amongst friends.

Within moments, the group was headed for the exit. When Zoey went to follow them, she was brought up short by Mark tugging on her hand. She looked back at him. "What's wrong?"

"Nothing. I just wanted to check with you and make sure this is still what you want."

"It's a little late to see if I want to come to California with you," she joked. When Mark didn't smile, she frowned. "Wait, why? Are *you* having second thoughts?"

"No, not at all," he said immediately, which made Zoey relax a bit.

"Okay, then what? I'm not understanding."

Mark gestured with his head toward one of his teammates, who was standing near the door with Zoey's luggage. "Rex is going to drive us home, since his car is here and mine isn't. We won't do introductions with Jess until tomorrow. But if you're uncomfortable going back to my house with me, I can have Rex take you to a hotel. I'd pay for it, so you don't have to worry about that. But the last thing I want is for you to feel awkward being alone with me in my house."

Zoey's heart melted for what seemed like the thousandth time in his presence. She put a hand on Mark's chest and leaned into him, tilting her head back so she could look him in the eyes as she said what she needed to say.

"Mark, if you dropped me off at a hotel, I'd probably change my mind about being here and go back to Alaska in the morning. I didn't come to California for a new start in my life. I came because this is where *you* are. Besides, I've spent the last week with you, why would I feel awkward about it now?"

He palmed the side of her neck with one of his large calloused hands and the feel of it made goose bumps break out on her arms. "I just don't want you to feel like you're stuck here. That you don't have any options. I didn't give you a lot of time to think about this. The last thing I want is for you to feel trapped. And staying with me in my house is a lot different than being out in the wilderness, and I think you know it. We aren't reliant on each other anymore. You can leave whenever you want. But if you decide to stay...it means something to me."

"It means something to me too," Zoey said. "It means that I want to explore the connection we made out there in the forest. I don't feel trapped and, if I'm being honest, I think being away from you tonight would make me feel lost. This might not be the wilds of Alaska, and I might not have to start my own fire, but I've still never been here and it's all new to me."

Satisfaction filled Mark's eyes. "Okay. But I meant

what I said. If things aren't working out and you want to go home, I'll help you get there."

"Without Colin there, Juneau feels less and less like home the more time I spend away from it. It's about time I cut the safety cord and experienced life. I've spent my entire thirty-one years in Alaska. I love it, but I'm excited about seeing new cities, experiencing new things. Do you know I've never swam in the ocean?"

Mark didn't say anything for a moment, and Zoey got worried. "Mark?"

Taking a deep breath, he said, "Sorry, I'm just thinking about how lucky I am." He winked. "Come on, I think Rex is about to say 'to hell with it' and let us walk."

Zoey wanted to tell Mark that *she* was the lucky one, but he was already turning to pick up her backpack and steering her toward the door with his hand on her back once more. Mark tried to put her in the front seat when they reached long-term parking, but she protested and sat in the back, listening to Mark and Rex talk about their commander, PT, and other general work stuff.

She was half asleep by the time Rex pulled up to Mark's house. She climbed out and got her first look at where he lived.

The house was small, but well maintained. It was two-story, brick, and had a lovely little porch in front. It wasn't fancy, and it was obvious the neighborhood was lower middle class, but secretly, Zoey was relieved. She'd never had all that much money in her life, and if Mark had ended up living in some huge mansion, she wasn't sure how she'd feel about that.

But no, the house was modest. Exactly like Mark.

"Thanks for the ride, Rex. I'll be late tomorrow. I'm

going to bring Zoey over to meet Jess and get her settled, but I'll see you after PT."

"Sounds good. I'll let the commander know, although I'm sure he's probably not even expecting you in tomorrow at all."

"I'll be there," Mark said firmly.

That was one more thing Zoey liked about him. His work ethic. It matched hers. She didn't want to sit around and do nothing. She'd be bored to tears in hours. She was glad she'd be meeting Jess tomorrow. She was anxious to start working, doing something productive.

"I'm glad you're all right," Rex told Zoey. "Thanks for looking after this big lug. Not sure what we'd all do without him."

"And you'll never know," Mark told his friend. "Now, get."

Rex laughed and gave them both a chin lift before he turned his body in his seat to look behind him as he pulled out of the driveway.

"Thoughts?" Mark asked

Zoey looked up at him. "About what?"

"The house. The neighborhood?"

"I like them both. They're down-to-earth. A lot like you."

He sighed in relief. "When we were first stationed here, I lived in the barracks for a while but that quickly got old. I didn't have a ton of money, but I had enough for a down payment. I wanted a small house that I could keep clean. I didn't want a cookie-cutter house and preferred an older home with more character. This neighborhood wasn't the best back then, but my realtor assured me that it was up and coming. She wasn't wrong. Jess has lived here for most of her life, and she has a ton of crazy stories about this neighborhood in the seventies and eighties."

"I can't wait to meet her," Zoey said.

"Tomorrow," Mark said with a nod. "Come on, I'll show you around."

Zoey followed him to the front door and inhaled deeply when they entered his house. It smelled like him. She'd gotten hints of it when they'd been sleeping out in the open, but ever since they'd spent the night in the hotel together, it was as if every time he moved anywhere near her, she got a whiff of him. Clean soap, mixed with his own natural musky scent.

Being here in his space, surrounded by his things, made her realize exactly how much she'd come to enjoy that smell. It signified safety to her. And stepping foot in his house, and smelling his scent so strongly, made her never want to leave.

"You okay?" Mark asked, ever watchful and aware of her feelings.

"I'm great," she told him.

"Good. Come on, I'll give you the dime tour."

It didn't take long for him to show her the three-bedroom, two-bath house, but Zoey fell in love with it immediately. It felt comfortable. Lived in. The wood floors looked original, complete with scuffs and scratches. The kitchen wasn't top-of-the-line, but it had everything Zoey could need or want to make quick and easy lunches and more elaborate dinners. The bedrooms were on the small side, and she managed not to blush when he showed her the master room with the queen-size bed.

When he was done with the tour, Mark pointed out the large front window at the dark house across the street. "That's Jess's house. I see her grass needs mowing, and I'll take care of that tomorrow when I get home from work. Make sure she doesn't get a bug up her butt to do it herself."

Zoey's brows went up. "She'd do that?"

"Yes," Mark said with a sigh. "She would, and has. It's annoying."

But she could tell that he wasn't really annoyed because of the slight smile on his face.

"You hungry?"

Zoey shook her head. They'd eaten right before they'd left Alaska, and she figured maybe their week of only eating berries, leaves, mushrooms, and the occasional fish or squirrel had shrunk her appetite. "I'm good. Thanks."

"Tired?"

She wanted to say no. That she'd love to stay up and talk to him. But the mere question made her immediately yawn.

Mark chuckled. "Come on, Zo. I'm beat too. I guess all that time out in the wilds of Alaska tired me out more than I'd thought."

She preceded him back up the stairs and headed straight for the master bedroom. Mark caught her hand and stopped her. She looked at him in surprise.

"If it would make you feel more comfortable, I can sleep in the guest room."

Oh, shit. Had she presumed something she shouldn't have? Did he not want to sleep next to her? They'd shared a bed the last two nights, and she'd just assumed they would at his place too. She squirmed, not sure about the right thing to say in that moment.

But like he usually did, Mark reassured her. "I don't *want* to, but I will if it's what you want or need."

Zoey's head shook of its own volition. "I liked waking

up next to you the last several mornings. And I know we're safe here, that no one would dare attack us in your own home, but I'd still feel more comfortable having you near."

Mark took a step forward, getting in her personal space, but Zoey didn't step back. She clutched his shirt at his sides as he took her face in his hands. "Hear me now—*nothing's* going to happen to you."

"You can't guarantee that."

"We haven't talked about everything that happened, in part because I'm waiting to talk to my computer genius friend, Tex, but I'll do whatever it takes to keep you safe, Zo."

"Do you think we're still in danger?"

Instead of shaking his head, Mark shrugged. That didn't exactly instill confidence in Zoey, but she did her best not to panic.

"I'm not sure. I mean, if someone targeted us because of Pop's will, nothing has changed. Except now we know what he left us. But the fact remains that we still got what we got and if someone isn't happy about that, then they could still want to hurt us. But the good thing is that I'm pretty sure we're out of their reach now. We're here, and they're still there in Alaska. And honestly, the list of people who might want us gone is fairly short, so that makes me even more sure we're safe here."

Zoey nodded. She hated that. *Hated* it. Because the short list of people who might be upset about Colin's will was full of people they knew personally. Unless there was someone in Colin's life who wasn't included in the will who felt like he or she should have been—and Zoey couldn't think of a single person—their situation hadn't changed. The likelihood was high that their potential killer was someone close to them. Which sucked. Big time.

Mark stared at her for so long, Zoey shifted under his gaze. "What?"

"The longer I'm around you, the more beautiful you get. How is that possible?"

His words made her uncomfortable. Zoey knew she wasn't beautiful. She wasn't unattractive, but she'd always been somewhat ordinary. Brunette hair that more often than not did its own thing instead of what she wanted it to, boring hazel eyes, a body that was curvier than it should be thanks to her love of carbohydrates.

"You don't believe me." It wasn't a question.

She shrugged. "I'm just me," she said lamely.

"Yeah, I know," he said mysteriously. Leaning forward, Mark put his lips on her forehead, and Zoey closed her eyes and inhaled deeply, drawing his scent into her very soul.

He chuckled. "Are you smelling me?"

Without thinking, Zoey nodded. Then winced.

"I like how you smell too," he said without a trace of embarrassment as he leaned over even more and nuzzled the skin between her neck and shoulder.

Tilting her head to give him more room, Zoey held on to his shirt for dear life. She felt like she'd melted into a puddle of goo at his feet, but within seconds, Mark stood.

He smiled down at her. "I don't know how you do it."

"Do what?"

"Make me forget everything. That I need to get you settled. That you're tired. That *I'm* tired. I think I could stand here with you all night and be perfectly happy."

"Me too," Zoey admitted softly.

"Come on. I know you brought some of your own stuff but if you don't feel like unpacking anything, you can sleep in one of my T-shirts tonight...if you wanted to."

The thought of putting one of his shirts on made her shiver. She nodded.

"Good. Do you need sweats or socks? I don't want you to be cold."

"I think I'll be okay. Um...are you staying with me?"

"Yeah, Zo. I'm sleeping here too."

"Okay, then yeah, I should be good. You're pretty warm."

He smiled then, and Zoey knew she'd never get tired of seeing it. "Yeah, I tend to run hot. I'll keep you warm." He went to a dresser and pulled out a gray shirt, and Zoey saw the word NAVY across it before he turned and headed to the bathroom. He disappeared inside and was back within seconds. "I'll head down to get your backpack so you can brush your teeth and finish getting ready for bed after you change. Anything else you need while I'm down there?"

Zoey shook her head.

"I'll be right back." Then he was gone.

Zoey exhaled sharply and headed for the bathroom. She had a feeling Mark wouldn't fuck around and he'd be back in a minute or two.

It was almost unbelievable how much her life had changed in the last week. She'd left Juneau to visit her mom. Her best friend, Colin, had passed away. She'd been left for dead in the middle of nowhere, she'd reconnected with her high school crush, helped save his life, she'd left her home state for the first time ever, and she'd fallen in love.

She stopped dead at that last thought and stared at herself in the mirror in Mark's bathroom.

The same old boring eyes stared back, and Zoey couldn't see any difference in herself since a week ago. She had a bit more color on her cheeks from getting sunburnt while tromping around outdoors, but otherwise she looked exactly the same.

Which was crazy, because inside, she felt completely different. For the first time in a very long time, she was looking forward to what the next day would bring. Everything seemed new and exciting, rather than the same old boring, day-to-day life she'd been living in Juneau.

But love? It seemed crazy. She was acting like an old maid who fell for the first man who'd ever paid her some attention. And the last thing she wanted was to be like her mother, constantly falling for a man's pretty words. But Mark didn't seem like the kind of man who would lead someone on or use them for his own purposes, as she'd seen men do to her mom. And he'd been extremely handsy since they'd been rescued, always touching her in some way. And would he say some of the things he had if he wasn't interested in her?

It was hard to say for sure. She didn't have a lot of experience with relationships and men. If she were here with Malcom, she could say without a doubt that he would definitely be leading her on, if only to get laid. But she knew Mark wasn't like that. He'd gone out of his way to make sure she felt comfortable and not to put any pressure on her.

"Here you go," Mark said, scaring the crap out of Zoey.

She jumped and almost tripped over her feet trying to get away from the doorway where Mark had popped in.

He reached out and grabbed hold of her arm, steadying her. The second she had her footing back, he let go and stepped back, giving her space. "I didn't mean to scare you. I'm so sorry."

Zoey shook her head. "No, it's fine. I wasn't paying attention."

"Second thoughts?" Mark asked quietly.

"No," she told him immediately, and a little desperately. "Not at all. It's just been a crazy week."

The lines around his eyes smoothed out. "Yeah, it has. Take your time. I'll go use the other bathroom." Then he was gone once again.

This time, Zoey didn't stand there staring at herself. She quickly changed into his T-shirt, feeling naked standing there in nothing but her panties and the shirt that came down to her upper thighs. She brushed her teeth and headed into the bedroom.

Mark wasn't there yet, so she slipped under the covers, taking another deep breath. God, she wasn't sure she'd survive sleeping in his bed, on his sheets. She hoped and prayed his scent would seep into her skin overnight so she'd have a piece of him to carry with her always.

Deciding that was weird, and she really was a creeper, she closed her eyes and tried to think about anything other than how right it felt to be in Mark's bed. And what a freaking miracle it was.

She heard him come back into the room and, without a word, he pulled back the covers and slid in next to her. His bare legs brushed against hers, and a warmth like she'd never felt moved up and over her body. When he physically moved her around to his liking, and she ended up with her head on his shoulder and her arm lying across his flat stomach, Zoey sighed in contentment.

"Comfortable?" he asked softly.

"Yeah."

"Sleep well, sweetheart."

"You too."

She felt his lips touch her temple, and she couldn't help but turn her own head and kiss his shoulder. His arm tightened around her for a second, then he relaxed once again. She wanted to stay awake. To treasure the moment. But he was too comfortable. And smelled too good. And felt too good under her.

She was asleep within minutes of closing her eyes.

CHAPTER FOURTEEN

Bubba reached up and knocked on Jessica Martens' door. It was eight o'clock, and he couldn't remember a morning he'd enjoyed more. Merely waking up with Zoey in his arms would've done it, but then he'd acted without thinking and kissed her awake, and she'd more than reciprocated. He'd made her a breakfast of scrambled eggs and bacon, and it had felt really nice to start the day with someone at his side.

When Zoey went upstairs to get ready, hearing the water running and knowing she was upstairs in his bathroom, completely naked, turned him on more than anything he could remember. When it was his turn to shower, the room smelled like the girly shit he'd bought her in Anchorage, and he'd had to jerk himself off simply to be able to walk upright.

While pleasuring himself had taken the edge off, the second he saw Zoey waiting for him downstairs, curled up under one of the throw blankets he had on the back of his couch, he got hard again. He wanted nothing more than to snuggle under it with her and show her exactly how much he liked having her there in his house.

But Jess and work were waiting. He wouldn't have been so keen on getting started with his day and parting with Zoey except he wanted to talk to Tex. He needed to get to the bottom of what had happened, and he had a feeling that would start with finding Eve Dane. And that's where Tex excelled.

"You ready?" Bubba asked Zoey as they waited for Jess to come to the door.

"Yeah. Are you sure I look okay?"

Bubba looked Zoey over from head to toe. She had on a pair of jeans and a short-sleeve green T-shirt they'd picked up in the Anchorage airport. It had a picture of a bear standing on its hind legs and the words, "Juneau what I'm saying?!" around it.

He'd thought it was funny and had bought it as a surprise present. She'd giggled when she'd seen it, and he'd been thrilled with her joy in the simple gift. She looked as beautiful as ever in it. She'd also been surprised that she didn't need to wear a jacket, saying that it would take some getting used to, not getting all bundled up every time she went outside.

The door in front of them creaked as it slowly opened. Bubba smiled at Jess and immediately stepped forward to hug her. He wasn't surprised when her arms latched around him with a strength that belied her looks.

"Hi, Jess," he said into her hair.

The older woman pulled back and stared up at him. She was tiny compared to him, he had at least a foot on her. But her big personality more than made up for her short stature. "It's about time you got home," she nagged. "Look at my grass. It's way too long, and I think a family of gophers have taken up residence."

"I'll take care of it tonight." Bubba turned, keeping one arm around Jess to make sure she didn't lose her balance. "This is Zoey. I told you about her when I called yesterday."

Watching with a careful hopefulness, Bubba grinned as Jess turned to Zoey and immediately hugged her. "It's good to meet you, Zoey. Anyone who can put up with this guy for a week out in the middle of nowhere has to be a saint. Come in, take a load off. I want to hear *everything*."

Bubba tried to follow them inside, but Jess put a hand on his chest and stopped him. "Girls only. Sorry. Besides, it's late. You need to get to work and do your super-soldier stuff."

He heard Zoey cover up a chuckle with her hand, and smiled at Jess. "Okay, I get the hint. I'll go. Zoey, you'll call if you need anything?" Rocco had gone to a store in Anchorage and gotten them both replacement phones before they'd left.

"Of course. But I have a feeling we'll be fine."

"Darn tootin' we will," Jess said. "I've got the grocery store on speed dial, and that hot young thing with an ass I could bounce quarters off of will bring me whatever I need. So shoo. I need some gossip time with your young lady."

Bubba didn't correct her. Zoey *felt* like his young lady. Leaning around Jess, he put his hand on the back of Zoey's neck and pulled her toward him. Bubba kissed her briefly on the lips. It was a short kiss, but he still felt sparks shoot through him as their lips touched. "I'll text you later," he told her.

Zoey licked her lips, and he swore he could see her

pupils dilate as she did. "Okay," she told him.

"Have fun. Jess, don't corrupt Zoey too much, okay?"

"Pish-posh," she scolded, but smiled as she said it.

"Bye, Mark," Zoey told him.

He gave her a chin lift and turned to head back across the street to his car. He found himself smiling the entire way.

It was easy to see that Jess liked Zoey on sight, which was a relief. The older woman wasn't one to beat around the bush, and if she'd sensed something about Zoey that she didn't like, she wouldn't have hesitated to tell him that she'd changed her mind and didn't need Zoey's help after all.

His girl was in good hands. It was time to get to the bottom of whoever had fucking tried to kill them once and for all.

Four hours later, after being caught up on what he'd missed at work over the last week, after reassuring his commander that he really was all right and explaining everything that had happened while he'd been in the wilderness more times than he could count to some of the other SEALs he came across, after he'd taken calls from Malcom *and* Sean with questions about the business up in Juneau, and after he'd called Zoey to make sure she was all right and her helping Jess was going to work out, Bubba dialed Tex's number and put the phone on speaker before placing it on the table top in front of him.

Rocco, Gumby, Ace, Rex, and Phantom were in the room with him, and everyone was eager to hear what the computer guru had to say.

"Tex here."

"Hey, Tex. It's Bubba."

"God, it's good to hear from you, man," Tex said. "It's frustrating as hell not to be able to do anything to find a person when they're literally in the middle of nowhere with no technology so I can track them and no witnesses to interview."

Bubba couldn't help but chuckle. "I can imagine."

"I wish you guys would reconsider wearing one of my fucking trackers. I could've pinpointed your location within ten feet and sent a helicopter to you that first night," Tex bitched.

Bubba and the rest of his team had always turned down Tex when he'd offered up one of his infamous trackers in the past. But after what he just went through, Bubba was seriously considering it. "I'll let you know about that."

"About fucking time," Tex muttered.

"What have you found out about Eve Dane or her plane?" Rocco asked. "Last we talked, you were still looking for both."

"Amazingly, she did a very good job of hiding in plain sight for an amateur," Tex said.

"You found her?" Rex asked excitedly.

"Yes, finally. But the bad news is that she's in the wind again."

"Fuck," Bubba muttered.

"Exactly. But it's only a matter of time, because she's not in the middle of the Alaskan wilderness. She's got to be using credit cards, driving a car, and eventually using a phone. I'll find her."

"Good. We need to know who hired her and why," Phantom said.

"You want to hear what I *was* able to find out?" Tex asked.

"Yes," all six SEALs said at the same time.

The other man chuckled then got serious. "Right. First of all, her name isn't Eve Dane. It's Eva Dawkins. Took a lot of luck to find her too. Most of the time when people use a fake name, they try to keep it as close to their real name as possible. So I looked at all female pilots in Alaska who are around twenty to thirty years old and whose names stared with an E. That got it down to about two hundred and fifty people. Narrowed that down to about ten people, but when I found out Eva Dawkins was the only one out of the bunch who'd disappeared off the radar completely, no credit card or cell phone usage in the last week, I figured she was the one. She's twenty-four years old and has two kids."

"Jesus!" Ace exclaimed. "Why the fuck would she do something so stupid? She's gonna get charged with attempted murder and ruin her life, her kids' lives, and probably her family's too."

"Well, she ran away from home when she was fifteen, never finished high school. Then hooked up with one bad motherfucker. One of the kids is his, the other she had before she started dating him. She got her pilot's license when she lived in Anchorage because she needed money to feed her kids, because her boyfriend sure wasn't giving her any. I guess there was some sort of free program that taught people how to fly. Since it's such a necessary mode of transportation up there, it's almost as common as learning to drive. Anyway, her asshole boyfriend was too busy selling meth to give a shit about her or her kids."

"Holy shit," Gumby breathed.

"Yeah, that's not at all close to the story she told us,"

Bubba said.

"Yeah. Anyway, she got good at flying," Tex continued. "Got hired on by a private company and was doing pretty well for herself. Then her boyfriend decided he wanted her to help him move his drugs. Expand his operations. For whatever asinine reason, she agreed."

"Let me guess," Bubba said. "She got caught."

"Yup. Got fired. She decided enough was enough and finally broke up with her boyfriend, but he didn't take that very well. Even though it was his drugs she'd gotten caught transporting, she had no proof. He used her arrest against her and got temporary custody of her kids."

"That's fucked up," Phantom said.

"Uh-huh. So there she was, no job, no kids, and pissed off at the world. And I'm guessing her ex is probably blackmailing her somehow."

"Right, then along comes someone who needs a pilot, and she needs money," Rex said.

"And if she was desperate, she'd probably do whatever it took to get her kids back," Ace added.

"Like get money to pay off her ex, or to hire a lawyer to fight back and get custody of her kids," Phantom added.

"That's what I figured," Tex agreed.

"Well, shit. Am I supposed to feel sorry for her?" Bubba asked a little indignantly. "She fucking left me and Zoey in the middle of nowhere to *die*. Her bad life choices don't mean she's off the hook for what she did."

"I never said they did," Tex said evenly.

"Then why did you tell us her fucking sob story?" Bubba asked.

"I'm merely updating you as to what I've found out. You want to discover who's behind trying to kill you, right?"

"You know I do."

"And that's what I'm doing. I'm guessing Eva Dawkins isn't the one out to get you. She's got no connections to Juneau that I've been able to find yet, and I don't think she even knew Colin. Someone else was calling the shots. But here's my real question...why fly you and Zoey out into the middle of nowhere and leave you to die? It makes no sense. I mean, if someone wanted the money you got from Colin, making you a simple missing person wouldn't make that possible. So nothing Eva did makes the least bit of sense. Unless someone hates you or Zoey so much that they just wanted you to suffer."

Bubba had known stranding them didn't make sense. Regardless of the method, while he wasn't exactly Prince Charming, he didn't think he'd ever made someone so angry at him that they'd go to great lengths just to see him suffer. And he couldn't imagine Zoey having someone who hated her that much.

"So here's my question for you," Tex went on. "When I find Eva Dawkins, do you want me to call in the authorities, have her arrested, let her lawyer up then sit in jail for a few months while her case goes through the court system? Or are you gonna give me the go-ahead to do what needs to be done to find out the information you want, so you can move on with your life?"

Bubba sighed. He had no idea what Tex had planned, but the last thing he wanted was to constantly be looking over his shoulder. Someone had tried to kill both him and Zoey. And the fact that they hadn't died and had managed to be present for the reading of his dad's will probably wasn't going to sit well with whoever was behind the entire scheme.

"I want this shit done," Bubba said after a moment.

"Right. And for the record, that's the smart choice," Tex told his friend. "The last thing I want is whoever's behind this to get a second chance to finish what they fucked up the first time. And I'm guessing you want to move on with your life with Zoey, as well."

"I do," Bubba said.

"I tracked Eva to Seattle," Tex said. "It's only a matter of time before I find out where she went next. I'm assuming she won't want to get too far away from her kids."

"Tex?" Ace asked.

"Yeah?"

"Are the children all right with the ex? I mean, with his less-than-safe occupation and the fact that he obviously has no problem separating them from their mother, are they safe?"

Bubba wasn't surprised his friend had thought about that. He loved kids. He was born to be a father. And with the addition of the three girls he and Piper had adopted from Timor-Leste, and the fact that his wife was currently pregnant, he was more conscious about children than the rest of them.

Tex hesitated before saying, "If things happen the way I'm thinking they will, the kids are going to be fine."

"What does that mean?" Ace asked.

"It means I'm gonna make *sure* they're going to be fine," Tex repeated. "Look, you guys know I work with all sorts of teams. Military, private security, and even some that work on the edge of the law. I know a guy who works out of Colorado Springs...*he* knows a team of men who won't hesitate to do what needs to be done when it comes to taking out the worst of humanity. I'm saying too much already, especially considering where y'all are sitting, but sometimes the evil in the world gets a little too much control and the good side needs a bit of help."

"What are you saying?" Rocco asked, leaning forward and lowering his voice. "That you know some vigilante group out there going around killing people outside the law? And you're supporting *and* helping them?"

"You *know* me, Rocco," Tex said tightly. "You know when it comes to protecting those I know and love, and my country, I'll do whatever's necessary. These guys have been burned by the very country and the laws that were supposed to protect them. They've taken it upon themselves to do what they need to do in order to sleep at night.

"I don't talk to them directly, but I *do* discuss injustices that I've run across with their acquaintance. What he chooses to tell them or not tell them is out of my hands. I know without a doubt that he'll either personally take care of making sure those kids are safe, or he'll get in touch with this team, and *they'll* take care of business.

"But I'll tell you this—I sleep just fine at night. Anyone who would not only sell drugs, but get his girlfriend involved, and then leave her hanging out to dry when she's caught, *then* manipulate the court system in order to steal her kids, isn't someone I'll cry over when I read his obituary in the paper. Understand?"

Bubba was seeing a side to Tex that he hadn't ever seen before. He wanted to say he was shocked, but he honestly wasn't. Tex had been around a lot longer than he or his team had. He'd seen and done things none of them knew about. If he was assisting a team of vigilantes who did their best to rid the earth of the worst of the worst, he didn't give one little shit.

What he *did* give a shit about was Zoey. And his

friends. And making sure no one hurt what he considered his. And maybe it was too much, maybe he'd lost his mind, but Zoey was sure as fuck *his*. Something had happened out there in the Alaskan wilderness. They'd connected on a level he'd never connected with anyone before. He'd be damned if someone hurt her. And if it took Tex doing whatever the fuck he had to do in order to make sure she was safe, Bubba would condone it a thousand times over.

"I don't care what you do or how you get the information, Tex. Just get it."

"I will," Tex reassured him. "I'll be in touch."

Bubba clicked off the phone and put it back in his pocket. The urge to text Zoey, to hear her voice, to make sure she was all right, was strong, but he resisted.

"Is anyone else concerned that Tex has finally crossed a line he can't ever come back from?" Gumby asked, his voice hushed.

Bubba opened his mouth to respond, but Phantom beat him to it.

"No. Fuck no. Tex is the most loyal and straight arrow I've ever met. Yeah, he does some illegal shit to get information, but he does it to save lives. We all know we've wished more than once that we could simply take out those who deserve to die, but our hands are tied. Imagine if they weren't. Imagine if we could simply end those who abuse women. Kill animals for the fun of it. Rape defenseless children."

Bubba heard the pain in his friend's words, but didn't know how to help him. But Phantom being Phantom, he rallied and his voice became stronger, more determined as he spoke.

"The goal here is to figure out who tried to kill Bubba. And if we need to enlist the help of a group of men we don't know and have never heard of, fine. All it means is that if we're questioned about them, we can't say shit. I'd jump through fire for any of you, *and* Tex. If he's okay with whatever he's doing to get information, I'll support him one hundred percent."

"Me too," Rex said.

"Same here," Ace said.

Everyone agreed, and Bubba sighed. "I can't believe this is happening, really. I mean, yeah, Pop left me some money, but most of it's tied up in his business."

"So who do we think did it?" Rocco asked.

"As far as I'm concerned, there's really only two people who could be *that* upset about Pop's will," Bubba said. "Sean and Malcom."

"You really think your brother would try to kill you over this?" Gumby asked.

"If you'd asked me a week ago, I would've said no way. But he wasn't exactly thrilled about the results of the will."

"What about other people your dad worked with?" Rex asked.

"It's possible," Bubba conceded. "Malcom brought up an interesting scenario that surprised me at the time...but the more I think about it, the more it worries me."

"What's that?" Rocco asked.

"Poison. Both Zoey and Mal said that Pop had been sick for a while, but he wouldn't go see a doctor. And after Zoey left to go to Anchorage to visit her mom, Dad took a turn for the worse and died. Malcom actually suggested that *Zoey* was working with Ashley, the nurse who helped Pop when Zoey wasn't around."

"It's not a bad theory," Phantom mused.

Bubba was about to lose his shit when his friend continued.

"The poison scenario, not Zoey being involved. There was an autopsy, right?"

"No," Gumby said. "Foul play wasn't suspected, and Malcom had Colin cremated almost immediately. Official cause of death was a heart attack."

"Any tissue samples taken before he was cremated?" Rocco asked.

"Not that I know of, but we can have Tex look into it," Gumby said.

"Shit," Bubba muttered. He hated to even think about this. It didn't seem real that he was discussing not only his father's death, but the possibility that he'd been *murdered*. "This seems more like a plot in a bad crime show than my life," he muttered.

"It's definitely looking premeditated," Ace said. "But we don't have proof that your dad was murdered. It could just be that someone took advantage of his death to try to get what they wanted."

"Right," Bubba said with a shake of his head.

"So who else could've planned this?" Gumby asked.

"I don't really know that much about Pop's employees," Bubba admitted. "I mean, the ones he dealt with on a regular basis. The suppliers or even the managers at the factory."

"It seems to me that Sean Kassamali is the prime suspect here," Rex said. "He's been in business with your dad since the beginning, right? What if he found out about the will, and that he wouldn't be getting as much of the business as he felt he deserved? He could've been really pissed off about that. It wouldn't make *me* happy to put in all that work, then get screwed out of what I might feel I deserved."

"Every single word you just said could apply to Malcom

too," Rocco said dryly.

"Fuck, you're right," Rex said.

"Wait, didn't the lawyer arrange for the private plane?" Rocco asked. "Or have his assistant do it? Could he be in on it too? Maybe he was upset that Colin didn't leave *him* anything? It's not common for lawyers to get a portion of estates, but he's been your dad's lawyer for about the same amount of time that he's worked with Sean."

Bubba knew this was what the team did when they were trying to figure something out, but the fact that it was *his* life they were dissecting was disconcerting. "I asked about the pilot and Kenneth's wife said Eve had come highly recommended by one of her husband's clients."

"Kenneth could've thought that everyone would just assume the plane had crashed, killing the pilot and everyone onboard, and he'd never be looked at twice," Rocco said.

Bubba's head hurt. He didn't like thinking about people he'd known for most of his life plotting to kill him.

"Maybe Bubba wasn't the prime target," Phantom said. "Maybe Zoey was. What do we know about her? Any ex-boyfriends in the picture? Her mother isn't exactly winning the award for mom of the year, maybe someone did this to get back at her?"

"Enough," Bubba said, standing, his chair making a screeching sound as it dragged along the floor. Which didn't help his aching head. "We could sit here all day and dissect my life, Zoey's life, and the life of every fucking person I've ever met, but it won't do any good without hard evidence. We have to wait on Tex and the cops in Alaska to figure this out."

"You can't put your head in the sand on this," Phantom insisted. "Shit isn't all sunshine and roses."

"You think I don't know that?" Bubba asked his teammate, resting his palms on the table in front of him and letting his head drop. "I'm perfectly aware that someone tried to kill me. That even if they weren't after Zoey, she was caught up in this bullshit too. I'm pissed off, even more so because it's likely someone I know. But I'm even *more* upset because I was robbed of the opportunity to pay my respects to my pop the way I should've. I'm angry at myself for not getting to Juneau to see my pop one more time before he died. And now I have to wonder if the same person who tried to kill me didn't also succeed in killing my father. So yeah, I know about the sunshine and roses thing, but I'd appreciate you not throwing it in my face."

Bubba was panting by the time he was done with his tirade, but he was just so fucking tired. Tired of the regrets. Tired of trying to think about who hated him so much that they thought it was preferable to kill him than to confront him.

"Sorry, man," Phantom said. "I was out of line."

Bubba sighed and ran a hand over his face. "No, you weren't. I was. *I'm* sorry."

"Tex'll figure this out. He'll use those connections of his to find the pilot and get the information he needs out of her. This'll be over before you know it, and you and Zoey can stop worrying about looking over your shoulder and instead concentrate on getting on with your lives," Phantom said.

Bubba knew his friend was doing his best to be supportive, and he appreciated it. "Thanks. I hope so. Are we done here?" he asked, looking at Rocco.

His friend nodded. "Yeah. You look exhausted. Go home."

"Thanks," Bubba said. He couldn't remember the last time he'd bugged out of work early, but he was tired and stressed and hadn't truly realized how hard it would be to be away from Zoey all day. After spending every minute of his time with her for a week straight, and being responsible for her safety and well-being, he was feeling their separation acutely. He wondered if she felt the same or if he was completely crazy.

Deciding not to call her and let her know he was leaving work early, he did his best to not break all the speed limits on the way to his house. He pulled into his driveway and parked and checked inside his house for Zoey. When he didn't find her, he immediately left and headed across the street.

He knocked on the door and waited impatiently for Jess to come to the door. When it finally opened, he was relieved to see Zoey standing there.

"Mark! It's early, what are you doing home? Is everything all—*mumph*!"

Bubba didn't know what came over him. The discussion with Tex. The stress of someone wanting them dead. Missing her. Seeing her smiling and happy and safe. All of it coalesced into a physical need to touch her.

His mouth came down on hers mid-sentence, and he sighed in relief when, instead of asking what the hell he thought he was doing, her arms immediately came up and gripped his biceps, pulling him into her rather than pushing him away.

She felt amazing.

The connection that he'd felt between them seemed to grow and solidify as they continued to kiss. Her head tilted to the side and he felt her go up on her tiptoes to try to get closer. Bubba wrapped an arm around her waist and pulled her into him so they were touching from their hips to their chests. Her hand moved to his back and he felt her fingernails digging in as she tried to fuse herself to him.

She tasted like tea and peppermint, and he couldn't get enough.

He had no intention of pulling away from her, but Jess's voice cut through the haze of lust and need that had overtaken him like a wet blanket.

"Not that I'm opposed to you two going at it on my front steps, but I'm guessing the other neighbors around here who aren't as open and easygoing as I am might have a problem with it."

Bubba felt Zoey jerk in his arms and he reluctantly pulled back. He stared into her eyes and was overjoyed to see the same need that he felt deep in his soul. Tenderly smoothing a lock of hair behind her ear, he leaned down and kissed her gently this time. A short touch of his lips to hers that did nothing to mollify the need inside him.

But somehow knowing that she felt the same desperation he did, that she wanted him as much as he wanted her, made him settle. She was here, safe, and he'd do whatever it took to keep her that way. If Zoey thought he was going to let her go back to Alaska after Tex figured out what the hell was going on, she was very wrong. Rex's words came back to him, and he refused to let her go and have one more regret heaped on his soul.

Turning his head but keeping his arms around Zoey, he said, "Hey, Jess. Thought I'd come home early today and make sure all was well."

The older woman cackled as if he'd said the funniest

thing she'd ever heard. "Good God, man, it's not as if we spent the day polishing our rifles and building bombs or anything. Zoey and I have simply been getting to know each other."

"And? Everything's good?"

Zoey hadn't said anything, but Bubba's attention was on Jess. He'd had a gut feeling that the two women would get along, but until he heard it from Jess's mouth, he wouldn't take that for granted.

She rolled her eyes and it made him think of Zoey. He relaxed. Yeah, it was fairly obvious that Jess and Zoey had most likely hit it off.

"Your Zoey cleaned my kitchen from top to bottom as I sat on my butt and watched. Then she made lunch, got me settled in my living room and tidied up as I napped. When I woke up and insisted she take a load off, we talked about what happened to her up in Alaska, about her mom, and you. We discussed politics and didn't even kill each other over it. I told her how much I missed Frank, and she made up a list of the things I need from the grocery store. She promised to take me there tomorrow, which is super exciting, but I told her that I wouldn't go *anywhere* without having my hair done first. It's been too long since I've been cooped up in this house, and I'll be darned if anyone will see my old lady hair."

Bubba beamed. "So things went well."

"Of course they did. Zoey's a doll. But there is one problem."

Bubba frowned, and he felt Zoey tense in his arms. "What?"

"I've lived on my own for almost six years. I don't need a babysitter. I *do* need a companion to keep me company during the day and to help get me to appointments and assist in keeping my house tidied. But you aren't the man I thought you were if you're seriously okay with Zoey living over here. Especially if that hot-as-heck kiss was any indication."

"Jess," Zoey complained, speaking up for the first time. "We talked about this."

"I know we did. But I disagreed with you. Your arguments were silly and wrong."

"What arguments?" Bubba asked.

"Nothing," Zoey said, but Jess, being Jess, talked over her.

"She said that you felt responsible for her, and the last thing she wanted was you helping her out of pity. I told her to open her eyes! That Mark Wright didn't do *anything* he didn't want to do, and if he spent a week with you in the woods and still wanted to bring you back here to Riverton and went out of his way to get me to hire you, then the last thing he felt for you was pity."

Zoey closed her eyes and whispered, "Kill me now."

But Jess wasn't done. "Were you lying when you said you'd had a crush on the man since you met him when you were teenagers? If not, then I don't get why you wouldn't jump at the chance to live with him now. I might be in my eighties, but I'm not dead. Me and Frank were doing the nasty every chance we had before we got married. If I'd'a had a chance to live with him before he put a ring on my finger, I would've taken it. The sex was *that* good. You want to know what the key to a good marriage is?"

"Seriously, just kill me now," Zoey repeated.

"Yeah, Jess, tell us what the key to a good marriage is." Bubba had turned so Zoey was slightly in front of him. He had his arm around her, his palm resting on her stomach, holding her tightly against him. He knew she could feel his erection against the small of her back, but he didn't care. Simply having her in his arms calmed him.

"Cunnilingus," Jess said with a completely straight face.

Bubba choked out a laugh and Zoey groaned.

"It is?" Bubba asked when he got control of himself.

Jess smirked. "Laugh all you want, but I'm right. Frank was a pro at it, and whenever I got mad at him, all he had to do was go down on me and within moments, I'd forget what the hell we were fighting about."

"Jess!" Zoey complained.

"Don't blush, girl. I'm right, you know I am." She turned her gaze to Bubba. "And you better not stand there and tell me you don't like cunnilingus. Because if so, you can turn yourself around and get the hell out of my house."

Bubba did his best not to laugh because he knew poor Zoey was embarrassed as hell. Her face was bright pink and he felt her shift uneasily in front of him. "It's one of my favorite things," he told Jess honestly, "but I'd appreciate it if we could change the subject because it's making Zoey uncomfortable. I already know how blunt you are, but maybe you can tone it down until Zoey gets to know you a little better?"

If anything, the smile on Jess's face got even bigger. "Standing up for your girl, I like it."

"Jess," Bubba warned.

"All right, all right. But to get back to my point. I don't need her here at night. I don't need a babysitter. You like her and she likes you and you're right across the street. If I need something—which I won't—I'll just call you and you can come running over. Besides, if someone is out to get you both, wouldn't it be better for you to have Zoey with you to make sure she's safe? Two women, one being in her eighties, isn't exactly ideal when it comes to security."

Dammit. Jess had a point. But Bubba still wasn't going to make the decision for Zoey. Did he want her with him? Fuck yeah. But he'd never forced a woman to do anything, and he wasn't going to start now.

He stared Jess down. "And if I said she couldn't live in my house? Would you really turn her out? Make her spend what little money she has on an apartment somewhere? Make her spend even more money on a car and gas? I know you, Jess, you wouldn't do that."

"Mark, stop it. If she doesn't want me here, I can find my own place to live," Zoey said.

Bubba ignored Zoey for the moment. He knew she'd say that, but he also knew his neighbor. Jess would no more make Zoey suffer than he would.

Jess narrowed her eyes. "Touché, young man. You know I wouldn't. Fine, if you don't want her, she can live here."

"I never said I didn't want her," Bubba countered. "But it's not cool to try to manipulate either one of us."

Jess grinned. "As if you'd let me manipulate you. So... she gonna move in with you or what?"

"You done with Zoey for the day?" Bubba asked instead of answering her question.

Jess's smile didn't dim. "Yes. Zoey put together a batch of soup in my Crock-Pot and it's been simmering all day." She looked at Zoey. "I'll see you tomorrow morning, right?"

"Yes, ma'am."

"I already told you not to call me that. You do it again and I'm gonna thump ya. See you tomorrow. Have fun tonight, kids!"

"You have everything you need from here?" Bubba asked Zoey.

She nodded. "Yeah. I didn't bring my purse or

anything, thinking if I needed it, I could just run over and get it. My phone and the key to your place are in my pocket."

"Great. Have a good evening, Jess," Bubba said as he steered Zoey out of the doorway and toward his house.

"You too!" she called before she shut the door.

Zoey didn't say anything as they went back across the street to his house. The second the door was shut, Zoey said, "I'm not sure this is going to work out."

Bubba led her into his house, keeping a firm hold on her hand, and seated her on his couch. He pulled the coffee table closer and sat on it, caging Zoey's legs between his own. He hadn't let go of her hand and gently caressed the back as he leaned in closer.

"Do you not like Jess?" he asked.

She looked up at him in surprise. "Not like her? I love her, and I've only known her for a day. I want to be just like her when I'm her age. She's funny, outspoken, and completely crazy. I respect that."

Bubba grinned. "So, what's not going to work out?"

"Mark, you heard her."

"Yup."

"You can't...I'm not... Shit."

"Don't be embarrassed by Jess. Yes, she's outspoken, but she's right. I didn't invite you to come to California out of pity. And I certainly wouldn't have hooked you up with my neighbor if I didn't want to see you every day. Get to know you better. She's just blowing smoke up our asses; you can totally live over there with her and she'd love every second of it. But the last thing I want is for you to feel coerced into doing anything."

Zoey stared at him, and he could see the indecision in her eyes.

"She was right about something else too," he said softly.

"What?"

"I want you," he said bluntly. "I came home early today because I couldn't wait any longer to see you. To check on you. To make sure all was right in your world. I'd like nothing more than to have you here in my house with me at night. If you want to slow things down, we can do that too. I'll sleep in the guest bedroom and you can have my bed. We'll eat dinners and breakfasts together, learn about each other, all our likes and dislikes. We'll watch TV and read books next to each other and go as slow as you want. Most of the time, I feel comfortable around you, Zoey. And I want that to continue."

"Most of the time?" she asked.

"Yeah."

"What about the other times?"

"Comfortable is not a word that comes to mind," he told her seriously. "Anxious, fidgety, aroused, excited, giddy, confused about what the hell you see in me, and turned way the hell on."

Zoey licked her lips, and Bubba couldn't take his eyes from them. He noticed that she was breathing faster and she gripped his hand even harder. "I've never done that."

Bubba frowned in confusion. "What?"

"Um...cunnilingus."

Hearing the very clinical word on her lips made Bubba want to laugh. But he didn't, this was way too serious of a conversation for him to fuck up by laughing at her. "No? Because you don't think you'll like it, or because the men you've been with didn't?"

"Um...both?"

"I wasn't lying, sweetheart. There's nothing I like

better than going down on a woman. And before you ask, it's been a hell of a long time since I've done it. It's a very personal thing that requires a lot of trust. I haven't trusted anyone like that in a very long time. But, since we're being honest here, I've fantasized about sharing that with you."

"You have?"

"Yeah, Zo. Maybe it's because of our experience out in the woods, but I trust you with my life. I can't think of *anything* sexier than eating you out, hearing you call my name as you orgasm in my mouth."

She blushed a deep pink, and Bubba had a feeling he'd gone too far. But she'd brought it up. He tried to control his raging libido and bring their conversation back around to the original point. "I want you in my house, Zoey. I won't manipulate you in any way. Tell me what you want, and I'll move heaven and earth to give it to you. Do you want to stay with Jess? Rent an apartment? Stay here?"

She looked him in the eye and softly said, "Here. If you're being honest and really don't mind me in your space, I'd feel more comfortable here."

"Why?" Bubba needed to know it was more than just because he could keep her safe.

"Because I *have* had a crush on you since I was in the tenth grade. Because you're generous and giving to a fault. Because when you kissed me, I couldn't think of anything other than you. And even though it might be a mistake and you'll find out I'm really just a small-town girl at heart and living here in Riverton scares the crap out of me, I still want to take that chance."

"You took on the Alaskan wilderness with me, sweetheart. The big bad city's got nothin' on you."

She smiled at him.

"And I'm kicking myself even more for not going back

to Alaska to visit my family, because if I did, I might've connected with you even sooner, and we would've had more time together."

"God, that's one of the nicest things anyone's ever said to me," she whispered.

"It's true," Bubba told her. Then he slowly leaned forward, lifted his chin, and waited for her to meet him halfway.

Something inside him settled as she immediately brought her lips to his. They exchanged a slow, sweet kiss, touching nowhere but their lips.

"So you'll live here with me?" he asked when he pulled back.

"Yes."

"Sleep in my bed?"

"Yes."

"With me?"

She blushed but said, "Yes."

"Good," he said in satisfaction. "I want to take things slow. The last thing I want is to take advantage of you or your feelings. Don't take that the wrong way. I want you, Zoey. Want to make you mine in every way a man can make a woman his, but I want you to make me yours too. And we don't have to rush into anything. It's been just over a week since we reconnected. Today was hard on me. Being away from you after all we've been through was tougher than I thought it would be."

"I'm glad it's not just me feeling that way," Zoey admitted. "I felt a little lost all day."

"Me too. That's why I'm proposing taking things one day at a time. We'll get to know each other little by little. I know you can make a fire and how you operate under extreme pressure, but I don't know what you like on your pizza and what your favorite movie is."

"Anything but anchovies or pineapple, and there's no way I could pick just one," she said with a smile.

Bubba wanted to stand up and throw Zoey over his shoulder like some sort of caveman, but he'd just told her he wanted to take things slow. That wouldn't exactly be slow. "What do you want for dinner?"

"Not fish or squirrel," she said immediately.

Laughing out loud, Bubba stood, taking her with him as he did. "Deal. How about spaghetti? It's not gourmet, but I'm thinking a huge bowl of carbohydrates sounds delicious right about now."

"Absolutely," she agreed.

Hours later, after dinner, and after he and Zoey had watched two *Die Hard* movies, Bubba was lying in bed, holding Zoey in his arms as she slept. He had a hard-on that wouldn't go down and his balls actually hurt from being denied release, but he'd never been more comfortable in his life.

He'd also never thought he could be as turned on by an inexperienced woman as he was by Zoey. Thinking back to Jess's advice, he could only mentally shake his head...and agree with her. He couldn't wait to get his hands *and* mouth on Zoey. But for whatever reason, holding her like this was almost as satisfying as any sexual encounter he'd ever had. He didn't know why, other than just because it was Zoey.

They'd shared something deep and profound, and he'd seen a part of her that he didn't think she showed to very many people. Her core strength. Her determination.

Turning his head and kissing her temple, Bubba was

rewarded with her mumbling something under her breath and snuggling into him even tighter.

Someone would pay for daring to try to kill her. He hoped Tex was able to find Eva Dawkins and get to the bottom of the plot sooner rather than later. But in the meantime, he'd keep Zoey safe. She was where she belonged. Right there next to him.

Eva Dawkins wasn't happy. She was running scared and pissed off that she hadn't gotten her money. Her kids were still with her psycho ex, and she had no idea what to do next. She'd hightailed it out of Seattle because staying in one place wasn't a good plan, and had been hitchhiking her way back up into Alaska. It wasn't smart to go back to the place where she'd been hired, but what other choice did she have? Her kids were there. And if she wanted to get them back, she had to face her ex. With or without the money he was demanding.

For the first time in days, the burner phone she'd been using to communicate with the woman who'd hired her rang, and Eva quickly clicked on the green button to answer it.

"Where's my money?" she asked in lieu of a greeting.

"There's no money," the woman said tersely.

"What? That's bullshit!"

"No, it's not. You didn't hold up your end of the bargain."

"The hell I didn't," Eva told her. "I did *exactly* what you told me to. I dropped them off in the middle of fucking nowhere."

"Yeah, well, it wasn't good enough. They were rescued, and the reading of the will went down as the law required."

Eva felt a pang of relief flow through her. She hadn't killed anyone. But she'd still certainly done something that was so fucked up, no jury would let it go. That, along with her record for transporting drugs, would get her thrown in jail without anyone thinking twice about it.

Shit. She was fucked.

She made a last-ditch effort to get the woman to wire the money she'd promised. "That's not my fault. I did what you wanted. You *owe* me."

The woman sighed. "You're right, you did. But here's the thing...*there is no money*. I gave what I promised you to the guys who were supposed to sabotage your plane—so all *three* of you would die when your plane crashed after takeoff."

Eva gasped. "What?" she whispered.

"That's right. If you'd have thought about it for two seconds, you would've realized that having Mark and Zoey declared missing made no sense. No money would be released until they were proven *dead*, and how could we do that if they disappeared into the Alaskan wilderness forever? No, I needed everyone to *know* they were dead, and not by some suspicious mugging or something. That fucking plane was supposed to go down in a ball of flames."

"I can't believe you," Eva said, stunned beyond belief. She was lucky to be alive.

"Believe it," the other woman sneered. "The only reason you're alive is because those assholes must've double-crossed me."

"Like you did to me!" Eva protested.

"Yeah, well...sorry."

She didn't sound sorry at all.

"You bitch!" Eva said. "You owe me, and I want my money."

"I don't owe you shit!" the woman told her. "I'm calling to let you know any association between us is done. If you breathe a word of this to anyone, I'll have you arrested so fast your head will spin. Who do you think the cops will believe, you or me? I'll tell you who, bitch. *Me*."

"But what about my kids?" Eva wailed in despair.

"They aren't my problem. Maybe you shouldn't have spread your legs for the first asshole who came sniffing around. You got yourself into that situation, you can figure a way out of it."

"I had! I did what you wanted," Eva said desperately.

"You're nothing but pure trash," the woman on the other end of the line said heartlessly. "Your kids never stood a chance. And *they're* going to be nothing but trash too. Use this as a chance to wipe your slate clean. Move to Maine or something and start over. It's probably the best thing you could do for those fucking kids."

After that soul-crushing retort, the line went dead.

Eva stared down at the phone in her hand and did what any other mother would do.

She cried.

Then she reached way down deep inside and vowed to do whatever it took to get her children back.

They *weren't* trash. They were beautiful and innocent, and Eva would do whatever it took to make sure they stayed that way.

The woman thought she could cheat her out of the money she owed her fair and square? Eva would *ruin* her. She didn't know how she'd do it, but she would. One way or another.

CHAPTER FIFTEEN

Zoey hid a smile in her teacup as she sat across from Jess on her couch a week later. The older woman had a habit of saying exactly what she was thinking, whether it was appropriate or not. And Zoey loved it.

"I'm not kidding, right to the vice admiral, Frank said, 'If you'll excuse me, Sir, I've been at this navy ball for four hours and haven't been able to think about anything other than getting my wife home and into bed.' Then he saluted the man, took me by the arm, brought me home and had his way with me."

Zoey couldn't hold back her laugh at hearing that. "Are you kidding me? I mean, you do like to joke a lot."

Jess held up a hand. "I swear I'm not kidding. I thought I was going to die of embarrassment, but apparently the vice admiral was jealous that we could leave, because he merely said, 'Have fun, sailor,' before we left."

Zoey shook her head and stood, taking Jess's teacup with her to get her a refill. It was hard to believe she'd only met the older woman a week ago. It felt as if she'd known her for ages. She wasn't hard to work for, not at all. In fact, most of the time Zoey felt like Jess didn't need her. Her house was already fairly clean, and Jess had no problem getting around. But after thinking about it for a while, she realized Jess was lonely. She had no family to visit and spent most of her time cooped up in her house.

Every day, they'd gone out and done something. Grocery shopping. A short walk in the park. They'd gone down to the beach and watched people surfing. Zoey had even taken Jess to the zoo. It was as nice to get out and see the city for Zoey as it was for Jess.

"Are you sure you don't want to come to the barbeque with us this afternoon?" Zoey asked as she sat back down next to Jess on the couch. The get-together at Gumby's beach house had been postponed a bit, and now it was going on as planned later that day.

"I'm sure. I invited Gretel over to play cards this afternoon."

Gretel was a woman who they'd run into at the library a few days ago. Apparently Jess had been friends with her years earlier, but they'd lost touch. The two women had been absolutely giddy to see each other and had made tentative plans to get together.

"She could come too," Zoey said, not wanting her new friend to feel left out.

Jess shook her head. "No, child. You go and have fun with the others. You need to make friends other than an old lady."

"I can have more than one friend," Zoey told her.

"Of course you can, but these women will be special in your life. They'll be your best friends, the aunts to your children, babysitters when you and Mark need time to yourself. They'll be your support system when Mark is deployed, just as you'll be for them. You need to cultivate their friendship, and you should start that as soon as possible."

"Jess," Zoey said softly, putting down their teacups. "I think you've misunderstood my relationship with Mark."

Jess merely raised one eyebrow in response.

"Seriously. I mean, we haven't...we aren't...we're just friends right now." She knew that wasn't exactly the case, but she didn't want to talk about her sex life...or lack of one...with the other woman.

"Trust me, that man is *not* just your friend," Jess said with conviction. "It's kind of cute that you've got your head in the sand when it comes to Mark, but at some point you're going to have to sit up and take notice of what's going on around you. I saw that kiss last week, that was not a kiss between friends."

"Oh, but...yeah, I thought so too. But he hasn't done anything since then. Not even a peck on the cheek. He said he wanted to go slow, but I didn't think he meant *this* slow."

"He's not sleeping with you?"

Zoey knew she was blushing again, but she honestly didn't have anyone else to talk to about this. "We're sleeping, but that's it. I was pretty sure we were headed toward a serious relationship, but now I'm wondering if I was just seeing what I wanted to when it came to us."

Jess nodded then leaned forward and took Zoey's hand in her own.

Zoey wanted to cry at the gesture. It had been a long time since someone had looked at her as tenderly as Jess was right now. She couldn't remember the last time her mom had actually sat down and had a heart-to-heart talk with her. The last she'd heard from her—a quick phone call the other day—she was in Fairbanks with Liam and things were going well.

"My Frank was an alpha man, just like Mark. He was protective and surly when it came to other men looking at me. After his deployments, it took him quite a while to get back into the swing of being home again. But even when he was at his grumpiest, I never doubted his love for me. He cooked me meals, he did the dishes, he vacuumed and did the laundry. He drove me to work when he could and picked me up. When I had nights out with my friends, he stayed up until I got home or volunteered to be the sober driver to get us all home safely. He held my hand in public *and* when we were here at home. To others, he was a Grumpy Gus, but to me, he was my Frank. A man like Mark wouldn't want to rush you. I'm guessing he's waiting for a sign from *you* to move things to the next level."

Zoey thought about Jess's words, and had to concede that she made a good point. Mark had been nothing but polite and caring toward her. He'd done all those things Jess had mentioned, except the holding hands thing.

"What if he's changed his mind? I mean, things were pretty intense in Alaska, and now that he's been home a little while, maybe he's decided it was just situational after all."

"He's interested," Jess countered. "I've seen the way he looks at you when you aren't paying attention. But that doesn't mean he'll sit around and wait forever. You're going to have to let him know that you haven't changed *your* mind. In today's world, men have to be very careful about making advances on women so as not to overstep their bounds."

A knock on the door interrupted their intimate talk. Before Zoey could get up and answer the door, Jess squeezed her hand. "Take some advice from an old lady, Zoey. I have a feeling it'll be up to you to make the first move, and you should do it soon. That man is the bee's knees, and if I were you, I'd be all over that."

Zoey chuckled. "The bee's knees?"

Jess smirked. "In my day, that was quite the compliment."

"It still is," Zoey told her.

Another knock on the door sounded, and they both heard Mark call out Jess's name.

"I need to get that so he doesn't worry," Zoey said.

Jess nodded and patted Zoey's hand. "Remember what I said. He's trying to be a gentleman and not rush you. Take hold of what you want, child."

Zoey nodded and got up to answer the door.

She pulled it open, and a little thrill went through her at seeing Mark standing there. He'd gone home after work and changed into a pair of khaki shorts and a white T-shirt. He looked absolutely yummy with his tan skin and the short beard he hadn't shaved off after their adventure in Alaska.

"Hi," he said, leaning forward.

Zoey tilted her head, making it easier for him to kiss her cheek, but instead his lips brushed against her own.

"Have a good day?" he asked.

"Yeah," Zoey said, her mouth dry. Jess's words echoed in her head, but she knew now wasn't the time to tell him that if he was holding back being intimate with her because he thought it was what *she* wanted, he was wrong.

They said their goodbyes to Jess, and Zoey ignored the smirk on the older woman's face and the way she waggled her eyebrows up and down.

Back at his house, Mark patiently waited as she

changed into a pair of shorts and a T-shirt and packed a bag with a towel, bathing suit, and an outfit to change into after spending a day on the beach. She couldn't help but notice that Mark grabbed one of his sweatshirts and stuffed it into her bag as well. She knew it wasn't for himself, that he'd thrown it in for her, knowing she'd probably get chilled and need it later.

Zoey was excited about the barbeque. She wanted to get to know Mark's teammates better, and couldn't wait to talk more with Caite, Sidney, and Piper.

From the second they arrived at Gumby's beach house, it was semi-controlled chaos. Piper and Ace's three children were running around with the never-ending energy only kids could have. Rocco was manning the grill, while Phantom and Rex had taken it upon themselves to look after the kids and make sure they didn't get hurt and were having a good time.

The remaining men threw a football on the beach, taking turns coming back to make sure no one needed anything at the house. After eating hamburgers and hotdogs, everyone went for a swim in the ocean, which was a new adventure for Zoey. The water was chilly, but not nearly as cold as it was up in Alaska.

After spending over an hour playing in the water and sand, everyone came back up to the house to shower and change. Finally, the kids were settled in the master bedroom watching cartoons, and the guys were gathered around the huge living room TV, watching football.

Caite, Piper, Sidney, and Zoey had decided to sip wine and sit on the back deck, enjoying the sunset. Well, everyone but Piper was drinking wine, as she was pregnant and had settled for bottled water. It was the first time they'd really sat down and relaxed all afternoon, and Zoey was more than glad for the time to talk to the other women one-on-one and get off her feet.

"How's working with Jess going?" Caite asked.

"Good. Really good," Zoey said. "She's a hoot. She's this teeny little woman with a huge personality. I swear I've blushed more around her than I have in my entire life."

"Have the cops found out anything else about whoever might've hired that pilot to leave you and Bubba in the middle of nowhere?" Sidney asked.

Zoey shook her head. "Not that I know of. I know there's a guy named Tex who is also looking into it, and Mark thinks he should find out something soon."

Piper nodded enthusiastically. "Tex is amazing. If anyone can find out who set it all up, he can." Then she proceeded to tell Zoey all about how Tex had arranged for the almost immediate adoption of her girls, and how he'd popped into one of their barbeques one day and she'd gotten to meet him. "He was a SEAL himself but lost a leg in combat. He's almost a God around here, and I can see why. I wanted to do something to thank him, but Beckett told me if I tried, Tex would do something completely over the top in return."

"Like what?"

"I asked the same thing, and Beckett said he once sent someone an exploding glitter bomb after they thanked him one too many times."

"Holy crap. No one wants that stuff in their house. It never goes away!" Zoey exclaimed.

"I know," Piper said. "Sinta begged me for some of that glitter glue stuff to use in a project, and I stupidly caved. I'm never going to get that shit out of my carpet."

Everyone laughed.

"Anyway," Piper went on. "I guess Tex doesn't do well with anything other than a simple thank you. Although I did have the girls each make him a card, and I got away with that."

"So you still have no idea who wanted you guys dead?" Caite asked.

Zoey shook her head and shrugged.

"That sucks. I know exactly how that feels," Caite commiserated. "But the good thing is that you've got Bubba at your side. How are things going with *that*?"

Feeling a sense of déjà vu since she'd just had this conversation with Jess, Zoey once again tried to explain how things were between her and Mark, and how she both wanted things to move faster but was *scared* to move things along because she didn't want to do anything that might screw up the connection she felt with him.

When no one said anything after she was done explaining, Zoey wasn't sure what to think. She'd felt a kinship with these women, and the last thing she wanted to do was say something that might mess that up. They'd known Mark longer than she had...well, that wasn't exactly true, since she'd known him when he was in high school, but still.

"So, here's the thing," Caite said after a long moment of silence had gone by. "I think none of us has jumped in with any sage advice because we know exactly how you feel. We were *all* in your shoes. Not exactly, but pretty much. I didn't know someone was trying to kill me for the longest time, which was crazy, but once I did, and Blake got all protective, I wondered if he was with me just to keep me safe or because he liked me."

"Same with me," Piper said. "Besides, we were so busy with the girls and getting them settled and acclimated to living here in the US. I was pretty sure that he'd only married me so the girls could get out of Timor-Leste."

"How did you...um...move your relationship to the next level?" Zoey asked, glad that she'd had some liquid courage.

"It just kind of happened," Caite said.

Piper nodded in agreement.

That wasn't what Zoey wanted to hear; it wasn't very helpful.

Sidney leaned forward. "I'll be the first to admit that I messed up pretty badly in my relationship with Decker. I did some really stupid things, and I'm grateful that he didn't immediately dump me on my ass as a result. But I'm seeing a counselor to talk about the shit that messed me up. I think the key to a relationship with men like ours is to communicate. To not be afraid to tell them what you want and how you want it. Whether that's sex or anything else. I didn't talk to Decker enough, and it almost ruined us."

Zoey bit her lip. "Mark is one of the nicest guys I know. He hired me to help his *neighbor* out."

"Where're you sleeping?" Caite asked.

Zoey knew she was blushing, but said, "In his bed."

"And where's he sleeping?" Piper asked.

"In his bed," Zoey repeated.

"Right," Caite concluded, sitting back and putting her feet up on the railing of the deck. "It's not pity, and he likes you."

"She's right," Sidney agreed. "There's no way he would set you up in his bed and crawl in there with you if he didn't want your relationship to be serious. It's not how our men are wired."

"I agree," Piper said. "He could've put you in his guest room."

"He offered to sleep there himself, but said in no uncertain terms that I'd take the master," Zoey admitted.

All three women smiled and nodded their heads. Caite leaned forward and held up her wine glass. Zoey tapped it with her own. "Welcome to the club, Zoey. We're thrilled to have you."

"What are you toasting?" a deep voice asked from behind them.

Zoey startled and almost dropped her wine glass. She turned and saw Mark standing there with his sweatshirt in his hand.

"To friends," Caite said easily.

"Ah, cool. Zoey, I thought you might be cold," Mark said as he held up the sweatshirt.

"Oh, thanks. I am a bit chilly."

He grinned and handed her the sweatshirt and held her wine glass as she pulled it over her head. It was huge on her, but she didn't care. It smelled like Mark, and other than him holding her in his arms, nothing could make her feel more relaxed than being surrounded by his scent. "Thanks," she told him as she reached for her glass.

He relinquished it, then surprised her by leaning down and kissing her temple. He turned to the others and said, "Don't get too drunk, ladies. Piper, I'm holding you responsible for making sure they can still walk in another hour."

Piper rolled her eyes. "Whatever. We're not doing shots of Jägermeister out here, you know. It's just a little bit of wine."

Mark eyed the empty bottle on the railing, and the one next to it that they'd just opened. "Uh-huh."

265

"Oh, shut up," Caite said. "And shoo, would ya? We're talking women stuff out here."

"I'm going, I'm going," Mark said. He ran his hand over Zoey's hair before turning and heading back inside.

"Oh, yeah, you have nothing to worry about, girl," Sidney said once Mark had left.

"Most of the time I think so too, but then days go by without him touching me even once, except for when we go to sleep. And I get paranoid," Zoey admitted.

"Bubba's one of the good guys," Caite reassured her. "He's doing what he thinks is right and honorable. But believe me, one of these days he's going to break, and when he does, it'll be glorious."

They talked for another forty-five minutes or so until the children wandered out of the house and onto the deck. Their show had ended and they were bored...and crabby. Not long after that, the party seemed to naturally break up. Everyone said their goodbyes, and Zoey was thrilled when all the women exchanged numbers with her and told her to call anytime, and that they'd be in touch.

Even before she'd left the beach house, Caite had sent her a text that told her to be patient, and to let her know if she ever wanted to talk.

It felt good.

Everything in Zoey's life seemed to be going very well...and that scared the crap out of her. In the past when things went well, something always seemed to come along and screw it up. But she was determined to stay positive and believe, for once in her life, that everything would work out for the better.

Bubba looked over at Zoey and smiled when he saw she'd fallen asleep on the way back to his house. Her cheeks were flushed from the alcohol she'd consumed and her mouth was slightly open as she breathed deeply.

He'd talked to his friends a bit about his situation with Zoey, and how he wanted her more than his next breath but was afraid of moving too fast. They'd advised him to continue to take things slowly, and that he'd just know when the time was right to go to the next step in their relationship.

The advice wasn't exactly what he'd wanted to hear. He wanted one of his friends to tell him just to go for it. But he also didn't want to screw up his friendship with Zoey. He valued that highly. Almost as much as he wanted to see her naked and writhing in ecstasy on his sheets.

When they got home, he glanced over at Jess's house and sighed in relief. She'd left the porch light on, as was her custom. She did that right before she went to bed at night to let him know all was well.

Bubba went around to the passenger side of his car and gently shook Zoey awake. He wrapped an arm around her to guide her inside as she was still mostly out of it. He helped her up the stairs and she collapsed onto his bed, immediately turning on her side and pulling the covers up to her face.

"Everything smells like you," she mumbled. "So good..."

Bubba stood at the side of his bed for a good five minutes and watched Zoey sleep. He wanted her. Bad. His cock stood at attention, and he knew without a doubt it wouldn't take more than a couple pumps to make him lose it.

He liked everything about Zoey. She was kind to

everyone she met, and that was so refreshing. She didn't talk bad about anyone, no matter what they looked like or what they did.

It was all he could do to not lean down, wake her up with a kiss, then strip her naked and make love to her until neither of them could move.

But it was too soon.

Honestly, it didn't feel too soon to him. Even though not much time had gone by since they'd been stranded, because of their experiences and knowing each other from high school, he felt as if he'd known her forever.

But he was supposed to wait.

Society said that jumping into bed with someone so soon after they'd started dating wasn't good for the outcome of a long-term relationship.

Even his teammates had advised him to wait.

He didn't want to.

But he would.

And the only way he'd be able to control himself was if he put some distance between them. It would kill, but he'd do it if it meant solidifying his connection with Zoey.

He forced himself to turn and head out of the bedroom and down the stairs. All he really wanted to do was change and climb under the sheets with Zoey, but he couldn't while still behaving himself. Not right this second.

He grabbed a beer out of the fridge and turned on the television. He clicked the channels until he stopped on a show he'd seen before. It was boring as hell, but he needed the distraction. He'd distance himself just a bit...enough to give Zoey a chance to acclimate to Riverton and her new situation. But he wasn't giving up his nights. He needed to hold her. To reassure himself that she was there and safe, and to give him a glimpse of what he had to look forward to in the future.

He'd have to cut that down a little, though. He'd stay up later, make sure she fell asleep before he came up. Then he could hold her as close as he needed to without her feeling pressure to move their relationship faster than she was comfortable doing. It might kill him, but for Zoey, he'd do it.

CHAPTER SIXTEEN

Two weeks later, Zoey was more confused than ever. Things had been going so well with Mark, and she'd been ready to try to let him know, subtly of course, that she was ready to move their physical relationship along. But ever since the barbeque at his friend's house, he'd seemed distracted.

He left early in the morning for PT and didn't come home for breakfast afterward, deciding to stay at the base and shower instead of returning to the house. He'd come home at night and they'd eat dinner together, then they'd settle in front of the TV and talk. That was all nice, but he'd been encouraging her to head up to bed early, and she'd been falling asleep before he came up.

She knew he eventually did come upstairs, because she woke up when his alarm went off in the mornings and was always in his arms, but the second the beeping of his watch sounded, he'd roll over and get on with his day.

It was depressing as hell.

She knew Mark was stressed. He told her he'd gotten at least one phone call every day from both his brother and Sean about the business. They always needed his signature on this or that form, or they requested he Skype into one meeting or another. Or they needed to discuss some change they wanted to make.

Mark had never been interested in his dad's business before, but now that he'd been forced into making decisions about it, Zoey could tell he had even less interest. But he was stuck. His brother and his dad's business partner needed him, or at least they said they did.

On top of that, Tex hadn't located Eva Dawkins yet. The night before, Mark told her that his friend was closing in on her location, and that it was only a matter of time, but she knew he was still frustrated it was taking so long. He needed to know who had tried to kill him so he could move on.

She had the thought that he was waiting for that mystery to be solved, so he could tell her that she was safe and could get on with her life. Maybe that's why he'd put distance between them. The idea hurt. A lot. But Zoey did what she always did when adversity came her way, she lifted her chin and got on with her life. She did her best not to stress over things that she couldn't control, and right now, she didn't have any control over the investigation into their attempted murder, Colin's business, the pressure being put on Mark because of it, or his job as a SEAL.

But she *did* have control over her relationship with Mark. She couldn't go on like this anymore. She needed answers. She still felt as deep a connection with him as she always had, but if he'd changed his mind about them, she had to know. She'd ask Jess if she could move in with her until she could find an apartment of her own.

The money she'd received from Colin's estate, along

with the money Jess was paying her, was enough to start fresh somewhere. Zoey liked Riverton. The weather was perfect and there were a ton of things to do. She didn't feel stifled as she had back in Juneau, and she loved not running into a million people she knew when she was out doing errands. There was something to be said for being anonymous while going about your business.

It was late and, as usual, Mark had stayed downstairs while she'd come up to bed. But instead of climbing under the sheets and falling asleep, Zoey was determined to get some answers. If Mark was done with her, she needed to know. Tonight.

She left the lights off and snuggled into the armchair in the corner of the room. She pulled a blanket around her and curled up her legs, turning on her tablet to play solitaire until Mark came to bed. She knew she might have a while to wait, but that was okay. She wasn't tired. Not when her heart was beating so fast and adrenaline was coursing through her veins. She wasn't a confrontational person, so this was kinda scary for her.

She could've gone downstairs and asked Mark what his deal was, but she wanted to see how long it would take him to come to bed.

Two hours later—the longest two hours of Zoey's life— she finally heard footsteps on the stairs. She put the tablet aside and waited. She watched as Mark eased into the room, being careful to stay quiet. Normally, that would've made her appreciate him all the more, but now, all it did was irritate her.

He went into the bathroom, closing the door all the way before turning on the light. Once more being considerate. When he exited, Zoey couldn't keep quiet anymore.

"It's late," she said softly.

He jerked in surprise, then turned to the chair she was sitting in.

"Zoey?"

"Yeah, who else would it be?"

"Are you all right? Are you feeling okay?"

"I'm fine. Mark, we need to talk." She winced as soon as the words left her mouth. All guys hated to hear those four words, but they'd popped out without her thinking.

In response, Mark clicked on the lamp by the side of the bed and walked over to her. He was wearing a pair of boxers and that was it. His body was absolutely beautiful, and it actually made Zoey's heart hurt looking at him. He was sleek and toned and the V muscles near his hips that pointed downward made her swallow hard. She wanted to put her hands all over him. To feel him under her and over her as they made love.

Knowing she had to concentrate, Zoey forced her eyes up to his face.

He was looking down at her in concern, seemingly not worried that he was practically naked. "What's wrong?"

"Us. This," she blurted. "This isn't working anymore."

Kneeling down in front of the chair, Mark put his hands on her calves. "You want to leave?" he asked softly.

Zoey shook her head. "No. Not at all. But you've made it more than obvious over the last couple of weeks that you don't want me here."

He frowned. "What?"

"Don't deny it, Mark. You've spent as little time here in the house as possible, and I can't help but think it's obviously because of me. You get up at the ass-crack of dawn and don't come back until right before dinner. Then we spend a few hours together, and I come up to bed and you *purposely* stay away until I'm asleep. If you want me to leave, all you have to do is tell me. I'm a big girl, I can handle it."

Mark sighed and looked down at the floor. Zoey's heart sank even further.

"I know Tex hasn't figured out who was behind everything that happened up in Alaska, but I promise I'll be fine. Nothing's happened since the reading of Colin's will, so I'm guessing that whoever arranged that shit is resigned to the fact that Colin gave us what he gave us. I've got enough money to rent an apartment. I'll keep helping Jess, because I love it. I love *her*. I've been looking online, and I can get a certificate in Gerontology. You've helped me realize that I can make a career out of something I love doing. I'll always be thankful for that."

Mark's head came up, and he pinned her in place with a look so intense, she froze.

"I've fucked this up," he said.

When he didn't say anything else, Zoey didn't know if she should agree with him or deny his words. So she said nothing. Just waited.

"It's true that I've been avoiding you, but not for the reasons you think."

Zoey could hardly breathe. Her heart hurt. She didn't like hearing confirmation of her fears.

"Zo, the last thing I wanted to do was rush you into a relationship you weren't ready for. Things happened very fast between us. They were very intense. And I didn't want you to feel beholden to me, or like you had to start a physical relationship with me because you were thankful."

"I'm grateful that you were the one stranded with me, but the last thing I'd do is go out with you, or have sex with you, as a result," she said softly.

Mark winced. "I've been staying away from you as

much as possible because it's literally the *only* way I can keep my hands off of you."

Zoey's eyes widened in surprise. He kept talking.

"I knew I needed to give you time. To let you make friends and acclimate to your new situation without pressure from me. So I left early in the mornings because if I had to sit across from you and watch you eat breakfast with a smile, and talk about all the fun things you had planned with Jess, I wouldn't have been able to keep from taking you right there on the kitchen table. I've been waiting until you're asleep to come to bed because if you were awake when I got up here, I would've taken advantage of you and seduced you before you were ready. I wasn't strong enough to sleep in the guest room, otherwise I would've done that too.

"The best part of my day is when I can come up to bed and climb under my sheets with you. Hold you against me. Hear your heart beat and feel your warm breaths on my chest. Not *want* you here? Zoey, I've never wanted anything more in my life."

His words took a moment to sink in, and then every muscle in Zoey's body sagged in relief. He hadn't been putting distance between them so it would be easier to let her down when he told her she should move out. He'd done it because he didn't want to rush her.

Jess had been right. She should've done more to make sure he knew she was ready for a physical relationship. Both of them had suffered needlessly over the last two weeks.

Her heart beating out of her chest, she uncurled her legs and scooted to the edge of the chair. She reached out and put her hands on either side of Mark's neck and leaned into him. "I'm ready, Mark. More than. Touch me. Make me yours. I want it. I need it. I need *you*."

One second he was crouched in front of her, and the next, she was in his arms and he was dropping her on the bed behind them.

The urgency in his actions was echoed in her own. Their mouths met, and she moaned deep in her throat. He speared his tongue into her mouth and devoured her. He kissed her as if he'd never kissed anyone before and never would again. As their tongues dueled, his hands reached for the T-shirt she was wearing. He backed away just long enough to tear the cotton over her head, then his mouth was once more on hers. Urgent desire drumming through them both.

Zoey's hands slid down his muscular back and slipped under his boxers to clutch at his ass cheeks.

It was Mark's turn to moan, and he picked his head up just enough to stare down at her. His pupils were dilated with lust, and she could feel puffs of warm air from his rapid breathing against her face.

Instead of leaning down to kiss her again, Mark inched his way down her body.

Zoey tried to grab his shoulders to keep him where he was, but he was too strong, and he ignored her nonverbal pleas. He settled on his stomach over her, and his lips latched onto one of her nipples so strongly, she gave a little cry and arched her back, pressing herself up and into him even harder.

His mouth felt so good. He licked and sucked at her as if he'd never get enough. His hands weren't still as he feasted on her. They plumped her breasts and, at one point, he even pushed them together and alternated sucking on one nipple then the other.

How long he played with her chest, Zoey had no idea, but it was long enough that she was desperate for more.

"Mark," she moaned, not sure if she was begging for him to stop or to continue.

Instead of moving upward, he slid even farther down the bed.

Zoey shifted uncertainly. She hadn't lied when she'd told him that no one had ever gone down on her before. She wasn't sure about this, was feeling a bit self-conscious about the act.

He gently eased her panties down her legs and licked his lips when she was finally naked underneath him.

"Relax," Mark murmured. "You're gonna love this. As am I. I've dreamed about this. About tasting you. About feeling you come apart around my fingers and mouth." Then he used both hands to shove her thighs as far apart as they'd go...and he merely stared down at her soaking-wet folds.

"Oh, shit," Zoey said, and closed her eyes. She was embarrassed beyond belief. The only person who'd looked at that part of her as closely as Mark was right this second was her gynecologist. And it wasn't the same thing. Not even close.

"Fuck, you're gorgeous," Mark said reverently. She felt one of his fingers glide slowly over her folds, smearing the wetness he'd found there. When she started to close her legs, he shifted slightly so his shoulder and elbow were holding her open.

"Don't hide from me," he growled. "I love this tuft of hair." He stroked the hair on her mons that she'd trimmed the other day. "And the fact that you're bare down here," his finger moved to once again glide over her smooth pussy lips, "makes me almost insane with lust."

Zoey didn't answer. Didn't think Mark really was waiting for a response anyway. She didn't know what to do with her hands. Didn't know what to expect. Was this normal? Did men usually examine their partners' sex before they went down on them? She had no idea, and that made her even more nervous.

But before she could ask what she was supposed to be doing, Mark's head lowered.

Zoey felt him lick her. His tongue was warm and soft between her pussy lips. It felt good, but not earth-shattering.

But then his mouth clamped over her clit and he sucked. Hard.

Her hips shot up from the mattress and she shrieked in delight, but Mark's mouth didn't let go. He latched on as if he'd found nirvana and nothing would tear him away. He went at her with unrelenting passion, and Zoey could only hang on for the ride. One hand gripped his head and the fingernails on her other hand dug into his shoulder as her hips undulated under his skillful mouth and lips. She couldn't stay still, wasn't sure if she was supposed to try or what. But the way he was sucking and licking at her clit made it impossible anyway.

At one point, she looked down and saw Mark's eyes were closed and he had the most blissful look on his face. His chin moved back and forth as he ate her out, and it was sensual as hell.

"Mark," she said again as she felt a monster orgasm rise closer and closer to the surface. She'd gotten herself off more times than she could count, but nothing had ever felt like this. Usually when she got close, she eased her vibrator off her clit a bit or slowed down the strokes of her fingers.

But as if Mark could tell she was getting close, he did

the opposite. He sucked harder and his tongue lashed against her sensitive bud even faster instead of backing away.

It almost hurt, but not really. Zoey didn't have time to warn him that she was about to come. One second every muscle in her body was tense and her ass was a few inches off the bed, and the next, she went hurtling over the edge. Her entire body shook, and she vaguely felt Mark ease a finger into her body, stroking her from the inside as she came.

Even then, he didn't let up. His mouth stayed latched onto her clit as if he was a cowboy riding a bucking bronco and had to stay on for the entire ride. Finally, when she felt her orgasm waning, Mark lifted his head and looked right into her eyes. Licking his lips, he didn't speak, but his satisfaction was easy to see. She could see her juices on his chin and glistening in his facial hair, and instead of being repulsed, it turned her on even more.

His finger continued to push in and out of her body, making shivers go through Zoey at the intensity of the feelings he was evoking within her.

"You're tight," he growled softly. "You're gripping my finger so hard, I can't wait until it's my cock in here."

Swallowing hard, Zoey nodded. She'd felt his erection against her and knew he was bigger than either of the two men she'd been with in the past. She was nervous, but she wanted him so fucking badly.

"Please," she whispered.

"Please what?" he asked.

"Inside me," she said, knowing she was probably beet red with embarrassment. She'd never been one to ask for what she wanted.

Instead of immediately moving up over her, Mark

continued to play with her with his finger. She was still spread open under him and it took everything within her to keep eye contact. She knew she was soaking wet after her orgasm, his finger sliding easily in and out of her body. She tightened her inner muscles to try to hold him inside, but he merely continued with his teasing.

"I want you more than I can possibly explain," Mark said. "But I'm perfectly content with stopping right here."

Zoey gaped at him. "What?"

"I never want to do anything you don't want to do. It's late. I've stressed you out over the last two weeks and if you need to sleep right now, we can wait."

"Are you kidding?" she asked incredulously. "If you don't get inside me in the next minute or so, I'm going to have to hurt you."

The serious look in his eyes was replaced with humor. "Yeah?"

"Yeah."

"I'm clean," he said.

Zoey frowned in confusion at him for a second, then realized what he meant. "Oh, yeah. Me too. And I had the Depo shot."

"The what?"

"Sorry, Depo-Provera. It's a birth control shot. I go in every three months to get it. It's helped regulate my periods. I'm good for another month before I need to go to a doctor and get another one."

Mark's eyes lit up. "I'll use a condom if you want me to. But the thought of being able to get inside you bare is the most fucking exciting thing I've ever heard."

Zoey didn't even hesitate. "Fuck me, Mark. Please."

He finally moved at hearing those words. His finger slid out of her body and before Zoey could register the emptiness, Mark was hovering over her. He'd slipped out of his boxers in record time and she couldn't help but stare at his cock. The head was slippery with precome and she could see the veins throbbing along his length. She didn't get nearly enough time to examine him though, because he leaned over her, propping himself up with one arm next to her shoulder, and she felt him probe at her opening with the tip of his cock.

"I'll go slow," Mark promised. He didn't give her time to agree or disagree before Zoey felt him begin to press inside her.

He went slow but steady. Once he started entering her, he didn't stop. Wincing a little at his size, Zoey did her best not to tense up. She lifted her hips to try to assist, and just when she was going to tell him to give her a moment to adjust, he was all the way inside. Zoey could feel his pubic hair meshing with hers, and she took a deep breath.

Looking up at Mark, she saw his jaw was clenched and he looked almost angry.

"Mark?" she said a little uncertainly.

"Give me a second," he said tersely.

Zoey realized that he wasn't mad, but on the edge, and that made her feel so much better. Just to see what would happen, she tightened her Kegel muscles around his cock and actually felt him twitch inside her. She giggled, and that made him press inside her even farther.

"Shit, Zoey. You feel so fucking good. I can't...I'm gonna...fuck! Hold on."

And with that, Mark moved one hand under her ass and squeezed the round globe while pulling her up toward him. His hips moved back, then slowly eased forward. After three or four slow thrusts, he lost the iron control he'd been holding over himself and began to hammer in and out of her.

It felt *so* good. Zoey had never been made love to with such desperation. Such passion. He fucked like he ate her out—without reservation or embarrassment. It *was* glorious.

Throwing her head back, she arched and gave herself over to the pleasure coursing through her body. Her clit was still sensitive from the tongue lashing Mark had given it. She felt his balls bouncing off her and the base of his cock brushing against her bundle of nerves with every thrust, making another orgasm well up inside her.

"That's it," Mark coaxed. "Come for me again."

Wanting that more than she wanted her next breath, Zoey moved one of her hands down between them and strummed her clit, giving herself the extra stimulation she needed to go over the edge.

One second she was there in the room, feeling Mark's hard cock inside her, and the next she was flying in blissful ecstasy.

She heard Mark shout as if from inside a long tunnel as he reached his own completion.

He lowered himself down and immediately rolled, bringing Zoey with him until she lay over him, boneless and panting.

"In case it wasn't clear, I want you here," Mark said when he'd caught his breath.

Zoey couldn't help it. She laughed. So hard, she felt Mark's cock slip out of her body. She hated that, but still couldn't stop giggling.

"It wasn't *that* funny," Mark said disgruntledly.

Zoey got control of her laughter and nodded. "I know. I just…I'm so relieved. It's never been like that for me."

"Me either," Mark said seriously. "That was a gift. *You're* a gift. Thank you, Zoey. I know I fucked up over the last two weeks."

She shook her head and lifted herself up so she could look into his eyes. "No, I should've done a better job in communicating with you about what I wanted."

"How about we compromise and say we both messed up, and we'll do a better job of talking about what we want and need from here on out?"

"Deal," Zoey said. Then sighed in satisfaction.

"Do you want to go clean up?" Mark asked.

"Would you be grossed out if I said no?" she asked in return.

"Never," he reassured her. Then he reached up and put his hand on the back of her neck and guided her head to his shoulder. "Sleep."

"We should probably talk about Tex and the business and all the calls you've been getting," Zoey said sleepily.

"Tomorrow."

"Okay." Zoey capitulated without complaint. She was tired. The stress and worry about where she and Mark had stood catching up with her.

CHAPTER SEVENTEEN

For the first time in two weeks, Bubba didn't set his alarm for o-dark-thirty and slink out of his house for PT. He woke up and texted Rocco to let him know he wouldn't be in until later, then fell back asleep with Zoey in his arms.

The next time he woke up was to Zoey kneeling at his side, her hand fisted around his cock as she stroked him to a rock-hard erection. She'd then straddled him and took him inside her body, riding him hard until she'd gotten off. Then he'd spun them around and taken her just as hard from behind until he'd orgasmed.

He definitely liked this new confident and sexy side to Zoey.

And he'd almost fucked it up. He'd been trying to take things slow, to make sure she wanted him as badly as he wanted her, but he'd been an idiot by not actually talking to her about their relationship.

When they were lying together, limbs intertwined, recovering from their morning sex, his cell phone rang. It was Malcom. Bubba ignored it.

Thirty minutes later, it rang again, and Sean's name came up on the screen.

Sighing, Bubba knew what he had to do. He'd been struggling with the decision ever since he'd heard his pop's will, but the time had come.

"I need to go up to Juneau," he told Zoey quietly.

She didn't even flinch against him. "When do we leave?"

"I want you to stay here. It'll be safer."

She propped herself up on an elbow next to him. "Actually, if you show up in Alaska by yourself, if the person who wanted to kill us finds out, he could come down here and take me out much more easily."

Bubba winced. "Would you please not talk quite so nonchalantly about being taken out?"

Zoey nodded. "I don't know why you need to go up there, but if no one knows you're coming, they can't arrange any shenanigans like they did last time. And it's really hard to arrange anything to be done on the house when I'm not there. I appreciate Tracy Eklund sending me some of my stuff, but I'd really like to go through the house myself and decide what I want to keep. What I need to give away and what I want shipped down here."

Bubba turned to look Zoey in the eyes. "Have you decided what to do with the house?"

"I think I want to sell it. I don't have much interest in being a landlord and renting it out, and..." Her voice trailed off.

"And?" Bubba prompted.

"I'd like to move here permanently. Even if you and I don't work out, I like it here. I like Caite, Sidney, and Piper, and I can get my certification at the community college here."

"You and I are going to work out," Bubba said sternly.

Zoey smiled up at him and curled a hand around the back of his neck. He loved that she liked to put her hands on him. He'd missed out on a hell of a lot in the last two weeks when he was trying to go slowly. Never again.

"So," she said, picking up her train of thought. "I could go with you and deal with the house stuff while you do whatever you need to do."

"I'm going to sell my part of the business to my brother."

Zoey didn't even look surprised. "Good," she said with a nod.

"Good?"

"Yeah. It'll never make you happy. It's obvious. Every time Malcom or Sean ring with a question or with something for you to sign, you get really stressed out. Your calling is to help people. To be a SEAL. I loved your dad, and I think he knew deep down that you'd never come home and go into business with him. And he was okay with that. He loved you exactly how you are."

"Thank you," Bubba said softly. "I'm still not sure bringing you with me is a good idea. I can't do what I need to do and make sure you're safe at the same time. It feels as if I'd be bringing you right back into the lion's den, and that would be stupid."

Zoey shrugged. "Then see if one of your friends can come with us. He can stay with me at the house while you're doing your thing. How long do you think we'll need to be there? Can one of your teammates take the time off with you?"

Of course. He should've thought of that. "I'm thinking we could leave on a Thursday and be back by Sunday night. There might be other short trips I'll need to take up there to finalize any paperwork or something, but Kenneth might be able to send the papers I need through the mail, and I can get them notarized down here and send them back. Who would you feel most comfortable going with us?"

"Phantom," Zoey said without hesitation.

Bubba was surprised. "Really?"

"Yeah. Ace, Gumby, and Rocco have their own families to worry about, and while I like and respect Rex, Phantom still kinda makes me nervous. He's super intense about nearly everything. But that's *why* I'd feel safe with him around. Nervous, but safe. He doesn't miss much, and his grumpy exterior will make even the most curious townsperson think twice about asking me a million questions."

Bubba nodded. He didn't like that she wasn't completely comfortable around Phantom, but he knew that was just his friend's effect on people. Besides, maybe a trip like this would let them get to know each other a little better, and she'd become more at ease with him.

"I'll ask him if he's free this weekend to go up there with us," Bubba said.

"Really?"

"Really."

"Mark?"

"Yeah, Zo?"

"I'm proud of you."

"Why?"

"Because you're doing the right thing. Malcom has been a part of your dad's business since he graduated from high school. I don't really like him much, but he really deserves it. If you're not keeping your share, I don't want mine either. Maybe I can sell it to Sean or something."

"Are you sure? You'd be giving up a lot of money in the long run," Bubba warned.

"I'm sure," Zoey said. "I've got all I need right here." Then she lowered her head and snuggled back into him.

Bubba knew he was the luckiest son-of-a-bitch to walk the planet. "I'll make the arrangements today. Make sure you warn Jess you won't be around."

"I will. I have no doubt that Caite and the others can pop in to check on her. What time is it?" Zoey asked.

Bubba was beginning to recognize that gleam in her eyes. "Eight-fifteen. Why?"

"Oh, no reason," she said as she inched her way down his body. "It's just that I've never done this and figure maybe you've got a bit of time before you have to leave for work to teach me?"

Bubba inhaled sharply as her hand closed around his quickly hardening cock. "I can be late," he choked out.

Zoey laughed. "Good. Tell me if I do it wrong."

For the next twenty minutes, Bubba could think of nothing else but how good his woman's mouth and hands felt on him. And he told her afterward that she'd done absolutely everything exactly right.

"Relax," Zoey ordered Mark when he squeezed her hand tightly as they made their way through the Juneau airport later that week. Phantom walked behind them as silent as his nickname implied. She knew Mark was keyed up, but they'd arrived without any issues and hadn't told anyone they were on their way.

But she knew better than he did how fast word could spread through the small town. She'd already seen two people she knew in the airport, and she had a feeling Malcom and Sean would know they were there before they arrived at Heritage Plastics.

Malcom had moved out of the apartment he'd been renting and into his dad's house after the reading of the will. Zoey and Mark hadn't planned on going to the house today, but instead, after visiting the factory, and hopefully setting up a meeting with Sean, Malcom, and Kenneth, they'd go to what was now Zoey's house and crash.

"Maybe this was a bad idea," Mark said under his breath as they waited in line at the car rental place, and after she'd said hello to yet another person she knew.

"It's fine," Zoey soothed.

"Mark Wright? Is that you?" a feminine voice called out.

Zoey turned to see Heidi Reynolds, a girl they'd graduated from high school with.

"Yeah...um...I'm sorry, I don't remember your name," Mark said, holding on to Zoey's hand as if it were a life line.

"Seriously? We only were in the same class for twelve years," the other woman trilled. "I'm Heidi. Heidi Reynolds. I can't believe you don't remember me. We went out our senior year. I'm sure you remember *that*." She winked suggestively.

Mark's tone didn't change. "No, I'm sorry, I don't."

Heidi looked taken aback. "Oh, well...anyway. I'm sorry about your dad."

Zoey was used to being ignored. Since she wasn't a "local," meaning she hadn't lived in Juneau her entire life, many people, especially those from her high school class, tended to dismiss her. It was ridiculous, really. She'd lived in the city for the last fifteen years, she would've thought that was long enough to lose the "newcomer" title, but apparently not.

"Thanks," Mark told her. Then he turned his back on Heidi and wrapped his arm around Zoey's waist, pulling her into his side. She couldn't help but grin at his actions. She was sure Heidi probably had a sour look on her face. She never did like being ignored, especially not by someone as good-looking as Mark.

"This is how it's going to be the entire time we're here, isn't it?" Mark asked after Heidi finally got the hint and walked away.

"Pretty much," Zoey told him with a shrug. "Colin did his best to let everyone know how amazing you were. He told stories about you to anyone and everyone who'd listen. You're a hometown hero, Mark. You're going to have to get used to it."

He sighed and pressed his lips together. "This is part of the reason why I never came home. I knew it was going to be like this. I mean, saying hello is one thing, but flirting with me or going overboard with the hero shit is too much."

"We won't be here that long," Zoey said, trying her best to soothe him.

"Good."

The person in front of them in line got his rental car keys and Mark approached the counter. Zoey stepped back while he dealt with the paperwork and payment. She turned to say something to Phantom and saw that he wasn't paying attention to her or Mark, but instead was on constant lookout. As if someone was going to jump out of nowhere and ambush them.

But then again, she supposed that had actually happened to them before.

Sighing, because it was obvious this wasn't going to be a relaxing trip, not with both Mark and Phantom on high alert, Zoey turned back to Mark.

He was accepting the keys to a mid-size SUV from the employee at the rental place. He wrapped his arm back around her waist and the three of them walked out of the small airport. The weather was cooler than it had been a month ago when they'd been stranded, but snow had yet to start falling in the area. Zoey was glad for that, as it would make it easier to get around.

They got settled in the car and Mark headed out of the parking lot.

"Are we still going to the factory first?" Zoey asked.

"Yeah," Mark replied. "I'd like to see it, and I'm guessing that's where we'll find Sean and Malcom. I want to get a meeting with them nailed down as soon as possible. The sooner I take care of this, the sooner we can get back to California."

"Are you really that concerned something will happen?" Zoey asked.

"I can't explain it, but there's just something about being back here that makes the hair on the back of my neck stand up," Mark said. "Not to mention that after we'd landed and I turned my phone back on, I had a message from Tex. He said that he finally found Eva Dawkins. I didn't want to mention it until we were out of the airport."

"He did?" Zoey asked with wide eyes. "Holy crap. What'd she say? Who hired her? Why'd she leave us in the wilderness?"

Mark squeezed her hand. "Easy, Zo. I don't know. He said he'd found her, but he hadn't had a chance to talk to her yet. He was sending someone to pick her up then he was going to question her."

"Pick her up? What does that mean?"

Mark chuckled. "Not what you think. Just that Tex knows people everywhere. He's getting a retired military guy he knows who lives in Anchorage to head to where Tex last pinpointed her. Once he convinces her that nothing's going to happen to her or her kids, he's going to connect her with Tex. Once *that* happens, and he finds out, finally, who was behind all this shit, he'll let me know. Until then, we just need to be extra careful."

"Do you think going to the factory is a good idea then?" Phantom asked from the back seat. "If someone's pissed that they didn't get a piece of your old man's pie, seeing you could make them act. The last thing we need is for someone to bring a weapon to the factory and start shooting up the place."

"We just landed. And although I know word travels fast, I think we'll be okay for now. Tomorrow might be a different story. I'm just going to meet with Sean and Malcom real fast, set up a meeting for tomorrow, probably at Kenneth Eklund's office, sign the necessary papers, then we'll be out of here."

Mark sounded wary but calm, and that made Zoey relax a little.

"I just need you to keep your eye on Zoey. If anything does go down, get her out of there."

"Of course," Phantom said, brushing his friend's words away as if he were annoyed he'd even said them. "Just watch *your* back."

Shivering at the conversation, and not wanting to think of anything happening to anyone, Zoey did her best to put it out of her mind. Mark reached over and turned up the heat in the car, and just like that, Zoey's mood was lifted.

He was always so considerate of her. It was hard to believe that he was hers.

They pulled up to the large factory on the outskirts of town and the three of them walked inside the building. After checking in with the security officer at the front, Zoey and Phantom were shown to a small room off to the side of the lobby, and Mark disappeared into the depths of the building.

"Will he be all right?" Zoey asked after she and Phantom had been left alone.

"Of course," Phantom said, but she could see the worry in his eyes.

Not able to sit still, Zoey paced while they waited for Mark to return.

"It's good to see you," Sean said as he shook Bubba's hand. "This is a surprise."

"Yeah, well, I've been talking to both you and Malcom every day for the last few weeks, I decided I needed to get up here and see to things in person."

"I wish you would've let us know you were coming," his brother said.

Bubba shrugged. "It was kind of a spur-of-the-moment thing. Zoey wanted to get some more of her stuff and see about getting the house on the market."

"Things are going well between you two then?" his brother asked.

"Very well," Bubba said with a smile.

"Seems as if your adventure in the wilds of Alaska was good for your love life," Sean joked.

Bubba stared at his dad's friend incredulously. "I can't believe you just said that."

As if he realized how horrible his words had been, Sean blushed. "Sorry, I didn't mean it like that. I'm just so relieved that things turned out all right and the two of you are okay."

Bubba eyed the man suspiciously. He knew Sean was pissed that his pop had left most of his part of the business to someone other than him. He'd put his blood, sweat, and tears into the company, and it couldn't have sat well that Colin wasn't leaving *him* the business.

"Anyway, I'm assuming you didn't come all this way to talk about inventory and about changing the shift times, like we talked about in the last phone call," Malcom said.

"No, you're right. I'm happy to sign any papers you guys have for me while I'm here, but I wanted to see if you were both free tomorrow to meet with me and Kenneth."

"The lawyer?" Sean asked. "Everything all right?"

"Yeah. So tomorrow? Maybe sometime in the morning, so I can help Zoey with her house?"

"Sure," Sean said, nodding. "Ten work?"

"Ten's perfect," Bubba said. "Mal?"

"I guess so. You're being mighty secretive. Why don't you just spit it out now instead of being all dramatic about it?"

Bubba shrugged. "I want to sell my shares back to you both. Zoey does too. It's more than obvious that the two of you know what you're doing here, and having to stop and talk to me about it and get my approval is just slowing things down. It's only fair."

Both men simply stared at him for a long moment. Bubba couldn't tell what either was thinking. "I'm going to talk to Kenneth about the details and how it'll work. I figured you guys would be happy about this...but by your reactions, now I'm not so sure."

Sean was the first to recover. He shook his head. "Sorry, Mark. It's just...this is a surprise."

"I know, and I'm sorry. I just don't have the time or energy to devote to the business like I should. I know Pop left part of it to me, but the two of you will do a much better job than I ever could. It's just not in my blood like it is yours." Bubba looked at his brother and waited for him to say something.

Eventually, Malcom frowned. "This is really coming out of left field, bro. I'm not sure what to say."

"Just think about it," Bubba said. "We can talk about the specifics and details tomorrow."

"All right."

"I'll see you both at ten then," Bubba said and turned to leave. He almost turned back to tell them about Tex, and how he'd found the pilot who'd stranded them, but something held him back. He could get into that tomorrow at the lawyer's office.

He walked quickly back to where he'd left Zoey with Phantom, feeling lighter than he had in almost a month. It wasn't as if he didn't appreciate that his pop had left him part of his legacy, but the truth of the matter was, he didn't need it. Nor did he want it. He felt a little guilty about taking anything from his dad. He could've been a better son, and even though he was trying to get over the guilt for not coming home before it was too late, he was still struggling.

Simply seeing Zoey made him sag a little in relief. He couldn't believe how much she'd come to mean to him in such a short time.

"How'd it go?" Zoey asked, rushing up to him in concern.

"It's good. I need to call Kenneth and set something up, but I said I'd meet them at the lawyer's office tomorrow around ten."

"I'll drive while you call him," Phantom said, holding out his hand for the keys.

Without hesitation, Bubba handed over the keys to the rental. "Come on, let's get out of here," he said, putting his hand on Zoey's lower back as they walked toward the door.

After saying hello to several people on their way out, and dealing with more condolences, Bubba was definitely ready to get to Zoey's house.

He called Kenneth on the way, relayed his wishes, and the lawyer said he'd draw up the papers and have them waiting the next morning.

Phantom drove up a steep hill to the house Zoey had been renting from his father, and just like the first time he'd seen it, Bubba had to bite his tongue to keep his opinions to himself. The house wasn't in the best shape. There were actual small trees growing out of the gutters. That wasn't too surprising, since the area was wet most of the year, but Bubba wished the house Zoey had been living in had been better maintained. The shutters on the windows were falling off and the grass didn't look like it had been mowed for at least a month.

There were old newspapers on the porch, and it was more than obvious to anyone driving by that the house wasn't being lived in.

"Well, shit," Zoey said as they pulled alongside it. There was no driveway, so Phantom parked on the side of the street in front of the house. "It usually looks much better than this," she said with a frown.

"I thought you'd paid for someone to check on the house?" Bubba asked.

"I did." Zoey sighed, and they all climbed out of the SUV. She took out her keys and made her way up the walk. "I thought it was all arranged. I'm going to have to call the real estate agent Tracy hired to look after the house and see what the hell happened. Maybe it was a miscommunication issue. Here's to hoping the electricity is still on."

She unlocked the door and started to enter, but Bubba gently stopped her. "Let me and Phantom check things out first."

She frowned, but Bubba was relieved when she nodded and stepped back.

"We'll just be a second."

Zoey pulled out her phone and pressed a few buttons before looking at both him and Phantom. "I've got 9-1-1 at the ready. All I have to do is hit connect."

Bubba would've chuckled, but Zoey was completely serious. He couldn't help himself. It had been too long since he'd kissed her, and she was completely adorable right now. He leaned down and palmed the side of her neck and tilted her head up to him.

He kissed her long and hard, thrilled when she reciprocated. It wasn't until Phantom cleared his throat impatiently that Bubba pulled back.

"You have your knife?" Zoey asked after licking her lips sensuously.

Bubba wanted nothing more than to push her up against the side of the house and taste her again, but he forced himself to take a step back. "Of course. I took it out of my checked bag as soon as it came off the conveyor belt."

"Good. Okay, I'll wait here."

Nodding at her, Bubba turned to Phantom. "Ready?"

The other man had his own KA-BAR knife in his hand and looked more than prepared to kick some ass. "Ready."

There was a saying, never bring a knife to a gun fight, implying that the person who brought the knife would be at a disadvantage, but both him and Phantom were more than lethal with their knives and had, more than once, either disarmed someone who had a gun or at least wounded them badly enough that shooting someone was the least of their worries.

Making his way through the house, Bubba kept his attention on clearing each of the rooms, making sure no one was lying in wait.

When they'd made it through the tiny house and they'd both put their knives back in the sheaths at the smalls of their backs, Phantom said, "Didn't Zoey say she'd also been paying someone to start packing up her stuff?"

Frowning, Bubba nodded. "Yeah. Doesn't look like much has been packed, that's for sure. Fuck."

Phantom clicked one of the switches and the room filled with light. "At least the electricity works," he said with a shrug.

"Probably because she was paying the electric company directly," Bubba grumbled. He headed for the front porch and let out a small sigh of relief when he saw Zoey standing exactly where he'd left her.

"Is everything all right?" she asked anxiously.

"Yeah, Zo. Everything's good," Bubba reassured her.

She nodded and pocketed her phone. "You say that, but your tone of voice says differently."

"It's just...whoever you were paying to get your stuff packed up most likely took your money and didn't do a damn thing."

Zoey simply sighed. "I was afraid of that. I'll call the real estate lady tomorrow and see what's up. I set up everything through Tracy, and she was supposed to get in touch with the realtor and they were going to see to it."

"Tracy?" Bubba asked.

"The lawyer's wife."

"Oh, yeah, that's right."

"Sean offered to have *his* wife help. I should've taken him up on it," Zoey said with a frown.

"I can also talk to Kenneth tomorrow and see what's up," Phantom told her.

"Thanks. I'd appreciate that."

Zoey walked into the house and put her purse down on a table against the wall and wandered into the kitchen. "I'm guessing there's not much to eat. Who wants to go out and get dinner?"

Bubba looked meaningfully at Phantom.

His friend smirked and said, "I guess that'd be me."

"Do you like seafood?" she asked Phantom.

"Love it," he replied.

"Good. There's a place called The Salmon Spot, and it's one of my favorite places to eat here in Juneau. I'll call and order us a mix of stuff and we can all share. Is that okay?"

"Of course," Bubba answered. He reached into his pocket and pulled out his wallet, grabbing his credit card and handing it to her. "Here, use this."

Zoey didn't reach for it. "I can pay," she said stubbornly.

"I know you can. But you aren't," Bubba said sternly.

They stared at each other for a long moment, a battle

of wills Bubba knew without a doubt he'd win. Then she sighed and snatched the plastic out of his hand. "Fine. But next time's on me."

Bubba didn't agree or disagree.

She wasn't paying. No way. It might be a little chauvinistic of him, but he was the guy, he paid for their meals. Period.

He listened with half an ear as she ordered their dinner. She gave Phantom very detailed directions on how to get to the restaurant, as if he was going to get lost and somehow drive his way to Seattle or something, which was impossible, as there were no roads in or out of the capital city. It was cute how she constantly forgot he and his friends were Navy SEALs. They'd navigated their way around the most remote cities and jungles with nothing but a compass, and sometimes not even that.

Bubba had a feeling Phantom would take longer to return simply to give him some time alone with Zoey.

The second the door had closed behind his teammate, Bubba took Zoey into his arms and backed into the living area. He fell onto the couch, Zoey still in his arms, loving how she giggled at his antics.

"Mark! Let me go. I need to get up and see about this disaster of a house."

"In a minute," he said, nuzzling the skin behind her ear.

Zoey turned her head, giving him room while saying, "We don't have time for this. The restaurant isn't too far away, Phantom'll be back before too long."

"We won't go too far," he told her. "I've been around you all day, but I still miss you."

He felt her melt in his arms. "That was sweet," she said softly.

"It's true. Now...kiss me, woman," he said, purposely lowering his voice so he sounded gruff.

She laughed again and sat up in his lap so she was straddling him. "With pleasure," she said before lowering her lips to his.

They made out on her couch for several minutes. Bubba knew he'd never get enough of her curves under his hands. He loved everything about her. Her shape. The little moans she made deep in her throat. The way she couldn't sit still as he teased her nipples—

Bubba froze when his thoughts sank in.

"What? What's wrong?" Zoey asked, looking worried.

"Nothing's wrong," he reassured her quickly, hating that he'd scared her for even a second. "I just...I love you, Zo."

She blinked at him. Her eyes wide as if she couldn't believe what he'd just said. "You do?"

"Yeah."

"Why?"

"Why?" Bubba laughed. "You want me to list all the reasons?"

She shook her head. "No, that came out wrong. I mean, are you sure?"

Zoey was freaking adorable, and Bubba felt freer and lighter than he had in a long time. "I'm sure, sweetheart."

"Well, that's a relief. Because I think I've loved you since we were stuck in the woods together. Which is insane, but honestly, with how much your dad talked about you and how awesome you turned out to be, how could I *not* fall in love with you? He had a picture of you that you sent him on his mantel, and every time I walked by it, I imagined what it would be like to see you again, even though I knew you weren't coming to Juneau anytime soon. Then your dad got sick, and I went to visit my mom, and...there you were. I didn't know what to say to you in the airport and just knew I'd made a fool of myself." She paused and winced. "Just like I'm doing right now."

"You're not making a fool of yourself," Bubba said.

She rolled her eyes and shook her head at him, and Bubba couldn't stop the laugh that burst forth.

"I even love it when you roll your eyes at me. You did that back when we were stranded, you know. I loved it then, and I love it now."

"You should know, I don't deserve you. But I swear that I'm going to do everything in my power to make sure you're happy. Most of the time I feel like I'm out of my depth around you. Like I'm this naïve little girl and you're this larger-than-life hero. But just know that I'm trying to toughen up. To get more worldly."

"Don't change, Zoey. I love you just how you are."

She stared at him for a second, then tears filled her eyes.

Bubba drew her down against him and didn't bother to tell her not to cry. He was overwhelmed with emotion as well. Zoey loved him back. He was going to spend the rest of his life with her, come hook or crook. No one would take her from him, and he wouldn't do anything that would make her want to leave him.

Easing her back so he could see her eyes, he said, "Being with a SEAL isn't easy, Zo. When I get called on a mission, I have to go. I can't tell you where I'll be or how long I'll be gone. Can you deal with that?"

"Yes."

Her answer was immediate and heartfelt.

"I appreciate that, but I want to make sure you know

what you're getting into with me before we make this permanent."

Her eyes widened. "Permanent?"

"Yeah. If, after a few missions, you still feel the same way about me and my profession, I'm gonna ask you to marry me. Our relationship has been fast, and while I'd marry you tomorrow, I want you to be sure."

"I'm sure," she said without any hesitation. "Mark, I've crushed on you for over thirteen years. You just said you love me and want to marry me. I'm not going to let something like your job get between us."

"Caite and the others will always be there when we're away," he told her. "You need anything, you can absolutely call them."

"I know. They're awesome. They've all been texting me nonstop since the barbeque. I've never had friends like them. They accepted me without reservations. Unlike anyone else I've known in my life, aside from your dad. I've always been the newcomer. The outsider. But to them, I'm already one of their inner circle. It's crazy, and so nice I can't even describe it."

"I'm glad. Zo?"

"Yeah?"

"How much longer do you think Phantom's going to be?"

She smiled. "At least another ten minutes, I'd say."

"Good. Time enough for me to get you off at least once."

"Mark! No, I—"

Her words were cut off on a groan when Bubba's fingers deftly undid the button on her jeans. He turned and dumped her on her back on the couch and slipped his hand inside her panties, groaning when he felt how slippery she already was.

As it turned out, it took Phantom another thirteen and a half minutes to return, but by then, Zoey was sitting primly upright on the couch once more with Bubba by her side. Her cheeks were a little flushed, but otherwise no one would be able to tell minutes ago she'd been writhing and screaming his name as she came all over his fingers.

Surreptitiously licking his finger, Bubba winked at Zoey when she blushed once more. Being with Zoey was exciting...and fun. He couldn't remember the last time being with a woman had been fun. He couldn't wait until later that night when they went to bed. He wanted to be inside her more than he could explain.

Forcing himself to be patient, Bubba went to the sink to wash his hands and help with setting up dinner.

The seafood smelled delicious, and Bubba realized his stomach was growling. This trip to Juneau hadn't turned out so bad so far. Tomorrow, he'd take care of his inheritance, then he and the love of his life could get back to California and get on with their lives.

Five hours later, Bubba was exhausted. He'd been helping Zoey pack up her things and she had the energy of that popular little pink bunny. They'd put things in piles to keep, donate, or throw away, and she'd been making a list of things that needed to be fixed before the house could be put on the market.

"Zo, enough, I'm beat," Bubba told her when it looked like she was going to start tackling the kitchen next.

She looked at him in surprise. "Oh, what time is it?"

"Late."

Zoey looked at her watch and winced. "Shit. I had no idea. I'm so sorry. Go on to bed, I'll be there as soon as I get through this one cabinet."

Bubba shook his head and took her by the hand and practically dragged her toward the back of the house where the master bedroom was located. Phantom had given up and said his good nights about two hours ago. He was probably dead to the world in the guest room upstairs. Bubba knew if he left Zoey on her own in the kitchen, he wouldn't see her the rest of the night. One thing about her, once she got her mind set on something, it was as if she had blinders on. It was both endearing and frustrating at the same time.

"Mark! Seriously, I need to finish sorting the cabinet. It'll drive me crazy if I leave it half-finished."

"Nope. I'm taking you to bed. Right now."

She didn't say anything, and he looked back at her as he entered her room. She was smirking, and he recognized the look of lust on her face.

"Take me to bed or lose me forever," she said dramatically.

Bubba frowned. "What?"

"Oh my God, you don't recognize that movie quote?"

"Obviously not," Bubba told her as he put his hands on the bottom of her T-shirt and slowly started pulling it upward.

"It's from *Top Gun*," Zoey told him, her voice muffled from the shirt being removed over her head.

"Hmmm." Bubba made the noise in the back of his throat, his attention on her tits and how they jiggled in her bra.

He couldn't take his eyes from her as she reached down

and undid the button on her jeans. "Am I the only one who's going to be naked here?" she asked as she climbed onto the mattress.

Quick as a flash, Bubba got his clothes off and was hovering over her. He was already hard and ready to go, but as usual, he wanted to make sure she got off first. His mouth was watering with the need to taste her. He eased his way down her body, his eyes glued to her own.

The smile fled her face and she licked her lips in anticipation of his touch.

"I love you, Zoey," he told her, before he buried his face between her legs.

"I love you," she replied.

Her words echoing in his head, he centered his attention on the prize in front of him. He'd never get tired of this. Of her. He licked his lips, and got to work showing Zoey exactly how much he loved her.

An hour later, with Zoey curled into his arms, snoring lightly, Bubba couldn't get his mind to shut off so he could get some sleep. Things were so great. Zoey was moving permanently to California, selling this house, packing up her stuff. She loved him, and he loved her. He wouldn't have to deal with the pesky daily things that came up with his pop's business after tomorrow.

But he hadn't heard from Tex again. And he had no idea if selling his ownership in the company would make whoever had tried to kill him happy or not. He hated not having the information he needed to make decisions. That's how people ended up dead. He felt as if his life was just starting, now that he'd met Zoey. The last thing he wanted was a lethal surprise to be waiting in the wings.

After his meeting with Malcom, Sean, and Kenneth in the morning, he'd call Tex and see what the man had been able to find out. He needed this situation to be done and over with once and for all. Only then could he truly relax.

It took another thirty minutes or so, but Bubba finally fell asleep. The heavy weight of Zoey comforting in his arms.

CHAPTER EIGHTEEN

"This place is called GonZo Café?" Phantom asked the next morning.

Zoey nodded. "Yeah, weird name, but excellent food. Their breakfasts are the best. I'll go shopping later today and get some stuff to tide us over for the rest of the weekend, but trust me, you're gonna love their food."

"Fine. Bubba, you good staying here?"

"Yup."

"He's good, but I'm starving," Zoey teased. "More movement, less talk, please."

She knew Mark was laughing at her, but she didn't turn to look at him. She was in the best mood this morning. Even though she hadn't been able to finish going through the kitchen and figuring out what she wanted to keep and what she was going to donate to Glory Hall and other homeless shelters in town, she couldn't be upset with the way the evening had ended.

Mark loved her.

It was almost unbelievable.

She'd never been happier.

Even though Mark was going to talk to Kenneth, she still wanted to call Tracy and find out what happened with the realtor who was supposed to arrange to get the house staged and ready to sell, but even that couldn't dim her happiness this morning.

Remembering the way Mark had gone at her the night before was almost embarrassing, but so freaking hot. Every time he ate her out, he made it seem as if he couldn't get enough. She had nothing to compare it to, but she didn't think most men were that enthusiastic about the task. She was very lucky.

She was still sore between her legs from the way he'd taken her hard and fast after she'd come on his mouth and fingers. It was sexy as hell, and it was hard to believe this was her life.

Nothing could get Zoey down this morning. Not even Phantom being grumpy about having to go out in the cold and pick up more food.

"You owe me for this," Phantom said as he got ready to head out the door.

"I know. I'm going to make a pecan pie this afternoon. Trust me, you'll love my pie."

"That's *my* pie," Mark said under his breath as Phantom turned to go.

Zoey was about to make a smartass remark about Mark quoting from the movie *The Revenge of the Nerds* when Phantom spoke.

"Watch your six. The air feels heavy today."

Zoey frowned. She didn't know what that meant, but Mark obviously did, because he said, "I will. You too."

Nodding, Phantom went out the door and closed it behind him.

"What was that about?"

Mark shrugged. "Sometimes we get feelings about things. Phantom's obviously feeling uneasy about something."

"Do you think you should postpone your meeting today?" Zoey asked worriedly.

"Absolutely not. The sooner I can get this done, and we get things here at the house wrapped up, the sooner we can get on with the rest of our lives. Together."

Zoey smiled and wrapped her arms around Mark's waist. She leaned into him and felt his cock stir. "I'm all for that," she said seductively. "Think you have time to give me another lesson on oral sex before Phantom gets back?"

Mark groaned, and she felt him twitch against her stomach. "I don't think you need any more lessons, wench. You're already perfect, and you know it."

Zoey knew he was being generous, but she didn't call him on it. She went up on her tiptoes and kissed him as he bent his head toward her.

They were so into each other that they didn't hear the back door open until it was too late. Mark spun around and shoved Zoey so fast, she didn't realize what he was doing until she was behind him.

"Jeez, Malcom! You scared me," Mark said, relief easy to hear in his voice.

Zoey's eyes about bugged out of her head when Malcom raised a pistol and aimed it right at his twin.

"Good. You *should* be scared," he said evenly.

Every muscle in Mark's body tightened, and Zoey had a sinking feeling that Phantom's mysterious feeling had been right on the money. Shit.

Bubba stared at his brother, his heart breaking at the realization that the person who wanted him dead was his brother. His *twin*. He'd been leaning toward Sean being the culprit. Not Malcom.

He held up his hands. "Easy, bro. We can work this out."

"It's too late for that. If you had just stayed gone, this wouldn't be happening right now."

"How do you figure?" Bubba asked. He needed to drag this out. The longer he could keep Malcom talking, the faster Phantom would return. Between the two of them, they could easily take Malcom down without anyone getting hurt. But at the moment, all Bubba was concerned about was Zoey. He couldn't move without putting her at risk, and that was the last thing he was going to do.

"With you and that bitch dead, I would've gotten all your money and the shares Pop left you, and *she* wouldn't've been around to collect what should've been mine."

His brother's reasoning was a little off. He was right in that if Mark was dead, his will left everything he had to his only living relative—Malcom. They may not have talked much, but he was blood. But if Zoey died, the house, money, and part of the business Pop had left to her would go to *her* relatives.

Maybe, in Malcom's mind, it was enough that Zoey herself wouldn't get it.

He needed to stall some more. "You wanted this house?" Bubba asked his brother.

"Fuck this house," Malcom sneered. "I don't give a shit about this dump. But I could've sold it and gotten the cash, just like she's planning on doing. That money should be *mine*."

"I told you why I was here yesterday," Bubba said. "At ten o'clock today, you can have what you wanted."

"No, I can't!" Malcom yelled, the gun wavering slightly as he spoke.

Bubba pushed Zoey farther behind him. If the gun went off, the last thing he wanted was Zoey accidentally getting shot.

"You want to sell your shares to me and Sean? What a joke! I don't have the money to buy you out. And even if I did, I shouldn't *have* to. Who was the son who was here when Pop needed help firing an employee? Me! Who was the son who was here to work a shift when someone didn't show up? Me! Who was the son who listened for hours and fucking hours as Pop talked about his precious business plan, and gave him advice on how to make more money? Fucking *me*! That's who. Not *you*. Not the golden boy who was off gallivanting around the globe playing hero. I'm gonna get your share of what should've been mine—without paying!"

Malcom's voice had risen with each sentence until he was practically screaming at Bubba by the end.

"If you'd hurry up and quit talking about it and just fucking shoot him already, this would be done," a feminine voice sounded from behind Bubba.

Shit. Things had just gone from concerning to critical in a heartbeat. Bubba spun sideways, keeping Zoey at his back.

Tracy Eklund was standing just inside the living room. They hadn't locked the door when Phantom had left, and she'd obviously just waltzed right on in.

He'd told Zoey that most people killed for money or sex, and it looked like in this case, it was both.

"Let me guess, you and my brother have been having an affair."

Tracy looked smug but didn't reply.

When Malcom spoke, Bubba turned his attention back to him. The situation sucked. They were in the middle of the two people who'd done their best to kill them. He couldn't protect Zoey from both Malcom and Tracy at the same time. *Shit, shit, shit.*

"I love her. She's the other half of my soul," Malcom said.

"She's way older than you," Bubba said, trying to get his brother to think clearly. "I'm guessing she approached *you*, didn't she?"

"Shut up!" Tracy screeched. "I'm not *that* much older than Mal. I'm only forty!"

"With those gray roots, you could've fooled me," Zoey said. "Kenneth's...what? In his fifties, like Colin was? What happened, your gravy train dry up?"

With that, Tracy reached over the counter and grabbed a big kitchen knife from the block that Zoey had wanted to pack away the night before but hadn't gotten the chance. "Shut up, bitch! You're nothing but a *leech*. Latching onto Colin and taking his money from the people who should have it. Namely, Malcom!"

"Easy," Bubba said, holding up a hand toward Tracy.

"I'm gonna carve you up, bitch," Tracy said with narrowed eyes fixed on Zoey.

Bubba put his hands behind his back and clasped Zoey's forearms. To Malcom and Tracy, it probably looked like they were holding hands behind his back...but Bubba was making sure he had a good grip on the woman he loved so if he had to fling her out of the way in a split second, he could.

Bubba's phone vibrated on the kitchen counter with an incoming call, the sound irritating, but everyone ignored it.

"Yeah, *she* came to *me* when we started seeing each other," Malcom said, the pistol wavering. "And things were great. But then you emailed Pop and mentioned a possible visit. He was so fucking happy, it was disgusting! He made an appointment that same day to change his will, swearing that if you came back and saw how great the business was doing, you'd fall in love with it and move home. He was delusional! Everyone knew you weren't coming back. But it was clear then that I had to do something."

Bubba's blood ran cold. "What'd you do, Mal?"

"Shut up, Malcom," Tracy warned.

Malcom ignored her. He stared into his brother's eyes. "She said it was the only way. That you'd always be the golden boy. His favorite. That I'd never measure up. I *had* to!"

"What'd you do?" Bubba demanded.

"It was only a little at first, to see what it would do. It worked really well. He got sick almost immediately…"

Bubba heard Zoey inhale sharply, but she didn't speak. He felt sick. "*You killed Pop?*"

"I had to!" Malcom shouted. "Tracy said it would be easy. That he wouldn't feel a thing!"

"But he did, didn't he?" Zoey asked softly. "Colin suffered. He must've been in so much pain."

"Yeah, but that was because I messed up and didn't give him enough. When you left to go visit your mom, it was time. I gave him enough arsenic to make his heart stop."

Bubba clenched his teeth together so hard they hurt.

"And it was all for *nothing*, because you guys didn't

fucking die!" Tracy spat out. "You *and* that bitch pilot were supposed to die after takeoff. The guys I hired to sabotage the plane took my fucking money and ran. Leaving you out in the wilderness to die was just the ridiculous plan we concocted so Eva would take the job. She had no idea that flight was supposed to be her last."

Bubba couldn't believe how heartless the woman in front of him was. She not only wanted to kill him and Zoey for money, but had no qualms in killing an innocent woman as well. Well, Eva wasn't completely innocent, she'd gone along with the plan to strand him and Zoey, but she hadn't outright killed them.

He felt Zoey shifting behind him, and he panicked for a moment, until he realized she was simply pressing herself even closer to his back. That was okay with him. The closer she was, the easier it would be to protect her.

The fact that he had to protect her from his own flesh and blood was insane. But at the moment, Malcom's pistol was more of a danger than the knife Tracy was holding. "I guess you were the one to tell Malcom what was in Pop's will, huh?" he asked her.

"Of course. I'm my husband's assistant, after all. Who do you think prepares all his documents?"

Bubba's phone vibrated again, and he wished like hell he could answer it. Whoever was on the other end was very insistent on talking to him.

"Kill them," Tracy ordered Malcom. "This has to end *now*."

"How exactly do you think this is going to end?" Bubba asked. He felt Zoey shift against him once more...then realized she was slowly taking his KA-BAR out of the sheath at the small of his back.

God, she was smart as hell—and also scaring the hell out of him.

"If you kill us, what are you going to do with our bodies? How are you going to explain our deaths? Sean and Kenneth are expecting me at the office in about an hour and a half. And you might get *my* shares of the business, but that won't give you enough to override Sean. And Zoey's will go to her mom. What then, Mal? You gonna kill Sean too? Then his wife, since *his* shares will probably go to her? When does it end? When will you get to stop killing?

"It's over, bro. Put down the gun and let's figure this out. Together."

"No. It'll work. It has to!"

"Don't listen to him, Malcom. He's trying to confuse you," Tracy told her younger lover.

"How am I doing that?" Bubba asked. "I'm telling him the *truth*. He wants the business, but if he kills us, he's *never* going to get it."

"We don't want the fucking business!" Tracy yelled a little hysterically. "I've got a buyer already lined up for our half of Heritage Plastics. He's ready to pay cash. We'll be able to leave this shit-hole town and start over somewhere else."

Bubba turned his head to stare at his brother. "I can't fucking believe this. If you wanted to leave, why didn't you just *leave?*"

"It wasn't that simple," Malcom argued, the despair and frustration easy to hear. "I'm not like *you*. I'm not strong. I didn't have a choice but to stay and work for Pop."

"There are always choices," Bubba said sadly. "And I can't believe you thought that killing me, your own flesh and blood, was your best option."

"Tracy said—"

"Listen to yourself, bro," Bubba demanded forcefully, interrupting him. "Forget about *her* for a second. She's a desperate woman, sick of life with her boring husband and wanting some excitement. She picked you, and you fell for it—hook, line, and sinker. She talked you into killing *Pop*! Into trying to kill *me*. Look me in the eye and tell me you're okay with killing me."

Bubba stared at his brother and willed him to snap out of whatever trance Tracy Eklund had cast over him.

Behind his back, he felt Zoey slip the handle of his knife into his palm.

Everything slowed down then. The familiar weight of the weapon in his hand made him feel a hundred times more confident in the outcome of the situation. He could take Malcom out with a flick of his wrist—and then deal with Tracy.

But the thought of hurting or killing his brother was devastating. No matter what decisions he'd made in the past—even though he'd admitted to killing their dad, and what he was planning right that second—Malcom was his brother. His twin.

"It's over, bro," Bubba said softly. "This needs to end now. I'll help you. Get you the best counsel possible. You weren't the brains behind this, we both know it. You'll probably get some jail time, but I'll do everything in my power to help you make a deal. A few years. That's it. Put down the gun, Mal."

"Don't you listen to him, Malcom," Tracy bitched. "*You* killed Colin. There won't be any deals. And *you* were the one who hired that pilot. He's lying to you. You're the one who'll go down for this, not *me*. Kill him now and we can leave tonight! We'll take the cash in Kenneth's safe and disappear."

An engine sounded from outside the house, and Bubba knew Phantom had returned. It had seemed like hours had passed since his brother appeared in the house, but he knew it had probably only been minutes.

"Do it!" Tracy screeched. "Don't be a pussy and fucking shoot him already! If you don't, you're going to jail for the rest of your life!"

Just as Malcom raised the gun once more, Bubba moved.

The knife in his hand sailed through the air and hit its mark dead on.

Even as Malcom was falling to the floor, Bubba turned and took a step toward Tracy.

But he'd been too slow. Zoey had beaten him to the punch.

He lost ten years off his life when he saw Zoey reach for Tracy's hand—the one holding the knife.

He took a step forward but Zoey was already executing the most perfect self-defense moves he'd ever seen.

As Tracy tried to bring the hand with the knife down to stab her, Zoey kneed her in the crotch as hard as she could. She obviously knew the move worked just as effectively on women as it did on men. Predictably, Tracy immediately hunched over in pain, the knife forgotten, and Zoey then rammed her knee into the older woman's face.

Tracy fell like a sack of potatoes to the floor, blood pouring from her nose, knocked out.

Zoey pried the knife out of Tracy's hand and spun as if she was ready to enter any fight going on between Bubba and his brother.

Bubba didn't have time to be impressed, because when he heard Zoey gasp and look behind him, he turned, ready to defend both himself and Zoey from Malcom.

But he didn't have to.

The knife he'd thrown into Malcom's thigh had done what he'd wanted...made Malcom drop to the floor. His brother could've started shooting wildly, but he hadn't.

Instead of training the pistol on Bubba, Malcom was holding it to his own head.

The front door opened, and Bubba knew Phantom would have his back. He didn't have to worry about Zoey, his teammate would make sure Tracy wasn't a threat.

"Put down the gun, Mal. We can work this out."

"No, we can't. She's right. I'm going down for this. All of it. As I should."

"She was the puppet master," Bubba told him. "We'll find a good lawyer who will show a jury that you were led astray. I'll even testify on your behalf."

"I will too," Zoey said from behind him.

Love swelled up inside him, but Bubba couldn't breathe. Not as long as his brother had that gun to his head.

"It's no good. I killed Pop!" A sob escaped him. "She's right about that. I could've said no. I could've stopped her when she came up with the plan to kill you and Zoey. I'm weak. And I'm tired. I'm so fucking tired."

"Tired? Mal—"

"Tired of being second best. Of this town. Of people looking at me like I'm worthless."

"No one does that," Zoey said.

"*Everyone* does that," Malcom countered. "Even you. I knew you liked Mark back in high school, but I didn't care. I wanted you for myself. But you still chose him in the end, just like everyone does. For what it's worth...I'm sorry. I'm sorry for being a dick to you, Zoey. I'm sorry for what I did to Pop. He didn't deserve it. And I'm sorry for hiring that pilot to do that to you guys."

"I forgive you," Bubba said. And he wasn't lying. He loved Malcom. He hadn't been the best brother, but then again, Bubba hadn't tried very hard to be there for Malcom either. Maybe if he'd gotten home more often, things between them would've been better. He could've seen the poison that Tracy had been to his brother.

"Thank you," Malcom said. His finger twitched on the trigger of the pistol...

And before Bubba could do more than yell "no!" the standoff was over.

Zoey screamed when the sound of the gunshot echoed through the room, and Bubba immediately turned to shield her from the horror that had unfolded in front of them.

"Oh my God! Oh my God!" Zoey chanted. "Call 9-1-1! We need to get him an ambulance."

"It's too late," Bubba told her. He didn't need to turn around to know what a bullet to the head looked like. What it did to the human body. He'd seen more than his fair share of gunshot wounds.

Walking slowly toward the front door with her, Bubba's only goal was to get Zoey away. To make sure she didn't get a glimpse of what was left of Malcom.

"I'll take care of the trash," Phantom said quietly as Bubba passed him, nodding to Tracy on the floor.

Nodding back, Bubba only stopped long enough to grab his phone from the kitchen counter. It was vibrating once again with an incoming call.

He looked down and saw that it was Tex calling. He

had a feeling the retired SEAL had finally had his talk with Eva Dawkins. But it was too late.

Feeling wrung out and empty inside, Bubba hustled Zoey out of the house. If it was up to him, neither of them would step foot inside it again. He was done with Juneau. With Alaska. It had brought him Zoey, his greatest gift, but also the greatest heartbreak of his life.

He heard Phantom talking to an emergency dispatcher from inside the house, but all Bubba could do was hold Zoey and thank God that she was all right. Malcom could've easily shot her. Or if she wasn't as fast as she'd been, Tracy could've sunk the knife into her body, killing her.

Burying his face in her hair, Bubba held on. When he began shaking, Zoey only held him tighter. He didn't know when the tears started falling from his eyes, but the woman who he loved more than anything in the world didn't let go, simply squeezed him tighter, giving him the stability he needed so he could fall apart.

CHAPTER NINETEEN

It had been a long day. The longest of Bubba's life. The police had arrived, and at first they'd thought *he'd* been the one to kill Malcom. He'd been cuffed and stuffed in the back of a police cruiser, and Zoey had absolutely lost her shit.

Apparently she knew most of the officers, and she told them if they didn't let him out, she was going to sue the hell out of them, the department, and the entire city. Bubba been proud of her, but he felt numb. He couldn't muster up the energy to be grateful when the officers had apologized and released him from the cuffs after they figured out Malcom's wound was self-inflicted.

Then he, Zoey, and Phantom had to tell their sides of the story at least four more times. Bubba'd been separated from Zoey, which had almost made him go ballistic. The detectives had asked him the same questions over and over until he wanted to scream.

Tex had gotten involved in the end, and he made some calls, and finally Bubba and Zoey had been free to leave. They were now in a hotel room in downtown

Juneau, as neither wanted to go back to her house, or his pop's.

Phantom had been typically reticent, but he'd also been a solid pillar of strength for both him and Zoey, which Bubba could never repay him for. He'd forced them both to eat something, since they'd never gotten around to eating the breakfast he'd picked up earlier. He'd called the team back in California and informed them of what had happened. Rocco had immediately offered to fly up to Alaska, but Phantom told him that wouldn't be necessary, as they'd be coming home as soon as they could.

Phantom had also called Sean Kassamali to let him know about the ordeal. He'd come down to the station and reassured Bubba that he'd take care of the business, not to worry. The ironic thing was, now that Malcom had killed himself, all of his shares in the company would go to Bubba. It was almost laughable, considering everything that had happened, but Malcom had been so sure his and Tracy's plan would work out. He didn't have a will of his own.

And since Bubba still didn't want anything to do with the business, Sean would end up owning one hundred percent of the company sooner rather than later.

Bubba was going to sell his shares to the older man for a buck...just to make it legal. Zoey planned on doing the same with her small percentage. If Malcom had come to the meeting with Kenneth, he would've found out Bubba was going to sell his shares to *him* for only a dollar as well. Not for some exorbitant price, as Malcom had assumed.

Bubba should've felt relieved he'd be done with the business once and for all, but instead he just felt sad.

"None of this should've happened," Bubba murmured.

He was sitting on the couch in the suite Phantom had

reserved for them in the hotel, and Zoey was curled up against him. The only time he felt as if he wouldn't fly into a million pieces was when she was in his arms. He'd never forget the look of despair in Malcom's eyes as he'd held that gun to his head.

Phantom stuck his head into the room. "Tex is on the phone. Feel up to talking?"

Bubba nodded. "Yeah, let's finish this."

Zoey tightened her arms around him, and her presence made this so much easier. Not okay, but better.

"You there?" Tex asked over the speakerphone.

"Yeah."

"I'm so fucking sorry I didn't get to Eva faster."

Bubba shook his head, even though he knew Tex couldn't see him. "Don't do that. This isn't your fault. It's my brother's. And Tracy's. None of this is your fault."

"You say that, but it doesn't make it true," Tex said. "Anyway, Tracy somehow knew Eva's ex. The connection is a little unclear. Malcom touched base with her for the first time and offered her money to do a job. Once she agreed, because she was desperate for cash, Tracy took over the arrangements. Apparently, Eva's ex said he'd give her kids back if she paid him three hundred thousand dollars. She, obviously, didn't have that kind of money, and Tracy and Malcom were easily able to convince her to do their dirty work.

"After leaving you guys in the middle of nowhere, Eva landed the plane in a tiny little town. The plane itself wasn't discovered until recently, confirming her story. Anyway, she went to Seattle, as she was ordered to do, to wait for things to calm down here, and was expecting to get paid for her part in the plot."

"Let me guess, she didn't get the money," Phantom said dryly.

"Nope. Tracy and Malcom had no intention of giving her any money because they thought she'd be dead right along with the two of you. In fact, there *was* no money to give her. Eva spent two weeks hitchhiking back to Anchorage. She wasn't sure what she was going to do, but that's where her kids are. She got hired at a strip club and has been living in her car."

Bubba couldn't help the twinge of pity for the woman. She'd made some horrible decisions, that couldn't be denied, but if someone took his children, he knew he'd do whatever it took to get them back. "Her kids?" he asked Tex.

"It's being taken care of."

Bubba thought back to what Tex had told them earlier. About the team of men he knew who had no problem taking care of scumbags like Eva's ex.

"The question now is...are you going to press charges?" Tex asked.

Bubba opened his mouth to respond, but Zoey beat him to it.

"No."

Bubba turned to her. "Zo—"

She held up her hand to stop him. "I know, Mark. I know what she did. We could've died. You almost *did* die. But we're okay. And honestly, what other options did she have? I'm not excusing what she did. It was horrible, and she should've gone to the cops before going through with your brother's plan, but..." Her voice trailed off.

"Is she sorry?" Bubba asked Tex.

"For what it's worth, yeah, I think she is. She seemed almost relieved that she'd been found. The first thing she asked was how you two were doing. She knew you had a bunch of shit in your pockets, Bubba, and she'd convinced herself that you'd be fine."

Bubba closed his eyes. He couldn't care less about Eva Dawkins. But for the sake of her kids, who would have no one if their mom went to jail, he sighed and asked, "What now?"

"I've gotten her a job in Florida," Tex said. "Nothing huge, but enough to keep her solvent. She and her kids will be flying there tomorrow. She won't have to worry about her ex ever coming into the picture again. With your blessing, she's getting a new start to her life. I told her not to blow it, because I'd be watching. One misstep, and I'll have her kids taken away and her ass thrown in prison faster than she can even blink."

Bubba couldn't help it. He grinned slightly. There was the Tex he knew and loved. "Good."

"Zoey? You okay?" Tex asked.

Bubba saw her look up at him, study his face, then she finally said, "I'm okay."

"I've got some paperwork to get done, so I'm going to get going. I'm sorry about your brother, Bubba."

"Thanks."

"Tex?" Phantom asked.

"Yeah?"

"Any word on that thing I asked you to keep your eye on for me?"

"Not really. I've heard rumblings of something interesting, but I don't have enough information to share yet. I'll be in touch the second I know anything concrete."

"Thanks. I appreciate it."

"Whatever. Don't be strangers, guys. I'll talk to you soon."

"Bye, Tex. Thanks for everything," Bubba said quickly before Tex hung up.

"Yeah, thanks, Tex," Zoey echoed, but her words fell on deaf ears as Tex had already ended the connection.

"Anything you need to tell me?" Bubba asked Phantom.

The other man shook his head. "Naw. It's nothing. Just something I asked Tex to look into for me."

Bubba studied his teammate for a long moment. It wasn't *nothing*. If Phantom had reached out to the computer genius, it was serious. But if Phantom didn't want to share, he wouldn't make him. He'd let him and the others know what was up when the time was right.

"I feel kind of sorry for Eva," Zoey said quietly.

Bubba rested his chin on the top of Zoey's head. He wasn't surprised at her words. She had a tendency to see the good in people. That was one of a million reasons why he loved her. A part of him had wanted to tell Tex to make the pilot's life hell, but it sounded as if her life was *already* hell. She was as much a victim in this entire thing as he and Zoey had been.

"Any word on what's going on with Tracy?" Bubba asked.

"Last I heard from Sean, her husband had contacted one of his big-time lawyer friends in Anchorage to take her case," Phantom said.

"Seriously?" Zoey asked. "That's bullshit. I mean, I get that they're married, but one, she was having an affair for who knows how long, and two, she had no problem killing us, your dad, and who knows how many other people! She was going to leave Kenneth and go to Mexico with Malcom!"

Bubba reached up and wrapped a hand around the

back of her neck and brushed his thumb back and forth reassuringly. "Easy, Zo."

"No. Seriously, he's stupid! He should've immediately filed for divorce instead of supporting her. Mark, if I ever do anything like what she did, don't you stay with me. You need to get the hell away from me and cut your losses."

Bubba couldn't help but chuckle. He also couldn't believe he was laughing after the day he'd had, and after everything he'd found out about his brother, his pop, and the reason why he and Zoey had been left in the wilderness, but he was. "You couldn't kill someone, sweetheart. No way, no how."

"I could," she argued stubbornly. "If Tracy had turned that knife on you, I *so* would've done whatever it took to take her down."

"Speaking of which...where *did* you learn to take someone down like that?" Bubba asked, his thumb continuing its rhythmic movements on her skin, doing his best to soothe her.

"Colin had a security specialist come to the factory and give self-defense lessons to anyone who wanted them. He let me tag along." Talking about his dad made her expression turn somber. "I can't believe he was poisoned."

Bubba sighed and tightened his arms around her. "Me either."

"I'm sorry, Mark."

"Thanks."

"I'm sorry too," Phantom said.

Bubba nodded. "In some ways, I'm glad Malcom killed himself," he admitted. "I know I couldn't have done it."

"You could've," Phantom told him in no uncertain terms.

Bubba looked at his teammate in surprise.

"Just because you're related to someone by blood doesn't mean they're automatically going to love you and want what's best for you. Sometimes you just have to do what you have to do."

"You have firsthand experience with this?" Bubba asked, because it sure sounded that way.

Phantom shrugged. "Families suck," he said, then stood up. "Not everyone has a loving parent to look after them. Evil is as evil does, and sometimes the innocent simply get stuck with the world's worst parents. I'm going to head to bed. You guys need anything?"

Bubba wanted to tell his friend to sit. To talk to him. To help him understand how and why Malcom had turned against him, because it sure sounded like he had some experience with relatives being assholes, but instead he just shook his head. "We're good."

"Zoey?" Phantom asked.

"I'm okay. Thanks."

After Phantom had closed the door to the other room in the suite, Zoey looked up at Bubba. "Is he okay?"

"I don't know. Phantom doesn't talk about his life. At all. But from things he's said here and there, it's been obvious he didn't have a good childhood. I'm thinking the two of us will have more to talk about now."

Zoey turned and straddled his lap. She wrapped her arms around his neck and rested her forehead against his own. "Are *you* okay?"

"No," Bubba told her.

"What can I do to help?"

"This. Hold me. Be there to listen when I need to talk. Tell me stories about my pop. And just be you, Zo. That's what I need."

"Deal." Then she draped herself over him, her nose

nuzzling the skin of his neck as she did her best to burrow into him.

Surprisingly, having her in his arms *did* help. It made him feel not quite so alone. He'd lost his brother and father, but he'd gained a partner. It was funny how life turned out.

CHAPTER TWENTY

Zoey smiled as she watched Mark light a fire in the fire pit outside their accommodations. It had been a tough month for both of them, but especially for Mark. He'd had to go back to Anchorage twice to talk to prosecutors who were preparing for Tracy's pre-trial hearing.

He'd dealt with putting his dad's house up for sale and going through both Colin's and his brother's belongings. Each time he got off the phone with someone from Juneau, or came back from Alaska, it took him a while to get back to being himself.

Zoey hated it, and wanted to see him happy and smiling again. So she'd arranged for this glamping trip in the hopes it would bring a little joy to his life. She remembered them having a conversation about glamping when they'd been in the Alaska wilderness and figured this would be a way to hopefully put their past behind them once and for all, and look forward to the future.

So far, her plan had worked. They flew up to Sacramento then drove the forty-five minutes to Colfax, California. A small, quaint town. She'd rented the Mongolianthemed yurt because it seemed almost ridiculous in the northern California setting. From the outside it just looked like a regular white tent, but inside, it was over-the-top colorful and ostentatious, and the first time Mark had seen it, the smile that spread from ear to ear had been worth every penny she'd spent on the place.

There was also a hot tub, outdoor shower, sauna, swimming pool, and hammock that they could take advantage of. But thus far they'd been content to laze around and hibernate away from the world. Inside the lavishly decorated tent, they could pretend they were the only people in the world.

Now, they'd ventured outside to sit around the fire and enjoy the night air. After Mark had gotten the fire going, he'd gone inside the yurt, grabbed a blanket from the bed, and sat behind her, wrapping it around them both. Zoey knew Mark wasn't cold, he was never cold, but she loved him all the more for going out of his way to make sure she was warm enough.

Looking up at the stars, Zoey relaxed against Mark and sighed.

"Happy?" he asked.

"Very. But I should be asking you that."

"Any time I get to spend with you makes me happy," he responded.

Zoey wrapped her hands around his forearms, which were across her chest. "I'm worried about you."

He rested his cheek against hers then said, "I know. And I wish we were starting our lives together without all this drama hanging over our heads."

"Everyone has drama," Zoey retorted. "Lives aren't all puppies and flowers like on social media. I just wish I could do more to help you."

Mark snorted.

Zoey frowned and turned her head to look at him. "What?"

"Zo, I'm not sure I could've gotten through any of this without you by my side. Knowing you're there for me is the best thing that could've ever happened in my life. And this trip has gotten me to thinking."

"About what?"

"Us. How everything in our lives is interconnected. How one little decision can change the trajectory of our lives for good or bad. If I'd refused the charter flight that Kenneth put together for us...that his wife arranged...I'm not sure we would be here right now. You might've died out there in the wilderness. Malcom and Tracy might've gotten away with killing Pop. There's a hundred little decisions we've made that have led us right here. And while I wish my pop was still here, and my brother hadn't been a complete idiot, I can't regret finding you through it all."

Zoey's eyes filled with tears. His words meant the world to her. For him to go through all the hurt he'd experienced, to lose his only family, and still be happy to have her in his life...it was almost too much.

"I love you," she said, squeezing his arms. "When I was in high school, I liked you because of the way you looked. As I got older, I admired you because of the stories Colin told me and what you were doing for our country. But now that I've gotten to know you, I love you because of the man you are."

"That means everything to me," Mark said. "I won't always have my muscles. My hair'll probably fall out and I'll gain a hundred pounds. The things I've done will be nothing but a memory and a footnote in some top-secret drawer buried in the Pentagon somewhere, but I'll always be exactly who I am. And who I am is a man who will do whatever it takes to keep you safe and happy."

That was it. Zoey was done sitting around the fire. Even though they'd just ventured out there, it had lost its appeal. She struggled to stand, needing Mark's help to get herself untangled from the blanket. She stood in front of him and held out a hand. "Take me to bed or lose me forever."

Since Mark had said he'd never seen the movie *Top Gun*, she'd made him sit down and watch it with her one night.

Without hesitation, he replied with Goose's iconic line from the movie, "Show me the way home, honey."

Then he grabbed her hand, yanked her forward so she fell over his shoulder, and he stood with her, heading for the opulent tent they were calling home for another couple of nights.

Giggling, Zoey propped herself up by putting her hands on his ass, and she gasped when he dumped her on the mattress inside the tent.

Looking up at the intense expression on her man's face, Zoey had a feeling they wouldn't be emerging from the yurt until morning. "Do we need to worry about the fire?" she asked, not wanting to kill the mood but concerned about leaving it unattended.

"I'll get up and take care of it...later."

"Okay."

Mark leaned over her, caging her in with his arms and practically touching his nose to hers. "I love you, Zoey Knight."

"And I love you back."

He shut his eyes for a moment as if in pain, but when they opened again, all Zoey could see was lust. For her.

Several hours later, Zoey lay boneless and exhausted in Mark's arms. He'd fallen on her like a man dying of thirst and the only way to quench it was by drinking the nectar from her body. He'd eaten her out for at least an hour before he'd allowed her to take a breather. But even then, he'd played with and fondled every inch of her body while she did her best to recover.

She knew some men enjoyed eating pussy, but Mark took it to a whole new level. He was insatiable when it came to her, and Zoey had never felt more cherished than she did when Mark was making love to her.

After she'd finally stopped shaking, Mark had entered her slowly and reverently. He'd stared into her eyes the entire time he made love to her, whispering words of adoration. Finally, when neither of them could take it anymore, he'd turned her over on her hands and knees and fucked her to within an inch of her life.

Zoey couldn't say what she enjoyed more. The oral sex, the slow, sweet lovemaking, or the hard and fast fucking.

She knew Mark wasn't asleep, as his thumb was making small circles on the small of her back as he held her to him. Out of the blue, remembering something Jess had said to them, she blurted, "So, I guess Jess was right? The key to a good relationship is cunnilingus."

He chuckled. "Actually, what she said was, the key to a good *marriage* is cunnilingus. And I'd have to agree with her." Mark leaned over and grabbed something from the small table next to the bed. She hadn't noticed it before, but now she could only stare at the small black velvet bag in his hands with wide eyes.

He opened it and pulled out a beautiful emerald-cut solitaire diamond ring.

Zoey gasped.

"I know this is fast, but fuck it. Our entire relationship has been unconventional. Will you marry me? I can't imagine going through the rest of my life without you by my side. I might be a tough Navy SEAL, but without you, I'm nothing. I don't care how long our engagement is. A week, a month, five fucking years, as long as you'll eventually be mine, I'll be happy."

"I'm already yours," Zoey told him quietly. "A marriage certificate won't change that." When she saw the uncertainty enter his eyes, she quickly went on. "But of course I'll marry you, Mark. I love you."

He smiled then and hugged her. Hard.

When he pulled back and slid the beautiful ring down her finger, Zoey couldn't help teasing, "But only if you promise to keep up that cunnilingus thing."

"As if you could keep me away from your beautiful body," Mark said with a grin. "In fact, I think I'm hungry again."

Zoey shrieked as Mark grabbed her around the waist and helped her kneel, then slid under her in a quick movement. She was on her knees above him, and he continued sliding down until he was between her legs. He stuffed a pillow under his head, and when Zoey looked down her body, all she could see was his eyes looking up from between her legs with an intensity that was almost scary.

"I love you, Zoey. With everything I am. I promise to do everything in my power to make you happy. I'll put you first in my life when I can, and I'll fucking kill anyone who tries to hurt you."

"I'm not sure about the killing part, but okay on the rest."

Then he smiled and pushed her thighs apart until she had no choice but to grab ahold of the headboard to stay upright.

"Hold on, sweetheart. I'm starving."

Zoey threw her head back at the first touch of his lips to her sensitive clit and did as he asked, hanging on for dear life.

After he'd rocked her world, again, and she was lying on her side cuddled up next to him, she stared at the ring on her finger. She was going to marry Mark Wright. The man she'd wanted for most of her life.

Life sure worked in mysterious ways.

"Are you sure you want to do this?" Rocco asked Phantom. They'd just gotten done with PT, and Phantom had pulled his friend aside to ask a favor.

"Yeah. I know the therapists on base have clearance, but I'd like you there to listen to whatever I say when the hypnotist puts me under."

"You're *that* sure you're missing something that happened back in Timor-Leste?" Rocco asked.

"Yes. I saw something, but in all the chaos when we had to get out of the orphanage because the rebels were closing in, I've forgotten what it was," Phantom told him.

Rocco frowned. "What is it you're hoping to find out from this?"

"That's the thing, I don't know."

"Phantom...Kalee's dead. We all saw her body. She's not coming back," Rocco said gently.

Phantom ground his teeth together. "I know," he lied.

The thing was, he'd had this nagging feeling that the woman they'd been sent in to rescue *wasn't* dead. But he knew if he said it out loud with no proof, his friends would think he was just as crazy as Kalee's dad.

Mr. Solberg had been released from the mental hospital and was back on his medications. Phantom wanted to go see him. To ask him about his daughter. To hear stories about what she was like. But he was too chicken. The last thing he wanted was to either give him false hope that Kalee was alive or to make the man have a relapse and end up back in the hospital.

But that niggling feeling inside him wouldn't subside. Wouldn't shut up. He'd second-guessed himself time and time again, and he'd done everything possible to remember the moment he'd found the pit with the bodies of the murdered children, but no matter how hard he tried, there was a tiny moment of time that was a blank.

One second he'd discovered the mass grave, and the next, he and his teammates were fleeing the area with Piper and the three orphaned girls.

"If you really want me to go, I will," Rocco said.

Phantom nodded. "I appreciate it."

"Just let me know the time and place."

"Will do."

The two men shook hands, and Phantom headed for his car to go home and shower before heading back to the base. They were gearing up for another mission. They hadn't been on one in a while, and he was more than ready to get back to what it was he did best. As soon as Bubba got back home from his short vacation, they'd hit the intel hard and most likely be shipped out within the week.

Unlike his teammates, who now had families and

women of their own, Phantom still looked forward to their missions. It would take his mind off the hole in his memory...and the undeniable fear that he'd somehow fucked up. Huge.

He'd asked Tex for his help and didn't know what "rumblings about something interesting" meant, but he knew Tex would tell him once he had something concrete. In the meantime, he needed to stay busy, meet with the hypnotist, and try to fucking move on with his life.

Rex had just gotten out of the shower and was eating his four-egg omelet standing up while watching the morning news when his cell phone rang. He and his teammates had gotten back from a short mission the day before, and he had the day off. He was looking forward to sitting around and decompressing.

"It's Rocco," his teammate said as soon as Rex answered. "You need to get back to base ASAP."

Rex was moving before Rocco had finished talking. He scraped his remaining eggs into the trash and asked, "What's up?"

"We're leaving as soon as everyone gets here."

"Shit," Rex said. There had been times they'd been called out to a mission without a lot of prep work, but their commander liked to have as much information as possible before sending them into danger. "What's up?"

There was a moment of silence on the other end, and Rex's stomach clenched in concern. Rocco didn't usually beat around the bush. It had to be something bad.

"It's Avery," Rocco said quietly.

For a second, Rex wasn't sure who his friend was talking about.

Then it hit him. "*My* Avery?"

It was a silly thing to say. Avery Nelson wasn't his. They weren't even dating. He'd flirted with her, and she'd flirted back. Rex had made extra trips to the hospital to see her, and he was working up the courage to ask her out. But she'd been gone for about a month and a half. She'd been assigned to a special detail that had gone to Afghanistan for a humanitarian mission...to help teach nursing skills to women.

But she was the only Avery he knew, and if Rocco was being extra careful in telling him what was going on, it had to be her.

"Yeah. She's MIA. Ten days ago, a small arms convoy was attacked near the clinic she was assigned to assist."

Rex's blood ran cold. "What's our mission?" he asked.

He was breaking protocol. Both he and Rocco knew they weren't supposed to talk over the phone about where they were going or what they were being sent to do, but he couldn't stop the question from popping out.

"Rescue," Rocco said briefly. "Friendlies in the area said she and a couple of others from the convoy were taken up into the caves in the mountains nearby."

"So she's alive?" Rex asked as he threw some necessities into a duffle bag.

"As far as we know, yes," Rocco said.

Taking a deep breath, Rex said, "I'll be there in thirty minutes or less."

"Drive safe," Rocco said, then hung up the phone.

Rex closed his eyes and thought about the last time he'd seen Avery. He'd gone over to the hospital to say goodbye before her mission. She'd been laughing with another nurse when he'd seen her, and he'd been struck once more by how pretty she was. Her bright red hair shone in the harsh fluorescent lights of the hospital and every time he saw her, he swore more freckles had popped out on her cheeks and the bridge of her nose.

He'd approached and, after seeing him, she had smiled so big, he felt as if he was truly the center of her world at that moment.

"Hey," he said.

"Hey back," she'd responded.

"Heard you're headed out soon."

"Yeah. The day after tomorrow."

Rex had opened his mouth to ask if she wanted to get some coffee or something before she left, but just then an alarm sounded from one of the rooms, and she gave him a look of apology. "Sorry, I need to go check that out."

"It's okay," Rex had said. "Be safe over there, and I'll see you when you get back."

She'd given him a look he couldn't interpret, but eventually nodded. "I'd like that," she'd said.

Then she was gone. Hurrying down the hall to check on her patient.

"I should've asked her out," Rex said out loud, opening his eyes and resuming packing for the unexpected mission.

He wasn't going to make the same mistake twice. He knew more than most how short life was. How quickly things could change. He'd been an idiot, and he hoped like hell he'd have a chance to fix things. He knew without having to ask for details from Rocco that they'd be going in to rescue Avery and the others.

"Hang on, Avery," he whispered. "Just hang on. We're comin' for you."

Avery Nelson blinked, but just like the last two hundred thousand and twenty-three times she'd blinked, nothing changed. She still couldn't see anything. Not a spec of light anywhere. Her head was throbbing, and she knew she'd gotten a concussion when an RPG had hit the clinic she'd been hunkered down next to.

The large piece of concrete that had fallen and hit her on the head hadn't done her any favors. She'd been disoriented, and when one of the terrorists who'd attacked the convoy had run across her, she hadn't been able to protect herself. He'd forced her into one of the trucks carrying the American weapons and had driven up into the mountains with her, the guns, and two other hostages from the convoy.

She'd been thrown into one of the hundreds of caves in the mountainside and beaten to within an inch of her life. She hadn't seen the other two hostages since she'd arrived, but she'd seen plenty of terrorists.

They'd stashed the weapons that had been in the trucks they'd stolen from the convoy in a cave near where they'd been holding her. And everyone who came to get a weapon had been invited to gawk at her. To hit her if they wished. To torture her.

As a part of her training, she'd been taught how to withstand torture. How to stay strong in the face of adversity. But she was almost at the end of her rope.

The men had taken her boots, and she was in nothing but the dark tan T-shirt she wore under her desert camo uniform and her cargo pants. She hadn't been raped, but the beatings and the mental torture had been just as bad.

They'd enter the small alcove where she'd been tied up

and sit just out of reach to eat their lunch. They'd pour out bottles of water at her feet, then laugh as she fell to her knees to try to suck the liquid off the ground. They'd bring her moldy bread and rotting meat, and take great pleasure in watching her attempt to keep from throwing it up.

The only thing that had kept her alive this long was the fact they left her alone at night. They'd make sure the chain around her ankle was secure, then leave her with only one guard outside the cave. When darkness fell, she'd silently crawl over to the wall of the alcove and lick the water dripping down the sides of the rocks.

She'd spied it her first day as she'd lay in the dirt in agonizing pain from the rock that had fallen on her head back in town and from the beating she'd gotten. The men didn't seem to even notice it. That water was her salvation. Without it, she wouldn't even have been able to stand. Her body would've begun shutting down by now.

As a nurse, she knew better than most what the human body was capable of, and without water, it was doomed to fail.

But yesterday, her hell had been different.

No one had come to pick up any weapons. No one had thrown stale and moldy food at her, laughing when she ate it as if it were the best thing she'd ever tasted.

In the early afternoon, a group of men had arrived but they didn't come into the back alcove where she was being held. Then there was silence after the men left.

Avery felt her hopes rise. If they left her alone, even for an hour, she would find a way to get out of the shackle attached to her ankle and get the hell out of there.

But instead, not too long after they'd left, there had been a large explosion, leaving Avery in pitch dark.

She'd been in darkness ever since. Without being able

to see the sun rising and setting, she had no idea how much time had passed. Didn't know if it was day or night.

But she wasn't going to give up. No way. Those assholes thought they'd killed her or buried her alive, but they were wrong. Their mistake was not shooting her in the head before they'd blown up the entrance to the cave.

Ever since she'd managed to use a rock to smash the links of the chain attaching her ankle to the floor of the cave, she'd been gradually, one rock at a time, doing her best to unbury herself.

It was slow going, but Avery didn't stop. Big rocks. Small rocks. Rocks so big she could only roll them out of the way by sitting on her ass and using her feet and legs to push. It didn't matter if she had to dig her way to China, she was getting out of this cave.

Except, with every day that went by, she got weaker and weaker. Her pants were loose enough that they were almost falling off her hips. She wasn't dehydrated, as she had all the water she could drink, thanks to the drip along the wall in the back alcove. But soon, even that wouldn't be enough.

Shaking, Avery forced herself to crawl toward where the opening to the cave had been and pick up another rock. She cradled it to her chest and shuffled backward, placing the rock behind her and off to the side, along with the others she'd moved so far.

She was exhausted, but refused to give up.

Eventually something had to give. Either the terrorists would come back—which was highly unlikely since they assumed she would die in their man-made tomb—or she'd move enough rocks to get out of her prison. What would happen then, Avery had no idea. The area was most likely crawling with terrorists or sympathizers. How she'd get back to the American base, with nothing on her feet but a pair of socks, she had no idea. But she wasn't going to quit.

Blinking once again and hoping like hell she'd see some sliver of light coming from the rock pile, which would mean she was close to breaking free, she sighed in disappointment when the utter blackness didn't abate.

Crawling back to the pile of rocks, Avery picked up a small one and threw it as hard as she could behind her. She was scared, tired, hungry, and her head was throbbing. But she couldn't give up. Wouldn't.

As she continued, she couldn't help but wonder if anyone knew she was missing. If anyone was looking for her.

Stopping for a moment, Avery sat back on her heels. She closed her eyes, not that it made a difference, since darkness was darkness, and prayed harder than she'd ever prayed in her life.

I'm here. I'm right here. Please, someone find me.

Then, taking a big breath and wincing at the pain in her bruised ribs from the beatings she'd endured, she picked up another rock.

*

Find out if the SEAL team can find Avery in *Securing Avery.*

(And of course *Securing Kalee is coming up as well...poor Phantom!*)

And as a bonus...want to find out more about Eva Dawkins? The pilot? Where she is now? What she's doing? If her ex continues to be a threat? Or if someone ELSE is a threat?Riley Edwards has written her story in my fan-fiction world and this story is one you will WANT to read! Pick up Maximus now!

. . .

Want to talk to other Susan Stoker fans? Join my reader group, Susan Stoker's Stalkers, on Facebook!

Also, be sure to check out a sneak peek below of my NEW Delta Team Two series starting in April with Shielding Gillian!

JOIN my Newsletter and find out about sales, free books, contests and new releases before anyone else!!
Click HERE

Want to know when my books go on sale? Follow me on Bookbub HERE!

Would you like Susan's Book Protecting Caroline for FREE?
Click HERE

Also by Susan Stoker

SEAL of Protection: Legacy Series
Securing Caite
Securing Brenae (novella)
Securing Sidney
Securing Piper
Securing Zoey
Securing Avery (May 2020)
Securing Kalee (Sept 2020)

Delta Team Two Series
Shielding Gillian (Apr 2020)
Shielding Kinley (Aug 2020)
Shielding Aspen (Oct 2020)
Shielding Riley (TBA)
Shielding Devyn (TBA)
Shielding Ember (TBA)
Shielding Sierra (TBA)

Delta Force Heroes Series
Rescuing Rayne
Rescuing Aimee (novella)
Rescuing Emily
Rescuing Harley
Marrying Emily (novella)
Rescuing Kassie
Rescuing Bryn
Rescuing Casey
Rescuing Sadie (novella)
Rescuing Wendy

Defending Zara (Mar 2020)
Defending Raven (June 2020)

SEAL of Protection Series

Protecting Caroline
Protecting Alabama
Protecting Fiona
Marrying Caroline (novella)
Protecting Summer
Protecting Cheyenne
Protecting Jessyka
Protecting Julie (novella)
Protecting Melody
Protecting the Future
Protecting Kiera (novella)
Protecting Alabama's Kids (novella)
Protecting Dakota

Stand Alone

The Guardian Mist
Nature's Rift
A Princess for Cale
A Moment in Time- A Collection of Short Stories
Lambert's Lady

Special Operations Fan Fiction

http://www.AcesPress.com

Beyond Reality Series

Outback Hearts
Flaming Hearts
Frozen Hearts

ALSO BY SUSAN STOKER

Writing as Annie George:

Stepbrother Virgin (erotic novella)

ABOUT THE AUTHOR

New York Times, *USA Today* and *Wall Street Journal* Best-selling Author Susan Stoker has a heart as big as the state of Tennessee where she lives, but this all American girl has also spent the last fourteen years living in Missouri, California, Colorado, Indiana, and Texas. She's married to a retired Army man who now gets to follow *her* around the country.

She debuted her first series in 2014 and quickly followed that up with the SEAL of Protection Series, which solidified her love of writing and creating stories readers can get lost in.

If you enjoyed this book, or any book, please consider leaving a review. It's appreciated by authors more than you'll know.

www.stokeraces.com
www.AcesPress.com
susan@stokeraces.com

facebook.com/authorsusanstoker

twitter.com/Susan_Stoker

instagram.com/authorsusanstoker

goodreads.com/SusanStoker

bookbub.com/authors/susan-stoker

amazon.com/author/susanstoker

CPSIA information can be obtained
at www.ICGtesting.com
Printed in the USA
LVHW081426030320
648850LV00008B/97